**Denise N. Wheatley** loves ha... storytelling. Her novels run t... strives to pen entertaining bo... the heart. She's an RWA member and holds a BA in English from the University of Illinois. When Denise isn't writing, she enjoys watching true crime TV and chatting with readers. Follow her on social media: Instagram @Denise_Wheatley_Writer; X @DeniseWheatley; BookBub @DeniseNWheatley; Goodreads Denise N. Wheatley

A *USA Today* bestselling author of over 130 novels in twenty languages, **Tara Taylor Quinn** has sold more than seven million copies. Known for her intense emotional fiction, Tara's novels have received critical acclaim in the UK and most recently from Harvard. She is the recipient of the Readers' Choice Award and has appeared often on local and national TV, including *CBS Sunday Morning*. For TTQ offers, news and contests, visit taprataylorquinn.com

**Also by Denise N. Wheatley**

**A West Coast Crime Story**
*The Heart-Shaped Murders*
*Danger in the Nevada Desert*
*Homicide at Vincent Vineyard*
*Hometown Homicide*
*Preyed Upon*

**An Unsolved Mystery Book**
*Cold Case True Crime*
*Bayou Christmas Disappearance*
*Backcountry Cover-Up*

**Also by Tara Taylor Quinn**

**Sierra's Web**
*A Firefighter's Hidden Truth*
*Last Chance Investigation*
*Danger on the River*
*Her Sister's Murder*
*Mistaken Identities*
*Horse Ranch Hideout*
*Cold Case Obsession*

**The Coltons of Owl Creek**
*Colton Threat Unleashed*

Discover more at millsandboon.co.uk

# FEARLESS PURSUIT

## DENISE N. WHEATLEY

# SHADOWED PAST

## TARA TAYLOR QUINN

**MILLS & BOON**

First Published in Great Britain 2025
by Mills & Boon, an imprint of HarperCollins*Publishers* Ltd
1 London Bridge Street, London, SE1 9GF

www.harpercollins.co.uk

HarperCollins*Publishers*
Macken House, 39/40 Mayor Street Upper,
Dublin 1, D01 C9W8, Ireland

*Fearless Pursuit* © 2026 Denise N. Wheatley
*Shadowed Past* © 2026 TTQ Books LLC

ISBN: 978-0-263-42018-0

0126

This book contains FSC™ certified paper and other controlled sources to ensure responsible forest management.

For more information visit: www.harpercollins.co.uk/green

Printed and Bound in the UK using 100% Renewable Electricity at CPI Group (UK) Ltd, Croydon, CR0 4YY

# FEARLESS PURSUIT

## DENISE N. WHEATLEY

To my parents, Ronald and Donna

## *Chapter One*

"Chief Miller! Would you mind taking a picture with me and my girls?"

Dani cringed at the request. She still hadn't gotten used to all the attention she'd gained after capturing the first serial killer to prey on Maxwell, Arizona, nearly a year ago.

*"Pleeease!"* the young woman begged in response to Dani's silence.

The chief tugged awkwardly at her black moto jacket, resisting the urge to dash out the door of the Zonian Bar & Grill.

"Of course," she finally said, relenting at the woman's hopeful dimpled grin. "Where should I stand?"

"Yesss! Right here in the middle of us!"

As Dani took her place in the center of the group, the crowd around them burst into cheers. The chief's face burned with embarrassment. She dismissed the applause with a wave, fixating on the woman's satin Bride to Be sash to avoid all the gawking.

The women around her adjusted their teal bridesmaid-style dresses, then kicked their cowboy boots high in the air. "Our girl's getting *marrieeed*!" one of them squealed. Peace signs and heart hands hovered over their heads like crowns while a fellow patron snapped photos.

Dani stood stiff as a statue, barely breathing while struggling not to squint at the camera's bright flash. Those flames of self-consciousness traveled down to her neck when she noticed her former classmates looking on. Their prying eyes felt more like glaring spotlights as they observed the awestruck exchange.

They'd gathered at the bar to celebrate their twenty-year class reunion. The Zonian was owned by their former senior class president, so after a weekend filled with cookouts, softball in the park and snowboarding at Cole's Ski Resort, it was only right that they end the festivities there. Dani just wished she could've celebrated privately like the rest of her peers rather than be singled out by eager admirers.

"Thank you so much, *Daniii!*" the bride-to-be sang out before slapping her hand over her mouth. "Oops, I—I'm so sorry, Danielle. I mean, Chief Miller. Congrats on being the queen of Maxwell!"

Dani's bemused head nod was punctuated with a chuckle. "The queen of Maxwell? That's a bit of a stretch, but you're welcome. And congratulations to you on your upcoming nuptials."

The chief's voice faded into the beer-scented air as the woman raised her drink, sending tequila dribbling down her arm. "Thanks, girl!" she exclaimed before twirling off to the pulsating rhythm of a hip-hop beat blaring through the speakers.

Just when Dani turned to rejoin her group, she noticed a set of dark, piercing eyes watching her intently.

"Ugh," she groaned, unable to swallow her disgust. The sight of Von Reed had that effect on her. Most women had the opposite reaction. They gravitated toward his smooth reddish-brown skin that deepened during the summer months and strong features that softened when he smiled. Even Dani couldn't deny that he had the whole tall, dark and handsome thing going on. Problem was, he knew it. And while others saw him as charismatic and confident, Dani found him annoying and arrogant.

"Why are you even here…" she mumbled to herself.

But Von had every right to be there considering he, too, was a former classmate. Regardless of that fact, his presence was unnerving. He and Dani's contentious history ran deep. Generationally deep. What had been ignited by their fathers was further fueled by the two of them. And Dani had no interest in snuffing out the rivalry.

*"Hey,"* her best friend, Chloe, whispered in her ear. "Have you noticed how Von's been watching you all night?"

"Of course I have," Dani responded with a slight eye roll. "How could I not?"

Close since childhood, Chloe had witnessed the contention between Dani and Von worsen over time. She'd missed a fair share of it after relocating to Chicago in her early twenties, becoming a big-city detective and losing herself in a toxic relationship. The move sent their friendship into a tailspin as it ruined plans to take over the Maxwell PD. They'd managed to reconcile, however, when Chloe returned home last October and began dating Dani's brother, Officer Troy Miller.

"Look at him," Chloe muttered, nodding in Von's direction. "Clearly he sees us watching him. Yet he's just standing here, shamelessly staring you down."

DANI'S HEAD WHIPPED BACK toward the desert-themed bar's succulent mural wall. It wasn't hard to miss Von's brooding six-foot-three presence, looming in front of a bright green prickly pear cactus. He stood with an air of cockiness, his thick hands tucked casually into his jeans as if he were posing for a magazine shoot. His penetrating gaze was like a freshly lit match, igniting a spark of annoyance in her gut.

It sent Dani spinning around, mad that she'd even acknowledged his presence.

"I wonder if Von's company is working security for tonight's event," Chloe said, craning her neck while pulling her long, straight bob behind her ears.

Shifting her eyes discreetly, Dani searched his broad chest for the Reed Protective Services' cream-and-navy shield. Von had been running his family's firm, better known as RPS, since his father's recent retirement. Tonight, his pale blue button-down was logo-free. "It looks like he's off duty. So I guess the only work he's putting in is studying every move I make. And of course his goofy sidekick is right there with him," Dani added, referring to RPS's vice president, Kevin Freelain.

"Oh, but of course. I do hate that Von is so handsome considering he's off-limits. I actually think you two would be good together. If you think about it, you two have a lot in common. Plus he's got those dark, deep-set eyes, that bright, mischievous smile—"

"Um, I'm sorry," Dani interrupted with a flick of her wrist. "But have you lost your mind? We do not give compliments to the enemy. Plus I don't have a thing in common with that man. Now you'd better quit while you're ahead before I tell my brother you've got a crush on Von."

"Now *that* would be a bold-faced lie," Chloe shot back before signaling the bartender and ordered another round of merlot. "Listen, it's Sunday. The last night of our reunion weekend. Let's not ruin it with all this talk of Von. Instead, we'll have another drink and toast to the fact that you actually showed up this weekend."

"Wait, what is that supposed to mean?"

"Please don't get defensive. It's a compliment. I'm proud of you for opening yourself up to a social life after cracking the biggest case of your career. So here's to more outings, more peopling, and dare I say it, you meeting the love of your life."

"Whoa, whoa, slow down, sis. I appreciate the intentions, but let's not go too far. Nevertheless, cheers."

Just as the pair clinked glasses, Troy approached, his tall, lean physique moving effortlessly through the crowded bar. "Wait, what are we toasting to? The fact that Dani is winning the stare-down between her and Von? Or that Maxwell PD's presence is so heavy tonight that we've managed to outnumber RPS's crew?"

"C," Dani rebutted. "None of the above. Von may be acting foolish, but I am in no way participating in a stare-down. And as for Maxwell PD, there is no competition. Contrary to what RPS may believe, they have zero authority in this town."

"True. But I can understand why they think they do, though."

"And why is that?"

Troy held up his hand, ticking off points on his fingers one by one. "For starters, some of the townspeople do have a tendency to call them over us when crimes are committed."

Through narrowed eyes, Dani glared at Troy, her sharp expression icy enough to turn the warm bar cold. The reaction silenced him. As Troy retreated against a stool, Chloe's knowing glance stated the obvious. Certain topics were touchy. The rivalry between the Maxwell PD and RPS was one of them. More specifically, the beef between the Miller and Reed families.

It all started when Dani's and Von's fathers entered the Maxwell PD's police academy together. Gene Miller and Hamilton Reed grew close during their journey to becoming officers. They'd remained tight up until the point where Gene was named police chief. It was a position that Hamilton had long vied for. He'd tried his best to get over the snub, despite being convinced he was the better man for the job.

Once Gene became boss, Hamilton felt as though he was too hard on him and overly critical of his job performance. Hamilton was convinced the reprimands would tarnish his record and block future job promotions. So he quit, cracked open his savings and established RPS.

For Hamilton, launching the company hadn't been easy. He'd never dreamed of owning a security firm. His goal had always been to work for the police department. But his confidence in the company grew when several officers quit the force and joined his team, which was a no-brainer after he offered a higher salary and flexible schedules.

The upside was that RPS became Maxwell's premiere protection service, providing security for the most prestigious businesses, events and private citizens. Yet the downside ran deeper than Hamilton's rivalry with Gene. Tensions between the men divided law enforcement officers throughout the town.

Chaos erupted when the townspeople became split over who to call when crimes occurred. Some reached out to the police department, but the number of officers had decreased due to the exodus. The force was stretched thin. Complaints began pouring in, accusing Maxwell PD of slow responses to crime scenes. As a result, some residents turned to RPS, knowing the officers were former law enforcement and familiar with the community.

*"Hellooo,"* Chloe said, snapping her fingers in front of Dani's face. "What's wrong? Did the wine just hypnotize you?"

"No, sorry… I was just thinking about this never-ending feud."

"I can't believe it's still going on. Especially now that both of your fathers have retired."

"Yeah, well, it seems to have gotten worse since I was named police chief and Von started running RPS."

"I can attest to that," Troy interjected, gently tugging at his goatee. "Dani went through hell after being promoted. Like our dad, she lost several officers to RPS after becoming chief due to their jealousy, resentment, all of that…"

"Yeah," Chloe said, nodding so furiously that her hair swept across her face. "RPS's security team was asserting their authority all over town, acting like they possessed the same amount of power as the force."

"Exactly," Dani agreed. "That's why Von and I have had so many unresolved confrontations that only made things worse between us."

She took a long sip of wine and swallowed hard, the burn in her throat matching the irritation in her head. Flashbacks to where it all started flipped through her mind like pages from her diary. The way they'd grown up together, attending the same schools and traveling in the same circles. Yet it was understood that there was to be no socializing between the Reed and Miller families.

That unwritten rule prompted Dani to keep her distance, which wasn't difficult considering she and Von were complete opposites. While he was busy being an attention-seeking athlete and party-hopping playboy, she was focused on her studies and rolled with a select clique of friends.

"And just like that," Chloe said, "he's gone."

"Who's gone?" Dani asked.

"Von. He's like the Black Panther. In and out before anyone notices."

"Don't compare that man to my favorite superhero. And I'm glad he's gone. I was getting sick of him staring over here all night. Anyway, speaking of leaving…" Dani glanced down at the time on her phone. "I need to get going. I've got an early morning. Budget meeting prep."

Troy slid his empty beer bottle onto the bar and threw an arm around Dani. "Before you even say it, I'm right behind you, Chief. Since I'm vying for that promotion to detective, I already know that getting to work early is a good look. You ready, Chloe?"

"I am. I've got an early day, too. The latest recording of *Preyed Upon* isn't gonna edit itself."

"Ooh," Dani breathed before waving goodbye to a group of classmates, then heading toward the exit. "I've been waiting for the next podcast episode to air. What's this one about?"

"A wealthy businessman in Atlanta who's also a major womanizer. He was known for dating several ladies at once, and eventually, that lifestyle caught up to him. One of his many companions ended up killing him."

Troy pulled open the door, the moonlight flickering across his gaping eyes. "*Damn.* I think I heard about that guy. Didn't the killer beat him over the head with an alarm clock or something along those lines?"

"Yes, she did. And her DNA was found all over his bedroom. But since her profile hadn't been entered into the national database, the suspect was able to elude law enforcement for almost a decade. During that time, she murdered a couple of her other lovers, too."

Dani clutched her black snakeskin purse, wincing at the lurid details. "That is just awful. I'm glad they were finally able to apprehend her, otherwise more people would have had their lives destroyed."

"True," Troy chimed in. He stopped in front of a faux Joshua tree, its twinkling lights rivaling the stars scattered across the sky. "Where'd you park, D?"

"Right around the corner. By the time I got here, the lot was full and every space on the block was taken."

"Well, we're in the lot, but we'll walk you to your car. Lead the way."

*"Please,"* Dani scoffed, swinging her bag in the air. "You don't have to do that. I'll be fine. I've got my bestie on me."

"So you've traded me in for a Glock 22?" Chloe quipped.

"Absolutely not. You and I are beyond best friends. We're more like sisters. I'm just waiting on *somebody* to make that official."

When Chloe wiggled her fingerless left hand in front of Troy, he grabbed her by the waist and pulled her close. "Patience, my love. And on that note, Dani, have a good night. See you in the morning."

"See you mañana."

"And hey!" Troy called out. "The day we decide to make things official is coming sooner rather than later. So don't you worry."

"Trust me, I'm not. You know better than to let a good woman get away!"

Their laughter floated through the night air, drifting into the distance as the threesome went their separate ways. Dani set off down the block, the darkness deepening with each step.

Mountain peaks loomed majestically in the distance as faint moonbeams illuminated their foreboding presence. Most establishments had already closed. Their pitch-black windows reflected the eerie silence blanketing the street, which had been alive with shoppers, diners and moviegoers just a few hours ago. The vibes now felt oddly still, with only the occasional flicker of headlights breaking the monotony.

Dani reached the corner and made an abrupt left turn. A sharp crack in the asphalt trapped her boot's heel, threatening to send her plummeting down the steep incline. She grabbed hold of the white stucco wall beside her, the rough surface scraping her nails as she steadied herself.

"Please do not roll your damn ankle," Dani uttered, blaming the misstep on lack of streetlights.

She activated her cell phone's flashlight, then tiptoed to her vehicle, aiming the beam toward the uneven pavement. Stopping in front of her burgundy Jeep, Dani leaned against the hood while digging through her purse for the key fob. It wasn't there. She patted down the pockets of her boyfriend jeans. Not there, either.

*Did I lock it inside the car?*

An out-of-towner would've been frightened by the stillness surrounding her. But Dani was used to it. Sunday nights on the main thoroughfare were relatively dead. Yet tonight, something about the silence seemed out of place. The desolation hit harder than usual.

Life in Maxwell was once safe and secure, to the point where residents left their doors unlocked and walked their dogs in the middle of the night. But ever since a serial killer descended upon their town last year, the community was on high alert. It didn't matter that the offender had been convicted and would spend the rest of his life in prison. Maxwell had been tainted, and there was no going back. The townspeople no longer felt protected beneath a comforting veil of security. They weren't an exception to the worst criminal acts. At this point, anything could happen.

The memory of all they'd endured sent a chill through Dani that could rival a subzero sweep. She tightened the belt on her jacket, then continued the search for her fob until it hit her palm.

Dani tapped the unlock button. Waited for the headlights to blink. They didn't.

"What in the hell…"

A vehicle parked farther down the block lit up. Dani took a closer look at the license plate. A pang of foolishness almost knocked her to the ground. She was standing at the wrong Jeep.

*At least nobody saw that*, she thought, laughing at herself before continuing down the street.

Dani could only see a few feet ahead thanks to her dying cell phone's fading light. That unsettling chill returned as she shuffled down the narrowing road. It resurrected thoughts of the bad omen still clinging to the town. Pushing the frightening thoughts aside, Dani quickened her pace, her heels clicking against the asphalt as she broke into a near jog.

A wave of relief rolled through her when she finally approached her vehicle. Dani's jagged breathing steadied once she climbed inside and slammed the door shut. She swiftly started the engine, then repositioned the rearview mirror.

Darkness covered the rear windshield. As her eyes adjusted, a shape emerged, silently rising from the back seat.

*What the...*

Dani grabbed the door handle, her heart thrashing against her rib cage, then fluttering uncontrollably. The rhythmless beat pounded her eardrums. She pressed her body against the door. But before she could exit the vehicle, a cold, sharp wire sliced into her throat.

Her neck hit the headrest. A stream of hot breath singed her eardrum when she was pulled against the back of her seat. Dani gasped, unable to release the scream trapped inside her throat. She slammed her hand against the passenger seat, desperately fumbling for her purse. One jerking motion from the attacker sent her arm flailing. A loud thud confirmed that she'd knocked the clutch to the floor.

Dani's nails sliced into her skin as she clawed at the wire. The assailant yanked harder, sharp steel ripping at her fingertips. Her breathing faltered. Grew thin. Ragged. Dani's surroundings blurred as her eyes rolled into the back of her head. The cord snaked around the back of her neck as cracked leather gloves scratched her flesh.

Just as she felt herself fading, the cord shifted a fraction of an inch. Dani inhaled sharply, oxygen tearing through her lungs like a silent scream. She gripped her throat. Slammed her hand against the door to try to escape. But she could barely move.

Tears of frustration sprang to Dani's eyes. She couldn't get away. Couldn't grab her gun and shoot the attacker dead. Dread burned her chest at the thought of him choking the life out of her, leaving her slumped in the seat. Dead.

Dani's eyes flew open when the wire's deadly grip released, its cold metal slithering away from her throat. The back door popped open. Her attacker fled from the vehicle and shot down the street.

Throwing herself toward the passenger seat, she ripped open her clutch and grabbed her Glock. Dani lunged from the Jeep so violently that she nearly hit the ground. She steadied herself, gasping as brutal pain throbbed inside her throat.

*Stay on your feet! Move!*

Dani pushed through the agony, her limp jog turning into a frantic sprint as she chased after the heavy footsteps. Their menacing beat echoed like a soundtrack from the past. To a time when Maxwell was under attack. And no one was safe.

The figure, dressed in all black, faded into the darkness. Taking a shot would've been too risky. So Dani held her fire. But the suspect didn't.

*Pow!*

"Drop your weapon!" she yelled after a bullet ricocheted past her ear.

*Pow! Pow!*

Dani veered off the sidewalk and ducked down behind a parked car. Peered over the hood. Listened as the fleeing footsteps waned, then disappeared.

Creeping along the side of the car, she drew her weapon and took aim. The street was empty. Just like that, her attacker had vanished as quickly as he'd appeared.

## Chapter Two

"Talk to me," Von said, sliding his laptop across the teak-wood desk and opening the calendar. "What's on the docket for this week?"

Kevin flipped open his embossed leather notebook and scanned the pages. "Let's see. We've got Grant Ferguson's antique car show happening this weekend, the We Got the Beat Music Festival, Andrea Jordan's wedding—"

"Wait, why does Andrea need security for her wedding?"

"Because she's afraid one of her exes may pop up during the whole *speak now or forever hold your peace* segment of the ceremony and mess everything up."

"Okay then…" Von muttered, typing in the event under Saturday's tab. "What else you got?"

"All of our regular gigs. We'll have officers at the banks, bars and retail stores. Oh, and Five Star Productions will be in town all week filming a movie at Cole's Ski Resort. So we'll need to send out a few extra guys to cover the grounds as well as the set."

"That shouldn't be a problem. Is that it?"

"Yep," Kevin confirmed. "That's it. Unless we get some last-minute calls now that the busy season is kicking off. You know the drill. Tourists hit the town—"

"And all hell inevitably breaks loose," Von injected before gulping down a half cup of lukewarm coffee.

"Don't you think you're being a bit dramatic? It's not *that* bad."

"That's debatable. You can't deny that things are getting worse around here——" Von paused at the ping from his laptop.

A notification popped up, alerting him that the latest edition of *The Maxwell Times* had dropped in his inbox. Von clicked the link. A photo of Dani flashed across the screen. The caption underneath it read, "How Chief Danielle Miller continues to keep Maxwell safe."

"What's wrong?" Kevin asked.

Von quickly relaxed his furrowed brow. "What do you mean?"

"Why are you glaring at your laptop with that scowl on your face?"

"No reason."

He reached for the lid. Before Von could slam it shut, Kevin grabbed the keyboard and swung it around.

"Ohh, no wonder," Kevin said, his frown now rivaling Von's. "Dani made the front page of *The Maxwell Times* again, huh. The last thing that attention-obsessed woman needs is another cover story, praising her for simply doing her job."

"Well…"

"Well what?"

"You do have to give her credit, Kev. This town had never been hit with a crime so brutal. And Dani did manage to solve the case."

"Did she? Or was it her brother and Chloe who cracked it?"

Emitting a condescending chuckle, Von slid the laptop toward the other side of the desk. "Okay, now you're just being cynical. RPS and the Maxwell PD may bump heads from time to time. But we can't take away from the fact that Dani worked the hell out of that investigation. She was under a ton of pressure, too, having just been named chief of police. Not to mention she had the attention of the national news media all over her."

"Hold on, Von. Are my ears deceiving me, or are you actually taking up for your archnemesis?"

"I'd like to think that I'm simply stating facts. Obviously Dani isn't my favorite person in the world. But we have to give credit where credit is due."

"If only your father could hear you now. Hamilton Reed did not build this great company and hand it down to you just for you to turn around and cozy up to your biggest rival—"

"Cozy up?" Von interrupted. "That's a bit of a stretch, isn't it?"

"I don't know. You tell me. Because it's sounding like the secret crush you've had on Dani since high school is rearing its ugly head."

Von snatched his mug and bolted from his chair. "Okay, now you've *completely* lost the script. I think we're done here. Plus I need more coffee."

Responding with a thin-lipped smirk, Kevin followed him out the door. "Whatever, man. Listen, I'll do you a favor and end the interrogation there. But don't forget, I've known you since we were eight. There isn't much you can hide from me."

"Come see me once you get the officers scheduled for those upcoming events," Von shot back over his shoulder while strutting through a maze of cubicles spread across the expansive, loft-style office.

"Way to evade the conversation!"

"I have no idea what you're talking about!"

But that was a lie. He knew exactly what Kevin meant, having spent years trying to hide his attraction to Dani.

As stunning as she'd always been, Dani never flaunted her beauty or intelligence. Von found that extremely appealing. Given the rift between their fathers, however, he couldn't bring himself to cross enemy lines and ask her out. Not that she ever would've agreed. That was made perfectly clear through her standoffish attitude and unbreakable familial bond. Getting anywhere near her was damn near impossible. So Von never tried. Nor had he revealed his true feelings to anyone.

Von knew Dani's disdain toward him stemmed from their fathers' feud. Nevertheless, he'd followed her lead, fronting as if he weren't the least bit interested. But deep down, he always wondered whether she was feeling him, too.

*Highly doubtful...*

Hovering over the coffee maker inside the break room, Von poured his third cup of the morning. It wasn't like him to down so much caffeine that early. But he needed it to settle his scattered thoughts. It didn't help that Kevin had stormed into his office the moment he'd arrived, throwing his entire routine off course. As the hours ticked by, it felt as though he was running on fumes.

*"Von!"* the receptionist's shrill voice boomed over the intercom. She still hadn't figured out how to use her inside voice with the new system.

The verbal blow sent a stream of hot coffee dripping down Von's wrist. "Damn it..." he hissed, flinging his burning hand through the air like a spinning windmill. As he set off toward the front of the office, Iga proceeded to make her announcement over the loudspeaker.

"Von, I transferred a call to your office from a Melody Anderson. I repeat, *Melody Anderson*. Since you seem to have stepped away from your desk, she'll be calling your cell phone and asked that you please pick up rather than send her to voicemail like you normally do. Thank you."

Bursts of muffled giggles arose from the cubicles.

"Please get back to work," Von said on the way to his office. The moment he closed to door behind him, his cell rang. Disregarding Melody's request, he sent her call to voicemail. Von didn't have time to keep explaining to his former fling why he couldn't see her any longer. Plus she knew not to call during peak work hours.

*"Von!"* Iga's voice roared through the intercom once again. "Sending a call to your office. It's Officer Bryant. He's at Cole's Ski Resort and says it's an emergency!"

Just as he reached for the phone, Kevin stuck his head inside the office. "I don't like the sound of that. Bryant never calls with an emergency."

The moment Von picked up the receiver, the officer yelled, "You and the team need to get to Cole's. Immediately!"

## Chapter Three

Dani lurched in her chair at the soft knock against her office doorframe. She glanced up, slamming her laptop shut at the sight of Troy.

"Hey," she muttered. "What's up?"

He entered slowly, eyeing her curiously while balancing a cup of coffee in each hand. "Are you all right? You look like you just saw one of those mummified zombies you used to dream about back when we were kids."

"I'm fine," she lied, still shaken up from the assault outside the Zonian two weeks ago. The lack of leads or suspects only made things worse, as did the alarming comments she'd just read on the Maxwell PD's online forum.

Troy set the coffee on the desk and glanced up at the wall. A satisfied nod preceded his grin of approval.

"What are you cheesing at?" Dani asked.

"That photo of me, you and Chloe at Cole's Ski Resort. Thank you for finally taking down the other one. This is a much better look."

"Don't mention it. Now that you're dating my best friend, I had no choice but to replace the picture with one that represents your new life. Anyway, what's going on? I'm short on time today and need to prep for our community beat meeting."

Taking a seat, Troy pushed aside several piles of paper before propping his elbows onto the desk. "First things first. What is going on with this office? It isn't like you to be this messy. Normally when I walk in here, everything's in divine order, you're disinfecting the computers, the phone, the drawer handles…"

"I'm just swamped, that's all."

"If you say so. But I'm worried about you, sis. I know you're still recovering from the attack. Yet you refuse to talk to someone."

"Here we go again." Hunching over in her chair, Dani rolled her head, wincing at the pain running across her forehead. She reached for her neck. Ran her fingertips along the faint scars lining her throat. When Troy's eyes tightened in her direction, she tore her hand away and sat straight up. "I appreciate your concern. However, like I said, I'm fine. Please don't worry about me."

"Yeah, well, I don't believe that. Look at you. You're obviously in pain, but you won't go see your doctor. A little therapy would do you some good, too. And this *office*…" Troy swept his arms over the desk like a game show host presenting a prize. "You are the epitome of a neat freak. Yet everything's in disarray. You've got old cups lying everywhere, stacks of reports that need to be filed, unopened mail and boxes piling up. Why don't I see if Chloe can come in and help you get organized—"

"Absolutely not," Dani insisted, tossing a few paper cups in the trash. "I've got everything under control and can have this office looking pristine in no time. As for the pain, I've just got a tension headache. Nothing a couple of ibuprofen can't cure. As a matter of fact…"

Dani ignored the disapproving click of Troy's tongue while reaching inside her drawer and grabbing the bottle.

She popped three pills, swallowing them down with a gulp of scalding hot coffee.

*"Gah,"* she gagged, the bitter brew scorching her tongue.

"See? That's what I'm talking about, D. You're off. Your head is all over the place. Let me go and grab you some ice."

"I'm good, Troy. Please. Sit back down and tell me what you need. And make it quick. My meeting's starting soon."

"I know. That's why I came to talk to you. All of Maxwell buzzing about the attack. And everyone knows we don't have any persons of interest to speak of. People are gonna be asking a lot of questions at that meeting and I'm sure they're all worried. How do you want to approach this?"

"Well, first of all, I think the assailant really wanted to scare me and undermine my authority. If that guy wanted me dead, I would be. He attacked me from behind with no warning. I was completely powerless. One or two more tugs from that wire and I'd be dead. And I blame myself for that. I got too comfortable. I should've had my gun in hand. Instead it was tucked away inside my purse, leaving me no chance to defend myself—"

"Dani, don't do that. This was not your fault. You have got to stop blaming yourself. Moving forward, we just have to be more vigilant. More aware of our surroundings. But you're right about the gun thing. Keep it out of your purse and on your hip, whether you're on duty or not."

A soft snicker escaped Dani's lips. She rolled her shoulders as the effects of the pain meds began to kick in.

"What are you snorting about?" Troy asked.

"You. My little brother, whom I still consider to be a rookie cop, giving me advice on how to handle myself."

"But am I wrong?"

"No, you're not wrong at all. And point taken."

Dani picked up her cup, this time blowing into it before

taking another sip of coffee. "You still haven't mentioned why you stopped by."

"Have you, um…have you checked the Maxwell PD's website this morning?"

*Damn it.*

She was hoping to have Chuck, their digital forensics expert, investigate the disturbing comments, remove them discreetly and then present the team with his findings before raising the alarm prematurely.

"I have," she rasped, unable to hide the quiver in her voice.

"So, what are you thinking?"

Anxiety rumbled in the pit of Dani's stomach. She opened her laptop and launched the Maxwell PD's website. A haze of disgust blurred her vision as she reread the comments.

*Imagine getting all that attention for catching a killer, just to turn around and get attacked. Chief Miller must feel like a real loser…*

*Taking all credit for making an arrest when your team actually deserves the accolades is WILD! Serves Chief Miller right that she was almost killed.*

*I just heard the news that Chief Miller was assaulted. Next time, I hope the attacker finishes the job. Maybe I should step up and do it for him…*

The words stung like acid, filling her with a bitter sense of vulnerability.

"I'm so sorry, sis," Troy whispered, his thumbs flying across his cell phone. "I'm texting Chuck now to see if he can delete those comments off the site."

"Thanks. I was planning on doing that right before you came in. And no need to be sorry. We need to be proactive. Find the evidence that'll tie this back to RPS."

Troy fingers froze mid-messaging. "Wait, what are you talking about?"

"Don't tell me you haven't put two and two together. This is the work of Von and his little flunkies."

"And what proof do you have of that?"

"Well, for starters, isn't it funny how Von disappeared from the Zonian right before we left? He had plenty of time to sneak inside my Jeep and lie in wait before he attacked."

Shifting in his chair, Troy bobbed his head, as if contemplating the theory. "I think that's a bit of a reach, don't you? Because again, where's the evidence? And why would Von do something like that? I get that our families aren't on the best of terms. But I don't think it's escalated to the point where he'd assault you."

"You're so naive, Troy. Von *hates* me. He hates all of us. RPS was built on the Reed family's disdain for the Millers. Von's father taught him the inner workings of the crime world—he'd be the perfect criminal. And the motive is obvious. You remember how jealous Von was when we caught the serial killer. He couldn't stand to see Maxwell PD get all that praise."

"Was it Von himself, or some of his officers?"

"Who cares!" Dani exclaimed. "The point is, RPS as a whole is salty and bitter. Since it's Von's company, he's included in that. The man is against me. He's trying to make me pay for my success. For *our* success."

"By viciously attacking you?"

Dani jumped up, her chair slamming against the wall as she paced the cluttered floor. "You don't have to believe me. The truth will eventually reveal itself. It's just a matter of time."

"Well, when it does, I'll be waiting," Troy retorted, catching a box of pepper spray teetering on the edge of the desk. "Until then, we should keep an open mind rather than jump to conclusions."

A knock at the door prevented Dani from arguing any further. "Come in!"

Chuck swung it open, his frizzy red hair blasting from his scalp like a fireworks display. "Hey, sorry to interrupt. Just wanted to let you know that everything is set up in the conference room for the beat meeting."

"Good, thank you." Dani paused, taking in his gaunt, anxious expression. "What's going on? You don't look like yourself."

"I'm cool. I just wanna make sure you are, too, after seeing those crazy messages on the website."

"I'm fine. Especially since I know who left them." A side-eye from Troy led her to say, "At least I *think* I know. I believe it's the same person who—"

"We should probably head to the conference room, Chief," Troy interrupted, standing before she could finish. "I'm sure the people have a lot to say, and we don't wanna be late."

A stare-down between the siblings commenced, sending Chuck tiptoeing out into the hallway.

"I'll see you two there," he said before jetting off.

Grabbing the agendas off the printer, Dani asked, "So is this what you're doing now? Interrupting your boss while I'm trying to speak with one of my employees?"

"I'd like to think I stopped you from making false accusations."

"I'd like to think of it as me stating my opinion. I'm curious to know what Chuck has to say. What the entire department has to say, actually. Because it's no secret that RPS is out to ruin Maxwell PD's reputation. What better way to do it than to take down the head of the department?"

"I hear you, Dani. But all I'm saying is that in order to back the claim, we've got to have the evidence."

"Thanks for stating the obvious. And that would be nice. But we've scoured the street where the attack took place numerous times and found nothing. My Jeep was thoroughly processed at the lab. Again, nothing. We've watched surveillance footage from every business in the area that had cameras and couldn't make out the suspect. At this point, I wish I could bring Von in for questioning. Find out exactly where he went after leaving the Zonian."

"And on what grounds would you be doing that?"

Breezing past Troy, Dani rolled her eyes. "My suspicions. But you missed the key words. I said 'I wish.' Not 'I will.'"

On the way to the conference room, she noticed a commotion brewing near the front desk as cops rushed out the door. The desk clerk, Natalia, pivoted from side to side, her fluffy blond bob whirling through the air like spinning cotton candy.

"Nat!" Dani said, making a beeline toward her while staring out the window. Officers were hopping inside their cars, flipping on the sirens and flying toward the exit. "What's going on?"

"Chief Miller! I thought you'd already left for Cole's Ski Resort!"

"Why would I be going to Cole's? Our beat meeting starts in a couple of minutes."

"Listen, I was just on the phone with Kelly—"

"Wait, who's Kelly?"

"She's the resort's concierge. While we were talking, I heard all this screaming in the background. I asked what in the world was happening. Apparently, somebody was found injured inside a stairwell. And he might be dead."

*"Dead,"* Dani shot back. "Did she give you any details? Did he get sick? Or was it a fall? Or…something worse?"

"I have no idea. But I did hear someone yell out that they'd seen blood coming from the victim's head."

Dani rocked back on her heels as the air grew thick with tension. A sense of dread engulfed her.

"Troy, can you go and get my things?" she panted before waving her hand at Natalia. "Go on. Tell me what details came in during the 9-1-1 call."

"I don't believe there was a 9-1-1 call. I only knew what was happening because I was on the phone with Kelly. When a few of our officers heard me getting worked up, they jumped into action and headed to the resort."

"I'm just confused as to why no one called emergency services."

A flustered Natalia grabbed a nearby file folder and began fanning her face. "I have no idea. Maybe since RPS was already on the scene, everyone thought the situation was under control."

"Wait, RPS is there?"

"According to Kelly, yes."

Dani's head whipped around, her fists clenching as Troy approached with her things. "We need to get to Cole's. *Immediately.*"

## Chapter Four

Von stared down at the victim inside the resort's back stairwell. An excruciating mix of shock and sadness swirled through his chest. Growing up, Cole's had been a second home for him, as his mother was a manager for the beloved establishment. It was still considered one of Maxwell's premier attractions, with tourists visiting from around the world. From the mountain retreat's picturesque timber-framed lodge to its elegant European-inspired furnishings, vacationers enjoyed breathtaking views of the snowcapped peaks and deep valleys surrounding the chalet.

Von had made countless friends there over the years while taking advantage of the various activities. Whether it was skiing, tubing and snowboarding in the winter or golfing, hiking and swimming in the summer, he'd mastered them all.

News of there being a dead body on the scene had sent him reeling. Von braced himself before entering the vestibule, pulling slow, deliberate breaths while studying the victim. It wasn't often that he'd been in the presence of a dead person. The sight was as disturbing as the stench of rotting copper drifting through the tight, stuffy space.

Covering his nose with his hand, Von fought the urge to gag in front of his team. As a leader, the last thing he wanted was to appear weak, as if he lacked the grit to maintain his composure. But seeing the pool of congealed blood splayed beneath the man's head sent his stomach roiling, making it difficult to keep his cool.

The chaos surrounding the scene rang out on the other side of the door, as Von's officers had managed to keep the guests at bay. "Just to confirm, someone did call 9-1-1, right?" he asked for the third time.

"Yes," Officer Bryant huffed. "At least I believe they did. When I ran past the front desk to see what was going on, the concierge was on the phone with law enforcement."

"I wonder why the paramedics aren't here yet? There's only so much our team can do—"

Von broke off mid-sentence when the Maxwell PD stormed through the door like an army of soldiers prepared for combat. Dani led the charge, her slender, curvy silhouette cutting through his officers like a blade. Von watched in awe as she carved a path around her men. Paramedics trailed closely behind, quickly administering aid to the victim.

*"Von Reed!"* Dani barked.

He stood at attention, as if it were his first day of boot camp. "Yes, Chief Miller?"

"Can you please explain to me why—" The question came to a sudden halt when she glanced down. "Oh my God…" Grabbing hold of Troy, she whispered, "Do you see this?"

"I do," he replied, rubbing his chin.

Von cautiously made his way toward the pair, his eyes darting between them and the victim. "What am I missing? Do you two know the victim?"

Dani and Troy exchanged glances. "I'll get the scene secured," he told her. "Then start up the investigation."

"Good, thank you." Pointing at Von, she said, "You, come with me," before marching up to the second-floor landing.

He followed closely, homing in on her trembling lower lip as she steadied herself against the wall.

"You do know who that is, don't you?" Dani asked.

"According to the guest services manager, his name is Gordon Edwards."

"Right. As in former *Lieutenant* Gordon Edwards. He worked for the Maxwell PD for over three decades before retiring. Lieutenant Edwards was my mentor. That man is one of the main reasons why I'm still on the force. He helped me through some of my toughest times."

Extending an arm, Von murmured, "I'm so sorry, Chief."

She brushed him aside with a dismissive swipe, as if he were a pestering gnat. "Thanks, but I don't need your sympathy. What I need is for you to explain why RPS decided to handle this situation on their own instead of calling 9-1-1."

"We did call 9-1-1. At least that's what Officer Bryant told me. Actually, it was the resort's concierge who made the call."

"*No*, the concierge just so happened to be on the phone with our receptionist. So that's strike one. Here's my next question. How did RPS get here so quickly? Do you have some insider on the premises who thought it would be a good idea to call you instead of the police department?"

"Of course not, Chief. This resort is one of my clients. RPS is here on site every single day."

"So you were here when the incident occurred?"

"No. Officer Bryant was. He's the one who called and told me what was going on."

Dani blew a frustrated sigh while tossing her sandy brown curls into a bun. Her wide-set hazel eyes raced between Von and the floor below as a glimmer of sweat traced the curves of her delicate features. Even in the midst of turmoil, he couldn't help but notice her beauty.

*Stop it. Get your head in the game...*

"So rather than dial 9-1-1," Dani said, "Officer Bryant calls *you*."

"Yes. Because again, he knew the concierge was reporting the situation to the Maxwell PD. Or at least that's what he thought."

"Okay, let's just end this conversation here since it isn't going anywhere."

Just as Dani grabbed hold of the railing, Von reached for her, gently pulling her back. "Wait, since my team and I were on the scene before you arrived, don't you want to know what we saw? And hear what we think may have happened?"

She hesitated, her right foot hanging over the top stair. A few moments passed before she took a step toward him. "Sure, Von. What are you thinking? Does this look like an accident, or something worse?"

"Oh, something worse, for sure. From what I can tell, it looks as if the victim was shot in the head."

"I cannot believe this," Dani muttered, backing into the wall before doubling over. "It is a nightmare."

Von slowly approached. When she didn't shun him, he rested his hand on her shoulder. This time, she didn't pull away. "You have my condolences."

Shooting up just as quickly as she'd collapsed, Dani ran her palms down the front of her navy blazer and charged back down the stairs. "Look, I need to get to work. Could you please gather up your men and leave my crime scene?"

*Are you serious?* Von almost blurted before biting down on his jaw. *Just let it go. She's already upset. Don't make it worse.*

Trailing her down the stairs, he heard the paramedic say, "There is nothing more we can do. The victim is deceased."

Von held his breath while awaiting her reaction. Dani responded with a nod, her face crumpling slightly as she motioned to an officer carrying an evidence collection kit.

Everyone looked on while he cracked it open, pulling out evidence bags, fingerprint dusting powder, lifting tape and swabs.

"Excuse me," Dani said to Officer Bryant, who was still hovering near the victim. "I'm going to need for you to leave. This is official police business. Plus you're in the way."

Just as the officer puffed out his chest, Von nudged him. "No problem, Chief Miller. Guys, let's give Maxwell PD some space."

Bryant tossed him a look of irritation. Ignoring it, Von headed toward the exit. As much as he wanted to jump in and assist, the chief had spoken. And contrary to what several of his officers wanted to believe, the Maxwell PD took precedence over RPS—especially when it came to crime scenes.

"Excuse me, Officer Bryant?" someone called out from the other side of the cracked door. "Could I speak with you for a minute? I'd like to share some information that might be relevant to what happened here."

The officer swung open the door, replying, "Of course," before stepping into the lobby.

"Hey, hold on!" Dani called out, running after him.

Von followed closely behind in the event he needed to play mediator.

"Mr. Finglass?" Dani said to the man.

"Yes, Chief Miller?" he rasped, pulling nervously at the gray beard hanging from his drooping jowls.

"If you saw something here pertaining to this incident, then you need to report it to the Maxwell PD. *Not* RPS."

"I'd rather not," Mr. Finglass shot back, shrugging his husky shoulders.

"And why is that?" Dani pressed.

"Well, considering how long it took law enforcement to apprehend the killer last year, I'm not convinced your department is capable of handling another murder. So I don't know. Maybe this go-round I should put my trust in RPS. Especially since they were the first officers here on the scene."

"Mr. Finglass," Von said, hoping to quell Dani's frustration as she tossed her hands in the air. "RPS doesn't have the legal authority to work this investigation."

"What do you mean?"

"What he means is," Dani interjected, "the Maxwell PD's legal authority is backed by the U.S. State Government. Therefore, we're the ones who enforce the laws, make arrests, process crime scenes... Do you see where I'm going with this?"

He stood there for several seconds with his jaw suspended in midair. "I—I'm not quite sure that I do."

"You know what..." Dani uttered just as Troy emerged from the stairwell.

He took one look at her asked, "What's going on?"

As she caught him up on the situation, Von turned to Mr. Finglass. "Sir, please. Whatever you wanted to share with RPS, just tell it to Maxwell PD. When it comes to the justice system, they handle the heavy lifting. My company does things like protect private properties and various clients. We don't have the legal clout that the police department does and can't enforce the law like they can. Does that make sense?"

The man's gaze lowered as he slowly uncrossed his arms. "Well, when you put it that way, I guess it does. Who should I talk to?"

Pointing in Dani's direction, Von called out, "Chief Miller? Mr. Finglass is prepared to speak with you now."

"Great. Thank you, sir. I'm going to have you talk to Officer Miller while I have a word with RPS."

"Oh no," Von grumbled under his breath.

Once Troy escorted Mr. Finglass toward a corner of the lobby, Dani approached Officer Bryant. "Would you mind answering a few questions since you were the first one on the scene?"

"I—I uh…"

"Of course he wouldn't mind," Von answered for him, his eyelids twitching with embarrassment. He'd trained his officers to stand up to anyone, and that included the Maxwell PD. "But I would like to stick around while you two talk." When Dani failed to respond, he added, "If that's all right with you, of course." Again, no response. "You know, since Officer Bryant works for my company and all—"

"Fine," Dani relented. "Let's step away from the stairwell and give my officers some space. Plus I'd like to talk in private."

Officer Bryant tossed Von a look of thanks as they followed her through the lobby. When Von saw Dani heading outside, he said, "Bundle up," before zipping his army-green parka.

The threesome tramped through the snow toward the sleigh ride's cedar pergola waiting area. Swirls of flurries whipped through the air, melting against their skin once they stopped underneath infrared lamps hanging from the structure's roof.

Gritting his chattering teeth, Von suppressed the urge to ask why they couldn't talk inside. The lobby's warm English brick fireplace was calling his name. But he already knew how she'd respond. Dani would insist that they needed to speak away from the gawkers. The real answer was that she probably didn't want anyone to see the Maxwell PD mingling with RPS considering they were bitter rivals.

Dani pulled her cell phone from her back pocket and hit the record button. After rattling off the location, date and time, she said, "I've got Officers Reed and Bryant from Reed Protective Services here with me. Officer Bryant was one of the first men on the scene, where former Lieutenant Gordon Edwards was found dead inside the resort's back stairwell. It appears as if he sustained a gunshot wound to the left temple. Officer Bryant, can you please tell me what happened from the moment you were informed that this incident had occurred?"

"Yeah, I uh, I..." His weight shifted from right to left as he peered over at Von.

*"Go on,"* Von insisted, his brows lifting expectantly as he encouraged him to speak.

"So, I was actually patrolling the area right outside of Cole's Sweet Shop when I heard screams coming from inside the main lodge. I made a run for it, charging through the lobby and pushing my way past the crowd that had gathered. It was actually a maintenance guy who found the body—"

"A maintenance guy?" Dani interrupted. "Do you know his name?"

"Mr. Stallworth, I believe."

"Got it. I'll be sure to speak with him. Now at what point did you conclude that the Maxwell PD had been contacted?"

"When I was sprinting past the concierge desk. That's when I overheard Kelly retelling the story and asking if the police were on the way."

Von held a hand in the air, interjecting, "Which could easily explain how Officer Bryant assumed 9-1-1 had been called. He had no idea that Kelly just so happened to be on the phone with your receptionist."

"Duly noted," Dani said.

Studying her stoic expression, Von couldn't tell if she really believed them. But it was obvious that she wasn't in the mood for questions. So he stood down and let her continue.

"What happened next?" she asked.

"When I reached the stairwell, I immediately began performing CPR on the victim. Then one of my partners stepped in who used to work as an EMT. While he administered chest compressions, I called Von. During that time, the victim was unresponsive."

"What about Cole's ski patrol EMTs?" Dani pressed. "Did anybody think to call them?"

"According to the staff, they were on the other side of the mountain treating a skier who'd been in an accident."

Von looked on as Dani's jaw clenched. He braced himself, expecting her to come undone. But instead she held her composure, urging Officer Bryant to continue with a flick of her wrist.

"So then my coworker pulled the cardiac defibrillator from the wall cabinet and tried using that, but it didn't work. The victim remained unresponsive. Soon after, your team arrived, along with paramedics."

"And as far as you could tell, the victim was already deceased when you got to the stairwell?"

"As far as I could tell, yes."

Grief took hold of Dani's somber expression as she turned away, her despondent gaze fixated on the snowy landscape. Once again, Von was hit with the need to comfort her. To assure her that everything would be okay. But he didn't dare try. Instead he stood there. Watching her stare into the distance. As if the pieces to solving the puzzle were hidden in the frosty terrain.

Regaining her composure, Dani spun around, a rekindled fire burning behind her eyes. "Is there anything else can you think of that might help us with this case, Officer Bryant?"

"Hmm, I think that's it."

"Okay then. Well, if something comes to mind, no matter how small, you know where to find me."

"I do."

As Dani set off toward the lodge, Von quickly added, "I'll do the same. And we'll all be sure to keep our antennas up in case any other intel emerges, whether it be around my office or out in the streets."

"You sure about that?" Dani asked over her shoulder.

"Of course I'm sure. Why wouldn't I be?"

She skidded to a sudden stop. Her hunter-green boots kicked up a cloud of snow that whirled around them. A few of the flurries landed on her lush lips.

*Look away...*

But he didn't, instead fixating on the flakes as they melted into her pink gloss. The visual activated a deep stirring sensation.

*You need to leave*, his told himself. *Just walk off.*

That feeling he felt was all too familiar. It didn't come around often. But when it did, he knew exactly what it meant. Strong desire, and innate attraction, toward whoever was standing in front of him.

"Officer Reed," Dani spat, "have you forgotten about the long-standing, toxic history between the Maxwell PD and RPS? To put it nicely, your company hasn't always been upfront when it comes to sharing intel with my department."

Von's lips parted. But nothing came out. He wanted to speak. Yet didn't quite know what to say. Because Dani was absolutely right.

A long stretch of silence ensued. Nothing could be heard beyond the eerie whistling winds swirling through the icy peaks.

"Excuse me," Officer Bryant said, "but um, Von? Should I excuse myself and let you two talk, or...whatever this is you're doing?"

"Yes," Von told him without taking his eyes off of Dani. "I think that would be a good idea." Once the crunch of snow beneath the officer's feet grew faint, Von stepped in closer. "Chief Miller, would you mind elaborating on that statement you just made?"

"I wouldn't mind at all. You do recall the various ways in which RPS has attempted to interfere in a number of past investigations, don't you?"

"Actually, no. I can't seem to recall that at all."

"So, you don't recall the rumors that were going around about how you and your employees were gathering leads on potential suspects linked to my cases, but weren't sharing them with the police department?"

"Once again, no. I do not."

As Dani moved in, her arms crossed tightly over her chest, Von inhaled a hint of citrus drifting from her neck. He swiveled slightly, hoping to avoid another whiff of the intoxicating aroma.

"Welp," she snipped, "fortunately for you, my memory does serve me correctly. I can recall all the ways in which RPS has tried to sabotage my cases. I'm pretty sure we both know why, too."

"Speak for yourself, because I'm completely clueless. Why don't you enlighten me?"

Dani let off a patronizing chuckle that misted through the air. "Von, when it comes to prior cases, you and your guys were always so desperate to catch my suspects and claim all the glory. You'd go behind our backs and interview alleged witnesses. Sneak onto crime scenes after hours to try to collect evidence. Call the forensics lab, trying to get test results. I should've arrested all of you for obstruction of justice, witness tampering *and* interfering with our investigations. The sad thing is, I wouldn't be surprised if your father was the one encouraging your criminal behavior."

"Chief Miller, those guys you're referring to were never official RPS employees. I'd hired them on a contractual basis to work a couple of events when I was understaffed. That's it. And as for my father, please don't bring him into this."

"Oh, it's a little too late for that. He brought himself into it. Back when my father was running the police department, Maxwell's criminal justice system was still of one accord. But then once your dad launched RPS, all hell broke loose.

Things haven't been the same since. I actually wouldn't be surprised if RPS was stirring all this up in an attempt to take down the force. The attack on me, the vile messages left on Maxwell PD's website, Lieutenant Edwards's murder…"

Dani's biting words burned away the numbness of the cold, leaving Von seething in his stance. "Hold on. You really think that RPS is behind all this?"

"I'm just saying that it wouldn't surprise me if you were—"

"Yeah, I think we're done here," Von interrupted, his Timberland boots pounding the snow as he backed away. "I don't know what you're going through, Chief Miller, but you're losing it. Which is sad, considering I could be an asset to you. But I'm not gonna stand here and let you take your frustrations out on me. However, I will tell you this. When it comes to these crimes? You need to take your focus off of RPS. If you don't, you'll never solve the case."

# Chapter Five

"Trust me," Dani said to Chloe and Troy, "I went off on Von so bad that there is no going back. At this point, he and I are enemies for life."

The three of them were sitting out on Dani's backyard deck, sipping wine and preparing dinner while watching the sun set. The yard had become a sanctuary of sorts, a place where she could unwind after long, hectic days.

She settled against her chair's red cedar frame, listening to melodic calls of northern mockingbirds. Her eyes followed the smoke drifting from the grill as it disappeared into her desert willow tree. The instant her lids lowered, visions of Lieutenant Edwards's dead body flashed through her mind like lightning, disrupting the moment of peace.

Over a week had passed since his murder, and no viable leads had emerged. The only DNA found near the scene belonged to the lieutenant. There were no fingerprints, foreign materials or identifiable secretions that could be traced back to the crime.

The lack of evidence cast a somber cloud over the department. Dani worked tirelessly to keep the morale afloat. But as each day went by with no new clues, fear began to drown out any remaining hope. The once-bustling energy around the station transformed into oppressive silence. The usual chatter and lighthearted updates morphed into clack-ing keyboards, muffled phone calls and a team on edge, desperate for a break.

But no one carried the pressure quite like Dani. While the police department worked as a whole, she was their leader. The expectations placed on her were greater. And the bur-den of every failure was hers to bear.

Dani's deepening concern over the recent murder left her confined to her desk, mulling over the case for hours on end. It had gotten so bad that Troy insisted she pull herself away and come home early for a home-cooked meal. Since she didn't have the energy to boil an egg, she'd agreed. And now, as the savory scent of halibut, Greek potatoes and roasted asparagus drifted through the air, Dani was glad she did.

"Personally?" Chloe said while refilling their glasses. "I don't blame you for going off on Von. However, you did *kind of* accuse the man of being a criminal, so…there's that."

"I said what I said. And I meant it. I wouldn't put anything past Von or any of his guys. It really pissed him off when I threw his father into the conversation. Being that he's such a daddy's boy, he'd do anything to please that man. And noth-ing would appease Old Man Reed more than taking down the Maxwell PD."

"Seriously, Dani?" Troy interjected. "You really think Von and his father are killers?"

"They could be," Dani insisted, stomping her bare foot against the mahogany planks. "Those men have huge egos. They'd do anything to shine a positive light on themselves and boost their business. Look at how Mr. Reed treated Dad back in the day. He left our father high and dry when he needed him the most. I know firsthand what it feels like to be a young new police chief. Your officers are all you've got. So to be betrayed and abandoned like that is beyond hurtful."

"Well, not to defend him or anything, but Mr. Reed was

hurt, too. He thought that Dad was being too hard on him, and I'm sure having to take orders from a friend was tough. Also, I don't even think our fathers hate each other like they used to. So much time has passed, it seems to be more like indifference these days than anything. But the bottom line is that I just don't think the Millers are killers." Tossing Chloe a wink, he added, "See what I did there?"

Shifting in her chair, Dani stared Troy down as he raised the top on the grill. "Troy, please. *Focus.* And I'm sorry, but whose side are you on?"

"Yours, of course. Which is why I can't stand here and lie to you. You've got to think rationally. I won't be convinced that RPS is involved in these crimes until I see some evidence that's directly linked to them."

"Best friend," Dani said to Chloe, "please step in and have my back on this. Do you think I'm wrong?"

*"Well…"*

"Oh, so now both of you are ganging up on me?" Grabbing her cell, Dani scrolled through the contacts. "I should call up some of my officers and talk to them instead of you two. Clearly I need to surround myself with more likeminded individuals."

Chloe threw her napkin over her head and waved it in the air. "Okay, okay, I surrender. Put the phone down, and let's seriously talk suspects. Aside from RPS, who else do you think may have wanted Lieutenant Edwards dead?"

"It could've been one of our officers," Troy suggested. "Not to throw Maxwell PD under the bus or anything, but think about how angry some of them were when you became police chief. Lieutenant Edwards was critical in you landing that job."

"That's true," Dani agreed. "But I just can't see someone on our squad being bitter enough to kill a retired lieutenant, just to get back at me."

"I can."

"Unfortunately," Chloe cut in, "so can I. This could be their way of getting back at the person who helped you, *and* burdening you with yet another murder investigation. Add in the attack and those messages on Maxwell PD's website, it could all be a ploy to get you to quit, which may be what they ultimately want."

Pulling her knees to her chest, Dani stared down at the plate of food that Troy set in front of her. "You know, when I think back on the day I got promoted, it was so bittersweet. I was thrilled, of course. So were a lot of my fellow officers. There were definitely those who weren't, though. But never in my wildest dreams did I imagine all this would come with the job."

"Who would?" Troy asked, handing Chloe her plate, then taking a seat. "If we're naming names here, I'd say Kenin, Henderson and Simons should be at the top of your list of haters." There was a noticeable tremor in Troy's hands as he cut into his potatoes. "*Damn.* I really do hate that we're even having this conversation. But it's a sad reality that we have to consider."

The sting of betrayal soured Dani's appetite as she pushed her plate away. Chloe, her expression softening, said, "Here's a thought. Maybe Lieutenant Edwards's murder was a personal attack that had nothing to do with the Maxwell PD *or* RPS."

"We've considered that," Dani said. "His ski club partners were there the day he was killed. They've all been cleared. We talked to his family. His wife said she was with friends that afternoon, and they backed that claim. Their oldest son, Martin, was at work. But…"

"But what?" Chloe asked.

"We're still looking into their youngest son, Evan. He has gotten into some trouble in the past. Drug-related. Lieutenant Edwards was pretty hard on him, right along with his dealer, who just so happened to be Evan's best friend. The dealer ended up doing time while Evan was sent to rehab."

"So you're thinking those two could be behind the murder?"

"It's a possibility. We're still working to verify their alibis. They were allegedly on a road trip to Orange County to visit a marijuana megastore that recently opened. Chuck already reached out to the store's security team to request surveillance footage. They haven't responded yet. If we don't hear back soon, we'll get Vista Del Sol's police department involved, then go from there."

"Here's a thought," Troy said before downing a mouthful of food. "Maybe the lieutenant's murder was a random act of violence."

"Could be…" As Dani settled into the conversation, she reached for her fork and stabbed at a stalk of asparagus. Hunger pangs hit after the first bite. "Mmm, this is so good, Troy."

"Thanks. I'm glad we're doing this…" His voice drifted as crinkles framed his downcast gaze. "There's something else I've been thinking about. And I hope I'm wrong about this, but it could be that we're dealing with a copycat killer here."

Dani winced at the thought, chasing it down with a long gulp of wine. "That would be a nightmare. It's actually crossed my mind more than once, but I'm not dwelling on it. My focus is on catching the killer before another murder occurs."

"*If* another murder occurs," Chloe said. "Let's hope this was just an isolated incident. Did the surveillance footage from Cole's security team reveal anything?"

"No, unfortunately. So many of the guests were walking around wearing ski masks, helmets and goggles, which made it almost impossible to ID them. Another thing I've been thinking about is if there were other witnesses who saw something and withheld it from us so they could pass it along to RPS, like Mr. Finglass attempted to do."

"Let's hope not," Troy said, reaching for a second helping of potatoes. "I can't imagine anyone would wanna play those types of games in this situation. Not after everything we went through. As for Finglass, I'd hate to call the man a liar, but his recollection of what he *thought* he saw was completely off. The bloody palm print he claimed to have spotted near the stairwell was a red arrow painted on the wall. Then the alleged argument he'd sworn he saw the lieutenant having with a ski instructor never happened. Edwards and his ski crew rented a private slope and no instructor had gone near the area. Finglass probably saw him talking to one of his guys."

"Yeah," Dani said, running her hand along the back of her stiff neck. "He just wanted some attention and accolades. On another note, I have got to stop sitting behind my desk so much and get some exercise. My entire body feels like it's been dipped in cement I am so stiff." Stopping mid-sentence, she reached over and nudged Chloe's arm. "Weren't we supposed to be signing back up for Spin classes this fall?"

"We were. I'm still waiting on you to tell me whether you wanna be on the Monday, Wednesday, Friday schedule, or Tuesday, Thursday, Saturday. So the ball's in your court, friend."

"Let me check my calendar tomorrow and get back to you."

"That's what she told me two months ago," Chloe muttered to Troy.

"I heard that," Dani quipped. "I need to figure out the next steps in this investigation. My entire squad is on edge.

And they're getting discouraged by the lack of evidence and leads. I've gotta do something to lift their spirits. Keep them motivated."

Troy stood and began clearing their plates. "Let's get aggressive then. Show the team that we're doing everything we can to solve this thing. We'll go back to Cole's and question the staff again. Drive out to Vista Del Sol and talk to the security team about that surveillance footage in person. Try to get a hold of Cole's maintenance guy again who discovered Lieutenant Edwards's body. I still think it's strange how he left the resort before we had a chance to really question him, and he hasn't been back to work since."

"I don't think he's our guy," Dani countered. "Officer Shields spoke to him briefly before he clocked out. I watched the body cam footage, and he was so shaken up that he could barely talk. Didn't seem like it was an act, either. And as far as him taking time off work goes, who can blame him? The man is probably traumatized."

"Well, when you put it that way…"

"Plus there was nothing at the scene that would indicate he was involved. He didn't have any blood on him, there was no weapon found in his possession, and his DNA didn't turn up anywhere near the scene or on the body."

Chloe emitted an ominous moan while pouring the last of the wine. "I'm about to say something that neither of you want to hear."

"Which is?" Dani asked.

"Back when I was working for the Chicago PD, any time we had a murder scene with no evidence left behind, we'd just have to wait it out. See if the killer would strike again. And hope that next time, he'd slip up and leave a trail of evidence."

"Hmph…" Dani pulled herself up from the table. "I think I need more wine. While I grab a bottle, I'm gonna call the head of the crime lab again. Ask her to go over the results one more time, just to make sure she didn't miss anything. I can't sit back and wait for another body to turn up. This isn't another random case to me. It's personal. And when I think about these recent crimes, one thing comes to mind— I may be next."

# Chapter Six

Von downed the last of his whiskey sour while staring at his phone. He and Kevin had just left a meeting with the Maxwell Historical Society to finalize security details for a high-profile exhibit opening, and swung by the Zonian for drinks before calling it a night.

It had been a long, hectic few weeks since the death of Lieutenant Edwards. RPS had been bombarded with security requests, and a wave of tension had gripped the town.

"I wonder what's going on with the Maxwell PD," Kevin said. "I haven't heard a thing about Lieutenant Edwards's case. Are there any leads? Suspects? Persons of interest? *Anything?*"

"I have no clue. But I haven't heard anything, either. When I think back on Dani's attitude at the crime scene, I'm sure she wants to keep it that way. At least when it comes to me. That woman hates my guts."

"Yeah, well, that's on her. You had every right to be at Cole's that day."

"It wasn't just the fact that I was there," Von said. "Somehow wires got crossed, and Maxwell PD wasn't immediately called when the victim's body was found. So Dani assumed that RPS was trying to investigate the scene on our own and purposely exclude the police department. That thought process led to her mentioning my father, then next thing I know, *boom*, she's accusing me of murder."

"Wait, *what*? I didn't know she took it that far."

Signaling the bartender, Von gestured that he needed a refill. "I'm telling you, Kev, our rivalry runs deep. So deep that I don't think *I* even realized how bad it was until now."

"But to accuse you of killing a man? Come on. *You*, a man whose father was on the force, who took over the family business and now works to keep people safe. Not to mention you volunteer with youth programs and look out for your elderly neighbors. You're probably the nicest guy I know!" Shaking his head in disgust, Kevin muttered, "I still don't understand what you see in that woman."

"What do you mean? I see in her what everybody else sees."

Rolling his head back, Kevin blew a rumbling grunt. "Ohh no you don't. Now before I get started, I will say this. Dani is attractive. But I can't name a man in this town who's actually attracted *to* her, other than you."

"Ha!" Von snorted so loudly that it turned a few heads. He ignored them while pushing Kevin's old-fashioned out of reach. "I think you may have had a little too much to drink, my friend. Because *me*, attracted to Dani? What in the hell would make you say something like that?"

"How about the fact that it's true? Do you really think you're inconspicuous enough to hide your feelings for her? Seriously, you've has a crush on her since elementary school—"

"Now *that* is a bold-faced lie."

"Is it though? Von, let's not forget that I'm your closest friend. I know you better than you know yourself. Plus, I see the way you look at Dani whenever she's around. The way you get all soft acting whenever she speaks to you, even if she's being rude as hell. Go on and admit it. You admire the woman. As a matter of fact, I think you're in love with her."

"Okay, now you're taking it way too far. Even if I did feel a little something toward her, it wouldn't matter. Thanks to our fathers, she is completely off-limits."

"But not once have you said you wouldn't want to be with her."

When Von broke eye contact and thanked the bartender for his drink, Kevin slid his phone in front of him.

"On another note, have you seen this?" he asked, enlarging the top story on *The Maxwell Times*'s website.

"No, I haven't," Von said before scanning the headline.

"Maxwell PD's Message Board Hit with Threats Against Police Chief."

"Damn. I'm reading through the threats now…"

*Police Chief Danielle Miller thinks she's a hotshot for solving that big murder case. Let's see whether it was a fluke, or if she can catch me, too.*

*Hey, Chief Miller! Be on the lookout, because I'm watching youuu. And when I get you, it won't be pretty.*

*I hope the chief enjoys being tied up and detained, because I've got a special spot in my basement waiting for her…*

Dread twisted inside Von's gut. He turned away, taking another long sip of his drink while thinking back on his conversation with Dani at the crime scene. It suddenly made sense why she was so defensive. The woman was probably terrified.

"That's pretty brutal," Kevin said. "I may not be too fond of Dani, but she doesn't deserve all that."

"I agree. I almost wanna call and see if she's okay. She has gone through so much hell already, and it's terrible that she's the focus of this misguided hate."

"Same. But do you really think Dani would want to hear from you? Especially if she thinks you're her suspect?"

"I don't know. If I had to guess, probably not. That doesn't mean I can't reach out in a show of support. What's happening here goes way beyond some ridiculous beef and her wild accusations. This is real. The woman's life is in danger. Not to mention Dani runs the police department. Like them or not, RPS is almost a subdivision of the force."

Kevin let off a dry chuckle while swirling the ice in his glass. "Yeah, maybe in your mind. But in reality, the Maxwell PD looks at us as being some substandard watchdog group, even though we're far from that. We are the gold standard of security firms. We're elite and highly trained, our clientele is ultraexclusive, and we provide the ultimate level of protection. Yet the police department continues to disrespect us."

"But that disrespect didn't start with us. We inherited it. So maybe it could end with us, you know? Dani and I don't have to keep fueling the fire that our fathers started. We could be the ones to put it out, and work to unite RPS and Maxwell PD."

"Good luck with that," Kevin retorted, turning his attention toward a group of women walking through the door. "Uh-oh…"

"Uh-oh, what?"

"Don't turn around."

"Why not?"

"Because your ex just walked in."

"Ugh," Von groaned, ducking his head in the other direction. "Which one?"

"That hostess you were seeing who works at Vortex Lounge. What's her name? Marissa? Miranda?"

*"Melody,"* Von corrected through tight lips.

"Yeah, Melody." Spinning on his stool, Kevin blew a low whistle. "Damn, man. I'm sorry, but she looks gorgeous, too."

Cutting his eyes over his shoulder, Von watched as Melody navigated her way through the crowd with ease. She relished the attention she drew, blowing air kisses to her admirers while swaying her lithe dancer's physique to the beat of the music. There was no denying her allure—the flawless raven pixie cut, radiant makeup, sexy black lace catsuit... But Melody's entire personality was built on her beauty, which had been a huge turnoff for Von.

"Tell me again why you two broke up?" Kevin asked.

"First of all, will you please turn back around before she sees us? I am not in the mood to answer a bunch of questions about where I've been and why I haven't called her. Secondly, there was no breakup. She and I didn't even date for a whole month."

Turning toward the bar, Kevin elbowed Von in the chest. "Quit being coy and answer the question. Why did you cut ties with her?"

"Long story short, she was too young for me. I didn't realize she was only twenty-four when I asked her out."

"Dude, haven't you heard? Age ain't nothing but a number."

"Yeah," Von huffed, "but not in her case. Melody was too superficial for my taste. Plus she runs the streets too much. She worked all hours of the night at the lounge, and when she wasn't there, she was out partying everywhere else."

"Nah, that's not it. You just don't wanna settle down."

"I wouldn't say all that. I'm just a busy man. I'm running a company and don't have much free time. But aside from not really being in a position to settle down, I don't want to settle. Why get involved with someone who I'm not really feeling?"

"You've got a point. But hey, don't pay too much attention to me. I don't know what's going on out here. I've been married and off the streets for a long time."

Von leaned in, raising his voice over the blaring techno music. "Yeah, you got lucky and found a good one right out of college. Some of us are still out here searching for our soulmates."

"At this point, you shouldn't be. You've met plenty of amazing women that you passed up for whatever reason. My wife and I alone have played matchmaker more times than I can count. But nobody's ever good enough for the great Von Reed. And I think I know why."

"Aww, here we go. I'm not even gonna take the bait."

Gripping his shoulder, Kevin replied, "You don't have to. I'll say it loud and clear. You're holding out for Dani."

"All right…" Von pushed away from the bar, his awkward chuckle masking the realization that he hadn't concealed his feelings as well as he'd thought.

"Oh no," Kevin grunted. "Brace yourself."

"For what?"

"Melody and her girls are making their way over here."

"Damn it. I should've left when I had the chance."

Von's muscles tensed as a slender hand drifted across the small of his back.

"Heyyy, Von-Von," Melody murmured in his ear.

Discreetly recoiling from her touch, he replied, "Hey, how's it going?"

"It's going well. But it would be even better if you'd buy me a drink, then explain why you haven't called me."

A fitting response eluded Von as he stood there, his mouth gaping and mind suddenly going blank.

"Aww, that's so cute," Melody purred, her sticky lip gloss clinging to his lobe. "I've rendered you speechless."

"No, you just caught me off guard, that's all. I didn't expect to see you here."

"Well, now that you're seeing me," she said, spinning a

slow 360-degree turn, "and you've had a few moments to think, answer the question. Why haven't I heard from you?"

"For starters, work has been crazy. And remember how we talked about this the last time we went out? I'm not really dating right now."

"Sweetheart, haven't you heard? *Nobody* is too busy for Melody Anderson."

Von tossed a wad of cash on the bar, caught Kevin's attention, and motioned toward the exit. "Listen, Melody. It was nice seeing you, but I just don't think I'm what you're looking for. I'm sure there are plenty of guys who'd love to take you out—"

"Oh, trust me, I already know. I've got several of them on the roster. But nobody puts Melody to the side and gets away with it. You need to call me and get back in the starting lineup."

"Yeah, well, I'll pass. Have a good night. Kev, let's go."

"Right behind you, boss."

"Your loss!" Melody called out.

Von responded with a brusque wave, his eyes meeting hers as she stared him down on his way to the exit.

## Chapter Seven

Dani strolled the produce aisle of Golden Canyon Grocers, debating whether to purchase another bag of apples after she'd let the last batch spoil.

"Leave it," she muttered, opting for a bag of pears instead.

Turning her cart in the opposite direction, she headed toward the hot bar and perused the array of dishes. While the rich, tangy scents of sweet-and-sour salmon, chicken Parmesan, and teriyaki shrimp sent her empty stomach rumbling, Dani kept walking. She had been to the store just the day before and hadn't returned because she'd forgotten something. She was back, avoiding the emptiness of her house.

It had been more than a month since Lieutenant Edwards's murder, yet she was no closer to identifying a suspect. Meanwhile, the threats against Dani not only persisted, but they were growing increasingly ominous. She had yet to tell anyone about the strange phone calls she'd been getting. Earlier that afternoon, her cell phone rang nonstop hour after hour while she was at the station. *Private Caller* or *Anonymous* flashed across the screen each time. When she'd answer, whoever was on the other end didn't say a word. But their deep, guttural breathing, which sometimes transformed into animalistic grunts, could be heard loud and clear.

Dani had every intention of turning the phone over to Chuck for analysis. But she already knew the number would probably be untraceable. Anyone bold enough to harass the chief of police would know better than to leave a digital trail. Nevertheless, she was obligated to pursue every possible lead.

Just when she reached the sushi bar, Dani heard someone call out her name.

"Chief Miller!" he repeated when she didn't acknowledge him the first time.

"Yes?" she said, twirling her cart around even though she was in no mood to socialize.

"I've been meaning to reach out to you. How have you been?"

Dani's fingers clutched the handle tighter, her eyes flashing with annoyance at the sight of Von.

"I'm fine. And you?" she said coolly, turning her attention to a row of sashimi.

"I'm hanging in there. Honestly, I'm still pretty disturbed by Gordon Edwards's murder."

"Are you really?" Dani shot back, her flat voice tinged with skepticism.

"Yes, of course. Officer Bryant is pretty shaken up, too, which is understandable since he was one of the first officers on the scene. I'm sure that Maxwell PD is working diligently on the investigation. Have there been any new leads, or—"

"How's your phone doing?" she interrupted, pointing toward Von's cell.

"It's—it's fine. Why?"

"Oh, I was just wondering. I'm surprised it isn't overheating, or on fire, actually."

Von held up the phone, his wide eyes shifting rapidly between it and Dani. "Um… I'm not quite sure what you're getting at, but like I said, my phone is fine."

"Yeah, okay. Maybe that one is. What about the other one?"

"*What* other one?"

"Your burner phone."

"Chief Miller, I have no idea where you're going with this, but I don't have a burner phone, and the cell that I do have is good. Anyway, sorry I bothered you. I'll let you get back to your shopping—"

"You think I'm an idiot, don't you?"

Von stopped so abruptly that his sneakers' soles screeched along the tile. "*No*, of course I don't. But I am starting to question your mental state."

Dani yanked her phone from her purse and stepped aggressively into Von's space. She froze when his biceps pressed against her breasts, shocked by the tingling sensation shooting through her chest.

Edging back, her eyes locked on the cell while Von's lingered on her. "Trust me, I'm perfectly sane. Which is surprising considering I've been harassed all afternoon. Do you see this?" she screeched as her thumb scrolled down the screen. "Call after call from anonymous or private numbers. When I'd answer, some maniac was on the other end, breathing a crazed animal." Dani's gaze darkened, rising to meet Von's. "Isn't it interesting that this started right after our confrontation at Cole's? And you're expecting me to believe you know nothing about it?"

"Yes. That's exactly what I'm expecting. Because it's the truth. And I'm sorry all this is happening to you, Chief. But please believe me when I tell you I have nothing to do with any of it."

"I'm sorry, but I'm just not convinced. If it isn't you, then it's probably someone from your company. Somebody who can't get past the bad blood between us."

Von leaned in closer, his husky voice low and riddled with

irritation. "All right then, prove it. Show me the evidence that backs your claims. I already know you can't. And that you're grasping at straws. You obviously have no leads. You can't even name a person of interest. So you're taking the easy route and blaming your shortcomings on my company."

Pushing her cart aside, Dani spun around and set off in the opposite direction. "I may not have the evidence yet, but it's just a matter of time. I'll figure it out. I always do."

"Chief Miller," Von called out, following her toward the exit. *"Chief Miller!"*

She ignored him, almost getting hit by a car while running through the parking lot. When she got to her Jeep, Dani stopped so suddenly that she almost fell against the hood.

The windshield had been completely smashed, its center appearing like a warped spiderweb as shards of glass hung from the frame. All of the tires were violently slashed. The burgundy paint was scraped away in jagged lines with what appeared to be a knife. Deep cuts revealed the raw metal underneath, leaving gashes that tore through the finish.

"Oh my God," Dani moaned, her weakening legs threatening to fold as she charged back inside the store.

Von, who was hovering near the entrance, tried to stop her.

"Chief Miller, what's going on?"

She rushed right past him and continued toward the customer service desk.

"I need to speak to the manager," she told the attendant. "Now! And where is your security officer? Is he on duty?"

"He's right behind you, ma'am."

Pulling out her badge, Dani attempted to introduce herself to the guard. He stopped her mid-sentence.

"Chief Miller, we all know who you are around here. You're our local hero. Or is it heroine? Hey, Maggie?" he said to the attendant. "Should I refer to Chief Miller as Maxwell's hero, heroine, or—"

*"Sir,"* Dani interrupted. "Thank you, but please, I need your help. Someone vandalized my car while I was inside the store. Could I take a look at the surveillance footage covering the parking lot?"

"Of course. I—I'm so sorry. Follow me."

While Dani made her way to the back of the store, she called Troy. The conversation was disrupted by the sound of approaching footsteps. Dani turned and saw Von trailing her, his eyes fixed intently on her.

"Hold on, Troy," she said into the phone before pressing it against her chest. "Von, what are you doing?"

"I'm coming with you. I saw what someone did to your car out there, and I didn't wanna leave you alone while you review the footage."

"That won't be necessary. My brother is on his way, and several other officers should be here shortly."

"Are you sure?"

"Of course I'm sure."

"Okay, well, the good news is, when this happened, you had eyes on me, so…" He hesitated, as if waiting on Dani to respond. She remained silent. "What I'm trying to say is, this proves that I'm not the one committing these crimes against you."

Dani ended the call with Troy, then stood in the control room doorway. "Von, while I review this footage and attempt to identify the suspect, why don't you go back to RPS headquarters. Check in with your staff. See if you can figure out where each of your employees was during this past hour."

"Okay, so now you're insinuating that one of my employees vandalized your—"

Before he could finish, Dani shut the door in his face.

## Chapter Eight

"I tried, Chief," Chuck said on the other end of the phone. "Trust me, I couldn't have dug much deeper. There just wasn't enough information available that could prove where the threats are coming from."

Dani swiveled on her cream barstool as she shifted between two open laptops, her personal cell phone and a stack of case file folders. Her kitchen had undergone a radical transformation, evolving from a warm, inviting space to a cutting-edge command center. She'd set up her devices along the beige granite island, with the Maxwell PD's message board displayed on one computer, her email inbox on the other, and the anonymous text thread open on her cell.

A dull ache pulsated throughout Dani's entire body. The numbing pain kicked in the moment she sat down and began reading through the scathing statements made against her. Each comment, each threat, left her agonizing over who was behind it all.

She'd been sure that Chuck would uncover some sort of lead. A digital trail, a cell tower's ping…anything that might point them in the direction of their suspect. But the perpetrator knew what they were doing. And if their goal was to incite fear in Dani, it was working.

After the run-in with Von at the grocery store, Dani found

herself rethinking his involvement. She couldn't shake the feeling that his concern for her seemed genuine. And then there was the fact that her vehicle had been vandalized while he was inside. While he may not have done it, she couldn't rule out the possibility that one of his cohorts was behind it. Whether or not Von was the mastermind remained to be seen.

"So hold on," Dani said to Chuck. "What happened when you traced those comments on the Maxwell PD's message board? Were you able to pull the IP addresses?"

"No, unfortunately. The users must've hidden them using a virtual private network. In some cases, these people are using double VPNs, which makes it even harder for their internet activity to be tracked."

Dani's head fell against her palm as she squeezed her temples in frustration. "What about the anonymous calls and text messages? Any luck tracing those?"

"No, and for similar reasons. The caller is either using a burner phone with a prepaid SIM card, or the phone's data is encrypted using a VPN."

"This is so damn aggravating," she said just as her phone beeped. Natalia's name flashed across the screen. Dani's stomach dropped when she saw the call was coming from the police station.

"Chuck, I'll call you back." She almost dropped the phone while fumbling to swap calls. "Nat, what's going on?"

"Chief, something's going down at the Blanche Hotel. I don't know all the details, but there's been some sort of incident. And I think it's fatal."

DANI TORE DOWN Rockfield Road, her siren blaring through the still desert air. The Blanche Hotel stood on the east end of downtown Maxwell. Several of her officers were already on the scene, as Mayor Cox had asked the department to keep an eye on things during his high-profile fundraising event.

The hotel's iconic red sign flickered steadily in the distance. Built in the 1930s, the Blanche had become quite a popular tourist attraction, second only to Cole's Ski Resort. Its terra-cotta-tiled roof, golden beige stucco walls and gracefully arched windows mixed timeless Italian elegance with old-world charm, earning the establishment a loyal following.

The beauty of the hotel diminished under the circumstances as Dani's black Ford sedan skidded to a halt, narrowly missing the colorful flower beds lining the cobblestoned driveway. Panic throbbed against her forehead at the familiarity of it all. Like the other crime scenes, this one hit like a violent storm. Blue and red lights flashed in the distance. Sirens cracked through the dark quiet. The imminent tragedy she'd soon face lingered in the air.

Without waiting for her officers to pull up, Dani jumped out of the car and charged the lobby. Partygoers' faces were a blur in the sea of madness. She almost collided with several of them as the dark woodwork and dimly lit sconces made it impossible to see through the turmoil. Footsteps pounded the glossy terrazzo tiles, each step growing more frantic than the last as attendees scrambled in every direction.

Dani climbed the stairs leading the grand ballroom two at a time. The commotion heightened as flustered guests draped in designer gowns and tailored tuxedos struggled to make sense of the scene.

The moment she approached the ballroom's vaulted entryway, Dani paused at the sound of a deep, familiar voice, vibrating through the air.

"Everyone, please! Listen up! Stay calm, and head down to the lobby using the staircase to your left. The elevators are to your right."

*Von...*

"What in the hell is RPS doing here?" Dani asked Troy when he approached.

"I'm not sure, but they seem to be doing a decent job of evacuating the area."

"Yeah, well, it's not good enough. Guests are still charging through the halls, causing chaos. Can you and the team help move everyone down to the lobby? Better yet, let's facilitate a full evacuation. I need them out of the hotel, now."

"You got it, Chief."

The moment Troy stepped away, Dani cut through the crowd and headed straight to Von.

"Once again," she said, "I see RPS beat me to the scene. How does this keep happening?"

"My men were already on-site. The mayor hired us to provide security for the event. One of my guys called to let me know what was going on. I just so happened to be close by, so it didn't take me long to get here."

"Wait, why would the mayor hire RPS when he had the Maxwell PD patrolling the event?"

With a slight shrug, Von replied, "Ever since that big crime case, he's been extra cautious, believing that one can never have too much security."

"So what you're telling me is tonight's incident occurred under Maxwell PD's *and* RPS's watch."

"Yes. Which is not a good look…"

Dani pivoted, uncomfortable under Von's intense gaze. "The victim is inside the ladies' restroom, correct?"

"Yes, she is."

"How in the world did someone manage to commit murder with all these people around?"

"The victim was found in a restroom located in the west wing of the hotel. The event is taking place in the east wing."

"Hmm, got it." Pulling a long stream of air, Dani's body

stiffened as she prepared for the worst. "Okay then. Let's walk and talk."

Guests stepped aside when they saw Dani and Von making their way through the crowd. She was careful when responding to their questions, telling everyone she'd share details once she knew more.

"Just keep walking," Von said, placing a hand on her shoulder while guiding her past the inquisitive attendees.

Several moments passed before Dani realized Von was still holding on to her. She surprised herself by not shoving his hand away.

When they arrived near the area where the ladies' room was located, it had already been cordoned off. Von raised the yellow caution tape over Dani's head as she ducked underneath it and entered the gruesome scene. The first thing she noticed was blood spattered along the soft peach wallpaper and white marble floor. The victim's glittery black pumps were sticking out from underneath a row of porcelain pedestal sinks. First responders hovered around her with first aid kits, portable oxygen tank, tourniquets and defibrillator set up nearby.

Dani's lungs restricted as her entire body went numb, cutting off her ability to feel. To breathe. To move.

"Hey, are you good?" Von asked.

The touch of his hand on the small of her back unlocked the traumatic hold on her limbs, pushing her farther inside the restroom.

*Pull it together. Do not let this man see you fold...*

A mass of blood had pooled beneath the victim's body, soaking her silver sequined gown. Dani's stomach clenched as she approached Officer Rose, their crime scene investigator. "Any initial thoughts? Gunshot wound? Stab wound?"

"Stab wound for sure. It looks to be several from what

the paramedics are saying. Right now, she's got no pulse and no heartbeat."

Moving closer, Dani zeroed in on the woman's face. Stared into her close-set, gaping eyes, almost too large for her gaunt face. Her pointy, slightly crooked nose and pinched lips. The sharp cheekbones, which were smeared with red lipstick. The longer she looked, the more familiar her face grew. And then it hit like a blow to the chest, leaving her fighting to breathe. "Is that—is that Brandy Orland?"

Officer Rose's bushy eyebrows shot up toward his creased his forehead. "It is. Do you know her?"

"I do. Brandy was a journalist who occasionally wrote for *The Maxwell Times*. She's interviewed me a few times in the past." Dani turned away, catching a glimpse of her reflection in the mirror. For a moment, she didn't recognize the shell-shocked person staring back. "The last time we spoke, I'd sung Lieutenant Edwards's praises for his mentorship."

"Oh, yeah. I remember it well. That was a really nice feature. People were buzzing about it for weeks."

Snatching a small notepad from her pocket, Dani's hand shook as she frantically scribbled her thoughts. "See, I knew the lieutenant's murder might've somehow been directed at me. And now this…this one looks like it is, too. I think somebody's trying to send me a message."

Dani pivoted toward Von, flinching at the sight of sweat beading across his forehead. When he blew a trembling breath and loosened his tie, she asked, "What's going on with you?"

"Nothing. Well, not nothing…something just hit me. This town has another dead body on its hands. I'm starting to wonder if this is a targeted attack on RPS."

"Wait, why would you think that?"

"For starters, both of these recent murders occurred on

my company's watch. That makes RPS look pretty damn incompetent. Who would want to hire a security firm that can't protect its clients?"

"You make a good point. But I don't think this is about you," Dani insisted, her bun coming undone as she shook her head emphatically. "This is about the Maxwell PD. More specifically, it's about me."

"How is that?"

"Didn't you hear what I just told Officer Rose?"

"No, I missed it. What did you—"

"Chief Miller!" Officer Rose cut in. "Can you come and take a look at this?"

"I'll be right there!" Dani's words tumbled out in a rush as her eyes remained fixed on Von. "I think you're way off base. And I don't know what else to tell you. But I do need to get to work—"

"We need to talk," he interrupted, his voice dropping almost to a whisper. "In private. Because I think *you're* way off base, and I need to set you straight—especially if you still believe that RPS has anything to do with this. Once we're done here, why don't we go and grab a coffee? Somewhere discreet, where no one will see us."

Dani hesitated. Meeting with Von privately felt like a betrayal to her father. And to the Maxwell PD. But if he held information that could help solve the case, ignoring him would be a betrayal to the entire town.

"Fine," she relented. "Let's meet up at Red Mesa Café. It's open twenty-four hours."

"Red Mesa Café…isn't that about forty-five minutes away, near the border of Sagebrush Valley?"

"It is. Didn't you suggest we meet somewhere discreet? It doesn't get much more inconspicuous than that dive."

"True. All right then. I'll see you there."

A CLOUD OF DUST billowed around Dani's sedan as she turned into the café's parking lot. Von was already there, sitting inside his car while typing away on his cell phone. He appeared startled when she pulled in beside him, his wide-eyed shock quickly melting into a sheepish grin.

"Sorry I scared you!" she called out through the passenger window.

"Scared is a bit of a stretch. More like surprised, that's all."

"Yeah, okay, tough guy."

Dani stepped out of the car, her feet tingling with surreality as she and Von walked toward the entrance. It still hadn't quite sunken in that she and her lifelong nemesis had set aside their differences—at least temporarily. When it came to the safety of her hometown, the provisional truce was well worth it.

*Keep your guard up*, Dani reminded herself, still not fully convinced of RPS's innocence.

"This place has certainly seen better days," she said, glancing up at the café's shabby wooden exterior. The peeling blue paint had succumbed to the desert's harsh sun and shifting sands. The signage, now tattered and frayed, had been worn down to a meager *Re esa Caf.*

"Yeah, but if the coffee is hot and the pound cake is fresh, then it'll do," Von replied, giving her a slight smile while holding open the frosted glass door. "After you."

"Thank you," Dani murmured, ignoring the shiver that raced up her arm when she slid past him. Decent terms aside, there was no way in hell she could be feeling any sort of attraction toward the man she'd hated for years. Yet if he was attempting to put her at ease after a difficult night, it was working.

She stepped inside, almost losing her footing on the uneven black-and-white linoleum tile. The café's interior may have been worse than the exterior. Old, scuffed-up wooden tables and chairs were scattered about haphazardly. Grungy booths lining the walls were riddled with cracked blue cushions. A few sleepy patrons were seated at a counter cluttered with tattered menus and scuffed dishware. But there was no ignoring the rich, roasted scent of freshly brewed coffee, which was what Dani needed the most.

"Good evening, folks!" a pudgy older woman called out from behind the counter. "Take a seat wherever you'd like. I'll be with you in a sec. Can I start you off with a couple of coffees?"

"That would be great, thanks," Von said before leading Dani toward a booth in the back. Once seated, he gave her hand a gentle nudge. "So, Danielle Sabrina Miller. Who would've thought that you and I would one day be sitting across from each other like this…"

"Without clawing each other's eyes out? I know, right? But wait, how do you know my middle name?"

"I know a lot about you. More than you probably realize…"

Von's eyes lingered on her perplexed expression a beat too long, only breaking when the server approached with their coffee.

"Do you two need to see a menu?" she asked, her wide grin putting her gapped teeth on full display. "And before you answer, let me just tell you that we're out of fried catfish and Italian sausages. But we've still got plenty of burgers and beef stew."

The thought of ingesting a heavy meal after leaving the crime scene churned Dani's stomach. As she struggled to shake off the lingering unease, Von replied, "I think we're good on food. Maybe just a couple of slices of pound cake if there's any left?"

"I just put a fresh one in the oven. I'll bring over a couple of slices as soon as it's done. Be back soon."

Rubbing his hands together, Von sat back, his head tilting curiously. "Back to our convo. Aside from this investigation, you and I have a lot to catch up on, don't we?"

"Not that I'm aware of. We came here to talk about this case. Not to catch up on old times. Or did I miss the memo?"

Her prickly response seemed to amuse Von as his lips spread into a charming smirk. "Come on, Chief. Don't do me like that. I'm just trying to break the ice here before we get into all the heavy stuff."

His words disarmed her. Put her at ease. She met his intense gaze. It was the same piercing look he'd given her that night at the Zonian, before the attack. But now she saw it in a different light. Behind his eyes, there was quiet sincerity. A softness that make him seem genuine and caring. And dare she say, appealing…

"Fine," Dani blurted. "You're right. We do have a lot to catch up on. A lifetime's worth, if you really think about it. But um…" Her voice drifted as she thought back on Von's panicked reaction at the crime scene. Nothing about it seemed forced, as if he had any involvement. "I should probably start by apologizing to you for my behavior. Particularly how I treated you that night at the grocery store. I was rude, and accusatory, and blamed you for things without any proof. And I, um… I hope you'll accept my apology."

Von straightened, his body leaning in toward the table as his smirk slowly melted into a full-bodied grin. "Wow, Chief Miller. Thank you for that. I really appreciate the apology, and of course I accept it. Believe it or not, I do understand where your defensiveness comes from. You've been hit with a lot. And now, with a fresh pair of murders on your hands, the threats against you…all that would set anybody off."

"Well I appreciate your understanding. And you're right. Things really have been tough. Not to mention confusing. I can't seem to wrap my mind around why someone would be targeting me."

"Maybe that's because these murders aren't about you."

"Here we go," Dani uttered, her lips twisting with doubt. She grabbed the creamer dispenser and banged against the side until clumpy white powder poured into her cup. "How could they not be when I'm so closely tied to both victims?"

"I don't know. You're the chief of police. In some ways, you're tied to practically everybody in this town! So it could just be a coincidence. But again, you know what isn't? The fact that both murders occurred on RPS's watch. I know I've got a few enemies out here. I could name several of your officers who aren't particularly fond of me. And you already know why. It's all about the power struggle between our respective agencies."

"Well, maybe your guys need to take responsibility for their part in that. The Maxwell PD has dealt with a lot of RPS hate. We don't have to get too deep into it. But our shared history is toxic. If we're being honest, most of that negativity was coming from *your* side of the fence. Not mine. My department's success in solving cases triggered RPS's need to overstep their bounds. That didn't sit well with the force."

Von snatched a wad of napkins from the holder and pressed them against his forehead. "Let me ask you this. Did you notice any of that behavior coming directly from me?"

"It doesn't matter. It came from your employees. They're a direct reflection of you."

"Point taken. And now that you've said that, I'll have a talk with my employees. Tell them to stand down and—" He stopped mid-sentence, staring up at the wall while tapping his fingertips against the table.

"What's happening right now?" Dani asked. "What are you doing?"

"I'm thinking. And I've got an idea. But I don't know if you'd be down with it."

"I'm listening."

"What if we put something together for our agencies? Like some sort of joint event? We could do it someplace neutral, like the Zonian. What do you think?"

Dani shifted in her seat, careful not to rip her black slacks on the torn cushion.

"That's um, that's interesting. Actually, it's a pretty good idea. But the question is, will my officers agree?"

"There's only one way to find out."

The pair paused when their server approached with two slices of pound cake. "Enjoy, folks!"

"Thank you," Von said, immediately digging in as soon as his plate hit the table.

When Dani failed to pick up her fork, he asked, "Aren't you going to have any?"

"I will. I'm still coming down off that scene at the hotel."

"Understood. So, with everything that's going on, how are you holding up? I know you're well protected since you've got the entire force looking out for you. But, emotionally. How are you doing?"

Cutting into her cake, Dani slid a small bite onto her fork. "For starters, being on the force doesn't give me an automatic sense of safety. It literally feels like I could be under attack at any given moment. There's an anxious feeling of vulnerability that comes with the job. But with that being said, I'm holding it together."

"Is there anything I can do to help? Like keep watch over your house, or provide you with personal security detail? Free of charge, of course."

"You know, as cool as it would be to go all Whitney Houston à la *The Bodyguard*, I think I'm good. I do appreciate the offer, though. It's interesting, you offering to protect me after I was convinced you were behind all this."

"Man, I *still* haven't gotten over the way you went off on me at Cole's."

Dani's embarrassment turned into a fit of wheezing coughs. "Yeah, I, um… I'm sorry about that, too. And not that I'm trying to run up a list of excuses or anything, but I was under a ton of stress that day."

"I know you were. But I'm not gonna let you off the hook that easily. Seriously, you went *in*. I mean, you talked about my father—"

"I know! I know. I shouldn't have gone there. It's crazy how after all this time, you and I never discussed the beef between our dads. I'm sure the stories you've heard are much different from the ones I've gotten."

"Oh, I bet they are." Von rested against the back of the booth and folded his arms over his brawny chest. "Since you bring it up, I'm curious. What did your father tell you about their rivalry?"

Dani was slow to respond, her eyes lingering on the outline of his biceps, bulging through his crisp white shirt. The way his rolled-up sleeves exposed his muscular forearms…

*What in the hell are you doing?*

She focused her attention on the space above Von's head to avoid looking directly at him. "Well, here's something you may not know. My father always thought that your dad saw his promotion to police chief as a result of favoritism, not merit, since he was close with a lot of Maxwell's movers and shakers. Plus your dad struggled with the idea of having a friend as his boss."

Von let off a condescending chuckle, then scarfed down a mouthful of cake, as if to avoid saying the wrong thing.

"I'm guessing your version of the story is different," Dani said.

"Yes, way different. The thing is, our fathers were both competitive. My dad always believed he was the best man for the job, but never doubted your dad deserved it. In the end, my father thought Mr. Miller was too tough on him. Because they were friends, maybe your dad pushed too hard to prove he wouldn't show favoritism. Either way, it didn't sit well with my father, and he felt he had to leave."

"Hmm, okay. They certainly did have two totally different perspectives. But it sounds like there were quite a few misunderstandings between them that could've been worked out had they just taken the time to sit down and talk."

"I agree," Von said. "But instead they let their emotions get the best of them and jumped to a lot of conclusions. Little did they know their personal feud would trigger enough fury to affect the entire town."

"To the point where it would last for decades."

"Yeah, well, us sitting down and talking like two mature adults is a move in the right direction. It could actually be the catalyst that'll turn this situation around."

Dani nodded, surprised by the weight of relief brought on by his words. She hadn't realized how heavy the burden of their rivalry had become.

"Look," Von continued after scraping his plate clean, "if nothing else, I'm just glad that you finally came to your senses and realized that I'm not some psychopath."

"Yeah, *you're* not, but…"

"But what?"

"You might be off the hook, but I'm still not sure about all of RPS."

"Chief Miller, are you serious? Do you really think that one of my employees, each of whom I thoroughly vetted, is a killer?"

"At this point, I'm not putting anything past anybody."
*Including my own officers*, she thought but kept to herself.
Dani wasn't ready to admit that truth to Von.

"Fair point. But as for me, I will continue to vouch for all
of my employees until the evidence says otherwise. Speaking of which, how long do you think it'll take the lab to send
back the results from tonight's crime scene?"

"We're expecting to hear something within the next two
weeks. The forensics investigator requested that they put
a rush on it. Hopefully we'll have more luck with this one
than the one at Cole's."

Sliding his coffee stirrer between his lips, Von said, "I'd
been wondering about that. So nothing came of the evidence
you collected at the lieutenant's crime scene?"

Dani's gaze fell to her half-eaten piece of cake. There was
no way she could respond while watching his full, inviting lips curl around that straw. "Nope. Nothing. The resort
doesn't have cameras installed inside the stairwells, so that
wasn't helpful. The footage from nearby areas didn't offer
any answers either. We did have a promising lead involving one of Lieutenant Edwards's sons. But his alibi checked
out. CCTV footage confirmed that he and a friend were in
California at the time of the murder."

"What about the maintenance guy who discovered the
body? I think his name is Mr. Stallworth?"

"Yes, that's him. He wasn't able to provide us with much
information. Some of my officers thought he could be our
suspect. But witnesses saw him inside the employee cafeteria at the time of the murder, so he was cleared."

"Got it…" Von grew quiet, running his fingertip along
a chip in his mug. "I know this is none of my business, but
when it comes to this case, I've been so curious as to what's
happening on the inside. It seems that this go-round, Max-

well PD is being pretty tight-lipped with the media and what information you're releasing to the public."

"We are. And that's because we don't want to say anything that might compromise the investigation. Our suspect may alter his behavior, destroy evidence or fabricate his story once he's brought in for questioning. Plus we don't wanna scare away potential witnesses who may fear we'd put them at risk by revealing more than necessary. So to avoid those types of pitfalls, we just remain quiet and hope that the evidence will speak for itself."

"Got it." The furrows etched into Von's forehead softened, giving way to a subtle hint of worry. "I hate to bring this up, Chief, but um…your vehicle being vandalized that night at the grocery store. Whatever came of it?"

"Ugh," she groaned, shoving a large chunk of cake in her mouth out of frustration.

"Just breathe," Von murmured, covering his mouth as if to stifle a laugh. "And please don't choke."

"What, you think this is funny?"

"No! Of course not. I'm just not used to seeing you going in on a piece of cake like that. It's actually kind of cute."

"Anyway," Dani said, ignoring the flirtatious glimmer in his eyes, "my Jeep is at the crime lab being processed now, so hopefully they'll recover some sort of evidence. As for the security footage from that night, all I saw was a figure dressed in dark, bulky clothing, hovering around my vehicle. He was wearing a baseball cap, a hoodie and large sunglasses that almost covered his entire face. That was pretty terrifying, watching him destroy my car like that. Especially since there was nothing I could do about it. I couldn't even get a good look at the person. But when I think about Lieutenant Edwards and Brandy Orland, I realize things could've been much worse."

"Oh, absolutely. What's clear to me is that you've got a

brazen murderer on your hands who's killing on a grand scale. It's pretty shocking how bold these crimes have been."

"And what's clear to me is that we're dealing with some-one who's pretty damn audacious. Someone who won't stop killing until we stop him. In the meantime, the entire force is on high alert. My house is under twenty-four-hour surveil-lance, seven days a week. My security system is on whether I'm home or not. Troy and Chloe barely want to leave my side. At this point, it feels like I'm in a witness protection program."

"Which isn't a bad thing…"

As Von's hand inched across the table toward her, Dani snatched her phone and checked the time. "Ooh, I didn't re-alize it had gotten so late. I need to get home."

"Yeah, I uh… I guess should get going, too. Thanks for agreeing to meet with me. This was good. Really good. A step in the right direction, if you will. And just so you know, if there's anything I can do to help, say the word. I may not be a part of the Maxwell PD, but I wouldn't mind stepping in to assist. So let me know. I'd be happy to slide into the rotation."

"I will do that. Thank you."

The gaze shared between them lingered, stretching sev-eral beats longer than necessary. Dani was the first to break, staring down at the bits of creamer floating inside her mug. Her skin burned underneath Von's unwavering stare. The intensity stirred emotions buried deep within her tough ex-terior, leaving her fingers fidgeting and stomach fluttering.

*Please look away*, her inner voice pleaded. But he didn't. She refused to make eye contact for fear of what might spark within her.

The spell broke when the server walked over and placed the check on the table. After paying the bill, Von stood. "You ready?"

"I am." A sense of calm fell over Dani as she followed him toward the exit. "And I'm glad we did this. Next time we see each other, hopefully it'll be under better circumstances. Like me telling you that we've arrested the killer. Wouldn't that be nice?"

"Yes, it would be. Because honestly? I don't think this town can handle a repeat of last year."

## Chapter Nine

The Maxwell PD's joint social with RPS was in full swing. Dani was pleasantly surprised by the turnout since it was her and Von's first attempt to mend the rift between their agencies. The Zonian was packed, with everyone clearly enjoying themselves as drinks flowed freely, games of pool were in motion, and the room vibrated with R&B hits.

But while the walls were lined with employees from both organizations, the bar felt divided. The police department dominated the right side of the room, and RPS occupied the left. No one was mingling across the divide.

Dani and Von were holding court in the middle of the floor, hoping their friendly interaction would inspire others to follow suit. So far, it hadn't. Troy was doing his best to break the ice, chatting with a few of the RPS officers. Yet no one seemed willing to take his cue, either.

"We need to do something to loosen things up around here," Dani said to Von. "Something that'll get our teams out of their little cliques. Maybe we should play one of the games we discussed."

"Good idea. Because at the rate they're going, we'll be here all night without making any progress."

"Which one should we start with? Two Truths and a Lie, Would You Rather, or Human Bingo?"

"I think Two Truths and a Lie would be a good one," Von said. "That way we can all learn a little something about each other. And I'm sure the stuff they'll come up with will drum up some laughs. Humor is always a great way to cut through the awkwardness."

"Good point. All right, let's do it."

Dani led him to the DJ booth and grabbed hold of the mic.

"Hey, party people!" she exclaimed, her voice booming over the raucous crowd. "Can I please get your attention? First of all, Von and I would like to extend a heartfelt thank you to everyone who came out tonight. We really appreciate each of you for accepting our invitation, and acknowledging our effort to mend fences between the Maxwell PD and Reed Protective Services. I'm sure you all realize this, but please allow me to reiterate the fact that our agencies are two of the most important organizations in this town. And while our history may be somewhat...*contentious*—"

"To put it mildly," Von cut in, drawing a laugh from the crowd.

"Exactly," Dani continued with an amused eye roll. "But that's why we're here tonight. To start a conversation, heal the rift, and move forward in a more positive way. This room is filled with so many passionate, highly trained officers who all have one thing in common—our love of Maxwell. So instead of just talking about it, let's actually be about it, starting with being a little kinder toward one another. You think we can we do that?"

A wave of hushed mutters swept through the room.

*"Really?"* Dani continued. "Now I hate to be the one who gets on the mic and says things like, *you can do better than that*, but people, I *know* you can do better than that. So again I ask, are you willing to show a little more love toward one another?"

Pulling the mic toward him, Von threw in, "Or at least a little more *like*?"

The crowd responded more enthusiastically this time, with cheers erupting and glasses raised high.

"All right then," Dani said through a satisfied smile. "That's more like it! Now I'm gonna turn the mic over to my cohost, Von Reed, who's going to share the deets on the icebreaking game we'll be playing."

"Thank you, Chief Miller. What's up, everybody? Just to echo the chief's gratitude, thanks again for coming out. And before I start, let's all give her a round of applause. While my name is on the bill, she pretty much planned this entire night on her own."

A thunderous roar shook the floor. Dani clutched her hands to her chest, mouthing the words *thank you* as Von quieted the crowd. There was something undeniably appealing about the way he stood there, confident and composed, commanding the room in his cool blue linen suit and fitted white T-shirt.

Coincidentally, she'd opted for blue as well. Her ombré bodycon midi dress went from powdery to sky to a deep shade of teal. She'd straightened her hair and applied smoky eyeshadow with a deep peach gloss. The look was sexier than normal, proven by her team's speechless reaction when she'd walked through the door. But no one's was as blatant as Von's. He hadn't taken his eyes off of her since he'd arrived.

"So listen up, everyone," Von continued. "We're gonna kick the night off with a game called Two Truths and a Lie. The way it works is that each person who's called to the DJ booth will share two true statements about themselves, and one false statement. The rest of us will have to guess what's factual and what isn't. Now since this is just for fun, there won't be much order in how it goes down. We'll just shout

out what we're thinking, see what the majority says, then have whoever's up to the mic give us the correct response. Got it?"

"Got it!" the crowd declared in unison.

It was the most enthusiastic reaction they'd gotten all night. Dani noticed the two agencies slowly merging as they moved to the middle of the floor. Several of them had even begun chatting with one another.

"It's already working," she whispered in Von's ear.

"Yeah, I see. Good job," he said, giving her a high five. "So do you wanna kick the game off, or should I do the honors?"

"Please, you do the honors. You're doing great. Everybody seems to be enjoying your commentary. Even my team."

"Thanks for the reassurance." Von punctuated his gratitude with a wink, then said to the crowd, "Let's get started! Go ahead and pull out the numbers you were given when you arrived. Numbers one through ten, we're gonna start with you. We'll give you a few minutes to come up with two truths and a lie. After that, line up next to Dani and me, then we'll go from there."

"Don't forget to tell them about the prize," Dani whispered in his ear.

"Oh, listen up! The winner of each game will receive a gift card to the lovely Canyon Catch seafood restaurant. So get loud, get rowdy, let your voice be heard, and most importantly, have fun. Good luck!"

Von handed the mic back to the DJ, who turned up the music. The crowd began bobbing their heads to Tinashe's "Nasty" while several guests made their way toward the booth.

"You know what?" Dani said. "I know it's still early, but I think it's safe to say that this event is a success."

"I think so, too. But let's not speak too soon and jinx it. The night is young. Anything can happen."

"True. However, I'm gonna err on the side of positivity and declare it a good night."

"You know what would make it an even better night?" Von asked.

"What's that?"

"If you'd dance with me."

Dani's heart rate sped up, thumping to the beat of the music as Von pulled her close. His arms circled her waist. Swaying gradually, his hips moved in a slow, provocative rhythm. She slid her hands onto his shoulders. Relaxed as her body fell in sync with his. When she sang along to Tinashe's hook, Von released a low moan, the warmth of his breath gently caressing her skin.

"Oh, so you've been a nasty girl, huh?" he quipped.

As Von spoke, his lips brushed against her neck. His touch sent a trail of quivers straight through her.

"Excuse me, Mr. Reed, but are you flirting with me?"

"Maybe. Would it be a bad thing if I am?"

"I don't know yet. But right now, considering where we are? You'd better cut it out."

"Are you sure about that?" Von debated. "Because I didn't hear an ounce of conviction in your voice. You're gonna have to come stronger than that if you really want me to stop."

"Hey, Reed!" someone called out from the DJ booth. "What's up? Are you gonna get this game going or what?"

Von tossed him a thumbs-up, then slowly pulled away from Dani. It took everything in her to release him from her embrace.

*Whatever the hell this is you're doing, stop it!*

As he stepped back to the mic, his gaze remained on her. "You still owe me the rest of that dance. So make sure you don't leave here tonight without settling your debt."

"Trust me, I won't."

The response was out of her mouth before she'd thought it

through. But it was too late to take it back. When Von licked his lips, Dani questioned whether or not she even wanted to.

Taking her hand in his, Von positioned her next to him. An awkward grin crept across her face. She scanned the room. Checked to see if anyone was watching them. Then locked eyes with Troy and Chloe. They were staring back at her, wearing matching expressions of disbelief.

Dani ignored them, making a mental note to explain whatever was happening between her and Von later. Or at least attempt to, given she didn't fully understand it herself.

*"Party people,"* Von sang into the mic. "Let's get things under way. First up, we've got my guy, Kevin Freelain. For those of you who don't know, Kevin is the vice president of RPS. He's also my right-hand man who helps keep the company running smoothly. Kev, I'm turning the mic over to you. Give us your two truths and a lie. And no pressure, but they'd better be good since you're this jumping this game off and repping my company."

Kevin's head rolled back before he replied, "Oh, no pressure, huh?"

"You got this, Kev!" someone yelled out, prompting everyone else to whoop and whistle in support.

"Thanks, guys. All right, here we go. Three things about me. Number one. I've never read a full book."

"Truth!" several people shouted in unison.

When a wave of laughter flooded the bar, Dani leaned into Von. "So far so good on the game."

"Of course. You were the one who came up with it."

"Well you were the one who come up with the idea to throw this event. So thank you. I really do think it's gonna help quash the beef between our agencies."

"I think so, too. Plus," Von said, "this night gives us a chance to spend some time together."

His fingertips brushed against her palm, sending a wave of

tingles to places she hadn't tingled in months. Dani couldn't decide if it was the gin and tonic fueling Von's boldness, or if he was genuinely drawn to her. Either way, the struggle to catch her breath proved the feelings may be mutual.

"As for my second truth or lie," Kevin continued, "I graduated college summa cum laude."

"Now we *know* that's a lie!" Officer Bryant hollered.

"You'd better watch yourself, B," Kevin retorted. "Don't mess around and let this game get you fired. Anyway, last but not least, number three. I have never been drunk."

"You're drunk right now!" Bryant shot back, ignoring the warning.

Boisterous laughter rocked the bar as the DJ dropped a beat. After giving Kevin an enthusiastic high five, Von took over the mic.

"Good job, man. Okay everybody, on the count of three, tell me which statement you think is a lie. Is Kevin stretching the truth about being a nonreader, a genius or a lightweight drinker? One, two, three!"

The crowd's loud rumbling was hard to make out. Dani and Von held their hands to their ears, urging everyone to yell louder.

"Is it me?" Von asked, "or am I hearing everyone say they think Kevin is lying about being a lightweight drinker?"

Taking over the mic, Dani replied, "I think you're right. The majority of our guests seem to think that Kevin is lying about never being drunk. So now it's your turn, Kev. Tell us, which is the lie?"

"The lie is, drumroll please...that I've never been drunk!"

The response incited a reaction so raucous that Dani had to cover her ears.

"Great job, everybody!" Von said. "Kevin, I'm gonna let you choose your winner, then take over the game while the lady of the hour and I take a quick break. Good luck!"

Taking Dani's hand once again, Von led her toward a se-cluded corner near the back of the bar. On the way there, she peered straight ahead, dodging the inquisitive stares of their guests while forcing a strained smile. Their shock was understandable. For years, the town had witnessed the volatile dynamics of Dani and Von's contentious relationship. Just a matter of days ago, Dani had added him to the list of suspects. Now here she was, not only tolerating his presence, but feeling a strange magnetic pull toward him—one that she couldn't quite explain or ignore.

"This hosting gig is exhausting, isn't it?" Von asked after they'd found two empty stools.

"Absolutely. It's fun, but it's definitely tiring. When you think about everything it took to put this night together, it's fair to say we're both worn out."

"Agreed. And since we've got such capable folks working for our agencies, I'm fine letting them take over for a bit while we cool out. Now, what are you drinking?" Von asked while flagging down the bartender.

"I'd love a mojito. Thanks."

After being served another round, Von held his glass to hers. "To us. For planning a fantastic event that brought both our teams together, and burying the hatchet. Hopefully for good. Cheers."

"Cheers to that." Dani took a leisurely sip, allowing the tangy fizz to settle on her tongue before swallowing it down.

Just as she went for another, Von asked, "So…are you seeing anybody these days?"

The question turned her sip into a gulp, which sent a mint leaf sliding down her throat. A coughing fit prompted Von to leap from his stool and massage her back until her breathing normalized.

"Are you okay?" he asked.

"I—I'm fine. Your question just took me by surprise. That's all."

"Really? I'm sorry. I didn't think I was being intrusive—"

"No, it isn't that. I'm just not used to us being this cordial and open with each other. Don't get me wrong. I'm actually enjoying it. But it's all so strange. You and I have spent our entire lives hating each other. So it's an adjustment."

"For sure. However, we agreed to turn all that around, starting with tonight. So get used to this. Also, stop trying to dodge my question. Spill it. What's going on with your love life?"

Dani's head tilted curiously as she studied his expression. The raised brows and parted lips indicated that he was truly clueless. But she was almost certain Von knew she was single.

"To put it simply," she said, "there isn't much going on with my love life. I'm not seeing anyone."

"Hmm, okay. Interesting…"

Dani could've sworn she saw a spark of satisfaction flicker across Von's eyes. He nodded, running the rim of his glass along his lips before taking a long, deliberate sip. Her gaze fell to his tongue. A piece of ice slid inside his mouth. He sucked it, slowly, his soft lips forming a pout as the cube rolled from side to side.

*What are you trying to do to me?* she fought the urge to blurt while pressing her thighs together.

"So um…are you seeing anyone?" she asked.

"Not at the moment, no."

"Are you sure? Because according to the streets, you're pretty popular out here on the dating scene."

"Is that what they're saying? Where in the world did you hear that?"

Spinning in her stool, Dani turned her back to Von while laughing hysterically. "Oh, *please*. Are you seriously asking me that? All of Maxwell is aware of your reputation for being a playboy. And from what I know personally, it's well earned."

"Is that what you know personally, or is that what you *heard*?"

"Look, there's no need to go back and forth on this. We both know the truth. So just answer the question!"

"I already did!" Von insisted. "The answer was no a few seconds ago, and it's still no. Now whether or not you choose to believe me, that's on you."

"Okay, that's fair. All I can do is take your word for it. But I do know you've got a pretty active dating life. Correction. That's what I've *heard*. Anyway, tell me. When was your last relationship?"

"Humph, let me think…" his gaze drifted as his expression slipped into a deep, thoughtful daze. "Honestly, I haven't been in a serious relationship for a while now. I've just dated casually here and there."

"And why didn't those situations turn into anything serious?"

The question was out before she knew it. Dani cringed, confused as to why she was suddenly so curious about Von's love life.

*You know why. So stop while you're ahead…*

"Since I've taken over RPS, I haven't really had time to even think about settling down. But I do take pleasure in the company of women. So when I connect with someone, I make it clear that I'm not looking for a commitment."

"Ahh, not looking for a commitment. Those are words that most women aren't looking to hear."

"They are. However, most women never admit to that. They'll oftentimes claim it's cool and they're not looking for anything serious either. Then after a little time passes, suddenly they change their tune. I'll give you an example.

A few months ago, I met a woman from Scottsdale at the Singalong Karaoke Bar. Her name was Jessica. She came to town often to visit her sister. During our very first phone conversation, I told her I wasn't looking for a commitment. According to Jessica, she wasn't either. So we started hanging out, and I tried to keep things casual. But she latched on pretty quickly and even starting talking about moving to Maxwell so we could be closer to each other. After that, I started to back off. But the more I faded, the harder she went. At one point, she even suggested that we move in together, and started dropping hints about marriage."

"Wait, and you two had been dating for how long at that point?"

Holding two fingers in the air, Von replied, "A couple of months. But after that, I had to cut things off. And I did so gently, reminding her that I'd been honest about my intentions from the beginning. She was a little salty for a while, and dropped a few angry texts and voicemails. But eventually, she got over it and moved on. After that, I met a woman named…" He hesitated, a self-deprecating smirk crinkling his eyes.

"Wait, why'd you stop?"

"Because you didn't ask me to run down my entire dating résumé."

Dani took another sip of her mojito, allowing the rum to dissolve her inhibitions. Sliding her stool closer to his, she murmured, "No, please. Go on. This conversation is getting interesting."

"Okay, as long as you're not judging me."

"I listen and I don't judge," she insisted, her thigh brushing against his.

"Cool," he rasped, resting his hand on her knee. "I appreciate that about you. So anyway, after Jessica, I met a woman named Melody. There's not much to say about her. She was a little too young and way too wild for me. That situation didn't last long at all. And then..." Von paused, covering a smirk with his glass before taking a hefty sip.

"What's with the sly grin?" Dani asked.

"I'm kind of embarrassed to tell you about my most recent dating adventure. Because you may very well judge me on this one."

"Uh-oh. Who was she?"

"Carmen Pendleton."

*"Carmen Pendleton,"* Dani squealed, clutching Von's arm. "As in our former high school classmate?"

"Yes. Her. I don't know if you remember this, but her dad used to work for RPS. He'd just left the navy and was one of the first officers my father hired back when the company first launched. So Carmen and I actually go way back."

"Ooh, okay. I didn't see that one coming. I never would've pegged her as your type. I mean, she's attractive and all, but Carmen was always so vapid and self-centered. Didn't she move to LA to pursue an acting career at some point?"

"She did. And she landed a few minor film roles, too. I actually saw her in one of them. *The Last Breath Before Midnight*, or something like that. It was a pretty cheesy thriller."

"Carmen moved back to Maxwell, didn't she?"

"She did. When she left for LA, I think she expected to book a ton of A-list roles the minute her plane landed. When that didn't happen, she moved back home. We went out a couple of times, but all she talked about was herself, her acting career, and how she was dying to get back to LA. This town isn't enough for her. It never has been. Those two dates told me all I needed to know. We weren't a good match."

He was cut off when a series of air horns blasted through the speakers.

"Von Reed!" Kevin shouted into the mic. "Your presence, along with Chief Miller's, is needed at the DJ booth."

"Welp, I guess our little break is over," Von said.

"I guess it is. This was nice. Thanks for sharing with me. And for admitting how you've been breaking women's hearts all over town."

"Why would you lie on me to my face like that?" he joked, taking Dani's hand and helping her up. "I may be a lot of things, but a heartbreaker isn't one of them."

Wrapping an arm around her, Von led the way toward the front of the bar. This time, she didn't avoid the crowd's probing stares. She was, however, taken aback when his fingertips caressed her shoulder, then slid up her neck.

When they reached the booth, their eyes locked. The air between them felt charged. Dani could sense herself slipping, succumbing to their burgeoning attraction. While Von's jovial smile and easy demeanor seemed friendly enough, the heat in his touch was far from platonic. Her mind spun with possibilities as she wondered what this all meant, and where things may go. But the biggest thrill was the uncertainty of how their night would end.

## Chapter Ten

"Von," Dani said as he followed her up the driveway toward her quaint bungalow. "I know you're tired. You really didn't have to follow me home. And you certainly don't have to walk me to my door. I told you, I'm fine."

He didn't respond immediately, instead staring up at her house. He'd driven past it countless times. But he had never been this close. Von studied the soft beige stucco walls, olive wooden shutters, and winding cobblestoned walkway leading to a charming arched door. Clusters of vibrant succulents lined a tiered rock garden. The warmth of it all enveloped him, driving an urge to step inside.

"I know you're fine," he said. "But I wouldn't have been okay letting you drive home alone."

"Letting me?" Dani asked with a smirk.

"You know what I meant."

"I do. And I appreciate it. However, you seem to have forgotten that I'm a police chief. Who's armed at all times."

"Were you a police chief when someone attacked you that night you left the Zonian alone? Or when your Jeep was vandalized outside of the grocery store? How about when those threatening messages—"

"Okay, okay," she interrupted, pressing her hand against Von's chest to silence him. "I get it. And again, I appreciate you." She spun around on her heels and dug inside her clutch. "I can't see a thing. I forgot to turn the porch light on before I left."

"Here, this should help." He pulled out his cell and shone the flashlight near her purse. The jingle of her keys soon followed.

"Thank you," Dani murmured, moving toward the door so suddenly that she nearly stumbled into him.

Grabbing her waist, Von pulled her upright, his body stiffening as she clung to him. "Whoa, you good?"

"Yep," she uttered, her embarrassment clear as she steadied herself. "I'm good. I didn't realize you were standing so close."

"Sorry about that. I didn't mean to startle you…" His voice drifted when he glanced down the block. "So the officer who's supposed to be keeping an eye on your house tonight called in sick?"

"He did."

"See, it was meant for me to be here tonight."

The buzz of Dani's phone cut into the moment.

"I already know that's Troy," she said. "He's probably checking to make sure I made it home."

"Tell him that you're fine. And that he doesn't have to worry about you tonight. I've got you."

"I'm sure hearing that is going to freak him out."

"Why would it?" Von asked.

"Um, I'm sorry, but have you forgotten that we've been sworn enemies? Finding out that you and I are suddenly cool would freak anybody out."

"Well, it shouldn't. Especially not Troy. I'm sure he saw us hanging out tonight and picked up on the good vibes."

"Probably so…" she agreed while typing away on her phone. "Thanks again for following me home. Feel free to get going. You've been at it nonstop all day, and I know you're ready to call it a night. I can take it from here."

"*No*... I'm gonna stand here and make sure you get inside safely. Lock the door behind you. Turn on the lights. And wave goodbye through the door."

Dani tucked the phone back inside her purse and stared up at Von. As silence fell over the pair, he noticed a sultriness in her gaze that he'd never seen before.

"You don't have to rush home if you're not ready," she said, her voice dropping to a soft whisper.

Stepping in closer, Von wrapped his arm around her waist. "What exactly are you saying, Chief Miller?"

"What I'm saying is, you can come inside if you want. Maybe have a nightcap. Debrief over tonight's event. That is unless you've got plans with Melody, or Jessica, or Carmen, or—"

"Okay, you can stop right there. I don't have any plans with anybody. And I'd love to come in and rehash our evening over a nightcap."

"Cool. Follow me."

When Dani cracked opened the door, a warm rush of air brushed against Von's skin. He entered after her, inhaling the sweet scent of lemon and vanilla. The dim interior slowly came into focus, illuminated by the warm glow of chrome lights suspended from the vaulted ceiling. Not surprising, the spacious living room was in perfect order. Everything was well appointed, with a touch of Dani's chic style spread throughout.

The swanky cream-colored furniture was lined with plush lilac throw pillows. A vintage leather coffee table was stacked with statement books and a crystal chess set. Floating shelves made of reclaimed wood were filled with an eclectic selection of novels, service awards and decorative knickknacks.

Stepping into Dani's world felt surreal, beyond just entering her space. Her carefully curated home gave him a deeper understanding of who she really was. Every thoughtful detail revealed a part of her that drew him in, bringing an unexpected sense of calm and intimacy. In that moment, Von felt as though he was exactly where he belonged.

"Have a seat," she said, kicking off her nude patent heels and heading to the kitchen. "Make yourself comfortable while I grab a bottle of wine."

Von sauntered toward the couch, his eyes fixated on the sway of Dani's hips. The pull in his groin heightened at the sight of her curves swinging from right to left, as if she were putting on a show for him. Rather than take a seat, he followed her past the dining area and into the kitchen.

"How does cabernet sound?" Dani asked.

"That sounds good, thanks."

His mind spun with thoughts of the private moments they'd shared earlier that night. The time they spent away from the crowd, stealing discreet touches while swapping personal stories. The drinks and sensual dances. Von never imagined he'd get so close to Dani, let alone step inside her home. Yet here he was, reminded that life had a way of turning the impossible into something real.

"Your place is really nice," he told her. "I have to admit, I'm a little shocked you invited me in. You've hated me for so long I figured the only way I'd set foot inside of here is if you kidnapped me."

"Don't give me any ideas," Dani said with a tipsy giggle. "No, but seriously. It does feel a little odd, you being here." Handing him a glass, she added, "But it's actually nice."

"Yeah, it is. Thanks for this. For everything. May this amazing night be the first of many more to come."

"Salud," Dani murmured before taking a sip of wine.

Von was so preoccupied with her lips, still stained with a

shimmery peach gloss, that he missed a question she'd just asked. His arm remained stuck midair. "I'm sorry, could you repeat that?"

"I said why don't we have a seat? And recap the night, or..."

"Talk about the investigation?"

Dani shook her head adamantly while leading him into the living room. "I'd rather *not* talk about the case. At least not tonight. If that's okay with you."

"Of course it is. As a matter of fact, why don't we shift gears altogether? Talk about us. And figure out where we should go from here."

"*We*, as in me and you?"

"No, we as in the Maxwell PD and RPS."

"*Ohh,*" Dani muttered, biting down on her bottom lip. "Got it. Sorry for the misinterpretation."

"No need to apologize," he told her. Von wanted to add that he'd love to explore their personal connection. Find out whether it was his imagination, or if something was unfolding between them. But he didn't want to rush into that conversation or make assumptions. They'd just made amends. Pushing too soon could jeopardize the possibilities. Plus he knew she was deeply entrenched in the case. Now might not be the best time to pursue something more.

As they sank into the couch, Dani's curious gaze caught his attention. The spark in her eyes threatened to turn his unspoken thoughts into words. But he refrained, shifting his focus to the silver framed photos lining her stone fireplace mantel.

"Hey, I think I recognize some of those smiling faces up there."

"I'm sure you do. Those pictures are like a timeline of my life. You see my parents in the first one, then Troy and me, Chloe and me, Chloe and Troy..."

"And your high school crew, better known as the Classy Clique."

Dani grasped Von's arm, erupting into an infectious laugh. "Wait, I cannot believe you actually remember that! Your memory is undefeated. You've spent this entire night reminding me of stuff I've completely forgotten about."

"Yeah, well, it's pretty easy to hold on to things that mean something to you."

After her long pause, Von realized he'd said too much. He wished he could rewind time and take it back. Their sexy interactions, mixed with the alcohol, had him talking too much.

"Or," Dani began, her head tilting inquisitively, "it could just mean that names like the Classy Clique are hard to forget because they're so obnoxious. Could that be it?"

He released a subtle sigh; he sat back and unlocked his shoulders. "I actually thought the name was cute. And very fitting. You all were pretty sophisticated. But you have to admit that your crew did walk around with your noses in the air, thinking you were too good for everybody."

"That is not true! We were just in our own world, focusing on our books and goals rather than boys and partying."

"Which, in all honesty, is what made you even more appealing."

"Appealing?" Dani snorted. "*Please.* You know you couldn't stand me back then."

"Actually, it was quite the opposite. I'm just a really good actor."

"Yeah, right…"

Von's expression grew serious, his smile fading as he peered over at her. "I never disliked you, Dani. As a matter of fact, I had a huge crush on you." *Still do*, he almost let slip. "But I never acted on it because I knew better. I couldn't betray my father by trying to get together with you. Not to mention I knew you'd never go for it. You were a daddy's girl. You wouldn't have crossed over into enemy territory and hung out with me."

"You're right about that. I actually feel a little guilty hanging out with you now. But at this point, the situation we're in—that all of Maxwell is in—is bigger than us. We can't afford to let a ridiculous beef between our fathers keep us divided. And it doesn't matter whether I'm the intended target or you are. Our best chance of catching the killer is to work together."

"Exactly. As the saying goes, there's strength in numbers."

Clinking her glass against his again, Dani replied, "That's part."

Von downed a mouthful of wine. It kept him from revisiting his earlier thoughts on whether their after-hours hangout was strictly a friend thing, or something more.

"Hey," she said softly, her fingertips gliding across his hand. "What's on your mind?"

*Don't do it. Do not mess this moment up by professing your true feelings to this woman.*

"I, um… I guess now that the event is over and the quiet has settled around me," Von said, "I'm back to reality. And the reality is that we do in fact have a killer on our hands. Possibly another serial killer, no less. So that's pretty deep."

"Yes, it is. But didn't we agree not to talk about the case tonight?"

"You're right," Von replied with a slow nod. "We did. So let's change the subject."

"Here's something funny that I forgot to mention—the stunned expression on Chloe's face when she saw us leaving together."

"If it was anything like Kevin's, I can already envision it."

Dani grabbed her phone and scrolled through her texts. "Those two… I felt like they were watching us all night. But

Kevin seemed more irritated than shocked. Jealous even. I know that man can't stand me. Plus he's possessive and doesn't like to share you with anyone else."

"Aww, come on. Do you have to be so hard on him?"

"Just calling it like I see it. Anyway, look at this. Chloe and Troy have both sent me several messages asking whether I came home alone."

"Are you gonna tell them the truth? Or will I be your dirty little secret?"

"There is nothing dirty about this hangout."

*Yet*, Von's mischievous side wanted to say. But he held back.

"It's getting late," he told her. "And I've got to be at the office early tomorrow morning to process payroll. So I should probably get going."

When he set his glass down, Dani refilled it, as if she hadn't heard what he'd just said.

"You can't go yet," she told him. "I haven't answered your question."

"What question?"

"About you being my dirty little secret."

"Yes, you did. You said there's nothing dirty about us hanging out."

"Now Von," she murmured, sliding in a bit closer. "Let's be real. Is that all we're doing here? Just *hanging out*?"

The question, along with her penetrating stare, sent a surge of heat straight to his head that settled below his belt.

"I, um… I don't know," he stammered, stuck between the notion of not saying enough and saying too much. "What do you think?"

"Let's just say that there seems to be more going on than just friendly banter over drinks."

Dani always had been a tough read. But her answer was as blatant as it could get.

"I was hoping you'd say that," Von told her, unable to hold back as his eyes roamed her body. "I think so, too. And might I add that you just opened a door I've been dying to kick down."

"Oh, have you now? I never would've guessed that."

"Well, it's the truth. But before we go any further, I have to ask you a question that you seemed to dodge while we were at the Zonian. Why are you single?"

"Oh, God," she groaned. "Are you going there?"

"Yes, I am. Look, you had no qualms grilling me over my love life. So it's only fair that I do the same to you. Plus, I'm very curious as to why a woman like you hasn't been snatched up yet."

"Hmm…well, the short answer is that I refuse to settle."

"And what's the long answer?"

Glancing down at her phone, Dani said, "You know, it really is getting late. Didn't you say you have to get up early and—"

"Don't even try it! I'm good. I don't need copious amounts of sleep in order to function. I've got plenty of time. So answer the question, please."

"I really do hate talking about this, but, since you insist… I'm single for the same reason that you are. Being the chief of police is a pretty big job. And I've dated, of course. But I date with intention. If I'm gonna take time out of my busy schedule to go out with someone, then it has to be mutually beneficial. So if I'm not getting anything out of it, or I don't see myself having a real future with him, then I'm not going to continue investing time in that person."

"Okay. I feel you on that. What about the last guy you seriously dated? Why didn't things work out with him?"

"Let's just say that he and I were complete opposites. He put on a good show in the beginning, though, convincing me that he was everything I'd been looking for in a man.

Intelligent, funny, close with his family, in tune with his emotions… But he couldn't maintain the facade for long. Cracks began to form in the foundation we'd built when I realized he really wasn't ready to commit. He was still into partying with his fraternity brothers and more interested in hanging out with his friends than with me. Telling the world that I was his girlfriend was more important than actually investing in the relationship. He seemed to think that dating a law enforcement officer was a good look."

"But not good enough for him to actually put in the work?"

"Apparently not. We eventually drifted apart, and I broke things off officially when one of my girlfriends saw him on a dating app after he'd insisted we start dating exclusively. Since then, I've gone out on a few dates here and there. But nothing serious. Like I said, if I don't see a future, I don't waste my time."

"Yes, like you said, you're dating with intention," Von repeated. "I like that. Okay, here's another question. Have you ever been in love?"

Dani's head fell against the back of the couch as she stared up at the ceiling. "Ooh, that's a heavy one. I was, actually. Once. Back when I was still hopeful and carefree, believing that the world was my oyster. His name was Joshua. He was a financial analyst. We met at celebrity basketball game, and our connection was electric. We could talk for hours about anything and everything."

"Hold on, now, you're making me jealous," Von interjected, only half kidding.

"Well, you asked! But seriously, no need to be jealous since things didn't work out. Anyway, the relationship was great. I actually thought it was perfect. Then we realized we had conflicting plans for the future. I wanted to live a traditional lifestyle, like what my parents have. Marriage, children, growing old together, then retiring and traveling the world. Joshua, however, was like a nomad. A free spirit. He wanted to pick up and catch a flight at the drop of a dime. Quit his job and live in different countries while living off of his savings. Stability wasn't his thing. Chasing after new experiences was. I tried to hang in there with him. But everything changed when I discovered he didn't want kids. That was the deal-breaker."

"Are children a must for you?"

"Yes, they absolutely are," Dani replied adamantly. "What about you?"

"Most definitely."

"Good."

A slow smile pulled at his lips, as if she'd just said she wanted to have children with him. He knew it was ridiculous to think of them starting a family together. But talk of having children somehow deepened the connection between them, as if he could feel the possibility buzzing between them.

"Now how about we put you back in the hot seat," Dani said. "Have you ever been in love?"

Von drew a long inhale, contemplating his answer carefully. "I have. But not as deeply as I'd like. You know that feeling they say you get when you know it's real? And you know you're with *the one*?"

"What, the butterflies, floating on air, head-in-the-clouds type of stuff?"

"Yes. All of that. That's what I want. And I'm willing to keep chasing it until I find it."

"Yeah, me, too," Dani rasped, her voice barely a whisper.

*Maybe we've found it in each other*, Von wanted to declare.

His longing for her burned through him like a wildfire, each flame stoking his burgeoning feelings. Von fought the overwhelming urge to act on them as his efforts to remain cool slowly unraveled.

When Dani stretched her legs across the couch, he pressed his hands together, battling his desire to pull her closer. Her dress rose over her thighs. Rather than adjust it, she tilted her head back and drained her glass, leaving him teetering on the edge of restraint.

A drop of wine lingered on Dani's lip. Von's finger lightly traced the curve of her mouth before he gently wiped it away. "You spilled a little."

"Thank you…"

She leaned toward him, her supple breasts pressing against his chest. Unable to hold back any longer, Von covered her mouth with his. His tongue parted her lips, then slipped inside. Just as he worried she'd pull away, Dani slid onto his lap.

The kiss deepened as their tongues intertwined, twirling softly, then retreating, then melding once more. Von felt himself hardening between her legs. The soft warmth enveloped him, as if they were already connected in the most intimate way. His lips swept across her jawline and down to her neck, his teeth gently nibbling her skin. An insatiable moan vibrated deep within Dani's throat. When she drew him closer he freed her breasts, teasing her taut nipples with his mouth.

Dani's body trembled as her hips moved to the rhythm of his touch. Lifting her off the couch, he carried her into the bedroom. In between kisses, they pulled each other out of their clothes. Von attempted to pause for a beat. Stand back. Take in every inch of her stunning silhouette. But Dani wasn't having it. She reclined across the bed and pulled him in while kissing him with a fiery urgency. Her touch spoke louder than words ever could, conveying everything she hadn't said—their desire for each other was equally aligned.

But what Von felt for her was more than just a physical

connection. Dani's presence evoked deep, emotional memories from their past. Back when he longed to break every rule written by their fathers and step over to the other side. Indulge in the thrill of her presence, despite it being taboo. And create a bond that he knew they were destined to share.

She was everything he'd ever wanted in a woman. Von just hoped she could get past their families' rivalry and give him a real chance. Because Dani had left him wondering whether or not he could be more than just her dirty little secret.

## Chapter Eleven

Chloe reached across Dani's desk and handed her a mocha latte. "You never did answer my question."

"What question?" Her shrill tone a dead giveaway. Dani knew exactly what Chloe had asked. She just didn't want to respond.

"Please stop playing dumb with me. For the third time, why didn't you call me when you got home from the Zonian?"

"Good morning, Chief Miller!" Natalia called out on the way past her office. "How was your weekend?"

"It was pretty good. And yours?"

"Same!"

*"Pretty good..."* Chloe muttered under her breath. "Girl, between you leaving the bar with Von, the fact that you've been uncharacteristically vague during our text exchanges, and your skin looking all dewy this morning, there is something you're not telling me. And I wanna know what it is!"

"Listen, now that you're dating my brother, I've had to cut off some of your friendship privileges. Starting with me letting you in on every aspect of my personal life."

"But why? I haven't done anything to ruin your trust. Plus you know I don't tell Troy everything."

"Now how would I know that? You two have probably

made some sort of pact, promising to keep your little pillow talks to yourselves."

"*Wrong.* I do still have a life outside of my relationship, Dani. Keep in mind that you and I were friends *long* before Troy and I started dating. Not to mention I don't believe in pillow talk. I'm an adult. I don't have to share every single thing with my partner."

"Okay, fine," Dani relented. "Close the door and I'll tell you everything."

Chloe sprang from her chair, pulled the door shut, then perched up on the edge of the desk. "All right, I'm listening. Spill it!"

"So, after Von and I left the Zonian, he insisted on walking me to my car. That turned into him following me home, which led to him coming inside."

"Wait, did he ask to come inside, or did you invite him in?"

"Von is a gentleman. He never would've asked. I invited him."

"Ooh!" Chloe exclaimed, leaning back so dramatically she almost tumbled off the desk. "Did I just hear you refer to Von Reed as a *gentleman*?"

"You know what? If this type of commentary is gonna go on throughout our conversation, then I'm going to end it right now—"

"No, no! Please, I'll stop. I promise. I'm just in shock right now. All my life, Von has been public enemy number one. So to go from that to hearing you invited the man inside your house is unreal."

"Well, if you think that's unreal, wait until I spill the tea on how the night ended. And how the morning began..."

"*Excuse* me?" Chloe screeched so loudly that within seconds, Troy came charging into the office.

"What's going on?" he huffed. "You two okay?"

"We're fine," Dani blurted before Chloe could say a word. "Your girlfriend was just being overly dramatic, per usual."

Troy's expression shifted from concerned to skeptical. "Are you sure that's all it is? Because the fact that neither of you can look me in my eye tells me that you're hiding something."

"Now that doesn't even sound like something we'd do," Chloe fired back. "And since when do I keep things from you, babe?"

"Is that even a real question? I know all about the whole girl code thing."

Dani gave him a dismissive wave. "I do appreciate you for checking on us. Now would you mind closing the door on your way out?"

"Should I take that as a not-so-subtle hint to leave?"

"Yes. You absolutely should."

"I've been kicked out of better places, you know," Troy joked, giving Chloe's shoulder an affectionate squeeze. "Are we still on for lunch at noon?"

"We are. But I need to make it quick. I've gotta get back home and edit my latest podcast episode."

"Ooh," Dani breathed, rubbing her hands together. "What's this one about?"

"It's a strange one. This case took place in the Midwest. It's about a group of friends who got together for game night, and the rules involved doing heavy drugs. After a few rounds of play, a few of them went outside to smoke cigarettes and never came back in. They were found the next day inside the homeowner's backyard, frozen to death."

*"Damn,"* Troy said. "That is brutal. Where did this happen?"

"Right outside of Chicago. And yeah, it was brutal as hell considering it happened during the middle of winter. I'll let you both know when the episode is up so you can tune in.

But anyway, I'll meet you at Autumn's Den at twelve—"
Chloe stopped abruptly and slammed her palm against the
desk. "Wait, we're being rude. Dani, do you wanna come
to lunch with us?"

"Oh…no. I—I can't. I already have plans."

"Since when do you have lunch plans?" Troy asked. "You
usually just grab something from the vending machine and
eat at your desk, or—"

"Babe," Chloe interrupted, tossing Dani a sly side-eye.
"You know your sister is busy. Leave her alone. We'll schedule something for another time."

He backed out of the office, his head bobbing in an exaggerated nod. "Yeah, you two are definitely up to no good. But
don't worry. I'm an excellent sleuth. I'll figure out what it is."

"*Or*," Dani said, "you could put those investigative skills
to better use and help solve this case."

"And on that ornery note," he called out from the hallway,
"Chloe, I'll see you at noon!"

The second his footsteps faded, Chloe jumped up and
closed the door. "Anyway, so you and Von spent the night
together, *and* you've got plans with him this afternoon?"

"Yes and yes."

"*Wooow*…this is unbelievable. I cannot believe you're
sleeping with the enemy. Literally!"

"Well, after everything we did, he's not so much the
enemy anymore. But hey, listen. You've gotta keep this under
wraps. I don't want anybody to know about us. The investigation is all I want my squad to be focused on. If news
gets out that Von and I are involved, that'll take the attention away from the case and bring a lot of scrutiny my way.
And that's the last thing I need."

"Of course. You know your secret's safe with me. But
here's my question. Is it safe with Von?"

Falling against the back of her chair, Dani retorted, "I

would certainly hope so. I doubt that he'd want that attention on RPS. Plus he should wanna stay under the radar since he believes these recent murders are targeted at him."

"*Should* being the operative word. But did you two actually establish that?"

"Not really, no. At one point, Von did joke about being my dirty little secret. However, we didn't get too deep into it."

"Well you've got to make that clear. I'd hate for miscommunication to stir up unnecessary drama and end things before they've even begun. Because honestly? You and Von have the potential to be great. He might even *the one...*"

Dani lowered her head and blew an exasperated groan. "Could you please slow down? Von and I literally just stopped hating each other. You're going from that to practically pushing us down the aisle?"

"See, now you're putting words in my mouth. I said no such thing. But from what I'm hearing, you two are moving at lightning speed. And I saw the way you were all cuddled up at the Zonian. Sharing drinks, slow dancing while whispering sweet nothings in each other's ears—"

Shooting up from her chair, Dani marched toward the door. "You should probably go home and change out of those yoga clothes so you won't be late for lunch with Troy. Why don't I walk you out?"

"I probably should. And I will. Right after you tell me what you and Von have planned this afternoon."

Dani's buzzing phone almost vibrated off the desk. Chloe caught it right before it toppled off the desk.

"Speaking of the devil," she said with a smirk while handing it over.

"I'm sure Von's just checking to make sure we're still on for today. He and I are actually going back to the Blanche Hotel to take another look at the crime scene. Then we're having lunch at the Sandstone Skybar afterward."

"Nice. Isn't that the hotel's rooftop café?"

"It is," Dani confirmed.

"Interesting choice. My former detective skills are telling me that you're the one who chose that place. And it's not because you love it. It's because you don't wanna be seen with Von. And since no one really goes there during the week except for out-of-towners, it's perfect. But if anyone *does* happen to see you there, they'll assume you two are discussing the case. Am I right?"

"Possibly."

"All right then. Do me a favor. Make sure you talk to Von about keeping whatever's going on between you two private. *Today.* Before wires get crossed, or expectations are misread, or word gets out and your relationship status ends up on the front page of *The Maxwell Times*."

Dani opened the door and stepped out into the hallway. "I will do that, friend. And even though you're being somewhat over-the-top right now, I appreciate the advice."

"Good. You're welcome. And hey, in all seriousness, it's been a long time since you've had someone good in your life. I know how much you've been wanting that. So I really am rooting for you two. Plus, you never know. Maybe this blossoming relationship will help mend your father's rift with Mr. Reed."

"We'll see. One thing at a time, though. Von and I have to actually *get* into a relationship first."

"Sounds to me like you're well on your way," Chloe said, leaning in for an embrace. "I'm happy for you. Now get back to work. I need to stop by Troy's desk before I leave, so don't worry about walking me out. I'll call you later."

Dani closed the door and practically floated to her desk. The flutters milling about inside her stomach hadn't stopped since her alarm went off that morning. Neither had thoughts of Von lying next to her, already awake as she'd gradually opened her eyes. The way he'd made slow, passionate love to her once more, their bodies moving in perfect harmony. Afterward he'd made coffee and omelets wearing nothing but a towel. It had been a long while since she'd had a man in her house, staying over and making meals. She'd forgotten how good it felt. It was all so surreal.

Looking forward to seeing you... she typed in response to his message.

Less than a minute passed before the phone vibrated against her palm. Excitement pulsated through her fingers as she gripped it tighter, anticipating his reply. But when she glanced at their text thread, there was no response from him. The last message in their chain was the one she'd just sent.

A small blue dot in the left corner indicated she had a new message. It had been sent from an unknown number.

Nice job catching Maxwell's first serial killer, Chief Miller. Now let's see if you can catch the second...

## Chapter Twelve

Von stood in the middle of the Blanche Hotel's ladies' room, staring down at Dani's phone. The chilling text she'd received left him seething, triggering dark thoughts of violence. He was overcome with the need to protect her. To keep her out of harm's way—especially now that she'd finally let him in.

"Have you told your digital forensics investigator about this message yet?" Von asked.

"I haven't, but I will. I guess I'm hesitant because I already know what the answer's gonna be. And I don't want to hear him say that the message was sent from an untraceable burner phone."

"But I have heard that Chuck is special kind of tech wiz who can figure out pretty much anything. So just see what he says. You never know. You may get lucky."

"We'll see," Dani replied, her tone uneven as she slipped on a fresh pair of latex gloves. "But I'm not very hopeful. Which, ironically, is the same way I'm feeling about this crime scene. And that's probably my fault."

"Why is that?"

"I shouldn't have come here with such high expectations. My team and I did an extensive analysis of this place the night Brandy died. We didn't collect any viable evidence then. So I don't know why I'd come back today thinking things would be any different."

"Maybe you thought having a second pair of eyes would help—eyes that aren't a part of the Maxwell PD. Since I was trained outside of the police academy, I bring a completely different perspective. Plus my dad taught me a lot of what I know about forensics. So don't give up yet. We're not done here."

"Thanks for that," Dani replied, her faint tone sprinkled with distress. "I'll try. But it isn't easy. I can't believe I'm going through this again, so soon after last year's tragedy."

Silence took hold of the room as water dripped eerily from a porcelain sink. Von thought back on that night. The mayor's most pivotal event to date quickly morphed into a horror show. All that blood spattered across the textured pastel wallpaper. Law enforcement officers meticulously swabbing the surface, so hopeful they'd uncover vital DNA evidence. Paramedics scrambling to save Brandy's life, suctioning fluid from her airway while administering endless amounts of oxygen. Bloodied white cloths, strewn across the patterned stone floor as they'd struggled to stop the bleeding. The chilling possibility that their suspect was still on the scene, putting more lives at risk.

The woman who had discovered Brandy's lifeless body spent several days in the hospital, recovering from the trauma. The people of Maxwell were on edge, ready to abandon their hometown after it had once again come under attack. The police department faced relentless scrutiny as the pressure to name a suspect increased with each passing day.

Von could feel the tension closing in. The unsolved murders loomed over him heavily, as if he were a part of the force. But the growing threats against Dani kicked his need to help solve the case into high gear. Von still couldn't shake the feeling that the crimes were somehow directed at him.

But there was no denying that the killer's motive was deeply rooted in a vendetta against her.

"We just need to find something," Dani said, shining her flashlight along the veiny marble tiles. "Even the tiniest bit of trace evidence that my team might have overlooked could lead us to the assailant."

Riffling through his forensics kit, Von pulled out an ultraviolet light. "It could. I'll use this to search the area again. Who knows. Maybe it'll pick up on bodily fluids that weren't in plain view or were hidden by other materials during the initial search."

"Good call. You may even find dried fluid that formed new patterns after being obscured by moisture."

"Let's hope…" Von switched off the restroom light and hit the power button on his device. A dark purple glow illuminated the space. He directed the beam toward the walls, the ceiling and the floor. "I know the restroom's been cleaned, but this light will detect fluid traces."

"Good. And just so you know, the blood that was collected from the crime scene belonged to the victim and no one else."

"What about the other evidence that was collected? Any fibers? Hair strands? Shoe impressions? *Anything* you could go on?"

"Nope," Dani confirmed. "Nothing that we were able to connect back to Brandy's murder."

"Humph," Von grunted, tossing the light back inside his kit, then grabbing a can of luminol spray. "You know, I hate to say this, but…"

"But what?"

"You may have to wait for another murder to occur."

"*Wow.* That is the exact same thing Chloe said. During her time with the Chicago PD, they occasionally had to use that tactic to track down their suspects."

"Yep. It's an unfortunate truth. Of course the best-case scenario would be you catch this maniac before another murder occurs. But consider the odds. No viable evidence was found at Lieutenant Edwards's crime scene. If we don't uncover anything here and no witnesses come forward, we'll be relying on the killer to slip up next time and leave behind a clue."

Dani look the bottle of luminol from his hand and sprayed it along the wall. "I'd hate for it to come down to that, but you both may be right."

The pair stood back, eyeing the wall while waiting to see if a blue glow would appear. A few faint areas glimmered under the chemical's pale crystalline, but nothing signaling bloodstains.

Tearing off her gloves, Dani raked her fingers through her hair. "This is so damn frustrating."

"Hey, come here…" Von placed his hands on her shoulders, gently massaging the tension from her muscles. "Don't get discouraged. You've done this before. You can do it again. And this time around, you've got a new heavy hitter on your team. We've just gotta keep digging. Our suspect can't keep this up for too long. Trust me, he's gonna slip eventually. And we'll be right there to take him down."

Her grumbling exhale indicated that she'd heard him, but wasn't completely convinced.

"What about Brandy's autopsy results?" he continued in a bid to pull her out of the funk. "Did the medical examiner discover anything significant?"

"Nothing that would lead us to a suspect. There was bruising along her upper back, arms and wrists, which would indicate a struggle. You already know about the stab wounds to the chest. There were eight to be exact. I was expecting for there to be some sort of cranial fractures to show she'd been struck in the head, which could explain how Brandy may have been subdued before the stabbing. But there were none."

"So the assailant must've sneaked up from behind and surprised her, leaving the victim no time to really put up a real fight."

"That's what I'm thinking," Dani said. "Brandy's hands were perfectly intact. No swelling or bruising. No traces of foreign skin cells underneath her fingernails. There were no signs of sexual assault, either, so this crime was not sexually motivated. Someone simply wanted Brandy Orland dead."

"Yes. But why? What enemies did she have? I dug pretty deep into her background. None of her reporting seemed salacious or worthy of her murder."

"Exactly," Dani said, her eyebrows shooting toward the ceiling as she tossed her gloves into a paper bag. "Which is why I don't believe the attack was about her."

"Point taken. Has the toxicology report come back yet? Maybe that'll tell us something. What that *something* is I don't know, but…" Von hesitated, staring up at the wall once again before turning the light back on. "I'm just grasping at straws here."

"At this point, we'll take any pieces of information we can get and hope that they fit the puzzle. I don't expect for toxicology to come back until sometime next week. Till then, like you said, we'll just have to keep digging."

"I'll continue to talk to my guys at RPS who were here on the scene and see whether there's anything they may have heard or observed that could be relevant. If I find anything out, I'll let you know."

"Thanks, Von. I'd appreciate that."

He braced himself, waiting for her to add a snide comment about his men hoarding information in an effort to be the hero. But she didn't, giving him hope that they'd turned a corner for good.

"I guess we can wrap things up here," Dani said.

Von's movements were heavy with disillusionment as he packed up his kit. Failing to uncover promising new evidence wore on his confidence. But the weight of disappointment in Dani's muted tone triggered his savior complex. His fiery determination burned hotter than their frustration, fueling his resolve to keep going. He had to. For the sake of Dani and their hometown.

"Hey," Von said softly, "keep your head up. We're gonna stay in this until the work is done and the case is solved. You've got my word on that. Now, I hope you're still up for lunch. I already called ahead and asked Sandstone's bartender to whip up a pitcher of virgin mojitos for us since we're still on the clock. Once we're off work, I'll take you out for the real thing. How does that sound?"

"That sounds amazing," Dani murmured, punctuating the response with a soft kiss.

The touch of her lips was all Von needed to soothe the sting of defeat as they walked out the door.

## Chapter Thirteen

There was no denying it. Dani was in over her head.

She blew an unsteady breath, watching as a stream of vapor billowed through the frigid air. Dani was planted on the high point of Cole's Ski Resort's Vesper Peak, also known as its max mountain. It was early Tuesday morning—almost two weeks since Brandy's murder. The ski area was fairly empty, as most guests were enjoying the resort's free continental breakfast buffet. But food was the last thing on Dani's mind. The thought of chocolate croissants and melon medleys churned her stomach. Her body needed movement—something invigorating that would leave her too exhausted to continue obsessing over the case.

Beams of sunlight shone across the tranquil pale blue sky, sparkling against a fresh blanket of snow. Majestic aspen and mixed fir trees lined the piste. Delicate whistles of western bluebirds drifted through the stillness. While she attempted to take in the beauty of it all, Dani's thoughts were overshadowed by her somber reality.

The state of the investigation was what lured her to the resort that morning. Cole's had always been her escape. A place of peace. And solitude. Somewhere she could go to get away from all the madness and think. Regroup. And refocus. There was a warm familiarity that had welcomed her since childhood, providing just the right amount of security. That was until Lieutenant Edward's dead body was found sprawled inside the stairwell.

The moment Dani had entered the main lodge, she shielded her eyes from the vestibule door, unable to bear the sight of it. Memories from that day sliced through her mind like a scalpel, each flashback cutting more meticulously than the last. The jagged, star-shaped bullet wound to the lieutenant's head. The fragments of gunpowder residue tattooed across his temple. The trauma of realizing some lunatic had intentionally killed a man she'd deeply admired. A man who'd been crucial to her professional journey and was a beloved pillar of the community.

Since that first murder, the gut feeling Dani got whenever trouble was brewing had been bubbling like lava, waiting to erupt. She was convinced that Lieutenant Edwards's murder, along with the ominous threats against her, were setting the stage for darker acts. Brandy Orland's tragic demise confirmed her worst fears.

*Do not start obsessing...*

The whole point of coming out to the resort was to unplug. But it was too late to press pause on her thoughts. They were already on a roll, running through her mind like a haunting montage. The chilling images of the night Brandy was murdered. Her body, sprawled underneath a row of sinks, immersed in a pool of blood...

"Stop it!" Dani screamed from the mountaintop, blowing exasperated puffs of air as the icy wind chilled her teeth. She bent forward, channeling her attention toward the blinding white snow. Forcing herself to shift the focus. Envision something positive. Something that was keeping her afloat amid the flood of madness.

*Von...*

Dani was still reeling from the unexpected turn her and

Von's relationship had taken. The whirlwind shift from sworn enemies to partners *and* lovers in such a short time had been both jarring and invigorating. His companionship was the balm that helped ease her stress. And his input had become an essential part of the investigation.

Unfortunately, those sentiments weren't shared by everyone. Animosity between Von's company and the Maxwell PD still lingered among some of their team members. Since the rivalry hadn't commenced overnight, Dani didn't expect it to come to an abrupt halt after one evening of pleasantries at the Zonian. Their joint social was a nice start. But creating peace would take time. And a resolution would require effort from both sides. For some, that was a lot to ask. Especially of their more resentful officers.

One thing Dani was grateful for was Von's open mind. He wasn't naive. He knew it was a possibility that one or more of his guys could be their suspect. When she mentioned it during their lunch at the Blanche Hotel, he didn't jump to their defense. Neither did she when Von brought up a member of the Maxwell PD being their suspect. She'd actually admitted to having the same thought.

"I'll tell you what," he told her. "If this keeps up, I will start secretly surveilling my employees. See if I can figure out whether or not it is in fact one of my guys. I'd suggest you do the same with your crew. Deal?"

"Deal," Dani had agreed.

Howling winds snapped her back to the moment as they swirled through the mountains' jagged peaks. She tightened the drawstrings on her bright red ski jacket, the breeze blowing all thoughts of the case from her mind. That was the magic of Vesper Peak. The steep, breathtaking slope may have been intimidating for some. But for her, it was pure solace.

Dani dug her steel poles into the powdery trail and pushed

off. Her heart raced to the rhythm of the skis cutting through the snow. Her strokes were swift and steady. The crisp pine air was intoxicating, injecting the thrill of the run with a euphoric high. She tightened her core. Leaned into the sharp turns, swaying from side to side as her knees absorbed the shock of each curve. The swoosh of her skis was melodic, easing her mind at every crest. Here, Dani was in control. Removed from her world and connected to nature. Able to think clearly. Contemplate who was after her. And why.

The rush down the piste grew faster. The speed was invigorating. Affirming. Alerting her that answers would soon come. With Von's help, she was getting closer to the truth.

Gravity took hold as snowflakes shimmered along the trail. For the first time in a long time, she felt a semblance of tranquility. A flash of freedom before the storm of the case descended upon her once she hit the base. Her breathing quickened. She inhaled the exhilaration and exhaled adrenaline, puffs of air fogging her goggles.

Her bliss was momentarily disrupted by a black dot appearing briefly through the corners of her eyes. Another lone skier, emerging from a cluster of lodgepole pines.

*Whoosh!*

Every muscle in Dani's body tensed as her right ski slipped across a mogul hidden within the snow. Shifting her weight forward, she turned the edge of her ski against it, rebalancing herself.

*Stay centered*, her inner voice whispered. No matter how many times she'd skied it, Vesper Peak was still a challenge.

Gripping her poles tighter, Dani eyed the winding trail up ahead. She leaned into the steep terrain, tucking the sticks under her arms as that pulse-pounding rush returned.

A shadow flickered, pulling her attention away once more. It hovered to her right. A swift glance revealed the skier she'd seen moments ago. He was catching up.

Dani's intuition kicked in, its intensity as suffocating as the thin mountain air. Sensing an imminent threat, she contemplated slowing her descent. Allowing the skier to pass her by. Because something wasn't right.

*Maybe you're just being paranoid...*

Dani reminded herself that she didn't own the slope. Another skier had the right to be on it. Yet that rationale failed to decrease the anxiety clenching her chest. She searched the mountain for other skiers. There were none. She and this dark figure were alone. The empty, wide-open clearing only amplified his ominous presence.

Her need to get off the slope grew urgent. Dani's feet widened as she bent down, tucking her body into a low stance while pressing her elbows against her sides. As her speed increased, so did the other skier's. The swish of their skis grew louder. Dani could no longer see him. Because he was directly behind her.

Her legs deadened as the impact of each bump rattled her joints. Determined to stay on her feet, Dani forced herself to keep cool calm. This could be nothing.

*It could also be something. Something treacherous...*

The base of the mountain appeared up ahead. A rush of relief shot up her calves as the numbness began to wear off. Dani's grip on the poles loosened just enough for her fingers to regain feeling.

*You're almost there...*

The picturesque wintery landscape blurred. Dani poured every ounce of her energy into reaching the bottom of the mountain.

*Get there...get there!*

Her determination faltered when a massive snow cloud engulfed her. The funnel of powdery dust sent her senses spiraling. Once the drift settled, that dark, hovering figure appeared next to her, expertly maneuvering the piste.

Startled, Dani pulled her skis inward, attempting to change directions. She almost lost her footing mid-switch.

*Reset!*

Her legs began to fold like tattered branches, succumbing to the weight of distress. Digging her poles into the snow, Dani regained her balance while picking up speed. So did the other skier, who moved with the same expertise.

As the pair raced down the mountain, Dani eyed a quick flash of silver. She attempted to scream. But the pounding in her throat silenced her.

The skier swung an arm through the air. A sharp, stinging pain hit Dani's torso. The impact sent her flailing, her skis cutting erratically through the snow as she struggled to stay on her feet.

"I've been hit," she panted, even though no one was around to hear her. "I've been hit!"

The cold, searing pain was unbearable. Bobbing back and forth on her skis, Dani fought the urge to fall to her knees. Unwavering determination took over, pushing her through the agony.

Just when her attacker swung an arm in the air, Dani stabbed him in the groin with her pole. He doubled over, emitting an animalistic growl in the process. She seized the moment and took off.

A treacherous curve came into view. Angling her skis sharply, Dani cut a high-speed turn that sent her skidding along its edge, leaving a plume of snow in her wake. She attempted to recover. But not before the hiss of her attacker's approach echoed from behind.

The pain in Dani's side took hold. Fighting the impulse to give in, she gritted her teeth, resolute in making it out alive. Her descent became a blur of agony. Ignoring the crackle of her assailant's skis nipping at her heels, she pressed on with renewed urgency.

*You're almost there. Just keep going...*

With a final burst of energy, Dani made it to the bottom of the mountain, practically plowing into the patrol office door.

"Help me, please!" she screamed. "Somebody help me!"

The second an officer came rushing out, her assailant made an abrupt U-turn.

"Ma'am," he said, "are you all right? Did you injure yourself on the slope?"

*"No,"* Dani moaned, barely able to breath. "I was… I was attacked. By him." She pointed in the direction of the suspect. Her glove hand wavered at the sight of him disappearing into a cluster of mixed firs. "You've gotta go—go after the person who…"

Dani paused, her head spinning faster than the flurries whipping around her. Disoriented, she struggled to focus on her surroundings. "Wait. I was…he was just…"

"I'm sorry, ma'am," the patrol officer said. "Go after the person who did what?"

"I—can you…call Von Reed," Dani muttered before falling to her knees and collapsing into the snow.

## Chapter Fourteen

Von charged down the hallway toward Dani's hospital room, checking the number near the door before knocking.

*Pull it together. Straighten your face. Don't lose your composure...*

"Come in!" she called out.

He turned the handle slowly, sticking his head inside before entering.

"Hey, how are you?" he asked quietly, hoping his soothing tone would mask the alarm coursing through his body.

"I'm all right," Dani said, barely turning toward him as she lay propped up against a stack of pillows. "A bit banged up, but I'll be fine. The doctor said the worst of it is the superficial stab wound that barely penetrated my abdomen. I've got my ski coat's synthetic polyester fill to thank for that."

"I'm so sorry, Dani. But it sounds like you got really lucky. So for that, I'm glad. I had no idea you were even going skiing at Cole's today. Had I known, I would've gone with you."

"It was a last-minute thing. I just needed to do something that would take my mind off the investigation. You know, get some alone time in to clear my head. Figure out the next steps..." Her voice drifted as she swiveled robotically, wincing with each movement of her body. "Why are you just standing there in the doorway? Come in. Have a seat. Listen to me complain about this nightmare of a day."

Von shuffled farther into the room, squinting as slivers of sunlight peeked through the half-drawn blinds. He hauled a heavy wood-framed chair toward the bed and took a seat, his eyes on the television rather than Dani. Focusing on an old episode of *Living Single* would be easier than admitting that he wasn't fond of hospitals.

The stark white walls, blur of lab coats, pungent odor of antiseptic and shrill beeping monitors brought back unpleasant childhood memories. Von had spent countless hours at Cedar Ridge Hospital with his mother during her nephrology appointments and dialysis treatments. After she'd received a kidney transplant, the incessant visits continued once complications arose. It had taken doctors months to figure out the correct course of immunosuppressant drugs. Once they did, she was finally able to live a normal life, and the hospital visits became less frequent.

"We've gotta catch this bastard, Von."

"Yes… I know we do." Finally turning to her, he studied Dani's expression. Her face appeared drawn, tight with worry, each crease deepening as she spoke. Unshed tears pooled in her dim eyes. Her lips quivered, as if holding back words she was hesitant to speak.

*"Ow,"* she wheezed, dabbing a quarter-size bruise splayed across her right temple.

Von jolted to his feet so quickly that the chair almost toppled over. "Are you okay? Should I call the nurse? Do you need more pain meds, or numbing cream for that?"

"No, I'm fine. What I need is to get the hell out of here. Get back on the street so I can hunt down this psychopath who tried to kill me."

"Shouldn't they be keeping you overnight? At least for observation?"

"I certainly hope not. Even if they try, I'm not staying."

The defiance in her toned prompted Von to pull the chair in closer and sit back down. "Listen, Dani. I've been thinking about everything. These attacks on you. The murders. The security of Maxwell, the community's diminishing faith in the police department... I think it's time that we switch gears. Step up our game. Create a new plan that could actually take down the suspect. One that won't require us to have to wait until another murder occurs."

"I've been thinking about all that, too. And I totally agree. In the meantime, I've got Troy and a few other officers reviewing the surveillance footage from the slopes today. They're at Cole's now, looking for witnesses who may have seen something. And we'll be sending my ski gear to the crime lab so they can process it for DNA evidence."

"Good. I hope something comes of it. Remember how we talked about surveilling our teams more closely to find out whether one of our own is behind all this?"

"I do."

"Well, I think it's time for us to put that plan into action. We need to put a couple of our employees who we can trust to work. Get them to spark up some *just between us* types of conversations around the office. Surveilling their movements is one thing, but getting inside their heads could give us the answers we're looking for, too. Alert us to who knows what and who's up to what. If one of our team members is the culprit, I highly doubt that he hasn't bragged about it or dropped some sort of hint to someone."

Dani shot straight up, gripping her left shoulder in the process. "*Ouch.* I like that idea. You and I could also start keeping a closer eye on our officers around the office. See if any of them are behaving strangely toward us, or just acting differently than normal. That goes for in person and on social media. You know how people love to post cryptic memes about what they're going through. We may luck up and find a few clues that way. I'm also not above putting GPS trackers on the cars of any officers who appear suspicious."

Whipping out his phone, Von launched the Notes app. "Those are some great suggestions. I'll keep a record of them."

His fingers sprinted across the keys, racing to keep pace with the whirlwind of ideas being tossed out. After several minutes, the steady rhythm of Dani's monitor morphed into a series of frantic, high-pitch beeps. Von glanced up at the screen. Her heart rate had increased to 115 beats per minute.

"Hey, Dani," he whispered, hoping his gentle tone would calm her energy. "Why don't we table this conversation for later and just focus on your recovery? We've got plenty of time to talk about the investigation."

"Actually, no. We don't."

"Look, your health comes first. What happened to you today was traumatic, both physically and emotionally. Your officers are perfectly capable of managing the case while you recuperate. And of course they'll have RPS's full support, too."

Dani's lips parted and shut repeatedly, as if she wanted to debate but couldn't find the words. Eventually, her icy scowl thawed, melting into a soft expression of acceptance. Falling back against the pillows, she uttered, "I hear you, Von. And I appreciate your concern, it's just hard for me to sit back and relinquish control. You know me. I think I can handle everything at all times."

*Tread carefully,* he reminded himself before taking her hand in his. "I know you do. And you probably can. But right now, it's important for you to do what's best for *you*. And that means falling back a bit and taking care of yourself. You've got a ton of perfectly capable people around you who are more than willing to take charge temporarily. Plus… I care about you, Dani. More than you know. It shook me to my core when ski patrol called and told me you had been injured. As soon as I heard those words, I knew you'd been attacked. The thought of you being in that type of danger yet again really—"

As his voice broke, Dani's grip on his hand tightened.

"Trust me, Von, I understand. I'm shaken up, too. But I'm not backing down. I can't. That's what this maniac wants. I won't let him win. Especially not now. The stakes are too high."

"Dani, please, listen to me—"

Her raised hand was all it took to silence him. "I'm sorry, but you can't talk me out of this. Now, I get it. Until the killer is caught, I can't move around town like I normally do. So I won't. But you need to trust that I can work and recover at the same time. I can't let up. If anything, it's time to push even harder."

A heavy silence fell over them. Von glanced up at the monitor. Dani's heart rate had normalized, dropping down to ninety-six beats per minute.

"Please stop watching that monitor like I'm about to flat-line," she insisted, running her fingertips along his forearm. "I promise you, I'm okay."

"I know you are. And I hear everything you're saying. You're a pro. So I get it. And I'll back off. But what I will *suggest*, however, is that you stick to your word and move around town differently. More cautiously. And never let your guard down. You're so used to being our police chief that you've forgotten you're still a target. The minute you let your defenses slip, you leave yourself wide open for any-thing to happen."

With a slight nod, Dani replied, "You're right. And I will take heed."

"See, that's what I wanna hear. Because together, we got

this. I'll be right by your side through it all. And not just as your security-slash-investigative consultant, either. I, um… I'd like to be something more. If you'll let me…"

Dani's gaze drifted toward the window as her grip on his hand loosened.

"Uh-oh," Von muttered. "Did I say something wrong?"

"No, you didn't. We just need to talk about what you're asking of me."

The mood in the room shifted. Their spirited conversation became overshadowed by her somber reaction. Sliding his hand out from underneath hers, Von said, "Why do I get the sense that you really are trying to keep me a secret?"

"That sounds so harsh. It really isn't like that—"

"What is it like then?"

"I just don't think it would be a good idea for us to go public with our relationship. At least not right now. I need for Maxwell PD's sole focus to be on this case. Not my love life. If we start dating out in the open, I'm convinced we'd be a distraction that might throw off the entire investigation. And that goes for RPS, too."

"Dani, we're adults. Almost everyone on your team is either married or in a relationship. The same goes for mine. So why should we be denied that? We have a right to be happy, don't we? Plus, last I checked, we're the leaders of our organizations. Why would we allow our personal lives to be dictated by our subordinates? And if somebody *were* to step out of line over what we do in our private time, they'd be dealt with accordingly."

"You're right," she replied in a hushed tone while picking at the label on her hospital bracelet. "But I would also hate for our situation to shift the focus away from the victims. On top of that, I'm already in the killer's crosshairs. If we take our relationship public, that could end up putting you in danger, too."

"Or maybe you and I coming together would be viewed as a power move. We'd become formidable allies. Because think about it. If the killer is one of our own, they're probably loving the fact that we're enemies and our agencies have been at odds. That puts part of our focus on the rivalry rather than the case. If we're together, *that* changes the game."

"In terms of the case? Yes. But on a personal level, I'm sorry, but I disagree."

Rubbing his temples in frustration, Von asked, "What if we do everything in our power to keep this situation under wraps, and somebody finds out about us anyway?"

"I don't know. We can cross that bridge when we get to it. If we ever do."

His fallen expression shifted from frustration to resignation. "Is that what this is really about? Or does it have something to do with your family, and you not wanting to disappoint them by getting involved with me?"

Her silence was all the answer he needed.

*"Wooow,"* Von breathed, grasping the arms of his chair before slowly standing.

"Wait, are you leaving?"

"No," he retorted while pacing the floor. "I just—I'm thinking…"

"Listen, I think we're focusing on the wrong thing. Let's get back to the real issue at hand. Apprehending the killer."

"Agreed." Stopping abruptly, Von turned and faced Dani. "Actually, why don't we put this situation between us on the back burner and revisit it once an arrest has been made?"

The second he made the suggestion, Von's chest caved, as if the words shot holes straight through his heart.

"You mean stop seeing each other romantically?"

"Yes."

"I don't know," Dani rasped, her tone tinged with sadness. "Is that really what you want?"

"Of course not. But when it comes to this case, if you think that would be best, then yes."

Dani's cell phone lit up, its hard-shell case vibrating loudly against the wooden tray table.

"That's Troy," she said after swiping it open. "He and Chloe just checked in at the registration desk. They're on their way up."

"Okay, well, I'll leave then…give you all a chance to talk privately."

"Von, you know you don't have to go."

"No, it's fine. I'll check on you later. Let me know if they decide to release you today and I'll come back and pick you up. Unless you'd rather have Troy take you home."

Slowly extending an arm, Dani gestured for Von to come closer. He obliged, taking her hand in his.

"I'd love for you to come back and get me. I'll call you when Troy and Chloe leave. Thank you for coming. I really appreciate you. And I hope our conversation didn't upset you."

"I'm good," he lied, brushing a kiss across her forehead. "We'll talk later."

"Hey," Dani said, gently pulling him back when he began walking away. "You do understand where I'm coming from with all this, don't you?"

"I do. But it still doesn't make it any easier. Anyway, I'm gonna go. I know you don't want your brother to see me here. I'll call you."

"Von, please. I just…"

He hesitated, waiting to hear her response. But when her voice faded, Von realized that Dani had no real argument left. Familiar voices out in the hallway sent him ducking out of the room and toward the stairwell, avoiding the elevator to steer clear of Troy and Chloe.

Confliction weighed heavily on his conscience as he

bolted down the stairs and trudged through the expansive sunlit lobby. The bright surroundings were a stark contrast to his own inner turmoil. A vision of him and Dani lying in bed together just days ago felt like a distant memory. In its place was the professional bond they'd built, alongside the promise to keep fighting for what mattered most—bringing the killer to justice. If that meant suspending their intimate relationship for the sake of the case, then so be it.

Nevertheless, the sharp sting of that decision lingered, a painful reminder of the boundaries they couldn't cross.

## Chapter Fifteen

Dani readjusted the bustline on her red silk cocktail dress and glanced around Gibson Country Club's elegant dining hall. The château-style room had been transformed into an elaborate art gallery in celebration of the club's annual auction.

Vibrant oil paintings on canvas, handblown glass sculptures and framed black-and-white photographs surrounded tables that were meticulously set with fine china and crystal stemware. A live string quartet positioned near the entrance performed soft classical music. Waitstaff glided through the crowd, offering champagne flutes that sparkled like stars underneath elegant chandeliers. The who's who of Maxwell mingled with the club's affluent members, who'd come together to support local artists and charities. It was a spectacular occasion that Dani seldom missed, as her family had been close with the Gibsons for over two decades.

It'd been quite some time since Dani had donned a fancy gown and attended an upscale event. She had been so wrapped up in the case that her personal life had taken a back seat—with the exception of her dalliances with Von. They hadn't spent much time together since she'd been released from the hospital a little over a week ago. He still checked in with her through text messages and sporadic phone calls. But the conversations had primarily been about the investigation.

Hitting a rough patch so soon after they'd finally reconciled didn't sit well with Dani. Their intimate nights together only complicated matters. Yet despite missing Von, the facts remained the same. A relationship between them would draw too much attention. And after all the drama their connection had stirred between them, Dani realized now was not the time to get swept up in an affair. Their focus had to stay on the case. There would be plenty of time for them to pursue something more once they caught the killer.

*If Von's still interested*, a nagging voice rebutted.

Dani's red satin pumps clicked across the polished hardwood floor, her toes tensed in anticipation of a confrontation. She hadn't realized RPS was handling security for the event and ran into Von the moment she'd arrived. Dani attempted to ignore the cloud of awkwardness looming over them when they greeted each other. But after she'd extended a hand to him, Von's snarky chuckle was a clear indication of his mood.

His posture had been rigid, and there was a sadness behind his eyes that seemed to linger even as his gaze drifted from her lips down to her breasts. Von's formal greeting, "Good evening, Chief Miller," felt worlds apart from the warmth of their recent exchanges. The chilliness in his tone assured her that she wasn't imagining the tension between them. Troy and Chloe had picked up on it, too, their raised eyebrows proof of the palpable strain.

"*Hey*," Chloe had whispered the moment Von walked off, "why is he acting so strange toward you? I hope he's not trying to pull back. Especially not now, after you two have been...you know..."

Dani remained silent, not in the mood to rehash their conversation at the hospital. Plus she'd needed a minute to cool off. To come down off of the high of seeing Von. To-night, there was no denying that the man looked more hand-some than she cared to admit. His expertly tailored tuxedo accentuated his muscular physique to perfection. A fresh haircut framed his handsome face. The scent of spicy san-dalwood pulsated from his neck, stirring something deep within her. It was the same cologne he'd worn the first night they'd made love.

"Dani!" Chloe called out, interrupting her thoughts as she approached the bar. "I've been looking all over for you. Are you okay?"

"I'm fine. Why?"

"Well, I'm assuming you're irritated after Von came at you with that dry *good evening* when you got here. And now he and Kevin are standing over there staring at us like we're under surveillance."

Dani's turned discreetly, peering at the men through the corners of her eyes. Sure enough, their gazes were fixed on them. Her mouth went dry at the thought of an actual fallout between her and Von. It would be her worst nightmare—their relationship going sour due to the fact that they'd slept together.

"Von better not have spilled a word to Kevin about what happened between us."

"Considering he's his best friend, I'd bet the house that he did. And let's not forget, you told me. So to be fair, neither of you kept it a secret, *if* he's guilty of running his mouth."

"Chloe, please. Now is not the time to try to rationalize with me. Let's walk around and get out of their direct view before I get irritated."

Dani fought the urge to look back and see if Von was still watching her. She and Chloe strutted toward the center of the room, pausing at an elaborate buffet table filled with savory hors d'oeuvres, beautifully arranged sushi and mouthwatering pastries. Nearby, several bartenders worked at mixing stations, chatting with guests while crafting signature cocktails.

"I really want a cosmopolitan," Dani said. "But I'd better stick to something nonalcoholic. Even though I'm off duty, I get the feeling that everybody is judging me. I hope nobody tries to question me about the case."

"Yeah, that would be rude. If they do, just hit them with a *no comment*. Anyway, speaking of the case, any updates from the crime lab?"

"Nothing useful. You already know we didn't get solid evidence back on the first two murders. And there wasn't any foreign DNA left on my clothing after the attack at Cole's. Surveillance cameras didn't capture anything that would identify the suspect since the attack occurred so far up Vesper Peak. And I swear, that psycho must be some sort of professional mountain climber. Because we're thinking he escaped off the side of the ski slope."

"Damn. Who the hell are we dealing with here? And what could his motive possibly be?"

"That's the million-dollar question. We just can't figure out the answer. Think about last year's killer. We never could have predicted his identity. It came as a complete shock. This one might be just as surprising. Or, maybe not…"

"What do you mean, maybe not?" Chloe asked, piling sashimi onto a plate.

Dani tossed a few mini spring rolls inside a napkin, then headed toward a high-top table. On the way there, she glanced over at the rustic limestone fireplace where Von and Kevin had been posted up. Kevin was gone. But Von was still standing there, watching her intently. When their eyes met, his expression softened. The warmth in his gaze curled her lips into a subtle smile.

"Oh, well," Chloe said. "And just like that, the two star-struck lovers have forgiven each other."

"You don't miss a thing, do you?"

"Dani, I am a highly trained former Chicago PD detective. Does that answer your question?"

"Yes, it does. But you've been nosy all your life, friend. So let's not act like your training with the force gave you that skill. Anyway, as I was saying. Motive. I'd *like* to think that no one has issues with me. However, that's clearly not true. We've talked about bitter officers on the force. And even though we had a great time at the joint social, all isn't well with RPS. Von keeps insisting that the murders are connected to him, but I'm not convinced. How would that explain the attacks on me?"

"Let me ask you this. Are you convinced that the murders are connected to the attacks?"

"Oh, most definitely," Dani affirmed. "Without a doubt."

Chloe bit down on a slice of salmon, then looked over her shoulder. "What about Kevin? Have you ever thought of him as a suspect?"

*"No,"* Dani said slowly, her features tightening with confusion. "Kevin may not be my favorite person in the world, but he and I have never had any real issues. And if this is some sort of dual attack against both Von and me, I don't think Kevin would do anything to hurt him. They've been best friends for as long as I can remember."

"Yeah, well, things change. Relationships shift. Von runs RPS, which means he's in a position of power. He's Kevin's boss. I'm sure that's not always easy—balancing the friendship and work relationship. So you never know. Maybe something went down between them and Kevin is trying to sabotage the company to get back at Von."

"I mean, it could be, but…that's a pretty wild assumption

to make considering there's nothing to back it up. And what does that have to do with me?"

"You don't think Von has talked about you to Kevin? He's been crushing on you since high school. He and Kev have probably dissected everything about you—from your family to Mr. Miller's position with the Maxwell PD. Bottom line? Kevin knows Von has feelings for you. So that's how this situation is connected to you. Now, I may be grabbing at straws here, but if Kevin's jealous of Von's success, jealous of the Maxwell PD's success, envious that his best friend is into the woman who's been the enemy...that's all the motive he'd need to be your suspect."

Dani slowly nodded while scanning the room. "Who knows, you could be right. Considering we don't have any suspects, I can't afford to court anybody out. So I won't dismiss your theory. By the way, where is Kevin?"

"I have no idea. Von is still standing alone over by the fireplace, staring you down. Maybe Kevin left."

A loud buzz swept over the room as the auctioneer stepped onto a small stage near the front of the room. The crowd whispered excitedly, gesturing at various art pieces while getting their paddles in position. When the stout, balding man held a hand in the air, a hush fell over the crowd.

"Hello, ladies and gentlemen!" he boomed into the mic. "Welcome to Gibson Country Club's twenty-second annual art auction, where your winning bids will benefit independent artists as well as several organizations, including Maxwell Children's Hospital and the Reed Center for Rehabilitation. My name is Curtis Feldman, and I'll be your bid caller for the evening. On behalf of the Gibson family, I would like to thank you all for being here, and express just how much your generosity means to them. With that being said, let the auction begin!"

The crowd erupted into a frenzy of applause. As the ovation faded, a blood-curdling scream tore through the room. In an instant, panic gripped the audience. People bolted in every direction, a sea of frantic bodies scrambling toward the exits.

Amid the chaos, Von charged Dani, his swift steps cutting through the mayhem. "Are you okay?"

"Yes, I'm fine. *We're* fine," she said, grabbing hold of Chloe. "But apparently somebody else isn't. We need to figure out what's going on."

"Help!" someone yelled. "We need assistance out on the golf course!"

"The golf course?" Dani repeated, her eyes darting with confusion. "Why would anybody be out there? It's pitch black, and the fairway is closed."

She and Chloe followed Von onto the terrace. Their shoes pounded the rich gray stone as they approached the wrought iron railing overlooking the green.

"What is going on out here?" Troy asked, rushing toward the group. "I was inside the cigar lounge and heard all this screaming."

"That's what we're trying to figure out," Dani told him. "We can't see a thing. It's too dark."

"On the way out here, I heard Mr. Gibson say he's gonna turn on the lights and figure out what's happening."

Suddenly, the range lit up. A wave of screams rippled across the terrace. There, near the eighteenth hole, lay a body sprawled underneath the flagstick.

## Chapter Sixteen

Von followed closely behind Dani as she charged the stairs and ran across the fairway.

"Troy!" she yelled. "Call for backup!"

A frantic rush ensued when guests rushed onto the green. "Everyone," Von called out, holding his arms out at his sides, "I'm going to need for all of you to go back inside. This is official police business. We need to stay out of the way and let the Maxwell PD do their jobs."

RPS officers stepped in and began ushering the onlookers back toward the stairwell.

"This cannot be happening," Dani said, hovering over the man lying on the ground. "This *cannot* be happening..."

Von joined her, peering down at him. He appeared to be in his mid-thirties. His strong, sculpted features—smooth, unlined and seemingly familiar—were frozen in an unsettling look of shock. His dark gray tuxedo was still in immaculate condition, not a wrinkle or speck of dirt in sight. There didn't seem to be any signs of a struggle or trauma. No bruising or wounds were apparent. No blood was present. And no weapons were in the vicinity.

Dani sprang into action and performed chest compressions as sirens wailed in the distance.

"He's not breathing," she panted. "And he doesn't have a pulse."

Von's stomach pulled at the look of alarm on Dani's face. "Keep trying. The paramedics will be here any minute. I wonder if the guy had a heart attack or something along those lines, since I'm not seeing any signs of trauma."

"Yeah, maybe he wasn't feeling well and wanted to get some fresh air, or…"

As her voice trailed off, Troy took a knee and stared at the victim. "Wait, isn't this—"

He was interrupted when a group of police officers and paramedics rushed down the fairway.

"Hey, let's give these guys some room!" Dani yelled before stepping away. Crossing her arms over her chest, she turned to Troy. "Yes, that's him."

"Wait, you two know this man?" Von asked.

Before responding, she asked Troy, "Can you and the other officers cordon off the area? And grab a forensics kit from your car for me?"

"Of course. Be right back."

Von waited for Dani to answer his question. She didn't, her eyes still fixated on the victim as paramedics quickly moved in. One of them pulled out a portable monitor, the device blinking to life with a series of beeps. Another cut open the man's shirt and swiftly attached the electrodes to his bare chest. The screen flickered, then displayed a flat line.

When Dani released a ragged stream of air, Von gently grasped her shoulder as they continued to look on.

"Let's check for a pulse," the paramedic said after readjusting the leads. She pressed her fingers against the side of his neck. Several moments passed before a shadow of worry flickered across her face.

"Okay, clear!" another paramedic shouted. He hit the button on the defibrillator. "One, two, three!" he counted, pressing the paddles against the victim's chest. Electricity surged through the cables. The monitor's screen flashed again. Another flatline.

*"Damn it,"* Dani huffed, turning away.

"Hey," Von said, wrapping his arm around her. "Come here. Are you all right?"

"No, I'm not."

"I understand. But hang in there. I know this isn't easy to watch, but from the looks of things, you may not have another murder victim on your hands—*if* the victim is actually dead. At least we're not seeing any outward signs of violence."

"That's true," Dani responded just as Troy approached with the forensics kit. "But I don't want to get my hopes up, so we'll see what happens."

"One thing's for sure, though. If this man is in fact dead, and foul play is involved? That would mean we've got yet another murder on our hands that occurred while RPS was on duty."

Dani remained silent.

"I know you haven't really bought into that theory," Von continued. "But you can't keep denying that these crimes are aimed at me. The suspect has killed someone at every major event RPS has recently worked."

"You know what else can't be denied?"

"What's that?"

"The fact that the victim is my ex-boyfriend."

Von's lungs emptied as he let off a stunned gasp. "I—I'm sorry. The victim is your *what*?"

"My ex-boyfriend. His name is Jeffrey Simmons. We dated for a few months, but the attraction just wasn't there. He and I remained good friends and still hung out on occasion. So, yeah. If he was killed, I'm dealing with yet another murder that's connected to me, too."

Her words triggered an intense urge deep within Von. His body grew tense while fighting the need to pull Dani close. Hold her until the fear disappeared from her eyes. He longed to brush aside the stray curls framing her face and tell her everything would be okay. But he couldn't. Not here. Not now. Despite the lines between them already being crossed, she'd made it clear that no public displays of affection would be tolerated.

"I should get to work," she said, slipping on a pair of gloves, then pulling a flashlight from the kit.

"Hey, Chief!" Troy called out from the brush near the side of the course. "You need to see this."

Von followed Dani as she rushed toward him.

"What's up?" she huffed. "What'd you find?"

Troy raised his hand in the air, the moonlight glinting off a sharp needle.

"Is that…a *syringe*?"

"It is. And I think we should get it sent to the crime lab first thing in the morning. As a matter of fact, I'll drive it down myself."

"Good idea. I'd love to know if it's somehow connected to Jeffrey."

"If it is," Von interjected, "that could explain why there's no obvious signs of trauma."

"Exactly," Troy replied, taking a step back. "I'll pack it up now."

"Chief Miller?" one of the paramedics called out.

"Yes?" she replied, her voice strained as she and Von rushed back over. "How's he doing?"

"Not good. There's still no pulse. We should get him to the hospital as soon as possible."

"Yes, thank you," Dani whispered, her head dropping toward the ground.

Von discreetly pressed his hand against the small of Dani's back. Something told him she could use the support. He braced himself, waiting for her to nudge him away. Instead, he felt her body relax against his palm.

"Hey," she whispered. "Let's talk. In private."

He trailed behind her to a secluded spot nestled near the side of the fairway. Dani's lips parted, but instead of speaking, she pressed her fingertips against her temples and stared off into a cluster of cottonwood trees.

"You good?" he asked.

When she finally spoke up, her voice was barely audible over the fluttering leaves. But Von heard her loud and clear when she said, "Not only do I think we're dealing with another serial killer here, but I think he's a pro. Better yet, we might be dealing with a group of pros."

"A group? So you think these murders are being committed by more than one person?"

"Possibly. Or maybe I'm just reaching. But how can one person continue to get away with these crimes at such public locations? During these crowded events, without *anybody* seeing something? I mean, it's as if the killer has eyes everywhere, and the person knows exactly when to strike without being noticed."

"You could be right. Especially when you consider there hasn't been any evidence left at the scenes. That would be hard to pull off if this was just a solo operation."

"*And* if the suspect, or suspects, didn't have a background in law enforcement…" Dani paused, clutching the sides of her face. "Hopefully the syringe Troy found will be the first real break in this case. But who knows? That needle could've been used by one of the golfers to inject insulin or something. So we can't bank on that just yet. I need to make sure doctors look for signs of a puncture wound that may have been caused by a needle. I want a toxicology screening done, too. I'm anxious to find out if Jeffrey was injected with some sort of drug or poison."

"I'll be sure to remind you of all that in case you forget."

Dani gave him a nod, then walked back over to him, her arms curled protectively against her chest. "I need to jump in and help the team. Would you mind going inside and taking the temperature of the crowd? I'm curious to know what's being said and whether anybody saw anything."

"Absolutely. I'll check back in with you soon."

Von backed away slowly, the soles of his black leather oxfords biting into the turf as he retreated. He had every intention on fulfilling the request. But he was having a hard time tearing himself away from Dani. He wanted to stay by her side. Comfort her. Look after her, even though she didn't think she needed any of that. Von was convinced she would later, when the dust settled and the scene at Gibson's was fully processed. Everyone would go their separate ways, and she'd have to return to her place alone.

*Not on my watch...*

Walking back over, Von tapped Dani's shoulder.

"Listen," he said, wincing at the grim intensity in her expression. "After we leave here, I don't want you to be by yourself—"

"Von, please. I'm not thinking about anything beyond this moment. I've got to stay focused and sort through this scene."

"I understand that, but when all this is—"

He was interrupted by the buzz of his cell phone. A text from Kevin flashed across the screen.

I stepped out of the club for a minute and just walked back into chaos. Somebody fainted out on the golf course? What's going on??

"Damn, word travels fast…" Von muttered, not realizing Dani was staring over his shoulder.

"So Kevin wasn't here when this happened to Jeffrey, *allegedly…*" she said.

The skepticism slicing through her tone didn't go unnoticed. "Apparently not."

"Humph. Interesting. Take this however you want, but I don't trust Kevin. We need to keep an eye on him."

"Wait, you're suspicious of *Kevin*?" Von shot back. "As in my vice president of RPS, Kevin Freelain?"

"Yes, him. Let's talk more about it later. But just know that I have my suspicions."

Von stood there, too stunned to move, let alone respond.

Another text from Kevin pulled him out of the stupor.

Where are you? One of the cops just told me that there's been an accident. What the hell is happening?

I'm out on the course, Von wrote back. I'll meet you inside the ballroom in a minute. Make sure you keep that news about the accident to yourself until further notice.

On the way to the terrace, Von slowed down when he heard one of Dani's officers say, "So I get that you think these incidents are all linked. But why would someone want to kill your ex? And why here, during the auction?"

"That's what we're trying to figure out. Maybe someone's attacking people I know to send the message that I'm next? And they're committing these crimes under RSP, as if they've got a vendetta against Von's company. Hell, at this point, they're occurring under the watch of Maxwell PD, too. So there are layers to these crimes that need to be peeled back. Immediately."

"I agree. Because this town is on the brink of going into full panic mode…"

The exchange sent a ripple of alarm through the cool night air. As the commotion raged on, Von's mind moved in slow motion. He couldn't grasp the reality that Maxwell was under attack yet again.

The sound of Dani's voice lifted the fog. He jolted, reminded that she had asked him to inspect the scene inside the club. But he couldn't move. It was as if his feet were planted to the course, ensnared within the tree roots twisting beneath the surface.

*"Von!"* she called out once more. "Please let me know what's going on as soon as you make it back inside."

There was an edge to her tone, as if she were irritated that he was still there. Her wide-eyed expression screamed *Get the hell off the fairway and do your job!*

"I'm on it," he called out, forcing his limbs to cooperate.

Right before entering the club, Von composed a message to Dani.

Please do not go home alone. Let me follow you there. I want to make sure you arrive safely.

He sent it, purposely leaving out the part where he'd be staying the night. Their hometown, which they'd believed was finally safe again, had been thrust into yet another terrifying nightmare. No matter what it took—even if he had to sleep on the porch—there was no way in hell Von would be leaving her side.

Von's phone buzzed with a response from Dani.

I'd like that, thanks. By the way, I just received word from the hospital. Jeffrey didn't make it.

## Chapter Seventeen

Dani's living room had been transformed into a war room of sorts as she was surrounded by case evidence. Several weeks had passed since Jeffrey's death at Gibson's, and the Maxwell PD was no closer to identifying a suspect. So she'd called her crew over in a bid to regroup, refocus and review everything they'd collected thus far.

Troy and Chloe had taken over the couch while Dani and Von set up shop along the floor. Dani had tasked each of them with specific assignments. As she examined crime scene photos and surveillance footage, Troy combed through police reports, Chloe reviewed autopsy results, and Von analyzed cell phone records.

Plates of half-eaten chicken pad thai and crab rangoon were strewn between empty water bottles and soda cans. The television and streaming systems were off and the team was locked in—taking notes, exchanging commentary and working to building a solid criminal profile.

When her phone pinged, Dani dived for it, groaning in frustration at the sight of a CNN news alert. No calls or texts from her digital forensics investigator. She refreshed her email inbox. Nothing there, either.

"Still no word from Chuck?" Von asked.

"Nope." Dani peered at him from across the coffee table. She wasn't surprised that he knew exactly what was bothering her. Their thoughts flowed like a synchronized dance. Over a short period of time they'd become completely aligned, able to read each other's thoughts and finish each other's sentences as if they'd been lovers for a long time.

"Wow," Chloe said, her lips bending into a mischievous smirk. "It's amazing how all it took was one glance for Von to know what's going on with you, Dani."

"Well, that shouldn't come as much of a shock," Troy said. "Didn't Von pretty much admit to stalking Dani over the years?"

"I *studied* Dani over the years," he quickly clarified. "Not stalked. There's a huge difference."

"Yeah, Troy," Dani chimed in, swatting her brother's leg. "Now cut it out and get back to work. We've got a crazed killer terrorizing our town. There's no time for jokes here."

"There's always time for a little laughter. The mood is heavy enough as it is. Nothing's wrong with sprinkling in some comic relief to lighten things up."

All eyes turned to Dani when she drew a sharp breath. Just as she fixed her lips to respond, Von raised a hand in the air. "All right, all right. Like the chief said, let's get back to business. Dani, what's the latest on Jeffrey's crime scene? Any new evidence come to the forefront?"

"Well, the surveillance cameras did capture him heading out to the terrace about thirty minutes before his body was discovered. He was seen taking a pack of cigarettes out of his jacket, so I'm guessing he went out there to smoke."

"Did the footage capture anyone going outside after him?"

"Nope. Which tells me whoever did this is familiar with Gibson's layout and knew how to get out there without being seen by the cameras."

Flipping her notebook to a blank page, Chloe asked, "What about the cameras out on the fairway? Did those capture anything?"

"They didn't. The video feed doesn't reach the eighteenth hole, where Jeffrey's body was found. And it was so dark out on the course that the footage didn't cover anything beyond the terrace."

"Okay, so…" Chloe hesitated, her eyes shifting around the room. "What did Kevin have to say for himself?"

"What do you mean?" Von asked.

Scooting toward the edge of the couch, Chloe said, "I'm referring to him disappearing around the time that Jeffrey's body was found. Did you talk to him about it? Or did you, Dani?"

The room fell silent. When Dani caught Von's eye, she read straight through to his thoughts. *I'll let you take this one, because if I do, it won't be pleasant.*

"We didn't talk to him about it," Dani told her, "but Von and I have been tracking his movements. Nothing about his behavior has been suspicious. He's been everywhere he's said he's going to be, and he isn't acting any differently than normal."

"Since we're doing some digging here," Von said, "what's up with those Maxwell PD officers who took issue with Dani after she was promoted? I believe it was Simons, Henderson and Kenin, correct? Have you all looked into those guys? Asked them any questions or monitored their movements?"

"Actually, we have," Troy countered. "Dani and I assembled a small team of officers who we trust to keep tabs on their whereabouts. We've been tracking them for weeks. So far, no one has done anything to cause suspicion."

Tapping his pen against the table, Von replied, "Yeah, well, I've been keeping a very close eye on Kevin, and like

Dani said, he hasn't done anything to cause suspicion, either."

*"Yet,"* Chloe muttered under her breath.

Von let off a sarcastic chuckle. "At one point, you all thought *I* was your suspect, didn't you? Obviously you were wrong then. So why is it so hard to believe that you're wrong about Kevin?"

"Look, I know that man is your bestie or whatever," Chloe said. "But I'm not putting anything past anybody. We see who Maxwell's first serial killer ended up being—"

"Whoa, slow down," Von cut in. "These are two completely different situations."

"Are they really, though?"

*"Guys,"* Dani interjected, her arms slicing through the air like a boxing referee. "Please. All this sparring back and forth isn't gonna get us anywhere. Now until we get some solid proof of suspicion, wrongdoing...*anything* that would point us in the direction of a suspect, we won't be making any more accusations. Got it?"

"Got it," the group muttered, each of them busying themselves to avoid eye contact.

After checking her email once again, Dani sensed the room's energy had turned toxic and knew she needed to shift topics. "So, I'm still waiting to find out whether Chuck was able to get something on those anonymous texts and calls. But I'm not getting my hopes up since he's come up short every time he's tried."

"But I thought he was working with some sort of new and improved software," Troy said. "That hasn't helped?"

"No. Or not yet at least. Like I've always said, whoever we're dealing with here knows exactly what they're doing. Remaining anonymous is their area of expertise. These obsessive hacker types have a way of staying ten steps ahead of law enforcement."

"True. You never know, though. Chuck is a pro himself. He doesn't usually take this long to get back to you with information, so maybe he's got something this time."

"Let's hope so." Dani picked up a magnifying glass and held it to a photo taken at Lieutenant Edwards's crime scene. The picture trembled in her hand as she homed in on his legs, twisted like crooked tree branches along the stairwell floor. His eyes were eerily wide open, as if fixated on the perpetrator who'd taken his life. His gaping mouth appeared as though it'd been calling out for help. But no one arrived in time. The terror emanating from the image was palpable. Intrusive. Personal...

Dani's throat burned as she muttered, "*Maniac*. Who the hell would do something like this? It is just pure hatred."

"Yes it is," Von agreed. "What's interesting is how each crime scene is so different. It's as if the suspect has no real modus operandi. Our first victim was shot in the head, the second was stabbed in the chest..."

"And the third was poisoned with strychnine—"

"Wait," Von interrupted. "He was? You didn't tell me that."

"I could've sworn I did. There's been so much going on that it's hard to keep up. But anyway, yes, there were traces of the drug in Jeffrey's system that came up in his toxicology report. And the medical examiner discovered a needle mark in the crook of Jeffrey's neck."

"Wow...okay. I'm not familiar with strychnine. How does it affect the body?"

"It's a white, odorless crystalline powder that can cause respiratory failure, and a lethal dose goes into effect quickly. Jeffrey's official cause of death was acute hypoxemic respiratory failure. And before you even ask, no. There wasn't any DNA evidence found on the syringe. So the killer must be using gloves when committing these crimes." Dani paused, shuffling through a stack of photos before pulling one from the scene of Brandy Orland's attack. "And while his murder was horrible, it wasn't nearly as gruesome as the others. There's no rhyme or reason to the way these victims were killed. But we all know the one thing that connects them."

When Dani pointed at herself, Von raised a finger in the air. "Yeah, I do know. All too well. I hate to sound like a broken record here, but I'd be remiss if I didn't mention the connection to RSP. My company almost lost the upcoming wine festival gig because these crimes happened on our watch. Whoever's behind this is going out of their way to destroy RPS's reputation."

"Duly noted," Dani said as frustration whirled through her chest like a tornado, poised to strike. She grabbed her phone and pounded the home screen. "Why in the hell hasn't Chuck gotten back to me yet?"

"Maybe he's still trying to figure out—" Von stopped abruptly when her computer pinged. "Wait, is that him?"

"Yes, *finally*…" Her fingers flew across the keyboard as she frantically scanned the email. Within seconds, she tossed her head back and stared up at the ceiling. "Oh my God…"

"Let me guess," Troy said. "He wasn't able to track down the owner of the cell."

"No, he wasn't. But that's not all." Spinning the laptop around, she shoved it toward Von. "You read it. I—I can't."

"Okay…" he replied pensively. "I've got an update, Chief. While I was searching for the owner of the burner phone, I fell into a bit of a rabbit hole and ended up on the dark web. I discovered something pretty unsettling on a bounty site. Someone listed all of your personal information—your full name, home address, phone numbers, email addresses, and a photo of you. They've offered a $50,000 reward to whoever can kidnap and murder you—'"

"Wait, *what*?" Chloe screeched. "Did you say kidnap and murder?"

"That's what it says," Von choked, reaching across the table and clutching Dani's hand.

Troy leaned in and gave her shoulder a supportive squeeze. "Was Chuck able to trace that back to whoever posted it?"

"Doesn't look like it. Apparently, the person said that anyone interested can email them for details and left an address. Chuck sent a message but hasn't heard back yet. He's extracting metadata in hopes of tracking the IP address back to the owner."

"I'm so sorry, Dani," Troy said. "Just know that we're all here to protect you in every way. What else can we do to make you feel safe in all this?"

"We can stick close by for starters," Von interjected, not waiting for her reply. "Which is why I really don't think it's a good idea for you to stay here alone, D."

"I second that," Chloe added.

Dani shot to her feet and stormed the kitchen, grabbing a bottle of wine. "I really hate this. I'm Maxwell's chief of police! I was trained to do this. I've got a security system in place, surveillance cameras all around the house, several weapons within reach. And yet here I am, needing to be babysat."

"This isn't about being babysat, Dani," Von responded, his low tone offsetting her hard edge. "We hate that this is happening to you, too. But unfortunately, it is. This killer is slippery. He has a way of getting around whatever safety protocols you've got in place. So we've gotta keep our eyes on you while staying two steps ahead of him—"

"But *how*?" Dani interrupted, balancing four glasses in her arms while making her way back toward the living room. "We haven't been able to pull that off so far, which is why we've got three deaths on our hands."

"By being more diligent in our pursuit," Chloe rebutted, taking the glasses and passing them around. "As the threats escalate, additional security measures would not only help ensure your safety, but they'd also give you extra peace of mind."

"Exactly," Von cosigned. "I think it would be a good idea for us to work in rotation, along with the rest of Maxwell PD. I know you've had officers sitting outside the house, but considering what we're dealing with here, it wouldn't hurt to have someone on the inside with you as well. The three of us could alternate staying here with you, just to make sure this lunatic doesn't follow through on his word."

"Or that someone else doesn't take him up on his offer and try to collect that $50,000 bounty," Troy added.

"All right, all right," Dani surrendered, taking a series of quick breaths to stay calm. "Fine. We'll work out some sort of surveillance routine."

She could sense the collective sighs of relief filling the room. But their comfort didn't erase her underlying fear. On the surface, Dani wore a tough facade. Yet beneath it all, she valued their persistence. There was no denying that the killer had the upper hand, and she'd become his number one target. What troubled her more, though, was that despite their tireless efforts—the digging, the researching and the analyzing—they still had no viable suspect.

"Keep the faith, D," Von said, as if he were able to read her thoughts. "Trust me, we're gonna catch this psycho before he or anyone else gets to you."

When he slid around the table and wrapped her in his arms, Dani caught a glimpse of Troy's and Chloe's expressions. They looked on with wide eyes, seemingly caught off guard by the unexpected show of affection.

Dani ignored them, resting her head against Von's chest. Her breathing steadied against the beat of his heart. As the pressure of the situation mounted, the past seemed insignificant compared to the urgency of what lay ahead.

In that moment, Dani let down her guard and allowed herself to be vulnerable. To admit that she couldn't do this alone. And that she needed the help of those around her.

## Chapter Eighteen

"Do you need anything else right now, Chief Miller?" the
server asked.

"Another Perrier would be great, thanks."

"You got it. Be right back."

Dani watched as she walked away, then checked her phone
again. Von was supposed to meet her at the Zonian almost
an hour ago. He'd been held up at the office, running background checks on several new employees he'd recently hired.
Von hoped that adding more officers would boost security
enough to deter the killer from striking again on their watch.

Any idea when you might be here? she texted. I'm almost
done with my salad and struggling to hold off on ordering
a burger until you get here...

The pair had agreed that making a public appearance
together would present a united front, signaling that their
agencies were collaborating to bring down the killer. It was
Thursday—the most popular night of the week at the Zonian.
Considering how bold their suspect had been thus far, Dani
figured he just might be there to indulge in the half-priced
cocktails, enjoy the karaoke battle, scope out his next victim.

That wasn't the only reason she'd invited Von to hang out.
Dani needed to catch him up on the afternoon's town hall
meeting. They were held once a month inside City Hall's vast

auditorium, and usually lasted about an hour. Since things normally ran so smoothly around Maxwell, attendance was oftentimes low.

That afternoon, however, there wasn't an empty chair in the building. Once the local government representatives, department heads and community leaders were done presenting, Mayor Cox opened up the floor for questions. And that's when all hell broke loose.

For over two hours, concerned citizens expressed their fears over the killer and questioned the Maxwell PD on what they were doing to protect the community. A few of them even made suggestions on how law enforcement could bring down the suspect. From consulting with a psychic to flooding the sky with drones to surveil every inch of the city, Dani had heard it all.

Mrs. Roswell, a lifelong citizen and self-proclaimed co-mayor of Maxwell, stood in front of the microphone reading a manifesto on how Dani should use truth serum on persons of interest and AI-powered facial recognition software to track their movements.

Her boldness prompted a slew of others to speak their minds, including Mr. Green, one of Maxwell's oldest residents. He'd teetered up to the mic on his cane while pumping a fist in the air, yelling, "Maxwell PD isn't doing anything to catch this animal. All of our lives are at risk. Either do more to keep this community safe, or I'll make a move to defund the police!"

Dani had tried her best to defend the department. Aside from offering up safety advice, she'd shared how extra patrol officers were out on the streets. Police presence was heavy at every event. A tip line had been established. The department was using advanced forensic techniques to gather evidence. And Maxwell PD had joined forces with RPS to help bring down the killer.

"Well, that simply isn't enough, now is it?" Mr. Green had rebutted before the townspeople broke into thunderous applause.

By the time the meeting ended, Dani realized there was no getting through to the community. When it came to the investigation, they weren't concerned with the department's intentions, plans or case updates. The Maxwell PD wouldn't be back in the townspeople's good graces until an arrest was made.

The buzz of her cell phone sent Dani lurching against the back of the booth.

*Please calm down...*

But these days, panic mode had taken over her normal disposition. Being in the middle of a crowded bar wasn't helping matters. Dani felt as though all eyes had been on her since the moment she'd sat down. It was no wonder, considering the investigation was being covered on the local news almost daily and the national news weekly. Every journalist, true crime expert, lawyer and law enforcement officer was asking the same questions. Who was terrorizing the town of Maxwell a second time around, and why hadn't the police brought the killer to justice?

*The Maxwell Times* had resorted to reporting on the case every single day. Oftentimes, their coverage was splashed across the front page. From "Has the Community Lost Faith in the Maxwell PD?" to "Is It Time to Bring in the Feds?," the headlines were becoming more scathing by the week.

Dani vented her frustrations on her Caesar salad, stabbing her fork into a thick clump of romaine lettuce. She was tempted to send it back and request another one with the dressing on the side. But she was too hungry to bother. She'd arrived at the police station that morning before seven o'clock, bypassing breakfast and working straight through lunch. By the time she had arrived at the Zonian, Dani was ready to order everything on the menu.

Her phone pinged again, this time with a series of texts from Von.

I am so sorry I'm running late! I ran into a glitch with these background checks.

Now the computer system just shut down...

Kevin had to leave and pick up his wife. I'm gonna have to finish this job solo. Be there soon as I can!

The server approached with Dani's drink. "Here you go. I'll come back over as soon as your guest arrives—"

"Change of plans. He doesn't know what time he'll be here. So I'll go ahead and order the turkey burger with cheddar cheese and a side of sweet potato fries."

"You got it. I'll get that order in and tell the cook to put a rush on it."

"I'd appreciate that, thanks."

Dani sipped her water while eyeing the crowd. A woman was standing on the stage, the straps on her red terry cloth halter top hanging down by her elbows as she belted out a drunken version of Alanis Morissette's "You Oughta Know." Hordes of people were waving their hands in the air while singing along with her. A few of them were huddled together, whispering while tossing skeptical side-eyes in Dani's direction.

*Ignore them*, she told herself as flames of irritation burned her neck. Just as she turned back to her salad, Dani's cell pinged again.

"Von," she muttered, "you'd better tell me you're on the way."

She swiped open the home screen without checking the notification. A text from an unknown number popped up.

Good evening, Chief Miller. I love that cool tan blazer you're wearing. How's your salad?

The phone fell from her hand and crashed against her plate. Gripping the edge of the table, Dani spun around and peered through the crowd. She didn't notice anyone looking back at her.

Who the hell is this, she typed, and where are you?

A reply came in within seconds.

It's me. The one you've been looking for. And I'm here, with you. At the Zonian.

Why don't you come over to my table so that we can talk face-to-face? Dani fired back.

Nah, no thanks. I'd rather do it this way. I'm actually enjoying watching you squirm in your seat while you wonder where I am. Is it frustrating, knowing that I can see you but you can't see me?

Anxiety clawed at her chest as Dani reread the message. Keeping her head down, she slowly raised her eyes and scanned the immediate area. Checked to see who was typing on their cell. That wasn't effective considering half the people there had their faces buried in their phones.

"Here you go," the server said, placing her burger on the table. "Can I get you anything else?"

"No, this is great, thanks."

The moment she walked off, Dani pushed the plate away. Her appetite had been devoured by a chilling sense of unease. Sliding her hand toward her hip, she gripped the handle on her Glock 22, just to make sure it was still there.

Her cell lit up with another message.

What, no response? And why aren't you eating? Is something wrong with your burger?

Dani took screenshots of all the texts and forwarded them to Von.

I need for you to get to the Zonian immediately! she told him. The killer is here, and he's watching me!

As soon as she hit *Send*, Dani called Troy and told him to get there, too, then put out a blast text to all her officers.

I'm on my way! Von wrote back. I'll have as many of my guys there as I can gather...

His message was followed by a slew of other officers, confirming they were en route.

Be sure to surround the entire building, Dani replied. I'll have the manager shut this place down. No one is coming in or going out until we find our suspect.

She hit Send and sprang to her feet. Then froze.

*Slow down*, Dani told herself. *Respond to his text. Don't let on that you're about to take him down...*

She straightened her pants legs as if that's why she'd stood, then gradually took her seat. Grabbing the phone, she replied to the suspect.

If you must know, my burger is undercooked. So I need to send it back. In the meantime, I wish you'd stop by and say hi. But I'm not surprised you won't. We both know you're nothing but a coward...

Dani sent the text while keeping her eyes peeled to the door. When her server came into view, she discreetly called her over.

"Is something wrong with your dinner, Chief Miller?"

"Oh, no, not at all. Everything looks delicious. But I do

need to speak with the manager. Would you mind sending him over?"

"No problem. I'll go and grab him now."

Dani's cell vibrated in her hand with a new message from the suspect.

What are you up to, Chief Miller? Texting nonstop, not sending the burger back after claiming it's undercooked... Are you putting together a plan to try to catch me?

As she surveyed the scene once again, sirens wailed in the distance.

"Damn it!" Dani hissed, mad that she hadn't told her officers to cut them.

A young man approached the table, sweeping his blond bangs away from his pale green eyes. "Hey, Chief Miller. I'm the manager, Bobby James. What can I do for you?"

"You're...the *manager*?" She'd never seen him before. He was all of five two and didn't look a day over fifteen.

"I am. And I already know what you're thinking. Just so you know, I'm twenty-two. I just look like a kid."

"Okay, well..." Dani paused, realizing that she hadn't thought out exactly what to say. She didn't want to alarm Bobby and cause a panic. But she needed to come up with something that would convince him to secure the place. "I, um, I was wondering if you could lock the front and back doors as soon as possible, and not let anyone in or out. I've been alerted that one of the patrons had a very expensive watch stolen, and I'm hoping to figure out who took it."

"Oh, yeah, of course. I'll lock them now. Is that your backup I hear pulling up?"

"Yes, it is. So why don't you go on and secure those doors so we can get this process started?"

He gave her a thumbs-up before rushing off. Just as she

grabbed her cell to call Troy, it vibrated with his name on the screen.

"Hey!" she yelled over the music. "Are you here?"

"I am. So is the rest of the team. We've got the place surrounded."

"Good. Turn off the sirens and lights and come inside. Is Von here yet?"

"I think I see him pulling up now."

A knot of tension loosened as Dani blew a heavy sigh. "Great. Send him in, too."

She headed toward the front door. On the way there, the manager flashed her a quick military-style salute. She mouthed the words *thank you* and waited for her officers to approach. Just when she spotted Troy, her cell pinged again with another text from the unknown number.

Aww, silly rabbit, tricks are for kids, and you just got played! You really think I'm dumb enough to stick around and get caught? I've been gone, bitch. Just wanted you to know you're being watched. As usual, I'm one step ahead. You hunt down killers like an amateur. While you're reading this, I'm zooming past all your officers. Your little sting was a waste of taxpayers' dollars. See you next time, when I might actually make a move and take you out...

Dani jumped at the sight of Troy banging on the door. She opened it, her sagging expression etched in defeat.

"Don't tell me," he said.

"Yeah," she croaked, stepping outside and peering down the street. "He got away. *Again.*"

Following her toward the curb, Troy asked, "Wait, how did the suspect know that you were here tonight?"

"I don't know. But trust me, I'm gonna find out."

## Chapter Nineteen

Von pulled into the Desert Grove Ranch, the crunch of gravel beneath the tires barely audible over the crowd's boisterous chatter. Maxwell's wine festival had started less than thirty minutes ago, and the parking lot was already packed.

After searching every aisle for a space, he managed to squeeze his car in between two oversize SUVs along the last row. He hopped out and hurried around to open the passenger door.

Dani was slow to exit. She didn't want to be there. She'd actually considered speaking with the Chamber of Commerce and having the festival canceled altogether. Another public event seemed too dangerous. The last thing Maxwell needed was another death on its hands. But Von had managed to talk her out of calling it off. The townspeople were already living in fear. Postponing such a huge tradition would only cause more alarm.

"Plus it'll make you look unsure of yourself," he'd insisted. "As a matter of fact, you'll appear unsure of your entire team, as if you're admitting that the Maxwell PD doesn't have things under control."

"Well, obviously we don't," Dani retorted. "We're investigating a third murder, and despite the escalating threats, the violence…we have no real evidence and suspects. This entire town thinks the Maxwell PD is a complete failure."

"Wait a sec, don't you think that's a bit of a stretch? Your department isn't new to this. You caught a killer before. And you'll do it again."

"That's the hope. Now let's see if it will become a reality. Because right now, all I know is that the fear among the community is rising. There are only so many PR statements we can release about how we're doing all we can to protect the town and solve this case. Eventually, everyone is gonna lose faith in us. A lot of them already have."

Brewing frustration stopped Dani from continuing. The daily criticism of the Maxwell PD was overwhelming enough. There was no need for her to pile on.

These days, even Chloe was being harassed. After word spread that she was the one who'd lured Maxwell's first serial killer to town, her *Preyed Upon* podcast listeners demanded that she cover the town's current murders. Chloe insisted the cases were still under investigation and there wasn't enough information available. But Dani knew the truth. Chloe was hesitant to speak on the department's failure to catch the suspect.

Forcing herself out of Von's car, Dani's stomach twisted into tiny tremors of tension. Memories of that chilling night at the Zonian still haunted her, two weeks later. Despite their best efforts, the Maxwell PD couldn't identify a suspect. Tracking the perpetrator through blurry surveillance footage inside the jam-packed, dimly lit bar had been impossible. Investigators weren't able to distinguish the perpetrator's DNA from the crowd's considering the vast number of people leaving evidence behind. And once again, the text messages that had been sent to Dani came from an untraceable number.

She did, however, figure out how the suspect had been keeping track of her whereabouts after Von discovered an AirTag tucked behind her license plate. A forensic analysis of the small circular device turned up nothing—no fingerprints and no trace evidence. Dani had no idea how long it had been there. But knowing that she was being hunted like prey left a cold, unsettling feeling in the pit of her gut, as did the realization that the killer was simply waiting on the perfect moment to attack.

The one thing she did have on her side this time around was the support of RPS. While Dani and Von had been leaning on each other more than ever, their dueling agencies just recently put an official end to their feud. The decision was driven by the killer's shared vendetta against both Dani and Von, prompting the Maxwell PD and RPS to team up for the wine festival in hopes of preventing another tragedy.

There was, however, one caveat—Kevin. Von was still convinced that he had nothing to do with the crimes. After he'd disappeared right before Jeffrey's death at Gibson's, Dani wasn't so sure. Uncertainty led her to ask Troy and Chloe to keep constant watch on him during the festival.

"You all right?" Von asked as they headed toward the entrance.

"I'm fine," she lied, unwilling to admit that her nerves were buzzing like a colony of frenzied bees. "I guess I'm not in the mood to be under everyone's microscope today. All the scrutiny, the judging… I just wanna do my job and catch this maniac."

"Just stay the course, Chief. You got this."

While his words were reassuring, they did little to dispel the chilling uncertainty looming in the air.

*Deep breaths*, Dani told herself. *Head up, shoulders back…*

As they approached the sprawling ranch's heavy wrought iron gate, she was hit with the rich aroma of wine mixed with the earthy scent of damp soil. Her darting eyes settled on the pastel haze stretched across the sky. The low-hanging afternoon sun cast a warm golden glow over rows of wine-tasting booths.

Attendees sauntered from one wooden booth to the next, sipping from their glasses while nibbling on a variety of cheeses. Their colorful, breezy attire was a stark contrast to Dani and Von's dark slacks and crisp button-down shirts. As the event's festive energy rippled through the crowd, it left Dani longing for things to be different. For there to be no criminal terrorizing their town.

"Looks like the organizers got a big turnout," Von said. "Which means we've got our work cut out for us."

"Yes, we do. So let's stay vigilant and keep our focus sharp."

"Absolutely." He hesitated, his words trailing off as he glanced around the sprawling event area. "You know, for some reason, I can't imagine the killer would be bold enough to try to pull something off today, knowing we're on high alert."

"I can. Remember the criminal profile we came up with that night with Chloe and Troy? The suspect loves sensationalism. And craves attention. He's a sociopath who gets a thrill every time he commits a murder. That excitement intensifies when he gets away with it. I believe he'll continue to chase that high until he can't anymore."

"Meaning when he gets caught?" Von asked.

"Exactly. But for today, I've got a plan. Our killer may very well be out here somewhere, hiding in plain sight. So I'll be zeroing in on each guest, hoping that something speaks to me." Dani pivoted, sweeping her arm across the rustic landscape. "So, what are you thinking? Should we split up and take a look around, see what we see, then reconvene a little later?"

"Why would we do that? Are you afraid to be seen with me?" Von's lips curved into an uneven smirk. But his blunt tone was unmistakably serious.

"Of course not. I just figured we'd cover more ground faster if we separate."

"I'd prefer that we stick together. You never know what we might run into out here."

"Okay then. Let's get moving."

As the pair set off toward South Holland Winery's booth, all eyes were on them. Most people spoke, but their greetings were chillier than normal. Dani wasn't surprised, nor did she bother mentioning it to Von. It was to be expected. The mood in town had been anything but upbeat in recent weeks. Being surrounded by so many familiar faces in one place only amplified the weight of the Maxwell PD's failures.

Dani cast the cold reception aside and plastered a pleasant expression on her face while moving through the crowd. Her instincts were piqued as she studied each passerby and took in every conversation. She was aware that their suspect knew how to blend in. So she searched for something deeper. Signs of someone whose behavior was slightly odd. A person who was overly fidgety, with jerking eye movements or uncontrolled bodily gestures. So far, no one was sticking out.

"I'm glad to see that all of our officers are positioned at their respective posts," Von said. "But have you noticed the strange looks people are throwing at us?"

"I have. And I don't know if it's because they're surprised to see us together, or upset that I've yet to solve this case. Either way, I'm being cordial all while ignoring it. My focus is on making an arrest. Not winning a popularity contest.

Last year the town hated me until the suspect was appre-
hended. Then all of a sudden I was the queen of Maxwell.
Their words, *not* mine."

"Yeah, I assumed that."

"My point is I don't expect this go-round to be any different than the last. So let's just block out the noise and stick
to the mission at hand."

"You got it, Chief."

Von rolled up his sleeves as the sun blazed overhead. Dani
stepped back, letting him take the lead as she observed him
effortlessly engage with the attendees. His presence was
commanding yet approachable. Authoritative yet charming. There was an air of confidence with each conversation
that drew people in, including Dani. She'd spent so much
time resenting him that she hadn't realized how well-liked
he was within the community.

While Dani had left the romance that sparked between
them simmering in the background, she couldn't ignore the
stream of emotions stirring within her. She was left questioning whether she'd made the right decision, putting him
on hold while allowing the investigation to consume her.

Deep down, she knew she had. There would be plenty of
time to explore their connection once the case was solved.
Or so she hoped...

But Dani's concerns didn't end there. She was still struggling with the idea of publicly dating Von. He'd chalked it
up to her reluctance in telling her father, and he wasn't completely wrong. She had no idea where her dad stood these
days when it came to the Reed family, and she wasn't eager
to find out for fear of his response. Dani knew she'd have
to share the news with him eventually—but it would be on
her own terms, in her own time.

"I know the day is still young," Von said. "But so far,

nothing is sticking out. I'm not seeing any strange faces or behaviors, no weird incidents…"

"Yeah, same. But like you said, it's early. Anything could happen. There's still plenty of time for things to go left."

"True…" Von shoved his hands inside his pockets and spun a full circle. "I've been meaning to ask about the list of vendors and staff members working the event. Were you able to get a hold of it?"

"I was." Dani pulled out her cell and forwarded him the list. "I just texted it to you. We can check that against all the booths, and each of the staff members are required to wear badges. So if we see people lurking in the background, or walking around unauthorized areas, they should be wearing a lanyard."

"Cool. I'll be sure to keep an eye out for that."

Dani's phone buzzed with a text from Troy.

Chloe and I are here and we've got eyes on Kevin. He's been chatting with a few vineyard owners near the north side of the ranch. We're being discreet, but we're on it.

Good, Dani wrote back. Thanks for the update. While you're at it, keep a close watch on our guys, too. If anything starts to look suspicious, alert me immediately.

"Everything all right?" Von asked.

The question startled her, almost rattling the phone from her hand. "Everything's fine," she blurted, shoving the cell in her back pocket. She searched Von's curious expression, wondering if he'd seen the text. Dani hadn't told him that Kevin was being watched by her team and certainly didn't want him to find out that way.

An obnoxious burst of laughter drew their attention to a group huddled nearby. Dani's instincts flared. Something about their exaggerated movements seemed off.

"Do you recognize any of those people standing near the Starlit Cellar's booth?" Von asked.

"I do. I think I've seen a few of them around Cole's. And...wait, isn't that Lieutenant Edwards's wife, Camille?"

"Judging by the pictures I've seen of her when I was looking through their social media accounts, I believe so. Ironically, I saw that she's connected to my father on LinkedIn, so I guess they know each other. Any idea who the man is holding her hand?"

Dani's eyes snapped down to their intertwined fingers. "Ooh, I didn't even notice that. I don't know, but he looks familiar." She pulled out her phone, opened Facebook and scrolled to the lieutenant's personal page. "Yep, just what I thought."

"What's that?"

"His name is Reginald Duvall. He's the president of the ski club that Lieutenant Edwards belonged to."

"That's...interesting."

"Very interesting." When Dani noticed Camille's eyes narrow in her direction, she subtly angled herself away. "Her husband's barely been gone for three months and here she is, cozying up to one of his closest friends. On a side note, Camille was never too fond of me. I think she took issue with the fact that Lieutenant Edwards and I grew close once he became my mentor. She always gave me the cold shoulder whenever we saw each other."

"Humph... So, if we're talking possible suspects, then it sounds to me like Camille could be in the running for a couple of reasons. One, she may have wanted to kill her husband to pursue a relationship with his friend. Two, if she's holding a grudge over her husband's role in helping you become police chief, then having another killer on the loose would be the ultimate revenge. Does that make sense, or am I reaching?"

"No, that makes perfect sense. And at this point, nothing is a reach. Especially since I saw her at the mayor's fundraising event *and* the art auction. Back when we first began investigating the lieutenant's murder, was our focus on the wrong family member? Should we have been more concerned with the wife rather than the son?"

"Maybe," Von said. "But I thought Camille had a solid alibi on the day Lieutenant Edwards was killed."

"She had a friend corroborate her whereabouts. But maybe I need to obtain more solid proof of that. Also, I should add that Reginald was at Cole's the day of the murder. Every member of the lieutenant's ski club was there."

"Ooh…and the plot thickens. What do you think? Should go over and say hello?"

"Good idea. I'll let you take the lead since she'll probably be more receptive to you than me."

The instant they reached the group, Camille yanked her hand from Reginald's grasp.

"Ch-Chief Miller," she stammered, her jovial expression bending into awkward surprise. "I—I'm surprised to see you here at the wine festival."

"Why? I always attend this event."

Waving a bony hand in the air, she tossed her head back and forced a giggle. "Oh right, right. I guess I was thinking you would be on duty, manning the station rather than indulging in alcoholic beverages."

She pressed her pointy elbow against Reginald's chest, prompting him to join in on the feigned laughter.

"Well, you're right about a couple of things," Dani responded, taken aback by the couple's matching neon white veneers. "I am on duty, which is why you don't see me drinking any alcohol. And I'm deep into the investigation, which is why I'm out here with my squad, patrolling the event rather than manning the police station."

Dani waited on her to inquire about the case since she hadn't once called in to the department for an update. Instead, Camille turned to Von and puckered her artificially inflated lips.

"Hello, Mr. Reed Jr. Are my eyes deceiving me, or has RPS landed on good terms with the Maxwell PD?"

"Hello, Mrs. Edwards. No, your eyes are not deceiving you. My team and I have joined forces with the police department to assist in the investigation. Chief Miller and I couldn't allow some rivalry to compromise public safety. So here we are. Doing all that we can to solve the case. Also, you have my condolences. I've heard nothing but wonderful things about your husband. Losing him has obviously been a huge blow to the entire community. How are you and your family holding up?"

Camille sucked in her jaws, as if the question had soured inside her mouth. "We're, um…we're holding up the best we can. The support of friends has been tremendous. I don't know if I could've gotten through this without them."

*Yeah, I bet*, Dani thought, watching Camille recoil beneath her steely gaze. Reginald's feet shuffled to the side, as if he were attempting to create distance between himself and the group.

A staff member from a nearby booth approached, offering wine samples. Camille took two and downed them both within seconds. While she made a feeble attempt at small talk by asking Von about his father, Dani's phone pinged. It was a text from Chloe.

Slight new development. We overheard Kevin talking to a couple of RPS officers. He mentioned Von hanging up photos of the victims in his office, just to keep the cases at the forefront of mind. Kevin begged him to take them down because he hated seeing their faces every day. I thought that was odd and worth mentioning… Nothing suspicious with Maxwell PD, though.

Good to know. Von and I have what could be a major new lead that we didn't see coming. Meet me by the information booth in thirty minutes and I'll tell you all about it.

## Chapter Twenty

Von's eyelids fluttered before gradually opening. He let off a deep yawn followed by a full stretch, awakening from the best sleep he'd had in weeks.

The corners of his lips curled into a satisfied smile at the sight of Dani's bare shoulders peeking over the soft gray sheets. He resisted the urge to slide over and kiss her neck, massage her awake and indulge in another round of lovemaking.

Their night together certainly hadn't gone as expected. From the moment they'd arrived at the wine festival to the moment they left, the pair had been on edge—cautious, mindful and keeping a watchful eye throughout. By the time the event was over, exhaustion weighed heavily on them both. But so did an overwhelming sense of relief as things ended without incident.

On the way home, their hunger pangs superseded the fatigue. They ended up grabbing dinner and drinks at the Copper Plate. Afterward, when Dani invited Von in for a nightcap, he couldn't say no. One thing led to another, and they ended up in bed together.

Von was hoping that Dani wouldn't jump up the second her alarm went off and kick him out. Nothing would make him happier than holding her in his arms a little longer and making love to her once again.

*Bzzz...*

Dani's vibrating cell sent her stirring. Von moved in closer as she arched her back, her breasts spilling out from underneath the sheet.

"Good morning," she murmured, her eyes barely open when she reached for her phone.

"Morning..." His muffled voice vibrated against her skin as his lips caressed her shoulder. "How'd you sleep?"

"Really well. Better than I have in weeks."

Pulled her toward him, he whispered, "I'm assuming that's because I was here with you?"

"Maybe so. I'm sure all the kisses and touches you showered me with until I couldn't hold my eyes open helped, too."

"And just think, there are so many more where those came from..."

She pushed her body further into his embrace while checking her phone. "Chloe's asking if I want to meet up for coffee before I go into the station."

"What are you gonna tell her?"

"That I'll have to catch up with her later."

"Good answer," Von said, gently nuzzling her ear.

Dani typed a quick reply, then set her phone back on the nightstand. Taking that as a cue to proceed, Von glided his body between her thighs. His arousal pressed against her, hardening when she drew him deeper. Her hands cradled his face. Pulled him into a kiss that began as a slow burn, their tongues tangling in a sensual dance. A rough, throaty moan hummed in the back of Von's throat when her hips rose to meet his. Just as their bodies began moving in perfect sync, Dani's phone buzzed again.

"Damn it," Von grunted, collapsing onto his back.

"Now I *just* told Chloe that I'm in the middle of something."

"Oh? You actually told her that I'm here?"

Dani's silence was all the answer he needed—she hadn't.

"Never mind," he muttered, rolling over onto his side.

"Come on, Von. It's not like that. I—I'll tell her later. I haven't been keeping you a secret."

"I'm really not a secret, though, am I? With the exception of last night, we haven't been seeing each other romantically. So technically, you have nothing to hide."

Dani remained quiet, her expression solemn as she reached for her phone again. Her refusal to communicate pushed Von to want to say more. To admit that his feelings for her hadn't changed. If anything, they'd deepened.

*Just let it go*, he told himself, clenching his jaw to keep quiet. She still seemed conflicted about her feelings for him. And he refused to put himself in a vulnerable position again, just to be rejected.

Dani moved toward him, the warmth of her hand resting against his chest easing his nerves. As their fingers intertwined, Von struggled to resist pulling her in again and returning to the moment they'd shared before Chloe's interruption.

The brief taste of what she'd given him weeks ago—a glimpse of the life they could share—left Von wanting more. But when Dani cut him off without warning, both his heart and ego were left bruised. Then last night, she'd revived him, quenching a thirst he'd been desperate to satisfy. Von hoped it wasn't just a brief reconnection, and that this time, she'd stay by his side.

He glanced over and noticed that her phone screen was black. "What's going on with your cell?"

"It's dead. I was so preoccupied when we came to bed that

I forgot to plug it in. So I don't know if that notification was another text from Chloe or a call that I missed."

"Just let it charge for a few minutes. It'll get some juice and you'll be able to tell. In the meantime, where did we leave off?"

"Right here, I believe…"

Dani slowly repositioned herself, her body curving over Von's. She straddled his hips. Took all of him in her hand while sliding down his chest. Just as she disappeared beneath the sheets, her phone rang.

"Ignore it," he insisted, shivering beneath the brush of her lips. "Just keep going."

"You know I can't do that." She crawled back up, reached for the phone, then jolted upright.

"What's wrong?"

"I've got a ton of missed called from several of my officers. Even Natalia called from the station. This is not good." Dani's fingers stumbled over the screen as she struggled to dial out. "*Troy*," she snapped, putting the call on speaker, "what's going on?"

"You need to get to Desert Grove Ranch right now! A woman's body was pulled from the reservoir this morning."

DANI'S HEART STUTTERED wildly as she and Von rushed to the water's edge. Officers and the medical examiner were already on the scene, hovering over the victim.

"Chief," Troy said, his expression eclipsed by a cloud of dread, "the medical examiner confirmed that the victim has no vital signs."

Pulling a sharp breath, Dani nodded, the musty scent of damp earth stirring a pang of nausea. She swallowed hard and approached the body. There was something hauntingly familiar about the woman. The way her dark, shoulder-length hair clung to the sides of her heart-shaped face. Her petite figure, on full display underneath the muddy lavender maxi dress clinging to her limbs. Those wide-set hazel eyes, half opened and lifeless, holding on to what she'd seen during her final moments.

"Is it just me," Dani said, the words tightening in her throat, "or do I look eerily similar to this woman?"

Von and Troy glanced at each other, neither of them quick to speak up.

"So it's not just me."

"I, um…" Von mumbled, "I didn't want to say anything, but yes, she does look like you."

"Yeah, I noticed it, too," Troy added.

"Do we have an ID on her?" Dani asked.

"Not yet. But no one here recognizes her. We're thinking she might be from out of town and here for the wine festival."

While crime scene investigators snapped photos with digital cameras, Dani fumbled for her cell, her fingers quivering as she took pictures of her own. "Who found her?"

"Two ranch workers," Troy said. "They were checking the water troughs when they came across her body."

Kneeling beside the victim, Dani studied her, wincing at the shock throbbing in her head. The resemblance between them was uncanny. It was as if someone had pulled Dani's reflection from a mirror and discarded it there.

"Somebody did this to scare me," she choked. "There's no question that all these murders have been personal. But this one? This crosses the line."

Von crouched down beside her and turned to Troy. "Did anyone notice trauma to her body when she was pulled from the water? Or could this have been an accident? I'm thinking that she may have drunk too much and fallen into the reservoir."

The hope in his voice was unmistakable. Dani couldn't help but appreciate his optimism. But there was no denying that this was a targeted attack. The killer's actions were far too methodical, and there was a twisted method to his madness. He'd intentionally murdered Dani's doppelgänger, fully aware that she would detect the resemblance. This wasn't just a crime. It was a message. And she'd heard it loud and clear.

Pointing toward the victim's throat, Troy added, "We did discover several red marks along the back of her neck. We're thinking that if this was a homicide, those may be the result of an attacker holding her head underwater."

Dani stood, her feet unsteady as she shook with a sudden surge of panic. "This is unreal. Four deaths in less than four months, and not a suspect in sight. No real evidence. Nothing. I've been racking my brain nonstop trying to figure out the motive behind these crimes. Is it some random local, enamored by all the attention the last killer got, so they're thirsty for a little notoriety? Is it someone who's related to the last killer, who might be out to avenge his arrest?"

"Those are all valid theories," Von said. "And let's not forget the one we came up with yesterday connected to the lieutenant's wife, her new boyfriend..."

"Let's not overlook the Maxwell PD and RPS officers who're still holding on to unresolved issues from the past," Troy chimed in. "One thing we do know for sure is that whoever it is, they know what they're doing. I'm still thinking they've got some sort of background in criminal justice."

"You're right. But that doesn't bring us any closer to identifying a person of interest," Dani countered, her gaze drifting as she turned away from the victim. "If anything, it only broadens our search. So let's think about it. We've got another death on our hands that's connected to an event that RPS was hired to work, and the Maxwell PD was patrolling. But this time around, none of us know this victim, correct?"

"Correct," Von and Troy replied in unison.

"However, this is our first victim that we're thinking isn't from Maxwell. And she just so happens to resemble me. To a T."

"Which could just be a coincidence," Von suggested.

"I highly doubt that. Our killer doesn't seem to be doing anything just for the sake of it. Every murder has been calculated. A direct hit that's targeted the two of us." Dani pointed at her brother without talking her eyes off of Von. "Troy, could you please excuse us?"

Without waiting for a reply, she grabbed Von's arm and pulled him away.

"What's the problem?" he asked, his head pivoting in confusion. "Did I say something wrong?"

"No, you didn't. But I've got a question for you that I need to ask in private. And I want an honest answer. Did you tell Kevin about us?"

Von grimaced, his expression contorting into a mix of shock and frustration. "*Wow.* That was the last thing I was expecting you to ask. What does that have to do with—"

"Could you please just answer the question? Does Kevin know about us?"

"Yes. He does. Now, why are you asking me that in the middle of a crime scene?"

"Von, think about it. Kevin can't stand me. He's *never* liked me. That man has despised me since we were kids, and it's all because of you. And because of your father's hatred toward my family. He's followed up behind you like a little lapdog for as long as I can remember—"

*"Dani,"* he interrupted. "Kevin is my closest friend and business partner. Not my lapdog."

"Correction. Kevin is your employee. Not your business partner. There's a huge difference."

"Look, I see where you're going with this, and you're wrong. Kevin's not your guy. He isn't a psychopath. He did not commit these crimes to retaliate against the Maxwell

PD or RPS. And he certainly didn't do it to get back at me because of my relationship with you."

"What about the victims' photos you had hanging up in your office?"

"What about them? And...wait." Von paused, running his hands down the sides of his face. "How do you even know about that?"

"Don't worry about it. Just explain to me why Kevin begged you to take them down, *knowing* they were inspiring you to help solve this case."

"First of all, he didn't beg me to do anything. Kevin mentioned that seeing the victims' faces made him a little uncomfortable. But that's because they serve as a constant reminder that we've got a deranged assassin running around town. *Not* because he's the one who killed them."

Moving in closer, Dani jabbed a finger toward Von's chest, her fiery glare burning with intensity. "Listen to me. I wanna know where Kevin was last night. I want a list of everything he did, from the time he left the wine festival to the time of our victim's death. Can you get that information for me, or do I need to bring him in for questioning?"

"I'll get it for you. And honestly, you don't have a valid reason to bring him in, other than your unsubstantiated suspicions. If you do, it really wouldn't been a good look. We just settled our differences with the Maxwell PD. After experiencing so much dissension, our agencies are finally on good terms. We're working together to solve this case. Please don't ruin that over some baseless personal issues."

*"Baseless personal issues?"* Dani retorted, flinching in disbelief. "I'd like to think that my reasoning behind his possible motives are logical and well thought out. But I hear what you're saying. And since our agencies are finally on good terms, I'll fall back and let you gather that information for me. In the meantime, I'll also be speaking with the

owner of the ranch and the workers who found the body, and collecting the surveillance footage from last night. If I can get some solid proof of who's behind this attack, then we won't have to worry about my unsubstantiated suspicions."

Von lifted his hands in the air, as if to surrender. "I hope you're not taking what I said personally. Like you, I'm trying to get to the bottom of all this and make sure we remain on good terms in the process. I'd just suggest that you don't lose sight of the other possible suspects we're investigating."

"Trust me, I won't lose sight of a thing. I am a professional. I'm not just focusing on your friend. Now if you'll excuse me, I need to jump in with my team. I'll catch up with you later."

Von's chest rose, as if he were about to make a statement. But Dani walked off before he could speak. She was done with the conversation. Arguing in circles wasn't going to solve a thing. Collecting evidence would.

She checked in with the medical examiner, who was busy running a swab underneath the victim's fingernails. After confirming that the victim was deceased, she called Troy over.

"I'm going to touch base with the ranch's staff and look into getting the CCTV footage. I'll meet you back out here and see what you've discovered. Any luck so far?"

"Not yet. But we're still searching. Hopefully something will turn up soon."

"All right. Keep me posted."

Dani marched toward the main lodge, ignoring the look of distress on Von's face as she walked by. She hated the fact that they'd spent such an intimate evening together, enjoying each other's company after thinking they had finally gotten a break from the case.

The pleasure, however, was short-lived. They quickly found themselves back at a crime scene, succumbing to the pressure of another murder. Conflicts flared between them, and as they grew more at odds with each other, it felt like they were no closer to capturing the killer.

Dani's determined stride slowed when her cell phone buzzed. She expected it to be Chloe, frantic for an update. But a text from an unknown number appeared.

Her heart hammered against her rib cage as she opened it. The phone almost slipped from her hand at the sight of a photo. It was an image of the victim who'd just been pulled from the reservoir. Another message soon followed.

Oops! I did it again. I committed another murder, thinking I'd killed YOU. Little did I know I murdered the wrong person! Oh well... But the good news is I'm getting closer to the right one. Chief Miller, count your days, bitch. You're definitely next...

# Chapter Twenty-One

Von trudged alongside Dani as they made their way down Willowbrook Nature Reserve's sandy walking path. The sun was barely up before she'd dragged him out of bed, insisting she needed to hit the trail and release some anxious energy.

The idea hadn't sat too well with him. Von had envisioned the pair sleeping in, then spending a lazy Sunday morning filled with hot coffee, an Uber Eats breakfast delivery, and a movie or two, then diving back into the investigation later in the day. But he'd agreed to Dani's suggestion, hoping the sun's warmth and the sweet, earthy scents carried by the breeze would be enough to soothe her frazzled nerves.

A week had passed since the wine festival, and the case continued to dominate their every waking moment. The number of theories they'd brainstormed and leads they had dissected were endless. The pair managed to move past their disagreement at the latest crime scene after she'd received the threatening text. That jolt of reality was a harsh reminder that they needed each other now more than ever, regardless of their differences. A fractured partnership between them would give the killer the upper hand, distracting them from their number one goal—capturing him.

Dani and Von had reexamined every crime scene that week, hoping to discover overlooked evidence. They hadn't.

They'd watched endless surveillance video footage once again. Questioned Cole's Ski Resort members. Called up a number of people who'd attended the mayor's charity event, the art auction and the wine festival, hoping someone would recollect something they'd seen or heard that could help the case. Once again, they hit a dead end.

The pair visited the crime lab to follow up on evidence collected at Desert Grove Ranch, but the results came back inconclusive. The medical examiner ruled the victim's cause of death as homicide by drowning. Her name was Stephanie Hunter, and she had in fact been visiting from Phoenix for the wine festival. As the text to Dani had suggested, it was a case of mistaken identity, and Dani was the intended target.

When she'd brought Lieutenant Edwards's wife in for questioning again, Camille insisted that she had been at a book club meeting during the afternoon of his death. To prove her innocence, the club's president showed police Ring camera footage from her home on the day of the meeting. Camille's entry and exit times confirmed she was not at Cole's when her husband was murdered.

Camille's boyfriend, Reginald, had left the resort late that morning to visit his mother at the Chandler Creek Nursing Home. Investigators followed up with the front desk clerk, who confirmed signing Reginald in at 11:21. That was well before the time of the crime.

During their interrogations, Dani pushed harder, zeroing in on their suspicious behavior at the wine festival. Both Camille and Reginald cracked under the pressure, admitting they were embarrassed that Dani had caught them together so soon after Lieutenant Edwards's murder. Admittedly, they'd turned to each other for support, which led to something more. What started as a simple need for comfort spiraled into a whirlwind romance—one they hadn't planned but couldn't seem to stop.

"We've got to do something big, Von," Dani said, her shrill voice shaking him from his thoughts. "Something risky and unexpected. Something that'll catch the killer off guard and get him on our turf."

Von peered at her while she readjusted her bright yellow leggings, mesmerized by the curve in her hips. He tried to keep his eyes on her face and focus on her words. But he couldn't resist admiring how her spandex workout attire clung to her alluring silhouette.

Instead of suggesting they turn around and go back to bed, Von asked, "What did you have in mind?"

"I don't know," she huffed rapidly, her words keeping pace with her racing feet. "Maybe we could set up some sort of sting operation, you know? Something on a grand scale, since the killer clearly likes to pull stunts at large events. We could put on a music festival featuring local artists, or a town picnic, or maybe a parade..."

Von stared up at the brilliant blue desert sky, as if the answer was hidden within the scattered clouds. He watched them drift aimlessly. Listened to the crisp dry grass and rustling leaves of shrubs. Took in the vast open flatland's muted palette of browns and tans, dotted with scattered cacti. It all brought on a calming sense of peace. He suddenly understood Dani's need to spend the morning there. It was the perfect place to think. To get grounded. And come up with a new plan of action.

After several moments of contemplation, Von slid an arm around her waist and led her toward a small wooden bench tucked beneath a paloverde tree. Its slender, twisted green limbs provided a fragrant umbrella of shade.

"Let's sit down for a minute," he said. "And talk this through. Because I think I've got an idea. RPS's twenty-fifth anniversary is coming up soon. What if we throw a party celebrating that? We could do something at the Blanche Hotel. Something fancy that would garner a good amount of press."

Dani's back straightened against the palm of his hand. "That's a good idea. A great idea, actually. You know what would be even better?"

"What's that?"

"If Maxwell PD teams up with RPS and we throw the event together. You know, just to reinforce the fact that our agencies are on good terms and working together to solve this case. I could even host it, if that's something you'd be interested in me to do."

"Of course I would. I'd be honored. Plus that would be the perfect setup for the killer. He'd go down in history if he pulled off another murder during an event of that magnitude."

"Thing is," Dani said, "we're not gonna let that happen. We'll have so many officers in place and ready to strike that it *couldn't* happen…" Her voice drifted as she picked at a chip in the wood. "But here's my question. Since both of our fathers would want to be there, how do you think they'd feel coming face-to-face with each other?"

"Honestly, considering how much time has passed, I think they'd be willing to put their differences aside. At least for one night. Don't you?"

"I do. How awesome would it be if they ended their feud altogether? Who knows, maybe our display of unity would force them to realize that it's gone on for entirely too long. I mean, seriously, at this point, do they even remember why they're mad at each other?"

"Ha!" Von chuckled. "Probably not. Maybe if they see the positive exchanges between our agencies in person, that'll help mend things."

"That, and the fact that they'll pick up on all the good energy and chemistry between us, too."

Von sank back, his eyes locked on Dani. "Hold on, are you saying what I think you're saying?"

"What, that I'm ready to go public with our relationship?"

He nodded, unable to formulate an actual response.

"I think I am."

*"Dani..."* Von sprang to his feet and lifted her in the air, twirling her around. "I know we're talking about a murder investigation here, and this is not the time to celebrate. But in the middle of all this madness, hearing you say that made me one happy man."

"Good," she replied, her voice muffled as it vibrated against his neck. "I know how much it means to you, so, it's time for me to get past my issues and start living for myself." She took a breath, her gaze meeting his. "I've been thinking a lot lately, about how much I've let fear control me. Fear of what people will think, what my family will say... Hell, even what strangers might think. I've been living for everyone else but myself, and I can't do that anymore."

"Can I just say that I love where your head's at?"

"Yeah, me, too. It's time for me to stop hiding. Stop worrying about everybody else's opinions, including my father's. If I keep letting that fear hold me back, I'll never live for me. And that's what I want. For the both of us. So, what's next? Should we start planning this event? Toss out some dates, make calls, take notes, coming up with an agenda?"

"Oh, trust me. We're going to do all of the above. But for now, let's just take a moment to celebrate the fact that I came up with such a brilliant idea, shall we?"

"You are so full of yourself," Dani said, her hands sliding across his shoulders. Just as their lips met, her phone buzzed.

"Can we *please* just have a peaceful morning for once!" Von exclaimed.

"It's probably Chloe. I'm supposed to help her brainstorm new ideas for her upcoming podcast episode."

"Good," he murmured in between kisses. "That doesn't sound too pressing. Which means you can save it for later."

"Now would you treat Kevin that way?"

"In this exact moment? Yes, I would."

"That just means I'm a better friend than you," Dani quipped, pulling her cell from her cropped yoga jacket. "See, I'm glad I checked. It isn't Chloe. It's Chuck. Maybe he's emailing me with an update."

"Okay, well, for Chuck, I'll back off."

Dani scanned the message, her smiling shriveling into a rigid line.

"Uh-oh," Von said. "I don't like that look. What does his message say?"

Shoving the phone toward his chest, she said, "Here. Why don't you read it for yourself," then turned away, refusing to look at him when he grabbed it.

"What's with the sudden cold should—"

"Just read the damn message, Von!"

"All right, all right! I will…"

Chief Miller, I've got an update for you. And it's pretty shocking to say the least. I was able trace that bounty post that I discovered on the dark web back to an email address. It's Info@ReedProtectiveServices.com. So looks like someone from Von's company may be behind this. I'm still working to connect the email to an IP address. I'll keep you posted on my progress, but that's what I've got for now.

Von dropped the phone down by his side and reached for Dani. "Babe, come on. I know you're not falling for this. I mean, do you actually believe that one of my officers would be behind all this? After all the surveilling I've done, and—"

"Just stop it," Dani interrupted, snatching the phone from his hand. "Stop trying to explain your way out of every single thing. I've suspected that Kevin was involved in this for quite some time, yet you kept trying to talk me down, insisting that I was wrong. Because he's your friend. He's your employee. He's so *loyal*."

"And my opinion of him hasn't changed. I still believe all those things to be true. What I cannot believe is that we're going through this again. And that you're actually falling for it! Our suspect has been after us both for months. Imagine how he felt when we finally put up a united front. He's obviously trying to tear us apart by hacking into my company's network, or…or spoofing RPS's domain name. I don't know. But please tell me you can see through these fraudulent tactics as clearly as I can."

"All I see is that your company's name is connected to a threat against me. So, no. You and I are not on the same page. At all. But things will become crystal clear once Chuck gets me that IP address. Although I've got a hunch that it's gonna fall right back on your so-called friend, Kev—"

Before Dani could finish, Von brushed past her and headed down the trail. "You're wrong, Chief Miller. And this time, once you realize that, I don't know if I'll still be here for you."

## Chapter Twenty-Two

RPS's anniversary gala was in full swing. Von glanced around the Blanche Hotel's elegant Aurelia Grand Ballroom, impressed with its transformation into a silver-and-white wonderland. Crystal chandeliers shone a soft glow over exquisite floral arrangements. A red carpet stretched across the entryway, where a professional photographer captured guests as they arrived. The tables were covered in rich satin linens, adorned with silver candelabra-style lamps and flickering votives. And the room was filled with attendees draped in dazzling evening gowns and impeccably tailored tuxedos.

As far as Von was concerned, Dani was the most beautiful of them all. He wasn't used to seeing her so made up. It looked as if she'd stepped straight off a runway in her strapless chartreuse floor-length gown. Its daring, high-cut slit rose up her leg, baring a flirtatious glimpse of skin. The keyhole cutout revealed a seductive peek of cleavage. Her hair, which had been pulled into a smooth, high crown bun, put her ethereal makeup, dangling crystal earrings and slender neck on full display.

A few weeks had passed since their fallout over the RPS email address incident. Determined to clear his company's name, Von had commissioned Chuck to conduct a comprehensive forensic analysis of every RPS employee's electronic

devices. Vindication came with the conclusive findings—
none of the staff members' network identifiers matched the
data extracted from the bounty post.

Dani's skepticism, however, lingered. "Who's to say one
of your guys didn't use an outside device?" she'd probed.

Von decided not to press the issue. The only way to truly
convince Dani would be to catch the killer. Nevertheless,
Chuck's findings had eased the tension between them. And
the facts still remained true. They were stronger together
and couldn't afford to be torn apart. They still had a deadly
predator to catch.

So far, tonight's celebration had gone off without a hitch.
Von almost forgot the real reason they were there. Both
he and Dani remained on high alert during the first hour,
making sure that the Maxwell PD's surveillance room was
properly set up inside the hotel's presidential suite. Snipers
were positioned around the building, poised and ready to
act if necessary.

But as the evening wore on, Von's guard slowly began to
slip. The joyous energy buzzing throughout the ballroom,
the congratulatory greetings from guests and the warm ca-
maraderie felt at odds with the unnerving possibility that
their killer might be among them.

The thrill of the night occurred when Von's and Dani's
fathers exchanged cordial greetings with each other. They'd
later sat at a table together, sipping cocktails and sharing a
few laughs over filet mignon. Von couldn't help but wonder if his connection with Dani had brought on the unexpected truce.

And now, as he watched the two men chatting amicably,
Von felt a sense of satisfaction. Even if the killer wasn't
captured that night, the settled beef would be well worth
the effort.

When the band launched into a soulful rendition of Bobby

Caldwell's "What You Won't Do for Love," Von strolled over to the bar and asked Dani to dance. He caught a subtle wink of approval from Chloe before escorting Dani onto the dance floor.

As they swayed to the music, Von's gaze drifted over the crowd before returning to her radiant face. He couldn't help but notice the glimmer in her eyes. It was a spark that he'd missed seeing over the past few weeks.

"You look stunning tonight," he told her. "I just had to get that in. And now that I have, I'll focus on the task at hand. Have you checked in with your team inside the surveillance room?"

"First of all, thank you. Secondly, yes I have. They said everything looks to be running smoothly. So far, no signs of suspicious activity."

"Good. But let's not allow that to go to our heads. Stay vigilant. Unlike the wine festival, our suspect may not wait until this event is over to make a move. We do know he's comfortable here at the hotel since he got away with murder once before. So at this point, anything is possible."

"Trust me, my eyes are wide open. We're all on full alert. On another note, can you believe that our fathers are actually sitting together, chatting each other up and toasting to RPS's anniversary?"

Von's lips spread into a satisfied smile as he glanced over at their table. "No, I absolutely cannot. Who would've ever seen this day coming?"

"Not me, that's for sure. For them or for us."

Sliding his finger underneath her chin, he raised Dani's head until their eyes met. "I've got a question."

"I'm listening…"

"I know that we're just getting back on track after the whole RPS email debacle. But I want to revisit the conversation we had about us moving forward together as a couple.

Out in the open. If that's something you're still interested in, do you finally feel comfortable telling your father about us? Tonight? Especially now that he and my father seem to have squashed their beef?"

"I do," Dani murmured, cupping his face in her hands. "But considering how all eyes are on us right now, we might not even have to. Whatever we decide, let's wait until the time is right and the coast is clear. I don't want to lose focus and allow talk of *us* to overshadow why we're here tonight. Does that make sense?"

"Yes, that makes perfect sense," Von said, drawing her closer as their bodies continued moving to the music. "I'm just glad that we're finally on the same page."

"Same. Because at one point, we weren't even in the same book."

"Ha! Facts…"

As the music slowly faded, Dani's father took center stage.

"Good evening, everyone!" he roared into the mic. "If I may interrupt for a brief moment, I'd like to say a few words."

"What is that man doing?" Dani whispered. "This was not a part of the agenda…"

"Yeah, well, neither was a reconciliation between him and my dad. So maybe he's been moved to get up there and say a few words. I'd say this is a good thing. So let's just go with it."

"Agreed. Not that we seem to have much of a choice," she said as her father continued.

"First of all, for those of you who don't know me, I'm Gene Miller, Maxwell's former chief of police."

The crowd burst into a round of cheers and whistles.

"Thank you, thank you. Now, for those of you who *do* know me, I'm sure you're well aware of the history between the Maxwell PD and the founder of RPS, Mr. Hamilton

Reed. If you don't, long story short, Hamilton and I *hated* each other. For years!"

When everyone broke into raucous laugher, Gene held a hand in the air to quiet them. "Hamilton was my biggest rival, my biggest competition, and here's something he may not know, my biggest inspiration. After tonight, I think it's safe to say that I've got my old friend back. Hamilton, I'd like to congratulate both you and your son, Von, who just so happens to be standing in the middle of the dance floor with my daughter, Chief Danielle Miller…"

"Oh, no he didn't," Dani moaned as all eyes turned to them.

"Ohh, but he did," Von uttered through a toothy grin. "Just smile and nod."

"Sorry to put you two on the spot!" her father interject. "But anyway, like I was saying. Hamilton, Von, congratulations on Reed Protective Services' anniversary. You built an amazing business from scratch, and despite our issues, I've always admired that. So, job well done, and here's to continued success."

"Hear, hear!" Hamilton shouted, leaping from his chair and thanking Gene with a big bear hug. As the men raised their glasses for a toast, the band launched into an up-tempo rendition of Louis Armstrong's "What A Wonderful World."

"Wow…" Von said, tightening his hold on Dani's waist. "I never would've seen that coming. For an impromptu speech, it was pretty fantastic."

"Yes it was," she replied, dabbing the corners of her eyes. "I didn't see it coming, either. If it weren't for some crazed killer terrorizing our town, I'd say that tonight has been pretty damn perfect."

"And I'd concur."

"Chief Miller?" Von heard someone chirp through his earpiece. "Come in, Chief Miller."

Her smile shriveled into a downward curve as she dipped her chin. "Chief Miller here," she announced discreetly into a tiny microphone taped inside her dress's bustline. "What's going on?"

"Chief, this is Officer Rose. We wanted to check in and let you know that everything still looks to be secure. No suspicious activity. The officers guarding the exterior haven't detected anything peculiar, either."

"Good, thanks for letting me know. We've got a couple more hours to go before the event is set to end, so let's stay alert. Keep your eyes open. You already know what we're dealing with, and tonight would be the perfect opportunity to pull off a sensational stunt yet. So stay sharp."

"Will do, Chief. We're on it."

"Ten-four," Dani said before taking Von's hand in hers. "It's good to hear that all is well."

"It certainly is. But like you said, we've still got a couple more hours to go. So we'll see if we get through the rest of the night without incident. And with that being said…" He held their clasped hands in the air. "What's up with the public display of affection? You sure you're ready for all that?"

She leaned in, her lips gently melting into his. "Yes, I am. Especially since I'm the one who made the move. Now, may I interest you in glass of fresh berry spritzer since we're not allowed to drink while we're on duty?"

"Yes, you may. Thank you."

Heads turned as they set off toward the bar hand in hand. While the whispers were low, the stunned expressions spoke volumes, loud enough for anyone to grasp.

"Do you see all the attention we're getting?" Von asked, his tone tinged with amusement despite hoping Dani wouldn't let the chatter get to her.

"I do. And I'm ignoring it. Consider tonight our soft launch."

"I think I like the sound of that." Von took his glass from the bartender and held it in the air. "A toast. To us. May we continue on this path, and ride it as far as it'll take us. No matter where it's going, long as I'm with you, I'm good."

"Cheers to that."

The clink of their glasses was drowned out by the blare of a fire alarm. Within seconds, the water sprinkler system activated.

The ballroom spiraled into hysteria. Guests ran for cover while hotel employees scattered in search of the fire. Pulling off his jacket, Von tossed it over Dani's head and led her to a side entryway.

"This is it!" he yelled, squeezing his eyes shut as water drowned out his vision. "The killer is on the move!"

"And so are we!" Pulling her gun from her black leather garter belt, Dani jumped into action. "You know the plan. Touch base with RPS and make sure your officers are in place. My team should already be in motion. I'll take the back stairwell and check in with my officers in the surveillance room. Keep your phone close. We'll circle back in ten minutes."

"Got it! Oh, and hey, Dani?"

"Yes?"

"Be careful, and… I love you."

She clung to his arm, her fluttering eyelids suddenly growing still. "Stay safe. And I love you, too."

# Chapter Twenty-Three

Dani's heart pounded against her rib cage like a frenzied bird struggling to escape its cage. She hit the stairwell and climbed the stairs two at a time. Sharp cramps shot through her calves from the strain of her pewter pumps. She gritted her teeth, pushing through the pain as she made her way to the third floor.

Bursting through the door, she tore down the hallway, her heels snagging on the plush blue carpet. The fibers almost yanked them off her feet while she sprinted toward the room.

Dani fought to control her erratic breathing as the pounding in her head grew louder. The rush of terror mixed with fierce determination clouded her mind, eclipsing all hope of calm. This was it. The killer had struck. Her chance to take him down before he took her out had finally arrived.

She threw open the door. Rushed over to the dining room table where her officers had set up shop. They weren't there.

Dani spun a three-sixty. The room was completely empty.

"Officer Rose?" she called out.

No answer.

"Officer Shields?"

Still no response.

"*Anybody...* Where are you?"

She dashed through the living room. Checked the bedroom, then both bathrooms. They were all empty.

"What in the…"

Pulling out her phone, Dani called each officer who'd been operating the room. No answer.

She ran to the computers and frantically scanned the monitors. Black-and-white feeds from various areas around the hotel flashed across split screens. Dani peered at the lobby. The officers weren't there. She checked the common spaces, elevators banks and stairwells. No sightings there, either.

Dani switched to the feed inside the ballroom. The entire area was consumed by wall-to-wall commotion as guests skidded across the slick parquet floors. Elegant updos were reduced to drenched, matted messes, while smeared makeup accentuated the horror etched on faces. Elaborate attire was soaked, clinging to shivering bodies. Amid the havoc, Von and his officers, along with the Maxwell PD, fought to usher attendees toward the mezzanine. Yet among the frenzy, there was still no sign of her surveillance team.

"This is Chief Miller," she barked into her mic. "Can somebody from the Maxwell PD please come in?"

"Chief, this is Officer Mixon. I'm still out back, patrolling the parking lot. Several of our guys were called inside the ballroom by Officer Miller after the fire alarm went off."

"I've lost contact with the majority of the team, and the surveillance room is empty. Has anyone seen Rose and Shields?"

"I have. They came out here and checked in before heading back inside to help get the crowd under control."

"Wait," Dani said, her voice rising over the sirens wailing in the distance, "why did they leave the suite? I need at least one officer keeping an eye on things at all times."

"According to Rose, a member of the hotel's staff came

up and told them that you requested their assistance inside the ballroom."

Dani's knees went limp as a flash of heat swelled in her gut. Steadying herself against the table, she iterated, "A hotel staff member? The only employee who knew we were inside this suite is the manager. And he wasn't instructed to do anything. Did you get a physical description of the staffer?"

"I did not. And I've lost contact with most of our officers, too. I don't think they can hear us over all the noise."

Spinning around in a panic, Dani surveyed the room, her eyes darting to ensure she was alone. "Listen, I'm heading back down to the ballroom now. What's the word around the premises? Do guests seem to think this whole alarm thing is suspicious, or that there's an actual fire somewhere in the hotel?"

"Honestly, Chief, I'm hearing a little bit of everything. But considering we've got a killer on the loose, most people are thinking there's more to it than just a fire."

"Got it. Thanks for the insight. I'll check back in with you soon."

On the way to the door, Dani dialed Von's number. The call went straight to voicemail.

"Von, it's me. Apparently, the hotel manager told my surveillance team they were needed inside the ballroom. I don't know where that order came from, but something is definitely off here. I'm on my way to the ballroom back down now. See you soon."

Dani disconnected the call. Walked past the emerald-green couch. Just as she reached the hallway, the suite went dark. She whipped around and stared into a black abyss.

*Get out!* that inner voice screamed inside her head.

Dani lunged for the door. The second her hand hit the handle, something was thrown over her head. Wrapped around her entire body.

"Stop!" she screamed, struggling to swing and kick her way out of the tight fabric. "What the hell are you doing?"

No response. Instead, Dani was knocked to the floor. Her nails clawed at the material as she fought to free herself. But every limb was constricted, wound like a vise, rendering her almost immobile.

"Let me *go*!" Dani shouted right before a raspy voice growled, "Shut up!"

Dani's body strained against the fabric. She attempted to lift her legs. Punch her fists. Anything to break loose. Nothing was working.

Wrapped up like a mummy, she was dragged across the room. The vicious tugging tore at her skin, igniting a scorching blaze of friction burns. Dani was being flung around like a rag doll, her limbs hitting floor lamps, furniture, police equipment and whatever else was in the assaulter's path.

"Please, *stop*!" she cried out angrily.

Dread coursed through her veins as the fabric clung to Dani's skin. Salty droplets of sweat stung her eyes, intensifying her confusion. The ability to breathe was stifled by her stuttering heartbeat. The dense air grew heavy with heat as the room seemed to be closing in. Every desperate move Dani made only wound the fabric tighter, trapping her in an oppressive shell of fear.

*Keep trying. Keep moving!*

Dani writhed her body in hopes of hooking on to something. While contorting with more urgency, she heard the attacker's breathing become increasingly strained.

*I'm wearing him down...*

"Ugh!" Dani grunted when her torso hit what felt like a doorframe.

*Boom!*

Suddenly, the sheet loosened. Dani kicked her way out. Felt around for her gun. It was gone.

Jumping to her feet, she searched for the suspect. When a faint bit of light flashed through the room, she noticed a dark figure hovering against the window, his body parting the curtain.

"Stand down!" Dani screamed.

"Or what?" he yelled through a distorted voice.

Dani stood with her fists clenched, prepared to fight for her life. Hoping that she wouldn't go down with a stab wound to the chest or a bullet to the head—despite standing there alone in the dark with no weapon, no backup and no way to contact Von.

*I cannot die tonight*, she thought before yelling, "Come on! Let's *go!*"

Footsteps pounded the floor as her assailant lunged at her. Dani couldn't make out a weapon. Only two fists. She went in for an uppercut.

*Bam!*

A kick to the stomach sent Dani doubling over. Excruciating pain shot straight through to her back. The attacker, dressed in a black-and-white hotel uniform, hovered over her.

"Chief Danielle Miller!" he screeched in a sinister high-pitched voice. "Who the hell do you think you—"

Dani cut him off with a blow to the right jaw that landed with a sickening crack. The impact sent him stumbling backward as he gagged on a mouthful of blood. Dani kept going, unleashing a flurry of blows that released the fear and anger she'd been carrying for months. Every murder, every attack, every threat… They'd all led up to this moment. Her assailant's groans of pain were music to her ears.

A left hook to the nose sent his head snapping sideways. A right cross dropped him to his knees. The final blow, a kick to the face, sent him crashing to the floor, where he lay motionless.

"Get up!" Dani roared.

He edged toward the love seat, his legs tangling in his boots while he struggled to stand. Following after him, Dani tripped on the sheet she'd been wrapped in. She snatched it up and shook it out in search of her gun. It wasn't there.

*Crack!*

The room grew even darker. Dani rocked backward, her vision distorted in the obscurity of the unfamiliar surroundings. Just as it began to clear, she caught sight of a brass lamp swinging in the assailant's hands. It came crashing down toward her head. With a quick twist, she ducked to the right, narrowly missing it by inches.

Dani dropped to the floor, the carpet's rough fibers scraping against her palms as she frantically looked for her gun. Loud rumblings from behind sent her twirling around, her leg extended in a powerful kick. Dani's stiletto sank deep into the suspect's chest, eliciting a guttural wheeze.

Her attacker collapsed, then rolled over onto his stomach. Instead of crying out in pain, he was giggling uncontrollably.

Dani paused. Listened closely. The tone was shrill and squeaky. And unmistakably feminine.

"Finally!" a woman grunted. "I got to you. The one who always thought she was better than everybody else, just because her daddy was chief of police. The one who constantly bragged about following in his footsteps. Welp, you made it, Dani. But, news flash! You're a complete failure. You barely caught Maxwell's first serial killer. If it weren't for your brother and his little girlfriend, that never would've happened. This time, you're dealing with a pro. Four murders under my belt and you *still* couldn't catch me. Two attacks, countless threats, and you never did track me down. See, Maxwell PD was right. You didn't deserve that promotion. Lucky for you, nepotism!"

Dani's chest constricted, imploding under the gravity of the woman's words. That voice. So familiar, yet forgotten, until now. Her presence. Bold, obnoxious, sucking the air right out of the room…

Slamming her hand against the wall, Dani fumbled desperately for the light switch. Her eyes widened when the shadowy figure struggled to her feet, then hobbled back and forth in a fit of rage, ranting as if she were reading from a venomous manifesto.

"But look at you now, *Dani*. Even with Von's help, you still couldn't track me down! And you know what? You never will. Because you're about to die. I cannot wait to wrap my hands around your throat and rob you of your last breath. But before I do that, I just need to know why the hell you thought you could take over Maxwell. This is *my* town, bitch! Always has been and always will be. You thought you'd snatched my crown with all that attention you got from catching a killer. Ha! Now the only attention you'll be getting is the news of your death."

"You are out of your *mind*!" Dani screamed right before the woman came charging at her. She stood in a fighter's stance, fists in the air. But her badly beaten attacker was barely hanging on. A swift elbow to the left temple sent her crashing to the floor.

Darting toward the nearest lamp, Dani jabbed at the switch. The room lit up. She spun around. Stared down at the woman who'd been terrorizing her for months.

There, holding her head in agony, was Von's ex, Carmen Pendleton.

"Carmen!" she choked, stumbling against the back of the couch at the sight of her former classmate. Her petite figure was swallowed by the oversize black suit, and her hair looked to be buried underneath a short brunette wig. "*You're* the one who's been behind all this?"

Dani stood in frozen shock, waiting on her to respond. But she didn't. Carmen's eyes were pinned to the floor. Following her gaze, Dani spotted a glint of shiny black metal beneath the love seat.

*My Glock!*

The women dived for it at the same time. Dani beat her there, grabbing the gun, and pointed it directly at her chest.

"Stand down!" she said right before Carmen lurched in her direction. "I swear, if you make one more move, I will shoot you!"

Carmen staggered to a halt. But her tirade continued. "To answer your question, Dani, yes. I'm the one who's been making your life miserable, just to prove your inadequacy. And I am proud to say that my mission has been accomplished."

"This is about Von, too, is it?"

"Of course it is! Because how could you actually try to take him from me?"

"*Take* him from you? You two weren't even dating!"

"If that's what he told you, then he lied. We were on a break, idiot. And then you came along with the whole damsel in distress act. *Ooh, Von, somebody's trying to kill me. Let's be friends!* I still can't believe he fell for it. Had it not been for you, he would've come back to me a long time ago. But…" Carmen's head fell as her eyes welled up with tears. Seconds later, she glanced up, her distressed expression transforming into a wicked grin. "That's why I had to teach his ass a lesson, too. Sabotage his work gigs. Prove that he's just as incompetent as you."

Carmen crept forward, her eerie gait resembling that of a predator, closing in on its prey. "You two deserve each other—"

"Listen to me!" Dani yelled, her finger tightening on the trigger. "Either back up or get shot. Your choice."

"Yeah, right. Girl, you don't have the guts to shoot me."

"But I do!" Von charged inside the room with his gun

drawn. "Now follow Chief Miller's orders and stand down!" He turned to Dani, whispering, "I got your voicemail. When you didn't show up inside the ballroom, I knew something was wrong." Tossing her a pair of handcuffs, he said, "Chief, do your thing."

Dani closed in on Carmen. It was a fight to cuff her as she thrashed about in a last-ditch effort to break free. Dani and Von's combined strength quickly overpowered her resistance. He pinned down her ankles while Dani seized her wrists. Carmen's struggle intensified, but slowly, her energy waned. Once defeat set in, she finally surrendered.

Dani exhaled sharply at the sound of the cuffs clicking shut. As Carmen's head drooped, her spiked wig slipped off, exposing a stocking cap that concealed a slicked-back bun.

"All I ever wanted was *you*," Carmen spat in Von's direction. "I did everything I could to destroy anyone who stood between us. I even put that fifty-thousand dollar bounty on Dani's head, hoping I'd finally get rid of her. But you *still* chose her. Why? Look at her! Why would you want that spoiled, entitled—"

"Hey!" Von snapped. "That's enough. Chief, should I call for backup?"

"Sounds like they're already on the way," Dani replied as heavy footsteps echoed through the corridor.

Tightening her hold on Carmen's arm, Dani said, "Carmen Pendleton, you're under arrest for the murders of Gordon Edwards, Brandy Orland, Jeffrey Simmons and Stephanie Hunter. And for the threats, attacks and attempted murder against me, Chief Danielle Miller."

## Chapter Twenty-Four

"Wait, so let me get this straight," Chloe said, stepping onto Dani's backyard deck. "You mean to tell me that Carmen confessed to being the killer, *while* she was attacking you?"

"Yes. That is exactly what I'm telling you. Her plan was to reveal the twisted motive, kill me, then flee the scene, just as she always had."

"Little did she know you'd live to tell your story."

"Yes, I did. My team did a great job erasing every trace of that bounty threat from the dark web, too."

Dani took a breath, her fingers trembling while pouring ice into a cooler. Recounting the night of the attack still had an emotional effect on her. It hadn't been a full two weeks since the incident. The haunting memory dredged up everything leading to that terrifying moment. The threats, the murders, the bounty on her head. Dani didn't know if she'd ever get past it all.

*You will. Baby steps. Just focus on today...*

At the last minute, Dani had decided to throw a barbecue for the Maxwell PD and RPS as a thank-you for all their hard work. The purpose of the gathering was twofold as they were also celebrating Troy's promotion to detective.

Dani scanned the portable buffet table, rearranging platters of corn on the cob, shrimp cocktail and Italian pasta salad to make room for Chloe's three-tier cupcake stand.

The rich, savory scent of steak filled the air as Troy manned the grill.

Guests were slowly trickling in. Everything was going smoothly—except that the men of the hour, Gene Miller and Hamilton Reed, had yet to arrive.

"Troy," Dani whispered, "are you sure Dad confirmed that he'd be here?"

"Yes. I'm positive."

"And he knows that Von's father will be here, too?"

"I didn't mention it to him, but I'm guessing he does know since RPS is being acknowledged, too."

Von slipped past Dani and set a tray of marinated rib eye steaks, lobster tails and chicken breasts next to the grill. "Everything is gonna be fine, D. I'm sure that both of our fathers will be here."

"You're right. I'm being paranoid. I just want everything to be perfect."

She surveyed the yard, her eyes lingering on each face while her hands fidgeted restlessly. Even with Carmen behind bars, Dani was still on edge. The constant urge to glance over her shoulder, double-check the car before getting in, keep her Glock within reach...those instincts hadn't faded.

"Babe?" Von whispered, giving her back a soft caress. "Everything all right?"

"Yes, it's just—I'm still a little anxious, that's all. And I hope we get a good turnout this afternoon. I want the day to go smoothly. I owe that to Troy, and to both of our agencies, to show them how grateful I am."

"Trust me, we all know that. And it's going to be a great day. So why don't you take a deep breath, relax and enjoy the party? The hard work is done. Carmen is locked up. While you're busy thanking and celebrating everybody else, it's time for you to relish that win. Now, since you like to indulge in a little dessert before the main course, how about I grab you one of those red velvet cupcakes?"

"Thank you, baby, but I'll wait," Dani murmured, brushing his lips with a soft peck. "I'm looking forward to that steak and lobster. But I appreciate all that you said. I needed to hear it."

"That's what I'm here for. Be right back. I'm gonna see if Troy needs help on the grill."

As soon as he walked off, Chloe swooped in.

"Here," she said, slipping a red plastic cup in Dani's hand. "I think you need to have a little wine. I can tell you're stressing out. But I'm glad Von's pep talk helped."

"It did. He could sense my anxiety. I honestly think all this tension stems from me blaming myself for not figuring out Carmen was the killer sooner."

"How could you, though? She managed not to leave any evidence behind. Plus she's the last person any of us would've suspected."

Dani's voice lowered as she pulled Chloe toward the side of the house. "There were definitely signs that I'd overlooked. The fact that her father worked for RPS and hated my dad because of the rivalry with Maxwell PD. That animosity trickled right down to me. Then there was the whole jealousy thing. Carmen resented all the attention I got after we arrested the first serial killer. In her delusional mind, she thought I was stealing her limelight."

"Makes sense. Carmen always did think she ran this town. But Maxwell wasn't enough for her, hence the move to LA. She never did land that A-list movie role though, did she?"

"Nope. Which is why she came running back home. Now here's an interesting side note. Carmen landed a small part in a low-budget thriller, where she played a murderous hacker. I watched it after her arrest, and so much of that film mimicked this case. That's where she learned the ins and outs of untraceable burner phones, fake email addresses and AirTags. She also knew to use public Wi-Fi to hide her IP address and wear discreet protective gear while committing the crimes. Between that and her father's knowledge of the criminal justice system, Carmen knew exactly what she was doing."

Chloe stood motionless, staring straight ahead while clutching the sides of her face. "What a psychopath. Didn't she try to launch some channel on YouTube after her acting career failed, thinking she'd become a big influencer?"

"Yep, right after she moved back home. It was called *Beauty Gets You Everywhere*. That didn't take off, either. She had about twenty-five subscribers. So she never was able to reclaim her it-girl status here in Maxwell. That's probably what really made her snap. As you know, nothing drives a narcissist to the brink of psychosis faster than the lack of attention."

"Facts. And what about Von? Were you able to prove that the crimes were aimed at him, too?"

"I was. Carmen admitted to it. She was pissed when he and I got close and took it out on us both. Her goal was to ruin RPS's reputation and put them out of business. You know, when I took her statement, she actually seemed to enjoy sharing details on how she'd gotten away with the crimes. I found out that she had been temping for an event staffing service. So she worked catering gigs at Cole's, the Blanche Hotel, Gibson's Country Club *and* Desert Grove Ranch."

"Oh, so she was already familiar with the layouts and knew how to get around the buildings."

"Exactly."

Chloe's eyes shifted away from Dani as she fidgeted with the drawstring on her army-green jumpsuit. "Hey, I've got a question. Did you ever apologize to Von for accusing Kevin of being your suspect?"

"I did. On behalf of you and me both, actually. And he graciously accepted the apology."

"Good. And *thank* you. Because I was right there with you, thinking that man was guilty. But anyway, back to Carmen. Please tell me that she's being held without bond."

"She is. And since I've got her full confession on record, she'll likely spend the rest of her life behind bars."

A loud buzz rippled through the backyard. Dani followed the crowd's gaze. A huge grin spread across her face when her father walked through the gate. Von's dad entered right behind him. The moment their feet hit the lawn, they were surrounded by guests, receiving warm hugs and cold bottles of beer.

"They're here!" Dani said to Von after rejoining him on the deck.

"Just like I knew they would be."

He leaned in and held her close, drawing plenty of raised brows from those standing nearby. Even a few low whistles blew through the breezy afternoon air.

Dani caught sight of her father raising a beer in their direction, just as Mr. Reed tossed them a thumbs-up.

"Could you ever have imagined our dads giving this relationship the green light?" Dani asked.

"Maybe not in the past. But there's no way I would've let anything stop us from being together. We'd have figured out a way to win them over."

The pair paused when Troy waved a pair of red grill gloves in the air. "Hey, everyone! The food will be done in about ten minutes. Why don't you all start lining up near the deck, and prepare yourselves for a delicious celebratory feast. While you do that, I'm going to pass the invisible mic over to one of our hosts, Von Reed, as he has a few words he'd like to say."

"Oh, you do?" Dani asked. "That's news to me." When she stepped to the side to give him the floor, he grabbed her hand and led her toward the middle of the deck. "What are you doing?"

"You'll see," Von told her, popping the collar on his blue shirt, then raising his cup in the air.

Dani, who wasn't a fan of spontaneity or surprises, shifted her weight while pulling at the frayed hem of her denim skirt.

*What is he doing?* she mouthed to Troy and Chloe.

They shrugged in unison, their shining eyes seemingly concealing a secret.

"First off," Von said to the crowd, "thanks so much for coming out today. To the Maxwell PD, as well as my RPS officers, it goes without saying that we are deeply grateful for your support in this latest criminal investigation. As we all know, Carmen Pendleton would still be on the run if it weren't for our fearless leader, Chief Miller."

Von paused as their guests broke into applause. When they quieted down, he took her hand and brought her closer. "Chief, once again, you have demonstrated extraordinary courage in protecting the people of Maxwell. While we honor the lives of those we've lost, it's important to remember that things could have been so much worse. But thanks to your efforts, they weren't. Your leadership made all the difference."

Holding her hand to her chest, Dani replied, "Thank you so much for that. But this was a team effort. And I know that came as a surprise to most, including me, given the conflict between our two agencies. However, not only did we join forces, but we also buried the hatchet, which brought our families together. I think I speak for us both when I say I'm extremely proud of that."

A thunderous roar boomed through across the lawn, followed by laughter when their fathers each took a bow.

"What's even better," Von added, "is that our hard work led to something more. Much more."

Dani held her breath as he handed Troy his cup, then reached inside his pocket.

"Danielle Miller," Von continued, "it's no secret that I have loved you for years. But I hid those feelings for obvious reasons. Now, *finally*, I am so glad that I can love you out in the open, and tell everyone here how much I care about you."

"I love you, too," she whispered, her heart thumping to the beat of his every word.

"There are so many things I could say to convey how excited I am for our future. However, I'll start here. Thank you for letting me in, and for allowing me the opportunity to show you who I really am."

Swallowing the knot of emotion in her throat, Dani rasped, "Thank you for looking past my feistiness and seeing me for who *I* really am."

The crowd's murmurs turned to stunned silence when Von dropped to one knee.

"Dani," he said, pulling a black velvet box from his pocket, "I never would've imagined I'd one day land the girl of my dreams. Yet here I am. And there's no place I'd rather be." He opened the lid, revealing a sparkling princess-cut engagement ring. "Danielle Sabrina Miller, would you do me the honor of being my wife?"

*"Yes,"* she breathed, looking on blissfully as he slid the ring onto her finger.

The crowd erupted into cheers as Troy popped open a bottle of champagne.

"Congratulations!" he exclaimed, pulling his sister into

a tight hug before whispering, "Make some time for me next week."

"Why?"

"Not to steal your thunder or anything, but I want you to go ring shopping with me."

"Aww, baby bro! Of course I will. And I won't say a word to our girl…"

Returning to Von's embrace, Dani raised her left hand, beaming as the diamond shimmered against their guests' cheering faces. Finally, all the torment leading up to this moment began to fade, replaced by the love of a man who'd been the one all along.

\* \* \* \* \*

# SHADOWED PAST

## TARA TAYLOR QUINN

To my mother, Agnes Mary,
and my daughter, Rachel Marie, my bookends.
May our hearts always be able to find each other.

*Chapter One*

"Did you take the test?"

Dr. Kara Latimer handed her husband the toothpaste, put her own toothbrush in her mouth, and nodded toward the plastic device sitting by the floral vase on her end of the double-sink vanity.

She wasn't looking. Had a C-section to perform on a six-year-old French bulldog in an hour, and didn't want to think about that, either. Poor Celia…mama had managed to bring the six pups she was carrying close enough to term to likely produce perfectly healthy pups, but the highly unusual double-size litter was taking its toll on the dog. And on Maggie, her owner, who'd requested that Kara spay the girl during the birthing procedure.

And…the forty-five seconds was up. She spit. Heard Ben do the same. While his water was still running in his sink, she grabbed the stick, turned it so she couldn't see the results right away.

Stood with her guilt as she prayed there wouldn't be a plus sign.

Ben sidled up behind her, pressing his gorgeously fit, nearly forty-year-old frame against her backside, his arms sliding around her belly as he peeked over her shoulder.

And then left half of her body cold when he let go with

one hand to cover her stick-holding fingers with his. "Uh, you need to turn it over, babe."

Babe.

Baby.

The plus sign glared at her. Growing bigger in her mind as Ben let out a loud whoop, spun her around, and hugged the air out of her.

She hugged him, too. Because he was so happy.

And she loved him so much.

"Oh, my God, I can't believe it!" His breath tickled her neck as his excited tone lit her own fire a bit.

She wanted the family Ben was so eager to have. "I know," she said, giving him one last big squeeze before kissing him, long and hard, and saying, "I'm sorry, sweetie, but I have to go." He knew how much the surgery was weighing on her. "We'll celebrate tonight, okay?"

She kissed him again, pushing her pelvis against his fly, distracting him long enough to get herself out of the house before her tears started to fall.

SHE WAS KEEPING something from him.

Her prerogative, of course. Healthy even, for married couples to maintain some autonomy.

Healthy on paper, at any rate. In his experience—and he'd had plenty—secrets between married couples often led to unhappy turns of events. The least of which was divorce.

And he had to keep perspective. He was so damned in love with his young wife that he'd been blinded by emotion on more than one occasion where she was concerned.

Ten minutes after Kara had given him the stick, Ben Latimer climbed into his new silver Mercedes-Benz and had some very clear come-to-truth moments. His mind had been clouded by doubts regarding Kara's lifelong dedication to him since a week or so before their wedding.

His worry had nothing to do with her actions, words, or choices of activities whatsoever. He was the one with ten years more life experience under his belt. The one who'd spent nearly twenty years as a senior partner and lead investigator in one of the largest, most successful law firms in Atlanta. He'd seen things. So many of them.

He'd had to delve deeply into the motivations that drove people to break the law—or just break vows, which drove others to break the law. One of the key determiners was the older man–younger woman scenario. In the beginning, it was all roses.

Until their different stages in life no longer allowed them to walk the same path. People changed as they aged. Their bodies aged, of course, but priorities were different, too. Perspectives had more experiences, which gave them more depth.

It was all a natural part of life. Nothing anyone could prevent.

And if one's aging was far ahead of one's partner's?

Until that morning, Kara had been the dream wife he hadn't ever thought to dream about. Far more mature than most twenty-nine-year-olds he knew, she'd been his support, his champion, the other half of his life for whom he could cheer. And the one for whom he would always drop everything to offer his assistance whenever the occasion warranted.

The doubt—the emotion that blinded him—had always been there, beneath the surface. Kara was gorgeous, successful, owned the only veterinary clinic in North Haven, the small town forty-five minutes southwest of Atlanta where she'd grown up—and where they currently lived. She knew so many people there and was known by even more.

There'd always been reason to think she could do better than a man so much older than herself. But the doubt had sprung to life during his bachelor party when one of his fellow firm attorneys had made a comment about how pathetic they were, working late and then just going out for a couple of beers rather than hitting strip clubs or hiring exotic dancers.

Kara had had a whole weekend at a rented beach house for her bachelorette party. He hadn't asked if there'd been any male professionals invited. She'd told him, though.

There hadn't been.

Just a lot of drinking, dancing, lying in the sun, and talking about sex.

He and the five guys who'd insisted that he have a send-off—one of whom had been Kara's brother-in-law, and the other four were married with kids—had talked shop mostly. And watched the end of a game on the bar's television set, doing a round of shots to toast the losing team.

So, yeah, he'd been aware from before day one of their marriage that there was a possibility that she wasn't fully seeing what she was getting herself into, marrying a man a decade older. He'd wondered at one time—or a million of them—if perhaps she'd been as much in love with the idea of marrying the best friend of her sister's husband—becoming a more solid, equal part of the everyday lives of the three who'd been close since college—as she'd been in love with him.

Driving to the firm, he forced himself to shake the doubts. To climb out of emotion and into rational thought. Something he excelled at.

And his first thought threatened to send him right back in.

What wasn't she telling him?

When he refused to sink back to a place where failure was far more prevalent than success, the next thought came. Why in the hell wasn't he asking her?

The answer he had didn't serve him.

He wasn't asking because he suspected the answer was going to confirm all his doubts. That Kara was going to tell him the time had come when she was starting to see that they were on diverging paths.

That plus sign had brought her no joy. While he'd thought it was their biggest crowning moment of all time.

He was going to be a father! He and Kara were starting the family they'd talked about raising together. The truth brought a surge of buoyancy. A huge smile.

Which, in the light of the facts in front of him, faded quickly.

He was turning forty. Wanted to be young enough to chase his kid down whatever kind of field the child wanted to run in. And to play tag with his grandkids, too.

Kara still had lots of time to start a family. Years ahead of her to win races against teenagers.

You could shoot down baseless doubts. Harder to avoid the truth.

He had to ask the question.

Pushing the button on his steering wheel, he asked the car's Bluetooth system to call his wife. And was relieved when she picked up on the first ring. As though he'd had doubts about that, too.

"Ben? I'm about to go into surgery. Is everything okay?"

Right. The French bulldog dangerously overloaded with six pups. For a split second he was envious of Kara's eagerness to birth those babies, but not his. Jealous of a dog in danger of losing her life.

He was not handling his disappointment in the morning's lack of celebration well.

Making it all about himself.

"I just wanted to make sure you're okay," he said then, all questions on hold until he had time to assess. Get out of his own skin. And firmly grounded back in reality.

"I'm fine," she said, sounding anything but. Possibly because he was keeping her from surgery. In order to confirm his theory, he glanced at the clock on the dashboard, then stared straight ahead at a lane filled with no traffic at all.

Clock read 8:04 a.m. Her surgery wasn't scheduled until nine.

They had to talk. But not on the phone. And the need was also not something he could just put baldly out there without actually having the conversation. "We need to talk" was generally not a phrase denoting happy words to come.

"How about lunch?" he asked her. "I've got a lead to track down not far from your clinic. I can swing by for you whenever you're ready. I'll make a reservation at Barney's." An upscale Irish restaurant not far from her practice. One of her favorites. And his, too.

The fact that his lead had to do with interviewing the wife of a murderer on the run didn't warrant a mention in the moment. She clearly had enough on her mind. He'd get the job done in time to suit Kara. And talk to her about it later. If it came up.

"I can't, Ben." Her words threw him into a feeling of cold storage. "I'm so sorry, hon, but I've got something in the works with my sisters, and you know how hard it is for the three of us to find times that gel…"

He did know. Melanie, at forty-five, was busy supporting her big-time sports agent ex-husband—who lived in Atlanta—and their teenaged sports star son. And Stella, thirty-nine, like Ben, had started traveling for work a lot more since her divorce from Ben's best friend.

What hit him most clearly, though, was the sudden call for time with her big sisters. Clearly, for some baby talk. Which could be a good thing.

"We'll catch up later this afternoon, then," he said, and

telling himself that he was making mountains out of mole-
hills, focused his attention on the workday ahead.

THE NORTH HAVEN COFFEE SHOP was three miles from the
little corner café Kara normally frequented. Central to where
the sisters had to be that day. Close enough to Stella that
she could ride her bike. Kara saw the familiar two-wheeled
transportation locked to a pole just outside the door as she
pulled into the parking lot a minute before she'd have been
late.

Taking the third seat at the table where Stella and Melanie
were waiting, she said, "I'm sorry for the drama, but I need
to talk to you two before I go home to face Ben tonight."

Kara could almost hear Stella's inward groan. Her older
sister by ten years, Stella was the activist, the middle child,
with her sassy, layered, short reddish-gold hair and blue eyes.
But she had a heart that bled for anyone who was suffering.
Kara had long ago figured out that Stella was the most sensitive of the sisters.

Melanie, the oldest at forty-five, leaned forward, her
brown eyes brimming with their usual compassion. "If you
lost Celia, sweetie, you have to know it wasn't your fault."

The French bulldog had been Kara's very first patient
when she'd opened up her own practice. "She produced six
healthy puppies," Kara told the two of them, glad that there
was good news to open what was going to be a difficult conversation. One she'd tried to have so many times over the
years but had always chickened out on.

But now, with her own birthing abilities being called into
play, she no longer had a choice.

Still, a minute or two to build up to the main event wasn't
a horrible idea. Since Melanie had presented the opportunity. "Her vitals are fine and she's contentedly nursing," she
continued. Thinking she'd end it there. But didn't. "I'm ac-

tually thinking about fostering a couple of the puppies if she doesn't have enough milk." The idea popped out before its time. She hadn't even mentioned the possibility to Ben yet.

Melanie's smile was supportive, and accompanied by lines on her forehead, too. "What does Ben have to say about that?"

Yeah. Leave it to the sister who'd raised her to figure out there was trouble in paradise. With a serious glance between the two of them, Kara said, "I haven't said anything to him about it yet." Their clue not to spill the beans in the event they talked to Ben before she did.

Stella picked up her soda-filled stainless steel mug and said, "Kara, you know I'm not going to be much help if we're here to talk about husband trouble."

"This isn't about Ben. Not directly, anyway."

She had their attention. And both sets of eyes focused on her. Exactly what she'd come for. And wasn't ready. "Ben's great. It's me…"

"What? Is something wrong? You're not sick, are you?" Melanie piped in.

"No." Kara took a long sip from the iced-caramel-and-vanilla-cream drink sitting in front of Melanie.

A move she hadn't made since she was about six.

Pushing the drink closer to Kara, sharing without comment, Melanie pinned her with the look that had always pulled the truth out of Kara. "What's going on?"

"It's about Mom."

Stella shared an immediate glance with Mel. Not just a glance. Some kind of silent communication. The same as they'd done Kara's entire life.

Stella had only been ten the last time she'd seen their mother. Melanie had to have spent a lot of time consoling her.

"What about Mom?" Mel asked, all nonchalant and innocent sounding, as though she was talking to her fifteen-year-old son, not her twenty-nine-year-old veterinarian sister.

Melanie had always been the keeper of the Mom secrets. The unofficial Tory Mitchell spokesperson for the family. The one Kara had gone to when she'd first had questions. Before she'd quietly started looking for them on her own. And had found far too little. And too much, too.

Too little to tell her anything. And too much to be able to let go.

"I need to know more." Kara's eyes wide, she implored both of them. "It's like I'm stuck in this place between where I came from and where I'm going. I know her death, the suddenness of the accident, was horrible for you both, and that it hurts to talk about her. But Ben…wants to have a family and I… I feel this void. Once I have kids…will I be there for them? I think I need to know my own mother before…" She shook her head, not quite tearing up, but feeling close enough to it. Stella was watching more closely.

"What do you want to know?" Mel's question came softly, filled with her usual empathy.

"She baked great chocolate chip cookies," Stella burst out.

"And had a beautiful voice, too," Kara added, nodding. "I know those things…you've told me many times. You just never say…was she…a good mom?"

"She was a great mom," Mel said, and Stella took another sip of soda. "She sure adored you." Mel's smile seemed genuine as she looked at Kara, and then, including Stella in her glance, said, "All of us. She loved being a mom and was always the first to volunteer when hair had to be done for dance recitals, or drivers were needed to get our softball team to an away game…"

Half-laughing, Mel glanced from Kara to Stella. And Kara had the distinct impression her oldest sister's good humor wasn't completely natural as Mel said, "Remember that summer we took a family road trip to Yellowstone and when we stopped at the roadside place for lunch, she pulled out a tablecloth and napkins and stuff before she'd let us dig into the cooler? Dad about flipped his lid because he was eager to get to the hotel before dark…"

Stella shook her head. "No."

They didn't have a lot of time. And Kara didn't need to revisit all the stories she'd already heard. She couldn't allow them to sidetrack her anymore. "I have to know more about the accident." Her tone, the determined look in her eye drew Stella's gaze straight to her.

"I've been through every newspaper I can find in the entire states of Georgia, Tennessee, Florida, and Louisiana—and did a countrywide search too—and I can't find any mention at all of a car accident attached to Mom's name. Or to the date she died, either. None that involved the death of a woman Mom's age…

"I found the obituary—not that I needed it since you'd already shown it to me," Kara continued, shooting her gaze back and forth between the two of them. "But even that… it was so…short. Just said that she died in North Haven, Georgia, as a result of injuries sustained in a car accident."

With another long, serious look, Kara said, "Aunt Lila told me a few years back that knowing the details would serve no purpose, and I tried to trust her judgment…but… I need to know. Did Mom kill herself?"

Lila. Honorary aunt. Her mother's best friend.

"No!" The word burst out of Stella. And Mel, too. Simultaneously. Glancing at her oldest sister, Kara felt her stomach clench. Mel wasn't known for outbursts.

And when it came to their mother, Mel had always been… calm.

Almost eerily calm, Kara realized, now that she thought about it.

She stared back and forth between the two women who'd been her role models—and trusted advisers—her entire life. Melanie's face was suddenly expressionless.

Driven by something stronger than herself, Kara held her ground.

And said, "I need the truth."

Stella slid down lower in her seat.

## Chapter Two

It turned out to be a good thing that Ben didn't have plans to meet Kara for lunch. He'd have had to cancel. The morning had not gone at all as planned.

Starting with the small stick he'd wrapped in tissue, shoved into the smallest sealed evidence bag he had, and slid into his inside suit coat pocket.

Yeah, she'd peed on it. Hence the tissue and sealed bag. But it was also the first sign of life his child had given to the world. He was growing sappy at the ripe old age of a couple months from forty.

And was holding on to hope that perhaps he and Kara would still have a major celebration with that stick as the life of the party.

Or he had been, until he stood almost toe to toe with Tina Hansen. The clearly frightened spouse of murder suspect John Hansen was pointing a rifle at him. Looking into that barrel, Ben's perspective had changed. He was currently pinning all his hopes on the chance that he'd make it out of the interview alive.

And that she would.

While the woman had gumption—and motivation—she did not have law enforcement training. She'd failed to check him for weapons after she'd answered the door with the rifle already aimed and ordered him inside. He'd been watching her trigger finger ever since. It was resting just below the metal igniter. The second he saw movement in any muscle in that hand, her time to feel in command was over.

He'd have his gun out before she had a chance to lift a finger. Any of them. Let alone the one trapped beneath that curved gun part.

And with a quick snap of his left hand, he'd take possession of the barrel of her hunting rifle, too.

If he had to shoot her to save his life, he'd do so. He hoped it didn't come to that.

"I'm not here to hurt you, Tina. Or to arrest you. I just want to talk." Her trigger hand didn't move. The one bracing the back of the gun lowered. Almost imperceptibly. But it was all the evidence Ben needed to know that the woman didn't want to shoot him.

Based on the awkwardness of her stance, the way her elbows were out from her body and nothing but her hands were actually touching the old gun, he'd bet she'd rarely handled it. If at all.

Showing her his private detective badge through the window before she'd opened the door had obviously not been the right move. "I'm not a cop," he continued. "I'm a private investigator, just trying to get some answers that might help me figure out something my client needs to know."

He wouldn't lie. Just wasn't the way he worked. But he chose his words carefully. As always.

His client was the Atlanta prosecutor's office that had contracted with his private law firm. They'd hired Ben to follow a convoluted and incomplete trail of evidence to find the accomplice of the serial killer they had in custody. They needed said accomplice to cut a deal and testify against the man who'd done all but one of the killings. John Hansen had shot in self-defense when an intended victim fought back against capture. He hadn't brutalized anyone. After the abductions, he'd been out of the picture. Detectives—and Ben, too, now that he'd seen the evidence—believed that John had been unaware of what, exactly, Stuart Miller had done with the prey after kidnapping them.

John's phone had never pinged anywhere near Miller's torture chamber but had signaled elsewhere during the times of the offenses. And John had alibis—surveillance camera at the bar he frequented more waking hours than he was at home—for the time the victims spent in captivity and times of death, too.

Ben held the older woman's gaze easily as she tried to stare him down. Law enforcement wanted nothing from her but her husband's location.

Personally, Ben would love to help her get away from the man. And would see what his firm could do to help her if, indeed, John was able to cut a deal that let him see the light of day again.

"You've done nothing wrong, Tina," Ben said then, his tone soft. "Can we please just talk?"

He wasn't surprised when she lowered the gun. The way it had been starting to shake the last thirty seconds or so, he figured it was too heavy for her skinny, frail arms.

Watching as she glanced toward the back door, and then the front, he wondered if she was expecting someone. Or, who she thought was watching her. He'd seen no evidence of cameras when he'd pulled into the drive of the rundown property five miles outside of town. But would check again, front and back, before leaving.

"Like I said, you're in no trouble at all," he said as she stood the butt of the rifle on the ground, holding the barrel with a tight grip an inch or so from the top.

Had she been someone skilled in handling rifles, she'd have gripped it a bit lower, enabling her—or someone with enough strength—to have the butt up under her arm and ready to shoot with one quick motion.

Raising her chin defiantly, Tina asked, "What you want to know? 'Cause I don't know nothin'."

"I need you to understand that you aren't in trouble now, but if I ask a question and you lie to me, you could be breaking the law."

"What law?"

His focus intent, he said, "Harboring a fugitive."

And...there...the drop of her shoulders, the glance to the floor and out the front window...gave him all the evidence he needed to press forward.

"Where's John, Tina?"

She looked him right in the eye as she said, "I don't know."

So she didn't know his exact location. But she knew something.

"But you know how to reach him."

She shook her head that time, rather than speak. But still held his gaze.

And it hit him. "You know when and where you're supposed to be to deliver whatever it is he's asked you to get for him," he said. It made sense. A man who spent the vast majority of his waking hours on a bar stool likely hadn't been prepared to live off the grid. He'd been on the run for a couple of days, at most, based on the last time he'd been seen at the bar. He'd need supplies.

Tina looked toward the window again. Back that time.

Which told him she was looking for a way out.

Not checking the route she knew someone had taken. Or someplace someone was hiding right there on the property. Ben had already had someone out checking the one falling-down outbuilding on the property. Before dawn that morning.

Before he'd seen the stick...

The thought came. And went.

"If you don't tell me what you know, you'll be breaking the law, Tina."

"You ain't a cop."

"No, but I'm working for them," he told her. Through the prosecutor's office. They were all on the same case. And his part in it had been fully sanctioned all the way to the top. "And can have a detective here in a matter of minutes, if you'd like me to call him. I was hoping it wouldn't come to that. You know, so no one sees police cars here."

Glancing out the window, Tina raised her chin as though nodding with it, and said, "Your fancy car's gonna do 'bout the same," she said. "People gonna ask 'bout it."

"Not if I'm out of here before anyone notices." Might already be too late for that. He figured they both knew that. But there was always a possibility that no one who knew Tina had driven by yet.

Unless, of course, she knew the place was being watched. That John was doing the watching?

"He told me to give you a message," Tina said.

That got his attention. "Me? How would John know *I* was going to be here today?"

"Not you, 'xactly. Just anyone who showed up."

Nodding, Ben said, "Okay, what's the message?"

"That if you hurt me, or threaten me at all, you can 'spect the same to happen to ones you love."

He'd already threatened her—with trouble if she didn't talk to him.

Chills ran through Ben. Kara. And…the baby.

Shaking himself, he got right back on track. "How are you going to be in contact with him again?" Ben asked, his tone no longer soft, or in any way conciliatory.

Tina shrugged. "Someone's going to let me know."

Taking a step forward, he grabbed her gun. Held it as he bit out, "Who? And when?"

"I don't know. Maybe when I go to the grocer. Or here. I'm only s'posed to be here, or the store."

"When do you go to the store?"

"Tomorrow. I always go Saturday mornings. It's the day they have all the expiring stuff out for cheap."

Bingo. He'd have someone watching the place, and someone else at the grocery store in the morning, too.

Holding up the rifle he said, "You got a license for this?"

And when she just stared at him, he said, "I'll be taking it with me then," and headed for the exit.

But stopped just before stepping outside, pulling a card out of his pocket and setting it on the small table by the door. "You get into any trouble, get scared, feel unsafe for any reason, you call this number," he told her. "It's the direct line to an officer working this case. He can have someone here in less than five minutes."

With one last glance at the card, not at Tina, Ben let himself out.

Stashed the gun in his trunk until he could turn it over as possible evidence—bit of a gray area concerning how he came to be in possession of it. He just hadn't wanted John to use the damned thing against Tina. No way she'd be able to use it to protect herself.

And left the property with several glances in his rearview mirror.

He did not have a good feeling about the interview.

The woman.

Or the morning in general.

KARA WAS HAVING a hard time remaining calm. After her point-blank request for more information regarding their mother, Melanie had insisted that they take a break from such a heavy topic of conversation and order some lunch. Kara had been about to argue when Stella had suddenly jumped up and brought menus, asking the passing waitress to hit them back as soon as she could.

But lunch was done, and so was Kara. She wasn't going to let her sisters in on anything she might or might not do regarding their mother, if they got up to leave without giving her something—anything—that would help her understand her mother's sudden, mostly inexplicable death.

Stella had cleared away their trash, and seemed to have been reaching for her backpack, when a firm glance from their older sister had her slinking back down to her seat.

Then, Melanie's gaze was on Kara only. It was as though Stella wasn't even in the coffee house with them.

"You remember when you were in high school and moved in with Darin and me?" Melanie asked, as though they were still discussing the dressing on their bagel sandwiches.

"Of course." Kara nodded, her wavy, long blond hair making her neck itch. "Josh was just a baby then…"

Melanie smiled, but awkwardly. She most definitely wasn't exuding her normal calm. Which made Kara wish she hadn't just eaten. "Right," her sister said, "but this isn't about that…"

"Oh. You mean…why I moved in? Because of Susan?" Eyes wide, Kara leaned in farther, and in an intense, though soft, tone, said, "Are you telling me Mom killed herself because Dad had the affair? No one ever told me she found out! And… I was born after that…" She'd only learned about the infidelity when she was in high school and had walked into a conversation between her father and Susan regarding friends of theirs who were getting a divorce. That's when she'd found out her father and his second wife had been a thing while her father and mother had still been married.

Stella cleared her throat, and Kara looked over at her

sister. "I went into Mom's room once, when she was pregnant with Kara. She was rubbing her belly and crying. She had this look on her face—it was like she was so in love, and in agony, too. I don't know what that means, or how it helps, but…"

The seemed to come from nowhere, a disconnect from the topic at hand.

While Melanie seemed to be scrambling to find words, Kara asked, "Wait…since Dad married Susan after Mom died…does that mean the affair never ended? And Mom found out? Right after I was born…suicide makes sense, postpartum depression…"

"Oh for God's sake, Kara, Mom didn't kill herself, okay?" Stella's words came out harshly.

Melanie patted Stella's hand and looked at Kara. "Aunt Lila isn't our biological aunt." Melanie threw out the seemingly inconsequential fact. This was old news to Kara.

"I know. She's Mom's best friend."

Melanie, who ended up on the receiving end of a hard glare from Stella, turned back to Kara once again. "Yes, but Lila was a foster child living in Dad's home when Mom met her at school. They became best friends. And that's how Dad met Mom."

"Lila was Dad's foster sister?" The news had so little relevance to the conversation, but was huge, just the same. Lila was kind of her aunt. Not biological. But more than honorary. And…

No. Melanie was not going to distract her again. "Melanie." She glanced to Stella then, and said, "Stella," then looking between them both, "Either you tell me what you know, or you don't. I'm not going to quit looking. I have to understand." Desperately, since she'd seen that plus sign.

Mel took a deep breath. "When Dad told Mom about Susan, Mom freaked out. Dad wanted to fix things, but she was too upset to talk about it. Lila took her to Florida for a girls' week on the beach…"

Melanie named the town, and Kara felt the blood drain from her face. The same name as the old hotel note she'd found when she'd started to get freaked out about being pregnant and had gone to their family storage unit. It had to mean something. Stella's tennis shoe slid softly against the back of Kara's ankle and stayed put.

"Mom…" Melanie had to stop. Frowned. "She wasn't like this, I swear, Kara," she said, looking her little sister deeply in the eye. Kara looked to Stella, and she saw her middle sister nod.

"Mom went a little wild. She'd married Dad at eighteen, straight out of high school. They had me almost right away, and, she never had like a spring break or anything…"

Stella shifted and Melanie got to the point. "Mom convinced Lila to use made up names while they were gone, so she could leave her old life behind, just for that week. And while she was there, she…saw things."

"Saw things?" Kara asked, frowning now, but still okay.

Melanie shook her head, glanced at Stella, who shrugged. "We don't know what things. That's the point. Really."

"What point?"

"Over a year later, after Mom came home, worked things out with Dad, and you were born, Mom found out about a murder that happened in Florida. Turned out, she was the only witness to something that could solve the case."

Eyes wide, Kara practically squealed, "Mom?" Others looked over and Kara quieted. As far as people in North Haven seemed to know, Tory Mitchell had died in a car accident. For some reason, her sisters and father and Aunt Lila wanted to keep it that way. Until she knew more, Kara had to trust that they had good reason.

She made herself sit calmly and listen.

"I don't know much else about it," Melanie said. "Just that the guy on trial was a rich, powerful, really bad guy, the kind that hired hit men." She stopped.

And Kara swallowed. Hardly believing what she was hearing. Like she was part of some kind of low-budget film instead of a loving family.

"You're telling me Mom was murdered by the mob?" Kara's voice was soft, her tone shocked and ragged.

Stella's foot left Kara's leg. "Oh Lord, Kara. Mom's not dead." Stella's bald words hit Kara like a blow to the head.

Her swift intake of air almost choked her. She could feel herself paling.

Melanie sat there, calm as always, as she said, "Mom made a deal with prosecutors in Florida that she'd testify, but only if she could be Jane Doe, and then go into witness protection."

Completely dumbfounded, and searing with an emotional pain she would never have thought possible, Kara whispered, "Mom's alive?" She looked between her sisters, who both just sat there, saying nothing while she read the truth in their expressions. "But…"

"Yeah, what about us." Stella's statement carried a load of bitterness. Something else new to Kara. Her sister was no Pollyanna, but Stella always looked for the way to fix things, or move past them, not get bitter about them.

Melanie cleared her throat, drawing Kara's attention as she said, "She told me she'd made a horrible, horrible mistake going away that week. And that she'd die before any of the three of us paid for it…"

"Like losing our mother didn't come at a huge cost?" Stella piped in anyway, eliciting a huge wide-eyed nod from Kara.

Exactly!

"She was worried about our lives," Melanie said, her gaze

staying on Kara, then. "They let her testify as Jane Doe. She gave a brief statement—filled with concrete proof—and they whisked her away."

"She could have taken us with her." Stella once again blurted out what Kara was thinking but was too stupefied to say.

"I was in high school," Melanie continued as though she hadn't been interrupted. "Darin and I were already together. Stella had just been accepted as the youngest member of the Georgia Interscholastic Debate Team. And you…you were too young to remember her. And Dad… Mom didn't have the right to take us from him. And she said there was no way she could take the three of us from our lovely home to a life where she'd be working full time just to make ends meet, leaving us home alone, with me having to take on a lot of the responsibility for you…" Melanie's gaze had become somewhat distant.

Which was pretty much what had happened, anyway. Minus the losing their lovely home part.

In that first second, Kara was envious of her oldest sister. Having had their mother to love and guide her for so much of their growing up. And then, in her mind's eye, she saw the rest. Melanie had been what…sixteen…and had had her life ripped away from her.

Kara knew that Lila had helped out a lot, but still, Melanie had pretty much become a teenaged mom overnight.

Stella leaned her forearms on the table. "She didn't bother to ask our opinion."

"Would you have gone?" The question came from Kara, but she barely recognized her own voice.

"Yes." Stella nodded. "I needed Mom way more than I needed any of the rest of it. But she put testifying for some stranger over keeping quiet and raising the family she'd created."

"No." Melanie's tone was louder, and so firm, others glanced in their direction. "She gave me the choice to go or stay," her sister said.

Stella gasped, staring open-mouthed, and Kara was watching her when Melanie said, "She made the most difficult choice a woman has ever had to make. Mom's testimony saved lives because of who she put away. A lot of lives. I know that much. And she sacrificed her heart and soul in order to do it."

Stella's harrumph seemed to break Melanie's hold on her temper. Putting her face right in Stella's, she said, "If Dad had chosen to go off to war to fight for his country, purportedly saving unknown lives, leaving us behind, and ended up not making it back, would you think less of him?" She bit the words, clearly in full fighting mode. A mode Kara had never seen before.

Shocked, scared, Kara stared between her two sisters. Needing them to be okay.

Melanie seemed to be daring Stella to say more. Kara waited for her middle sister's well-known mouthiness. Stella wasn't cruel, or mean-spirited. She'd just always refused to be silenced. Had to speak what was on her mind.

When, for once, Stella kept her mouth shut, Kara felt the full weight of how much her life had just irrevocably changed.

# Chapter Three

*You hurt me, or threaten me at all, you can 'spect the same to happen to ones you love.* Ben didn't have to listen to the recording he'd made of the interview with Tina Hansen to hear her words again. They played in his mind all thirty minutes of the drive to the outskirts of Atlanta where he was meeting with prosecutors on the case.

It wasn't the first time he'd been threatened. Or had his family threatened. But it was the first time since he'd been married. And most definitely since he had a family on the way.

He commanded his car's Bluetooth to call Kara. Her phone went straight to voicemail. Which left him more uneasy. "Hey, babe, call me when you get this. And watch your back. I've got an uneasy feeling about this case. Probably just being overcautious, but something doesn't feel right. I love you."

He almost deleted the message during playback. It didn't sound anything like him. But he couldn't not warn her.

And didn't want to be an alarmist, either.

He'd had his share of drama growing up with an insecure mother and actor father. Enough to last a lifetime. Which was part of the reason he'd become a lawyer. Because fact was provable. Law was based on fact, and provided the boundaries for behavior.

Telling the message to Send, Ben stepped up his speed, needing to get done with the meeting ahead and back to North Haven. To Kara.

What the hell!

He'd seen a plus sign, and had gone from elated to being pulled in by the gates of hell less than two minutes later. And couldn't seem to get himself back in sync.

As he neared the city, he started to try Kara a second time, but pushed his steering wheel to click off the call before it connected. The threat Hansen had supposedly sent through his wife likely meant nothing. There was no way Hansen had the means to find out who Ben was, or where he lived, let alone who his wife was. Ben had flashed his badge at Tina from too far a distance for the woman to have read it clearly.

And gave her the officer's card he'd been instructed to leave. Not his own.

Unless... Stuart Miller had someone keeping him informed—someone from his attorneys' office maybe—and knew that Ben had been hired by the prosecutors' office. No way Stuart gave a damn about Hansen, or his wife, but if he thought that Hansen would roll on him?

He'd have a hit out on the guy.

*He'd have a hit out on anyone who tried to use Hansen.*

Was that why Tina had been so scared? Because she knew that her husband's life was in danger? Had someone come to their home? Threatened both of them? And that's why Hansen had run?

The thought, while just conjecture, rang with truth.

And Ben tried Kara one more time.

BEN WAS CALLING. For the second time. Kara couldn't pick up. Couldn't deal with baby questions, or give his joy the consideration it deserved, until she had herself under control.

How did she explain to the man she adored—and wouldn't

willingly hurt at any cost—something that she didn't understand herself?

She'd gone to her sisters for what she'd expected to be
hard answers. But clear ones. And had found out that her
entire life had been a lie.

That everyone in it, those she'd loved most, the ones who'd
raised her, who'd been her safe space, those she'd trusted
forever, had all been lying to her?

Lie. Lie. Lie.

The word was a monotone theme song running through
her head.

She felt foreign in her own skin. Her own car. Nothing
was as she'd thought it to be, because she wasn't who she'd
thought she was.

Her mother was alive?

Could even be living in Atlanta? Or some other small
town close by? Had she been surreptitiously keeping track
of Kara her whole life?

Shaking her head, Kara slammed on the brakes. She'd
almost run a red light.

Granted, she knew very little about witness protection.
Only what she'd seen on television shows that were made
to play up the dramatic aspects of life. But it didn't make
sense that one could stay safe if they had any eyes on their
old life at all.

Tory Mitchell was likely not even in the same state. And
certainly didn't go by that name anymore.

Not trusting herself to safely maneuver the small bit of
traffic that drove through their small town every day, Kara
drove down to the beach, parked, and, leaving the beach
proper, sought out an old cement bench in a sandy cove. It
was her secret place. She could see the water, but couldn't
be seen. Taking her first easy breath since she'd brushed

her teeth that morning, she sat her butt down, welcoming the slight sting of heat through the thin cotton of her skirt.

And gazed out at the reservoir that filled over seventy miles of shoreline.

What a day. Starting with the damned plus sign on a stick. And the rest…

She couldn't wrap her mind around it. Or find herself within it.

She'd always been the one whose mother died right after she was born. As though the tragedy somehow defined her.

She'd expected to get her sisters to admit their mother had committed suicide, and then to show them the scribbled sheet of paper she'd found from what looked to be off a bedside notepad from a hotel in Florida. She'd planned to demand that they give her some real memories of the woman Tory had been. Starting with why their mother had hidden that one piece of paper inside a box of maternity clothes up in the attic of the family home to begin with.

The clothes had been there for her daughters to use, if they wanted to do so, when it came time for them to give birth. But the scribbles on a single sheet of notepaper?

Already feeling unsettled before she'd taken the pregnancy test Ben had insisted on, she'd gone, the week before, to the storage facility where things from the family house had been stored just to get that box. Hoping that seeing the clothes her mother had worn while she'd been pregnant with Kara would somehow give her some confidence in her own mothering capabilities.

Or, at the very least, help her to bond with the woman who'd given her life, but of whom she had no memory of knowing.

Instead, that box, those clothes, the note, along with the other snooping she'd done in news archives and microfiche

of old North Haven school yearbooks over the past week—
had all driven her further from her goal.

Far from curing her mother issues, they'd only escalated
them.

Rather than feeling closer to Tory, she'd felt adrift. Floating out at sea with no paddles or navigation system.

She'd been afraid.

And still was. That was really the gist of it. Kara, the
fearless, young, go-for-the-gold Mitchell sister was scared
of something as natural as becoming a mother.

She'd left her sisters without telling them anything she'd
gone to lunch to share.

Her mother was alive!

Ben should know.

She didn't want to call him.

Which worried her.

She'd had to refuse his lunch date offer. Hadn't told him
she was leaving the clinic a little early. Or let him know
she'd be home for dinner.

Guilt rose, holding hands with her fear while shock looked
on.

Their mother had been forced by her conscience to leave
her three daughters as though they'd never existed. Ripping
out her own heart for the good of many more.

And leaving a lot of pain behind, too.

Kara, aching beyond comprehension at just the thought,
had no idea what to do with any of it.

With a heart dropping like lead, she stared at the beach
in front of her, seeing shapes, not things.

The week in Florida—incidentally where the hotel-room
note had originated. Testifying. And not coming back after
it was over. Three strikes, Mom's out.

For a second there, Kara almost shook her head. How

could her world be inexplicably collapsing around her because of a plus sign?

How could she not be happy to know she was having her own baby?

Because she wasn't. But she couldn't be the family's young darling anymore, either.

With a baby on the way, she had to figure out how to be a mother...

Kara heard a loud rustle. Oommff! Something came down over her head. Tightened. She saw purple. Fighting with both arms, she screamed. Felt big hands on her biceps, holding off her attack, jerking her arms backward. Her phone fell out of her grasp. Her tailbone hit the hard cement of the back of the bench. And something wrapped tight around her wrists. Desperate, she hooked her calves beneath the bench. Held on tightly with her knees. Felt the cement scrape her skin as she refused to give in, but the arms hauling her upward were stronger. Just as she was off the bench, and ready to kick backward, he grabbed her legs, shoved her knees to her chest, and dropped her. On her side. Scrambling to move, Kara came up against hard plastic. A prison of it. Beneath her. Surrounding her. She was in some kind of barrel. Hands grabbed her head from above, shoved some kind of rope in her mouth on top of whatever he'd thrown over her head. Tied the rope behind her neck. Cutting off most of the air intake through her mouth. She tried to think. Breathing in cloth through her nose, staring at purple. Until...seconds later, she saw nothing at all...

BEN TRIED KARA for a third time before going into his meeting. When her phone went straight to voicemail again, he gave a thought to phoning Stella. Kara had had lunch with her sisters.

And stopped himself before he'd even clicked for his contacts.

They weren't in high school. If his wife was choosing to take some time away from him, no matter the reason, he had to respect that.

Not call a mutual close acquaintance with whom his wife had just had lunch to ask how Kara was doing.

Except…what if she was in some kind of trouble?

*If you hurt me, or threaten me at all, you can 'spect the same to happen to ones you love.*

Ben stepped outside the city building to call Stella. Squinting against the sunshine, he pulled his sunglasses from his pocket and hid behind the shades. Watching everyone come and go. Checking out faces. Vehicles he could see leaving from the parking lot.

He wasn't a paranoid guy. Neither was he himself that morning.

Stella's phone had connected. Rung three times.

Something did not feel right. Because he was going to be a father and the world was suddenly seeming entirely different?

Babies were helpless. Fragile.

And children…young, innocent, trusting…

"Ben? What's up?" Stella's upbeat friendliness sounded forced. But then, she'd only been divorced from his best friend for a year. The breakup had happened right after he and Kara were married. He hadn't taken sides. But he and Thane were as much in touch as always.

"Kara's not answering her phone." The blurtation was not what he'd intended.

"I'm sure she's just with a patient. An emergency surgery or something…" The woman's words were appropriate, the way she'd said them…right after meeting with Kara who hadn't been herself all day…

Fear stabbed Ben's gut. "What's going on, Stella?" If he'd been in court, his tone would have had a witness spilling the truth.

"Wow, what's wrong with your day?" the outspoken, and loyal as hell, woman said.

He didn't waste time with an answer. Just waited.

"I was with her less than an hour ago," Stella said then. "She left in one piece."

He stood there biting back…he didn't know what. A whine? A worry? A demand…

He ended up saying, "She scheduled a last-minute lunch with the two of you." Not that private meetings with her sisters were any way inappropriate. She had every right…

But the baby was his, too. He and Kara should be dealing with the situation together.

"She just wanted to talk about our mother."

*Their mother.* Tension eased out of Ben so quickly he was almost lightheaded. A woman facing becoming a mother for the first time—one who'd grown up without her own mother—it all made perfect, healthy, intelligent sense.

In a moment of extreme change, Kara had needed something he couldn't give her. And had sought it out. He'd married a strong, capable woman. He would have smiled, except that he hated that he couldn't make her having grown up without a mother better for her.

It wasn't that she didn't want their baby—that she wasn't as excited as he was—it was a maternal thing. Something he would never be able to fully comprehend. With thoughts of a baby celebration back on the table for that night—and feeling like himself again—Ben hung up. Turned to go back inside.

And stopped.

Kara's seeking motherly talk from her sisters might explain her odd behavior that morning. Even her not picking up the phone the first time he'd called. She might have still been at lunch and the conversation wouldn't have been one she'd have interrupted to answer her phone.

But the last one? Stella had said that she'd left Kara an hour before—or close to that.

After one push of his thumb, Ben held his phone to his ear and listened to the ring on the other end. His call was answered before the second sounded. And he'd hung up within seconds of asking for his wife.

There'd been no emergency at the clinic. Kara wasn't even there. She'd taken the afternoon off.

Running for his car, Ben put in a call to North Haven police and then called the prosecutor with whom he'd been going to meet. Kara wasn't at the clinic. Her sister, with whom she'd had lunch, thought she was. She wasn't answering her phone.

And...

*If you hurt me, or threaten me at all, you can 'spect the same to happen to ones you love.*

He wanted to call Stella back. And Melanie. To have them out looking for their sister. But couldn't chance leading them into possible danger as well.

The police were on it. He'd already given them Kara's routine. Places she might have stopped on her way back to the clinic. Routes she'd likely have taken. Except that she'd taken the afternoon off. How did he know where she'd been headed?

Slamming his hand down on his steering wheel, he cursed his waffling that morning. Letting baby news interfere with his normally sharp thoughts. Worse, letting it interfere with his own ability to trust himself. To trust the judgment that had been guiding him his entire life.

Pedal to the floor, he sped toward home, angry with the miles separating him from where he needed to be.

And scared to death, too.

His wife, his child—his entire heart—was on the line, and there he sat, miles away in his luxury car. Unable to do a damned thing to help them.

Instead of being his reliable self, he'd gotten all caught up in some kind of bizarre, teenage type drama where his wife didn't want their baby because she no longer wanted him. Instead, he'd let Kara and the baby down.

He'd panicked. Second-guessed himself. Lost his window of opportunity.

For no good reason.

He was damn sure old enough to know better.

## Chapter Four

He'd slammed the lid shut on top of her, leaving her in total blackness. Kara's prison had tilted, was being dragged through branches, twigs, and sand, out of the cove. She had to think. To be ready.

For what, exactly?

She'd dropped her phone during her attempt to fight back. All she had on her was her key fob.

Wrenching her left arm almost out of the socket, she got her right hand around to her pocket. Tears of pain sprang to her eyes as she pulled out the device, but she ignored them, pushing to open the manual key that was provided for use in the event of low battery on her SUV's electronic entry. What she'd do with it, she didn't know.

Jab it somehow. As soon as he opened the barrel.

His face would be best.

Or…

The barrel banged into something. Stopped. Then, with a lift and a thud, landed again. Hard. Jerking her left shoulder against the barrel, shooting another sharp pain through her back and down her arm. She ignored the tears.

*Think. Stay in your brain. Your brain. Anatomy. Anatomy.*

*You know.*

The carotid artery. Yes. The carotid. All mammals had them. Humans. Dogs. In the throat. A hard enough jab could kill. Had to go deep enough.

She'd have a good chance with a scalpel. But a blunt-edged piece of thick steel?

Her head bumped against the side of the barrel as her mobile prison hit something. And then the rough passage turned smooth. They were on the cement. The sidewalk. It led to the parking lot.

She was gliding, not being dragged. A barrel on wheels. A trash barrel?

Had there been a city truck when she'd pulled in?

She couldn't remember. Hadn't paid attention. Not at the coffee shop. Not when she arrived. Or when she left. Not driving.

She'd pulled off at the beach because she'd almost had an accident. Because she hadn't been focused.

There could have been someone dressed in a city worker uniform.

An employee dragging a trash receptacle wasn't going to get much attention.

She had to get attention.

She shoved her feet with all her might and barely made a sound. There wasn't room. With her arms stretched behind her, the way she'd been dropped, on her side, fetal position...

She had to sit up somehow.

People. She heard voices. Her prison kept gliding.

Words. She couldn't make them out. Male. Female. Growing weaker.

Where was he taking her?

The big trash receptacle in the parking lot. Brown. A truck came with claws and emptied it when it got full.

More speaking. A laugh. Growing fainter.

"AHHHHH!" Kara gave everything she had to the animalistic sound that ripped through her throat. And to the thrashing that had her head and her shoulders bashing against the hard plastic holding her captive.

The gliding stopped. She froze. Held her fob. Sobbing, but ready, too.

He might be stronger, untied, able to stand...

But she wasn't going to die without a fight.

BEN WAS TEN minutes from town when his car system announced a call from the North Haven Police Department.

He pushed the steering wheel to take the call before the automated voice had finished naming the caller. "Yeah?"

"It's Doug, Ben." Doug Zellers. He recognized the detective's voice. They'd worked a case together shortly after Ben and Kara had married.

"Yeah," he said again. No time for pleasantries.

"We've got her. She's okay. At urgent care now—she strained her shoulder—but otherwise is fine. If you're close, you can meet her there."

He heard it all. Passed by everything but the "she's okay" in those first seconds. Concentrated on his driving. Signaled the turnoff for a country road that made a more direct route to the medical center. And then posed the question that had to be asked. "What happened?"

She could have been in a car accident. He knew, just by Doug's subdued tone that it was worse than that.

"We're still looking at that," Doug said. "She gave a brief statement, of course, and they've done an X-ray... Officer Allen is with her now and will be bringing her to the station as soon as they're done there."

There. The medical center. He was breaking the speed limit by a lot and was still seven or so minutes out...

"What we know is that she was sitting on that old cement

bench in the cove. Said someone came up from behind her, put a bag over her head, tied her hands, gagged her, and threw her in a trash bin. He was apparently wheeling it toward the parking lot when he got spooked. She was making what noise she could, and by the time someone heard her, there was no one else in sight. Just the trash bin on the edge of the parking lot. With her tied up inside."

He almost puked all over himself. No way he was stopping to do so. Swallowing back bile, jaw clenched, Ben said, "You talk to witnesses?" He was an investigator. He would find whatever answers there were.

"Yeah. No one noticed anything. We had patrols out looking for her in every place you mentioned. The beach was one of them. A squad car had already pulled into the lot by the time someone heard her. She said the barrel had only been still for a minute or two before she was rescued. Best we figure, the guy saw our car pull in, got spooked, and walked off and left her there."

"I'm assuming forensics is all over the barrel? And cameras on the lot?"

"Yes to the forensics, though Kara says he was wearing gloves. And the cameras had just been disabled. As though they'd been following her and saw their chance."

The abduction had been planned. The how was quick work.

Had Stuart Miller's legal team found out that Ben was working the case? And the serial killer had somehow gotten the news to Hansen?

Thanking Doug, asking to be kept informed, Ben then hung up and put in a call to the prosecutors' office. They needed to know everyone Stuart Miller had been in contact with. Phone calls. Visitors. Any outgoing mail.

He'd be looking at Miller's legal team. And looking for Hansen, too.

Just as soon as Kara was settled someplace safe.

THERE'D BEEN A SCENT. Having a few seconds alone in the urgent care cubicle, with a police officer right outside and—she'd been told—Ben on the way, Kara caught a whiff of alcohol. Welcomed it. A strong smell that felt…normal to her. She was around it every day at the clinic.

It had never brought tears to her eyes before. As she closed her lids against the new onslaught, she told herself it was a natural reaction to having been abducted—and rescued before anything horrible happened to her.

But it was the familiarity of the alcohol smell that was making her weepy with thankfulness. With relief. Making her feel warm where she'd been growing colder and colder all day.

Because…it completely cleaned out another smell from her system. There'd been a smell. In the bag put over her head? Before that?

A weird combination…like…chocolate mixed with musty cologne and cigarette smoke?

Realizing how off-the-wall the thought was, Kara shook her head. Had there been a smell? Or had she just been half-way hallucinating in there?

In.

Shivering, she shook her head. Cleared it. She'd been thinking about chocolate—she remembered that. Had tried to focus on something good, something she liked. Had thought about the chocolate shavings she liked on top of her hot chocolate. Something she only ordered at her regular coffee house.

She'd been inside a trash can. Explained the sense of cigarette ash. Trash.

And she'd seen a patient that morning…an older German shepherd with an even older male owner—who'd been wearing a shirt that looked like he'd had it on a few days. Musty cologne.

She was fine.

Not losing lucidity.

She'd barely taken an easy breath before she heard commotion outside in the hallway, muted voices. Her door flew open with such force, she drew in a loud sharp breath. And saw Ben.

Her Ben. The brown eyes seeing straight into her heart. She let him. Seeking his as well…and came up blank. Like he'd blocked her.

Understandable. He was in work mode.

"You're okay?" he asked, eying the sling holding her left arm steady at her side as he sat in the chair next to hers. And glanced from her to the bed she'd already vacated.

"Yes," she told him. "I strained my upper arm and shoulder, but there's no tendon damage. I was reaching for my fob. I'm a little sore. But the sling is overkill."

He grabbed her free hand. Squeezed it. And let it go. As though he wasn't sure what physical contact she could take. Or would welcome.

Wrapping her right arm around his neck, she hugged him. Held on. Felt his arm slide behind her back. Squeezing her into him gently. All the way.

And for a second, she just wanted to lay her head on his shoulder and stay there. But knew she couldn't. Her abductor could still be close by. Every second counted if they were going to catch him.

As though he'd read her thoughts, Ben said, "They want you to wait on results of the X-ray, just to be sure."

She'd been told. And had a feeling he'd been made privy to her response as well. "I said no," she told him. "I'm fine and want to get to the station. I know my body, Ben. I'm okay. And if there was some unknown damage in my shoulder, I can always come back."

He was an investigator. He'd get that she understood how important it was that she be thoroughly questioned while the incident was still so clearly in her mind.

Interrogation could help her recall something she didn't know she knew. Real memories that could be critical to finding out who'd tried to kidnap her. Not like her own segue to remembered scents prompted by the familiar smell of alcohol.

Ben was shaking his head slowly, and she shook her own, too. Harder. "He could already be out there trying to get his next victim, Ben. I got lucky. The next woman might not be." And then, at his frown, softly added, "I've got medical training. I'll call the doctor at the first sign of anything not right." It was a promise to him.

And to the plus mark, too. She'd seen the stick. She had an obligation.

"I'd feel better if you stayed here long enough to get the all clear," Ben told her. And she knew he was thinking like the new father he was going to be—not like the top-rated lawyer and investigator she needed in that moment.

"He didn't hurt me physically, Ben," she said, looking him straight in the eye. "He put a bag over my head. Tied my hands behind me. Picked me up and, shoving my knees toward my chest, dropped me a couple of feet into the barrel. That's it. I never even saw him."

"But you knew he had gloves on."

"I felt the leather against my skin when he secured my wrists."

"What about his voice?"

There. That's what she needed. Ben, single-focused. In top form. As she'd heard him so many times in the past.

"He never spoke."

She shivered. Felt the bag slide over her head. Tears filled her eyes.

Ben pulled her to him then. Right up onto his lap. Holding her close. Like a baby. When she hadn't mentioned the one she was carrying.

She laid her cheek against his shoulder. He kissed the top of her head.

But neither of them said a word.

KARA WAS TRAUMATIZED. How could she not be? First thing Ben had to do was comfort his young, pregnant wife.

Then he had to find Hansen, find out who'd sent someone after Kara—Hansen or one of Miller's goons. He had to tell his wife that her abduction was because of him. Because of the case he was working. He'd brought the danger home to her.

And they had to talk about the baby.

Not in any particular order. All three matters were of crucial priority.

But taking a moment, or however many she needed, to comfort her, to be thankful that she'd escaped before anything horrible had happened to her—that definitely came first.

She'd been lying against him less than a minute—barely enough time for him to get a few easy breaths in—before she sat up. "I need to get to the police station," she said. "Time is critical."

He wanted her to have an ultrasound. Something, anything to check that the baby was okay. But after she'd told him what had happened, he knew that his preference was overkill. More important was managing her stress level.

She stood up, took the fob out of her pocket like she could just walk out to the parking lot and have her car be there.

Half believing she would just walk out and leave him sitting there if he didn't choose to follow, he asked, "Did you tell the doctor about the baby?" He at least had to know that much.

She was at the door. "Yes," she said, then pulled on the handle and stepped outside.

Ben was right behind her. Intending to give her a ride. But the officer outside the door came forward and said, "You ready to go?" She'd made other plans, apparently.

Made sense. While she wasn't a suspect, she was technically still in police custody. The victim of a violent crime. She didn't have to ride in the squad car, but seemed hell-bent on doing so.

She turned back to Ben. "You're coming to the station, too, aren't you?"

The question, reassuring him that he mattered to her, stirred sense back into him. The woman wasn't herself. But she was standing on her own two feet—which said a hell of a lot about her. "Of course," he told her. "I'll take you back to get your car from there," he added. Needing to be an important part of her recovery.

He needed to tell her about his part in her abduction, too. Before the police did. "How about if you ride with me now?" He made the suggestion that should have come from him from the beginning. And would have. If he hadn't been busy doubting where she stood within their relationship. Doubting that she was still with him for a lifetime.

His lifetime, at any rate. If they lived normal lifespans, he'd be gone a decade before she'd... No.

Kara hadn't answered his question. He saw her glance at the uniformed officer, who shrugged, said it was up to her, and then walked toward Ben as though she was as much his wife as she'd always been.

Because she was.

They were just having one hell of a hard moment. On a

day that should have been one of the best memories of their lives. No fault of hers. His career had nearly cost her her life.

And he had about seven or eight minutes to tell her as much. Or Doug would when she arrived at the station.

Kara didn't link her hand in the crook of his elbow, or hold his hand as they walked out. Nor did she let Ben get close enough to wrap an arm around her. She stayed evenly spaced between him and the police officer. Who was busy telling Ben the protocol for the next few minutes. They'd be driven from the cruiser at the curb to his car in the parking lot. Then followed to the station.

He was to go in the west door. Someone would be standing by watching for them, to let them in.

Good plans. Speaking to the very real danger that still lurked all over them.

Something Kara had yet to find out.

During the minute or so he rode in the back seat of the cruiser—with Kara up front with the officer—Ben entertained the idea of calling Melanie. Working out a plan to whisk Kara away to some safe house in another state for a day or so. At least. Long enough for him to do his job, get Hansen in custody, find out who'd abducted his wife, and slap shackles around that man's wrists, too.

Without killing the bastard. Which was what he wanted to do.

He was still on that train of thought—the safe house, not the murder—liking it more and more, as Kara climbed into what he thought of as her seat in the Mercedes and pulled the seat belt down around her. With her right hand only. She was holding her left arm almost completely still.

Because her shoulder hurt more than she was saying? He took note. But left it alone. He had bigger issues to tackle first.

And as had been happening since she'd looked at that stick and acted so completely out of the ordinary, he looked at Kara differently as he started the engine. Had things been changing gradually without him noticing? It had taken a major moment to get his attention?

And the gods chose to send two of them in one day to make sure they had his attention?

They had him. By the balls.

"We need to talk, Kara," he started in before he'd even pulled off the lot.

And she started shaking her head even before he'd finished the sentence. "Not now, Ben. I need my mind on what just happened. We have no idea what I might know that can help catch this guy."

He glanced at her, his stomach sinking deep. She'd thought he'd wanted to talk about the pregnancy test results.

And she wasn't willing to do so.

Just as she hadn't been that morning in their bathroom. Or when he'd called her later.

She'd run to her sisters instead. Needing to talk about their mother. A woman both Stella and Melanie remembered.

And Ben had to chill. To give Kara time to deal with some things he would never ever be able to fully comprehend. Or experience. Growing up without a mother. Becoming one. And how the two were interrelated. He could support her struggle, but he couldn't help her with it.

But her sisters could.

He pulled to a stop at the light just outside the medical center and turned to her. "For the record, what we need to talk about is what happened on the beach." She turned to look at him, and let him hold her gaze, so he continued. "And as to the other…you take the time you need, Kara. I'll be here. No pressure."

She didn't tear her gaze away right away. She swallowed. Glanced toward the front windshield, then back at him just as the light changed, and he had to keep his focus forward.

"What do we need to talk about right now?" she asked then. Acknowledging that there was another elephant on the table between them?

"I have a lead on your abductor."

He heard her gasp. Spared a brief glance to see her, open-mouthed, stare at him, just before she said, "You do? Oh, thank God, Ben, who is he?" Her voice thickened with tears on the last part.

He didn't want to speak again. To go from hero to zero in her eyes. But he did. "I don't know, yet. But I know where to start looking. The appointment I had this morning...the case I'm working on...the guy I'm charged with finding is an accomplice to a serial killer just brought into custody." He heard another gasp. Wouldn't have looked over even if he could. Just had to get it out.

"I went to see the accomplice's wife this morning. He'd left her with a threat to issue to anyone who came looking for him—speak to her, and he'd be after their loved ones."

He pulled to a stop at the street before his right turn into the station. Turned toward Kara and saw her watching him.

Not with horror, but...compassion in those big brown eyes framed with her soft, long, flowing hair. God, he loved her.

"Don't blame yourself, Ben," she said then. Her tone weak, not herself, but her sincerity was clear. "I knew the dangers inherent in your career before I married you. And I know that between you and the police, you'll get this guy. Put them both away forever so that the rest of us can live safe, normal lives."

He listened because he had to. And because he wanted to. Needed to. She'd said some of the same before. But after what had just happened...

"The world needs you, and others like you. People who have the ability and the willingness to fight the fight for good, Ben."

Before he could respond, the squad car behind him honked, and he had to pull into the police station.

And give up the brief bit of privacy he'd had with his wife.

Long before he was ready.

## Chapter Five

She'd remembered very little else. The barrel had been empty. The gloves felt like leather. He'd come from behind the bench. She hadn't heard him. Just a rustle as the bag came down. The covering over her head had been purple.

She didn't remember seeing a city worker, or trash collector at all that day. Not at her clinic. Not at the North Haven Coffee Shop. And not at the beach.

But then, she'd been…preoccupied. Hadn't paid any attention at all to surroundings. Her thoughts had been inward. And lost in lies.

The only good piece of evidence she'd had to offer was that when the guy had stood behind her, after he'd tied her hands behind her back, and just before he'd lifted her into the barrel, her head had been below his chin. Almost directly. Which put him a head taller than her five foot five.

Doug and Ben were both energized by the small piece of evidence.

And she was certain he was a man. She'd felt that evidence during that brief second, too. Almost at her tailbone.

Which gave them an idea of how long his legs were.

She'd forgotten that last part completely until Doug and Ben were on either side of her, taking her through the abduction for the fifth or sixth time.

And then they were done. She was free to go. Ben would take her to get her car. He'd go back to work. And...so would she.

"We need to get you out of town," Ben said as they walked down a vacant hall toward the private west door through which they'd entered.

She stopped. "Out of town?" She frowned up at him.

"They missed you this time, Kara, but chances are they'll try again." He was frowning, too. The look that meant he wasn't going to be easily swayed.

A look that gave her insight but had never stopped her from standing her ground if she believed the situation warranted as much.

"Doug didn't seem as sure of that." She said the first thing that came to mind. "He said that it's just as likely they'll go for someone else. You aren't the only one working the case."

"I'm the only one who approached Tina."

"He also said that they aren't going to risk getting caught by trying to come after me again. They know we'll be on high alert. Have extra security measures in place. I feel like I'd be safer here, frankly, than anywhere else. If I'm off in hiding, and they find me, I've got less chance of surviving." She was spitballing. Sort of. There were safe houses. But they were breached sometimes. And if that Stuart Miller guy had friends in high places, it seemed more likely to her that a safe house abduction would be much easier for someone on the payroll, than finding her out in plain sight. With a whole lot of eyes that could be on her. Everyday eyes. Cameras. The people who knew her.

Ben stood silently. Staring her down.

Not something he'd ever done before. They talked. Each side got aired. And they found ways to make things work. "I've got security cameras all over the clinic," she reminded him.

"You're caring for two now, Kara." He sounded like... her father. In a tone he'd never ever used with her before.

She felt slapped. Insulted. "You think I don't realize that?" she asked him, calmer than she'd have expected. Most particularly with what she'd just been through. The terrifying moments. The struggle to grasp that it had happened at all.

And to feel safe now that she'd been set free.

Yet, maybe because of the near-fatal episode, Kara was avoiding all drama. From within herself. And coming at her, too. Her mind and body's way of keeping her together, she supposed.

Her mother...the baby...neither of those mattered if she wasn't alive. She had to deal with one thing at a time. Recovering from being abducted came first.

Ben continued to watch her. His lips tightening. Loosening. His eyes seeming to speak, but she couldn't decipher their message. Until he said, "I'm not sure what to think."

He'd just spent a hellacious hour, too. Knowing that his wife—newly pregnant—had been abducted. With all the crime and tragedy he'd seen in his career as a gun-carrying private investigator, she could only imagine the horrors that had run through his brain.

With him powerless to help.

She knew that Ben hated that most of all—feeling powerless.

Putting her hand in the crook of his suited elbow, she turned toward the door. "Let's just take a few breaths, okay?" she suggested. "I need to get back to the clinic. To Celia. These next twenty-four hours are critical for her and those pups. I might need to supplement formula if she doesn't have enough milk for all of them." Concentrating on her job helped. Gave her confidence. And a sense of her own well-being and health. "I'm as safe there as I'd be anywhere," she added when Ben started to walk slowly toward the door with her. "You can hire someone to stand guard, if you'd like."

That was it. The best she could do in terms of compromise.

Ben could take it or leave it, but she was going back to work. And would hire her own guards if it came to that.

It felt like if she didn't carry on, with all that had happened that day, she might just lose her sense of control over reality.


SHE WAS RIGHT. Her clinic was safer than a lot of places. Except that it was *her* clinic and anyone who'd want to find her would know right where to look.

Maybe that was the point. Keep her close, with eyes all over her. Rather than sending her off where no one knew her. And where, if her location was breached, she'd only have a few guards to keep her safe. With no witnesses.

By all accounts, no one should have been able to identify him as Tina's visitor that morning. Let alone find his wife and have time to make a plan to follow her, to snatch her when the occasion arose. Which meant that someone on the inside, someone who'd found out he was working for the prosecutor on the case, was feeding information to criminals.

Could that same person, by the same unknown means, find out where Ben had her hidden away, if he could somehow get her to go? Enlisting her sisters was still a possibility. He'd never known Kara to directly refuse to do something, or not do something, if they both felt strongly about it.

Partially because they didn't play the ultimatum card often.

Did he really want her far away from him?

No. That answer was immediate. Clear.

So... "Are you planning to spend the night at the clinic?"

She'd said the next twenty-four hours were critical. She could assign technicians to stay, but she didn't always.

They'd stepped outside and Ben hustled her into his car, before hurrying to the other side and climbing in.

She was looking at him. "I'd like to spend the night at the clinic," she said to him. Then added, "You planning to stay with me?"

There were two cots that he knew of.

She wasn't completely shutting him out. "I'd like to," he told her, his mind buzzing over the arrangements that should be made over the next few hours. While their home had as much security as the clinic, it was on half an acre of property in a quiet neighborhood of large, wooded yards. The clinic, while far less convenient and comfortable, was right in town. With the added benefit of traffic cameras.

Still, they'd need toiletries, clothes, food. And off-duty officers taking shifts to watch the place. At least for the night.

Glancing at her as he drove—before returning his gaze to the busy traffic on Main Street and watching for any hint that someone might be following them—he discussed details with her as though she was any person he'd just agreed to protect.

Because it was what she seemed to need.

She'd held his arm as they'd left the station—a normal activity when they were walking together—and yet, she'd felt…distant. Separated. Apart.

Because of the abduction?

The baby?

Or had her pulling away been going on for a while and he'd been too caught up in his own world—work, schedules, obligations, and their pleasure excursions—to notice that she wasn't sharing with him as she used to do?

A beat-up blue truck had been behind him since he'd turned out of the police station. He hadn't thought anything of it except that when he'd slowed, it had as well. He'd taken a side street around the corner to Main and it had done the same. And when he changed lanes, it did, too.

It didn't come close enough for him to make out the driver. But he said, "Take a look in your side-view mirror—that blue truck, see it?"

Kara glanced without making it obvious. "Yeah." She said the word slowly. "Why?"

"Have you ever seen it before? Today in particular?"

"No." She didn't hesitate on that one. "I think I'd remember. It's got a dog collar hanging from the rearview mirror."

A large one. Multicolored. He hadn't noticed. But Kara would.

Relaxing his diligence not at all, Ben drove on.

CELIA WAS DOING very well. Her incision looked good. And with the technician's and then Kara's help, all six pups were getting their turns at her teats, though only getting colostrum for the time being. It would be another two to three days before the transition to milk would happen, and that's when Kara would really be able to determine whether the small mother would be able to produce enough nutrition to feed all six of her pups.

Maggie, Celia's owner, was in for an hour late that afternoon. She hadn't heard about Kara's mishap, and Kara hoped it stayed that way. The town was small, but the police were doing what they could to keep things quiet. And out of the news. All those at the scene were asked not to speak of the incident as the case was ongoing. They were under no legal mandate to comply, however.

Kara had called her sisters while still in Ben's car to let them know what had happened. Stella was at a fundraiser to support a fight against book banning. And Melanie was in Atlanta with her ex-husband and son at a sporting event.

They'd both said they were coming home immediately, but with Ben's input, she'd managed to convince them that she was fine, at work, and in no need of company.

Physically, she'd been telling the truth. She'd taken the sling off when she'd arrived at the clinic and was doing just fine without it. Her shoulder was sore, but didn't prevent her from doing anything.

She'd be careful not to overextend her left arm, or to lift with it, and figured she'd be back to normal within a day or two.

Ben had come in around seven, bringing pasta and salads for dinner—handing her the piece of dry, butterless French bread that she always had with pasta—and spent the time filling her in on details of the investigation into her abduction.

Basically, no news, but he went through everything that had been looked at, giving reports on each item, just the same.

It was good to know that the police and prosecutors' office were being so thorough, both in North Haven and in Atlanta, where the Miller case would be charged and tried.

The topic of conversation made it a little more difficult to eat. But she forced herself to do so. Slowly. Small bites. Well chewed. As much to keep Ben from calling her on her appetite as the knowledge that she had a second life depending upon her diet.

He'd brought clothes and toiletries, too. She didn't even look in the bag to see what he'd chosen for her. Couldn't find the energy to care.

She was too busy expending everything she had on keeping her spirits above water.

Her entire life had been a lie.

She'd been abducted.

The plus sign.

Ben.

She felt like a Ping-Pong ball. Unless she focused on work. It was all that felt halfway normal to her. The only place she could contribute anything of value.

Ben went to work on his computer as she put leftovers in the refrigerator with the other dairy and fresh vegetable staples he'd brought in with him. She threw the used containers and disposable utensils in the trash, then checked on Celia. Changed papers in the bigger kennel where the bulldog and her babes would sleep for the night.

And, grabbing her bag, she went into the shower just outside the small operating room in the clinic. Decided to throw away the linen pants and short-sleeved pullover shirt she'd had on all day.

Funny how you could be abducted, thrown in a barrel, and not get your clothes dirty. Not in any way that the eye could see. She'd never see them as anything but tainted again.

Her shoulder felt better under the hot spray, and she lingered there for a bit. Until she knew she could put off bedtime no longer and, in the cotton dog-print pajama pants and matching, short-sleeved top Ben had brought her and a pair of flip flops—a gift from Melanie the year she'd graduated from veterinary school—she traipsed through the quiet hall to her private office.

She'd already set up the two cots. Had hauled out the sleeping bags she kept in the closet for those rare occasions she had patients overnight. And walked in to find Ben already encased in one of them, a T-shirt over his normally bare chest, with his laptop open on top of it.

"You want the light on or off?" she asked, feeling more awkward than she had the first night she'd ever slept with the man.

They'd been married a year, and in less than a day, he'd

become somewhat of a stranger to her. Her fault. She got that. Just didn't know how to fix it.

How to fix herself.

Closing his laptop, he said, "Off is fine."

She flipped the switch gratefully. Leaving only a dim light from the hallway coming in from under the door. She didn't want to look at him, or have him looking at her, as they ended the day without a kiss good-night. The first time... since they'd started dating three years before.

She could go to him. Kiss him. *Should* do so.

But didn't. It felt forced. The kiss wouldn't be honest. And she couldn't bear to have lies between them. Hard enough that there were things she couldn't talk about, couldn't explain—even to herself.

"I just checked with the guards outside," he said as she slid into her bag. The furniture in the room—her desk jutting out from one wall, a couch on another, and life-size anatomy mold of a dog taking up yet another—left no option but to have the cots perpendicular to each other. "They're in place, all is quiet."

He had a radio he could talk into that was directly connected to earpieces the guards were wearing.

Guards outside watching over her—the necessity for them—was not anything she wanted to think about. Most particularly not in the dark.

Maybe she should have left the light on.

"I'll need to check on Celia in a couple of hours," she said then. "But she's doing great. All six pups have nursed. She seems to have fully accepted them."

"There was a chance they wouldn't?" His question came at her loudly in the small room. She might have imagined the sharpness in his tone. Didn't think so.

"The chance is more prevalent with C-sections," she told

him. "Some dams even attack the pups if they near her incision point."

Quiet fell then. Leaving her to wonder, a couple of minutes later, if Ben was asleep. He'd always been able to drop right off. She'd just thought…that night…there'd be…more.

She'd been dreading the moment where they were going to talk about the stick they'd seen together that morning. Mostly because she had no idea what to tell him. He'd been so elated.

"Did you tell your sisters?" His voice came softly that time. Kindly. And she relaxed some.

"Yeah, they know. They were glad to hear that Celia made it in general."

"I meant about the baby."

*Baby.*

She tensed all over again. He said, "Isn't that why you had lunch with them today?"

Right. She could see why he'd think that. And needed to tell him that her mother was alive. She just couldn't talk about it. Not then. Not with everything else going on.

She couldn't answer his inevitable questions. About any of it.

"No," she said, after too long of a pause. Then, finding the response too unequivocal, added, "Not yet. And… I'd appreciate it if you didn't say anything. This soon…"

His silence worked as well as any words would have done.

Kara couldn't get the note she'd found in the maternity clothes off her mind. But didn't know why. Her sisters had explained Tory's visit to Florida.

It was like…a private message between her mother and her. It wasn't. Her mother would surely have expected Melanie and then Stella to use the clothes first.

Melanie hadn't done so. Kara hadn't asked why.

Nor was she sure why she hadn't told her sisters about

the notepaper she'd found. She'd looked up the resort. Had even looked on the internet for photos from the summer before her mother was supposedly killed. Thinking maybe she'd taken the family there for vacation. And that the hotel posted guest photos with permission. A memory that might bring renewed pain to her sisters. But help Kara.

There'd been guest photos. None of her mother or sisters.

And Ben's silence was starting to get too loud for her to just lie with it.

Taking a deep breath, she tried her best to find some kind of clarity for him. Why hadn't she told her sisters she was pregnant? "I need some time to get used to the idea myself, Ben, before I deal with their involvement." And since their lunch, she needed time to digest the news they'd given her.

"I see," he finally responded, uncomfortably long seconds later.

"I don't think you do." How could he, when she didn't even understand? He was a brilliant lawyer, and had ten years living experience on her, but he'd never been pregnant.

Didn't even practice medical law.

Whereas she…she'd delivered six babies that day. Granted, of the canine variety, but…panic hit…

What in the hell was wrong with her?

"Will you answer one question?" He sounded tired.

And…older.

"Of course."

"Do you plan to have this baby?"

She closed her eyes. Couldn't believe he was even asking. "As opposed to?"

"Not."

The flare of anger that passed through her came and went. Given the way she'd been acting, the question was probably…more fair than she wanted it to be.

"I'm not even considering that option," she told him softly.

"And even if I was, I'd consult with you first. This is your child as much as it is mine. But no. *Not* is not on the table."

"Yet you aren't happy."

"Not at the moment, no." Not. Not. Not.

She could feel his pain mingling with hers. Knew she was ruining what would have been one of the happiest moments of his life. Hated herself for that.

But couldn't go another moment being the person everyone wanted her to be.

How could she be responsible for the happiness and emotional health of another human being if she wasn't even sure where others stopped, and she began? Her whole life she'd been coddled. Watched over. Babied. Had her battles fought for her by her two very protective, much older sisters.

Her whole life she'd been lied to.

And had been floundering so much from the news, she hadn't even noticed that she'd been followed.

What if she really couldn't stand on her own two feet? How, then, would she teach someone else to walk?

She had eight months to figure herself out.

And get it right…

Or turn out like her own mother? A woman who ran off…

Panic swarmed heavier within her.

"I love you, Kara."

She wanted to tell him to come hold her.

Wanted to crawl into his waiting arms, and…what?

Lose herself some more?

She swallowed back tears, found her voice, said, "I love you, too."

Then closed her eyes.

## Chapter Six

Ben didn't sleep worth a damn. Shutting off and slipping into a natural unconscious state wasn't a problem for him. But that night on the cot in Kara's office, staying asleep became an issue. He'd doze off. And fifteen minutes to an hour later, would find himself lying there fully conscious. The physical conditions could be to blame, but Ben knew the foldaway bed wasn't the issue.

He'd almost lost Kara that afternoon.

And had apparently been losing her for some time before that, too. Had he been so content—okay, happy—in his own view of their relationship, that he'd failed to consider her? To really see her?

To be aware of her needs?

Clearly, he'd failed to understand something.

The woman was the most compassionate individual he'd ever met, and she wasn't happy to be pregnant with her own child. He just did not get it.

He understood two things, though. First, she was in danger and he was not going to let anything happen to her. That the danger was because of him was an issue to be dealt with at a later date.

And second, she'd made it clear that whatever was bothering her was not something she could discuss with him at the current time. Maybe the reason had nothing to do with him. Maybe it did. Maybe he'd failed to create a safe place for her within his personal world. Again, something to delve into in the future.

Up at dawn the next morning, Ben quietly left the office where Kara was sleeping after her last check on Celia. Out of earshot of his wife, he radioed with the off-duty officers he'd hired privately to keep Kara safe, heard that there'd been no suspicious activity during the night, and had one of them come inside long enough for him to jump in the tiny shower in the back of the operating room.

A shower that had been installed as a safety measure. In place in the event anyone would be exposed to anything contagious, dangerous, or lethal in the operating room. Because Kara was just that conscientious.

In the gray suit and tie he'd brought in the night before, he stood in the small break room where they'd had an uncomfortable dinner, and drank coffee. Planning his day.

Two things. Simultaneously. Find the scum who'd attempted to hurt his wife. And give Kara the emotional space she needed from him.

As he stood there, leaning on the counter, his gaze landed on a wall hanging by the one table for four in the room. A depiction of a butterfly. And the verbiage *If you love something, set it free. If it loves you, it will fly back.*

It was like Kara had gotten up in the night, purchased the damned thing just for him, and hung it up so he'd be sure to see it. She knew he couldn't start his morning right without that coffee. A minimum of two cups.

He set down his first, still half full, and walked out the door.

WITH THE OFF-DUTY officers hanging around unobtrusively, Kara saw patients Saturday morning. No one was allowed in the building that the staff didn't recognize as an owner of a current patient. Thankfully, there were no new patients on the schedule.

Her staff had been apprised of the near abduction—as a random attack—the afternoon before, and were asked to keep the information quiet and let the police do their jobs.

North Haven was a small town. News would travel—but hopefully not in a loud way. Or too fast for investigators to find out who'd been pulling a trash can in the parking lot the previous day.

Several people expressed concern and compassion for her as she worked, and she smiled, thanked them, assured them she was just fine.

She wanted to be.

Needed to be.

Her shoulder pain was minimal. There wasn't a single bruise on her body—not even where her wrists had been bound—though the area was a bit sensitive to the touch.

As she worked, she started to feel better inside, too. To regain a sense of self, of being in control, and was able to give genuine smiles, to feel the joy as Celia's owner—the last appointment of the day—came to pick up her girl and the six pups.

"You get the pick of the litter if you want it," the woman, Maggie, said to Kara. "I know things are chaotic right now and you don't have to decide for several weeks, but keep us in mind…"

Kara hid the sudden spurt of tears the offer brought by reaching down to pet Celia, and take one last glance at the pups, as she said, "I might just take you up on that offer, thank you!" And was still pondering the response, minutes later, back in her office.

She'd always wanted a dog of her own but hadn't seriously considered getting one. Didn't even know if Ben would welcome a dog into their home.

They'd talked about starting a family—his concern about his age a major factor to him—but never about what that family would actually look like.

She'd loved their plans. Her sudden reticence, as plan became reality so quickly, was a complete shock to her.

And something she was going to have to come to terms with immediately.

So, thinking, she closed her office door and pulled out the folder she'd started the previous week when, late for her period, she'd experienced the first unexpected stirrings of unease about actually having a child growing inside her.

Needing her.

Calling her *Mom*.

She'd gone online for old yearbooks, first. Found a couple of photos of her mom—one with her parents together at some kind of pep rally. Had printed them all. She'd seen photos of her mother, of course. In an album that Melanie had. There hadn't ever been any around the house while she was growing up. Mention of their mother had always upset Stella.

And there was Susan…the sticky widget that no one ever mentioned…the woman who'd broken up her parents' marriage in the first place, who had then, after their mother's death, become their stepmother. Kara had grown up thinking—rightly or wrongly—that part of the reason no one mentioned Tory was because it would upset Susan.

For whatever reason, her stepmother had never become a mother figure to her. Maybe because Kara represented a union between her mom and dad that took place after the extra-marital affair her father had initially had with Susan?

She'd been all of eight when Stella had graduated and left for college. Melanie and Darin were already married, and Kara had spent as much time at their house as she had at her father's.

Because everyone, but her—everyone including Susan—

knew that Tory was still alive. The marriage between her mother and father had never been terminated through death. Or divorce. But by some means that the government had in their process of making people disappear. Some things were starting to make sense—in the present.

Tory had never been a figure in Kara's life. An entity. A memory kept alive for the daughter who hadn't known her. The mother just died, and others took over. Tory hadn't had a place.

She'd been a ghost.

One who was haunting the hell out of Kara.

And then Kara walked into a coffee shop for lunch with the sisters she'd known and trusted her entire life—trusted *with* her life—and had come out with a live mother? And an entire life that had been a lie?

If they hadn't known…but they had. All of them. Her father. Aunt Lila. Susan. Melanie and Stella. They'd all been lying to her her entire life.

The first three hurt. But Melanie and Stella…she had no idea how she would deal with them. Their cuts went much deeper. Soul deep.

Which meant, for the time being, she wouldn't do anything where they were concerned. She wouldn't seek them out. And she wouldn't avoid them when they sought her out.

What she could do was find out about her mother. She had to know the woman who'd given birth to her—then left her behind.

And the first place she looked was in the exclusive, out-of-the-way Florida beach town where her mother and Lila had spent their week away. Homed in on the hotel from which she'd found the odd note the week before, scribbled on paper torn from a hotel pad. Melanie said there'd been a murder. It had to have been late the summer before she was born, based on the fact that her parents had gotten pregnant with her shortly after—since she'd only been a year old when her mother left.

The victim must have been someone important, since witness protection was involved.

Surely it had made the news…

Maybe just something as simple as knowing what her mother must have seen, who was killed, would help her understand the good that came from the ultimate sacrifice Tory had made. That could help Kara find the piece of herself that was missing. The part of her that could see herself as a real mother, of a real baby.

Not just the distant caregiver of animals.

Kara found old crime reports. Headlines that sounded as though they could be what she wanted. She read through article after article. Expanded her search to all of Florida, and then nationally. Whoever had been killed had been important enough for someone very powerful to have ordered the hit.

But it wasn't until she looked specifically for the county where she supposed the murder had to have taken place, a year after she was born, adding in the name of the hotel to her search, that she found something.

A two-paragraph article in a county weekly, mentioning a trial at the courthouse. The proceeding only lasted a couple of days, instead of the weeks residents had dreaded.

A man had killed his little brother. And the star witness was named Jane Doe.

Shaking, she stood. Paced her office. Cried some. Went back to her desk and read again. Took the information from that short clipping and did broader searches. Looking for on-line court records. And finally realized—just as Tory had been whisked away—everything else about the case had been sealed.

Which in itself told her something.

Maybe what little she'd found would be enough. Given a

few days to digest everything she'd discovered in the past twenty-four hours, she might just come out a more complete, stronger woman, who'd embrace being a mother with all of her heart.

Who could celebrate the news of the upcoming baby with her husband first, and then start planning for her future with excitement and anticipation, instead of dreading it.

Maybe.

At the moment, all Kara felt was shock. And a strange disassociation with everything that had been familiar to her.

She printed out the article. Put it in her folder. Held the heavy material close to her heart.

Then dropped it to her desk as though it had burned her.

For a second, she felt guilty. Like she'd somehow, with her searching, betrayed all of those who'd loved her, who loved her still.

Then she shook her head. Refusing to give into drama. She was hurting no one.

The case had closed successfully, thanks to Jane Doe. The guilty man had been put away for the rest of his life without possibility of parole.

And her mother was safely ensconced in her invented life. Kara couldn't expose her or unknowingly lead anyone to her even if she wanted to. She had no idea who Tory Mitchell had become. Or where she'd moved.

Nor was she sure she wanted to ever know.

Hopefully, what she had was enough.

And given a little time, she could find a way back to her husband—and the building of her own life. One based on truth, not lies.

TRUE TO HIS personal directive to give his wife space, Ben didn't bother Kara while she worked on Saturday. He kept in contact with the guards watching over her, instead. Getting a text message report every quarter hour, for every hour that he was away from her.

There'd been a rough couple of minutes when, after the last client left, a tattered blue pick-up with a dog collar hanging from the rearview mirror pulled onto the North Haven Veterinary Clinic lot. He'd already alerted the local police to keep an eye out for the vehicle, still not convinced it hadn't been following him and Kara to the clinic the day before.

He'd had a text five minutes after the most recent communication regarding the truck's appearance. But before he'd made it to his vehicle at the office that he was using at the local precinct—a favor from Doug that tension-filled Saturday—he'd received an all clear.

Turned out the vehicle belonged to Celia's owner. A Maggie Crawford. The woman had been there to pick up her French bulldog and pups.

Ben found it odd—someone who had the money to own and breed such an expensive species of dog, driving such a beat-up vehicle—but didn't let himself linger over inconsequential details just because they touched his wife in some way. Kara needed his attention on finding Hansen.

On determining if he, or someone else associated with Stuart Miller, had ordered that Ben's loved one be hurt—as a warning that he better back off or else.

A shockingly strong part of him wanted to do just that— back off, take Kara, run to a faraway place and never look behind them again. But he knew that if he was going to be any kind of husband—and father—he had to keep his eye on the ball.

Running from one dangerous episode, rather than fighting to stop the danger, only led to a more dangerous society in the future.

He had to do his job. And protect his loved ones while making sure that the world in which they lived remained a safe place. For them. And for all the innocent, great people just like them, living normal lives in a society that wasn't driven by fear.

To that end, he listened to instincts, which drove him to phone records. Namely, Tina Hansen's. It helped having immediate access to databases his emergency warrant had provided. Tina's registered cell phone had not received or made any calls in the past week.

And yet calls pinged from a tower right by her house. One, within a minute of Ben's having left. And then back and forth over the next hour. All to and from the same number. A burner phone that had been making calls pinging to that same tower for the week Tina's registered phone had been silent.

It didn't surprise Ben a bit to find that John Hansen's registered phone had been silent for that same amount of time.

"Gotcha," Ben said out loud to his small, closed-door space.

But he didn't stop there. He checked traffic cameras along the roads leading to Tina's place just outside of town. And at the grocery where she shopped.

He noted vehicles, taking down all license plates, and ran searches on them.

Ran facial-recognition software where he could.

And came up empty-handed.

So he expanded his search. Looked for any known associates, any businesses, churches, or charities that had any mention of or association with Tina or John Hansen. Including possible distant relatives.

A detective on the case in Atlanta was going over Hansen's bank records, ostensibly to search for anything associated with Stuart Miller and the serial killer case. If he happened to find something suspicious in the past twenty-four hours, anything relating to North Haven, he'd be sharing that information.

They already had proof of association between Miller and Hansen—the one murder that Miller's attorneys had claimed Hansen had committed while refusing to admit to any of the murders of which their own client was guilty. Miller had rolled the bus over Hansen. Hoping to walk.

The man was that confident that there'd be no evidence that could convict him in court. But he could provide clear-cut evidence that would implicate Hansen.

Which was why Ben had been called in in the first place. He was an expert outside investigator who also knew the law intricately and would make certain that whatever path a piece of evidence took, it would be admissible and stand up to any curve the defense might throw in court.

At the moment, Hansen's bank records were being dissected for any proof, or even hint thereof, of him having paid someone to abduct Kara.

Overall, Ben spent hours on Saturday poring over long tedious work, and yet, with every detail he was able to cross off as being of no use to him, he knew he was getting closer and closer to the one speck that would lead him to his suspect. With everything he read, he was learning the man. The choices he made, the way his head worked. Hansen was guilty. Of murder, at the very least. There was no doubt about that. And, one way or another, Ben would find him.

He didn't doubt that, either.

Tina hadn't yet left her house that day. Hadn't made the grocery run she'd said she was going to make to meet up with her husband. Nor had anyone shown up resembling the man, or waited around suspiciously as though expecting someone to appear. That alone was evidence.

And a reason to bring the woman in for questioning, too. She'd lied to an investigator. It wasn't a crime—he was a private hire. But it bore a need to hear more. Most particularly with the threat she'd issued, shortly after which Kara had been abducted. Because the abduction had taken place in North Haven, Doug was handling the interrogation.

Tina Hansen was due to arrive within the hour, and Ben planned to be present for the interview. Watching from another room via video camera.

The plan changed when, twenty minutes before Tina was due to arrive, a 911 call came in from guards outside the North Haven Veterinary Clinic regarding a disturbance at the back side of the building. Where Kara's office was located. A fire was burning outside not far from the window.

Doug was at his door as the details were still coming in and Ben tore out with the detective, eager to accept the ride in a car with a legal right to speed, and a bubble and siren to avoid a crash while doing so.

Thank God he'd hired the off-duty officers. Had they not been outside to notice the fire within seconds of it having started, Kara's clinic—most particularly the office in which she was spending the afternoon catching up on paperwork— could have gone up in flames.

A fire truck had already been dispatched. And the indoor guard was escorting Kara out to a front reception area, from which he'd get her into an unmarked car as soon as it pulled up to the door.

"Possible customer in reception," the call came urgently over Doug's car radio. "Puppy lady…"

The words were cut off by the sound of an explosion. Loud enough that the sedan seemed to rock with the noise.

And then there was silence.

## Chapter Seven

Kara had been in the bathroom off the operating room, reapplying makeup to cover up the evidence of the tears she'd shed, when she heard a guard calling her name. Sounding urgent.

She'd just jerked open the door, calling, "I'm here!" when a boom sounded, and the building seemed to rock on its foundation.

Gunshots! She dove under the operating table. Shaking. Hugging the lab coat she always wore at work around the beige pants and white blouse Ben had packed for her, she crouched, shin and stomach toward the floor, knees to her chest. And pulled a box of exam gloves down to cover her head while she listened for the direction of the gunfire.

She heard crumbling. Like falling debris. And then footsteps pounding at a run. Smelled smoke. But no more shots. Before she could determine her next best move, the door to the operating room burst open.

"Dr. Latimer? Kara? You in here?"

Who was asking? She didn't recognize the voice. What if it was yesterday's kidnapper, back to kill her? Panicked, she remained in a tops-of-both-feet-to-the-floor fetal position, eyes wide open, and held her breath.

"Kara!" Officer Allen, from the day before. She recognized the voice. But was she being forced to call out to Kara?

Footsteps sounded around the room, walking by her toward the bathroom from which she'd come. "Find her!" Officer Alexander, a man who'd been on duty the evening before and had let her know he was there again that afternoon, came closer to the operating table.

And Kara waited. Frozen in place.

Men's black heavy-duty work shoes appeared, and then a pair of knees covered in light brown pants. "Kara?"

She looked up at the face she recognized, reading for any sign of regret on his face. Of sorrow that he was being forced to do something he didn't want to do. If they'd gotten to the guards, threatened their families, she couldn't blame them...

The brown eyes staring back at her were forthright, focused, and filled with urgency. "A bomb went off," he told her, reaching for her arm. "We have no way of knowing if there might be more explosives. We have to get you out of here."

With a nod, she climbed out from her cover under her own steam. And allowed herself to be rushed outside.

Unable to stop the tears from filling her eyes as she caught a glimpse of the damage done to her reception area. And waiting room.

She allowed herself to be led out through a side door. Saw an unmarked car pull up, with the passenger door flying open before the car had come to a stop.

Recognized Ben as he flew toward her.

And knew that, no matter their personal situation, she was going to be the wife her investigator husband needed so he could get his job done.

No way she was going to bring a child into a world where the good guys ran and hid.

BEN COULDN'T GET to Kara quickly enough, even seeing the officers who had her surrounded and covered as they walked her through two lines of fire trucks and out to Doug's waiting car. There was no time for the unending hug he needed to share with her, just a quick squeeze of her hand as he pushed her ahead of him into the back seat of the car, saying, "Get down and stay down."

Officer Alexander rounded the car and jumped in on the other side of Kara, and Doug had the car in gear and moving before Ben, sandwiching his wife in, had his door shut.

As the vehicle sped away, Kara started to lift her head up from her lap, and he pushed her back down. And then relented with, "Slide down in your seat. You need to keep your head below windshield and back window levels."

His blood was thrumming, his heart pounding, but he was damned well going to be at his best, using his years of training and experience to keep her safe.

In less than a minute, they'd devised the plan to get Kara out of the clinic without being seen.

They were going to the North Haven police station first. For reconnaissance. And to wait for reports from the crime scene.

"Was anyone hurt?" Kara asked, looking between Ben and Alexander, the officer who'd been closest to her as they'd escorted her out to the car. For a second there, in the midst of hell, Ben felt a stab of jealousy, which disgusted him.

Something he would have to look at later.

"Dillon Williams, a rookie, was in the waiting room, hoping to escort you out. He caught more of the blast than anyone. Has at least one cut that needs stitches," Doug said from the front seat. "Everyone else is accounted for."

Except the driver of the blue pick-up truck that had just blown up in Kara's parking lot. He and Doug had been a couple of blocks away, had heard the explosion, and Ben knew, as soon as he heard mention of that blue truck, that Kara wasn't just being targeted physically.

They were after her emotionally, too. At a time when she

was already off her game in that area. The whole thing was making him sick.

Furious.

Determined.

And angrier, still. Rage seethed within him as he sat there next to her, prepared to take any bullet that might try to hit her, and dreading the upcoming conversations.

Trying to hurt or kill someone was one level of bad. Attacking them psychologically was a layer that only those with diabolical hatred, experience, and an enjoyment of careful planning generally took on. It became part of the game. The thrill. It became an addiction.

One with which Stuart Miller was clearly afflicted.

Part of the goal had to be to make the man think he'd succeeded where Kara was concerned. "Get a second ambulance there. In the parking lot," Ben said, sitting forward to glance at Doug as he drove. "Have them put a body on a stretcher—Officer Allen," he clarified as the ideas hit like bullets. "She's the right size. Put a sheet over her head and have her carried out. Make a big show, officers around, concerned. Upset."

Whoever Miller had working for him—even if it was Hansen—would have been told to watch the scene. To make certain that their target was down.

If they didn't see that evidence, Miller would up his attacks. Both psychologically and physically. "Have it speed straight to Atlanta," he added, as he heard Doug give the orders over the radio. "To the coroner's office."

Technically, it was Doug's case, not Ben's, but the detective had made it clear that he not only respected Ben's greater experience, but welcomed any input he had regarding the case. As soon as Doug finished the orders, Ben called the lead prosecutor he was working for in Atlanta. Filled him in. And hung up, satisfied. Kyle Hernandez was one of the best. He'd known exactly where Ben was going without him having to say so aloud. And had just assured him that the coroner would follow protocol as though he'd just received a high-priority dead body.

It was just a start. A temporary measure. But it allowed Ben to move forward in his pursuit of evil.

Without strangling at the thought that he'd almost lost his wife—and unborn child—for a second time in twenty-four hours.

KARA DIDN'T NEED Ben's thought processes spelled out to her. She knew that body on the stretcher was a stand-in for her. She got the goal.

Was impressed by and proud of his quick thinking.

She didn't like the way he hovered over every aspect of every moment she spent from that point forward and over the next hour. Walking her to the bathroom had been over-kill. Keeping her out of the tense conversations going on behind closed doors, some of which had to do directly with her, bothered her.

More than a little bit.

He hadn't even allowed anyone to question her without him present. His takeover, without making her privy to any-thing being discussed, reminded her far too much of how her sisters had arbitrarily decided what she would and wouldn't know about the truth of her parentage.

Secrets, lies—where loved ones were involved—were just not acceptable.

After an hour of being coddled and sheltered, she was about ready to pound on a door and demand to be set free. She wasn't a prisoner.

Thankfully, common sense rescued her from the wayward thought. She was there for her own safety. Because of what could only have been another attempt on her life.

And while she was currently in the midst of major internal struggles, she most definitely did not have a death wish.

She needed—wanted—and was deeply grateful for the professional physical protection the police department had been and was continuing to offer her.

And yet, when her phone rang and Melanie's name came up, she tensed again. Needed to be left alone to deal with the situation, at least long enough to find out for herself what was going on. To take it in. Make some kind of sense of it.

To figure out how she felt, what she needed to do, before someone else told her what that would be.

She answered with a kind tone, anyway. "Hey, sis," she said, flooded with love for her big sister. And thankful that Melanie was always there. Always ready to take on any battles that came their way. Always caring.

Yet, before Melanie could start in, she quickly said, "I'm fine. Not even a scratch. And holed up safely inside the police station."

"I know," Melanie said. "Ben told us."

*Us.* And *Ben?*

Even as she had the reaction, Kara knew she wasn't herself. Her family was all in. Always had been. It made sense that they'd call Ben—the investigator—to get the facts before offering Kara the comfort she needed.

Besides, if Kara had been injured, or dead, she wouldn't have been able to give them the status report they'd so clearly need first.

But still… "Ben called you?" He should, at the very least, have spoken with her first.

Though, she'd never had an issue with Ben calling anyone in the past. They all reached out to each other. It's what they did.

And suddenly she was having a problem with that, too?

"No!" Melanie's heightened sensitivity reached Kara on

some level. She took a deep breath as her sister said, "I was at the bakery, picking up…well it doesn't matter what I was picking up…someone came in and said there's been a bombing at the vet's and…"

*Oh, God.* Her heart dropped, and then broke some, as she pictured her sweet older sister actually experiencing the situation she was describing.

"You called Ben," she finished when Mel's words broke off.

"Yeah. And Stella beeped in. She's in Tennessee for a rally, but someone called her…" The rally. Stella was at a rally. And her ex-husband, Thane, was there, too. It was their first time working together since the divorce.

Normally, Kara would have been thinking about Stella. Hoping for a peaceful and successful weekend for her outspoken, but so sensitive, middle sister.

Instead, she'd been so wrapped up in her own drama, in the lies she'd been told, that she'd barely had a thought for either of her sisters. Outside of the purview of the lies they'd told her.

"I'm fine," she told Melanie softly. Instilling strength into her tone. A sense of self-assurance she most certainly wasn't finding inside. "Shaken up, of course, and waiting to hear the extent of the damage to the clinic, but unharmed."

"But on top of yesterday…how's your arm?" Melanie cut herself off to ask.

"Fine." Sore, when she moved it right then, but Kara told her sister the truth. "I haven't even thought it about it." A little bit of arm pain didn't fall anywhere close to her radar at the moment.

"Ben says that this is all because of a case he's on," Melanie said then. "I told him that Stella and I would go with you, wherever was safe, and keep you company while he gets this bastard."

The statement set her off again. Taking a deep breath,

Kara said, "I'm not going anywhere with you and Stella." She wasn't sure where she was going, but she wasn't going to be shipped off like some recalcitrant child.

Or an adult with nothing meaningful to contribute. She was being threatened. She had to do something. Even if it was just to sit in a family waiting room at the station and be available to identify a suspect, or answer some innocuous question that could be the missing piece that broke the case. She'd been with Ben long enough, shared his work enough, to know how the process worked.

"I have business to take care of here, Melanie," she said. Everything had changed. Kara felt different. "As soon as the clinic is no longer a crime scene, I'm going to need to get things in order so I can get back to work. I have clients to call. Patients to refer to Atlanta, if I can't get to them myself…"

She had to be an adult and in control of her own life.

"You seriously aren't thinking about just going back to work as though nothing happened," Melanie said, then added, "Well, not as if nothing happened. I get that there will be arrangements to make, and the clinic to secure, but you can't just hang around here, Kara. The guy has missed twice. Strike three and you could be out."

Spoken just like the ex-wife of a big-time sports agent. And knocking Kara right out of the park, too.

"I'm not suggesting that I'm going to walk blithely out of here and continue my life like nothing's happened," she said, frustrated that, having talked to Ben, Melanie probably knew more about what was currently going on than Kara did.

Feeling guilty for his part in what was happening, Ben would want to shield her from whatever he felt he could. A week ago, she might have at least been warmed by that sentiment, if not by the unnecessary sheltering. The sheltering had been happening since she was born. She'd just learned to take in stride, and mostly blow off, by the time she'd kissed her first boy in junior high.

Or so she'd thought.

"You have to go into hiding, Kara, and let Ben and the police do their jobs."

"I've agreed to protection, but that's it," Kara said, feeling resolute, and somewhat more peaceful with the statement. "I'm not going to run and hide."

"What kind of thinking is that?" Melanie's tone rose. "Of course you're coming with us. Stella is on the phone right now making arrangements to rent a bungalow in upstate New York. We'll have around-the-clock protection and lots of time to—"

"Stop." Kara had reason to be irritated, and didn't bother to hide the fact. "I am not going, Melanie. Nor are you and Stella going to watch over me. There are trained professionals being paid to do that."

"Of course there are. An entire detail is going to be coming with us."

"No!" Kara stood, then paced the room she'd been occupying alone for far more time than she should have been. At least in her opinion. Maybe taking it out somewhat on her big sister as she continued with, "You and Stella think I'm some fragile thing that needs you both watching over me! I'm twenty-nine years old, for God's sake, Mel! I'm a veterinarian, in a successful practice. That I started from scratch. On my own." With help from a lot of referrals from the two of them, yes, but if her skills hadn't been top rate, if she hadn't been capable, those referred clients would have ended up going elsewhere.

Taking a breath while her sister's undoubtedly shocked silence hung on the line, she softened her tone. "It's time you all treat me like an equal, Melanie, not like some kid who still doesn't know what she doesn't know."

A long pause followed. And she pulled the phone away from her ear to check that the call was still connected. Was about to apologize, when Melanie said, "Now you're like the rest of us, huh? An adult who doesn't know what she doesn't know." There was humor in her sister's tone. Begrudging, maybe, but there.

"I'd like to think so," she said quietly. And then more boldly, "Most definitely on the not knowing what she doesn't know part." Hell, she didn't even know her own mind, her own reactions at the moment. Didn't recognize most things about herself.

Her dread at being pregnant. Yelling at her sister.

Drawing away from Ben.

What in the hell was she doing to herself? To her life?

"For my part, I'm sorry, Kara. I had no idea I was in any way impinging on your autonomy. Truth is, I rely on your judgment. But… I've had to bite my tongue twice in the last few minutes, to keep from doing exactly what you say we do. Overprotect. Watching out for you is kind of like breathing, you know? But since I'm not too fond of the idea of walking around with a swollen tongue, I'll try my best to do better."

Kara sat. Mouth open. Staring at the floor. Stunned.

"You still there?" Melanie's voice came differently over the line. A little less filled with boss, and more with friend-who-wasn't-sure-they-were-okay.

Or at least, in that moment, Kara heard her that way. "I'm here," Kara told her. And then added, "I don't want you to stop caring, Melly, to stop being there. I just need…"

"To be treated like the capable, successful adult you've become."

With tears in her eyes, Kara nodded.

Then quickly blinked away the emotion, straightening her spine, as a knock sounded on the door.

And fear shot through her.

## Chapter Eight

Ben felt like he was walking into the principal's office. It had been that long since he'd had to answer to anybody who had any kind of power over him.

He'd been his own boss since graduating from law school. Had partners in his firm. And many, many friends and associates. Equals, all.

But Kara…she'd made a place for herself much more deeply inside him. A spot he couldn't just shut down.

For the first time in his adult life, he was truly vulnerable with another human being.

One who was standing in the room he'd just entered, her phone in hand, looking as though she'd seen a ghost. Not something a susceptible guy wanted to see by way of greeting from the woman he was powerless against.

Her gaze hardened almost immediately—which made matters worse. "I am not going to be shipped off someplace with my sisters." Her tone brooked no argument.

He wasn't about to give her one. "I know," he told her, breathing a little easier as he put two and two together. His earlier call from Melanie, the phone in Kara's hand…

He'd already figured it out before she said, "Melanie seems to think differently."

"I was in the middle of a report from the crime scene investigators when she called. I heard her suggestion and told her I'd call her back. Which I have not yet done. Obviously."

Kara's gaze softened some. Not like it might have done pre-stick, as he was beginning to think of the morning before in their bathroom. But then, she'd been endangered twice since then. The woman deserved a hell of a lot more slack than she was taking.

"I'm not getting my sisters involved in this, Ben."

He'd hoped to convince her to hide out in some luxury resort with guards around her. Might need to rethink that one. Maybe.

She might change her mind. Kara was usually amenable when she had all the facts in front of her.

To that end…

"Celia's owner, Maggie, is under investigation." He put the worst right out there. Which wasn't at all how he'd planned to break the news.

He'd been thinking more of leaving that piece until last… just a tail end tidbit to soften the blow.

Open-mouthed, Kara sat. Stared up at him.

Then shook her head. "No," she said. "No way that woman is involved in wanting to hurt me. She trusted me with her heart when she left that mama and her babies with me."

There. Right there. The Kara he'd sworn to himself on their wedding day that he'd spend the rest of his life protecting. He'd thought his job would be guarding her heart from being hurt.

The reminder brought a change in his messaging. "I'm not saying she was involved." He gave her the hope he'd thought best not to dangle, just in case. "Just that she's been brought in for questioning."

Her gaze narrowed, and he sat, prepared to give her what she was clearly going to demand from him. Or she'd bypass him and go to Doug if he didn't comply. The Kara before him most definitely was not the woman he'd gone to bed with two nights before.

And the fact had no place in that room at that time.

"Remember the blue truck that I thought was following us yesterday?"

Kara pulled out a chair, sat perpendicular to him. He bizarrely noted that the chair was the one closest to him as she said, "The dog collar."

"Right. It's Maggie's truck."

Kara shook her head. "That doesn't mean she was following us."

"A man was driving the truck yesterday," he told her. "Maggie claims that she has new neighbors down the street. They came down, a man and woman, in a newer-model sedan and asked if they left their car with her, would she let them borrow her truck just long enough to haul boxes out of storage and unload them."

Kara nodded, not as though she already knew what he was telling her, but more as if she was on board with the information.

Refraining from taking her hand, which every instinct he had was driving him to do, Ben continued. "She drove the truck to your clinic today to pick up Celia and her babies."

Another nod, with very little expression was Kara's only communication.

"Your protection detail saw the truck and after going through protocol with your receptionist regarding Maggie being a legitimate client, they deemed the truck safe."

Kara shook her head then. "Maggie didn't do it. She put Celia, a dog who's been a member of her family for years, and those pups, in that truck. She wouldn't harm them any more than she'd put a gun to her own head." Kara's eyes widened as she said the words. "Unless someone else had a gun to her head?"

Brimming with compassion as he looked at her, he said, "That's what we're trying to find out. A fire was set outside your office window. We think by a small device that was either thrown by someone hiding nearby, or possibly dropped from a drone. The officers on outside duty went immediately to the fire, grabbing a fire extinguisher, and also fanned out from there to determine the source. In the meantime, Maggie's truck was back on the lot. One of the officers saw it, figured that the client had returned for something, and continued his search for who'd thrown the small firebomb. Two minutes later, the truck exploded all over the front of your building. Your front door was blasted out, and much of the waiting area and reception was damaged."

Ready for her tears, for pain and anger, Ben watched Kara sit there, clearly digesting, but not falling apart.

"No one was badly hurt," she said. "It's all fixable."

True. And exactly the tactic he'd planned to use to comfort her through her grief. He was missing the boat all over the place.

Had he known the woman he was married to at all?

"So did Maggie's new neighbor borrow the truck again this afternoon?" she asked, instead of weeping all over him.

"According to her, he did. Only problem is, upon canvass of the neighborhood, we found out that she doesn't have any new neighbors."

"She was duped," Kara said. "I know this woman, Ben. She's kind. Gentle. And generous to a fault. She just offered me pick of the litter, which is worth a lot of money to any breeder, let alone a woman who scrapes to get by. She's giving me what would probably be a couple of months' worth of bill money for her, just for saving Celia's life. I can give you more examples. Actions over time that speak to her character far more than a truck on my lot this afternoon. Good Lord, I was abducted and hauled off the beach like trash. My clinic was just bombed. It's not a stretch to think that Maggie was duped."

She was right, of course. He and Doug had already reached the same conclusion.

But something else had just become very clear to him. His wife did not need, or appreciate, the kid gloves he'd been wearing around her.

And so, from that point on, he'd keep them off.

SHOCK WAS A funny thing. Horrible on one hand, in that it encased a body in a cage all its own. A prison with see-through white cotton walls.

And it put distance between you and everything else. Even from objects, from people, that were close enough to touch.

But on the other hand, the encasement offered a body—a mind—protection. Things didn't hit as hard, or hurt as badly from inside its hazy womb.

And Kara could still think. Speak. Stand up for herself.

"I'll need to get back in there," she said to Ben as he sat, seemingly at a loss, watching her. "I need my client book and—" she thought of the folder she'd dropped to her desk "—other things. From my office." The clinic was closed on Sundays and Mondays. "I need to see whether I can have someone fix the place well enough for me to open on Tuesday. Obviously, the damaged part of the building will need to be cordoned off, but we could use the side entrance. Set up a table for reception. And use exam room six for a waiting area…" Gathering strength as valid plans started to formulate, she looked over to see Ben's frown.

"The idea is to hope he fell for our ruse with the covered body in the ambulance. Until we know differently, you're presumed dead, Kara. It needs to stay that way until we find Hansen, or link Miller to all this somehow and follow the trail to figure out who else he hired to get me to back off from this."

Right. The officer with the sheet over her head being carried out of her clinic. It was a testament to the fog she was breathing through that she'd dismissed that part. Probably because she didn't put a lot of stock in it. They had no way of knowing if the bomber had even seen that move.

And the folder...regarding her mother...she'd dropped it onto her desk. "I still need some things," she told him. "I'll be careful not to appear to be alive, but I'm in the middle of preparing schedules, and I've got bills to pay." She was spitballing. She needed that folder. It was the only hope she had of setting herself free from whatever darkness had a hold on her future as a mother. A wife.

"Make a list and I'll have a crime scene investigator get back over there to collect everything."

With a breath of relief, she nodded, the details he'd just given her finally finding roost in her brain. And not making sense. Frowning, she said, "I thought you said this Miller guy was diabolically smart."

"He is."

"Well, this is a pretty brainless plan, isn't it? To think that me being dead is going to help you all find this guy? He didn't think to look at you, before going after your family? To know that you aren't just some struggling PI, but a man with more power of your own than he'll ever have? And even if he did that, and he succeeds in scaring you off—after all, he's already a murderer, what's one more body to him—but with all the ruckus he's caused, the prosecution is just going to be that much more determined to hire someone else to take over. A dozen someones at once, even, since this thing has escalated so quickly. Is everyone hoping he won't threaten the next guy's family, and the next?"

He didn't seem surprised by her theory. As though he'd

already been there. Which, if she'd been in her right mind, she'd have surmised before thinking she knew better than him how to do his job.

With a nod, and a kind tone, he said, "I'm still openly on the case. He had to know his threat didn't work. But to your point about intelligent, intricate planning…or lack thereof… that's why we're leaning more toward Hansen working alone on these attacks. This isn't the work of someone like Miller, who's slow and methodical. This is someone who's desperate."

He was scaring her. "He's managed to get close enough to possibly kill me twice in two days. And he hasn't been caught. He outsmarted a trained protection detail today."

"He's outsmarted the Atlanta police department, too, up until this point. But the more desperate he gets, the more likely he is to make a mistake. And Tina Hansen has been brought in for questioning. We have his wife, Kara. We're closing in on him."

She heard the almost-pleading tone in his voice, and said, "What do you want from me, Ben?" She wanted to give it to him, whatever it was. Even as she lacked confidence in her ability to do so.

He opened his mouth. Closed it. Then, with a change of expression from frown to almost peaceful certainty, he said, "I want you to agree to around-the-clock protection. I'm talking secret service type. And to stay hidden in one of the three resorts on the beach here in town. I'll set up secure suites in all three of them. Your choice which one you actually stay at when. You'll move around between the three as necessary."

Talk about details…

He'd already had the plan before he'd come in. Or Doug had. More likely Ben had framed it, because it was the kind of arrangements he'd make, but he didn't seem fond of the plan, just the same. And for a second there, he felt like her other half again. Or she felt like his.

Cocking her head, she said, "You were kind of hoping I'd agree to go away with my sisters, weren't you?"

He didn't quite grin. But almost. "As your husband, I'd give everything I have to have you do so."

"But?" she asked, clearly hearing one in his tone.

"There's a chance that he didn't see the body in the ambulance, that he doesn't know we staged your death. If that's the case—and we'll get wind of that pretty quickly based on his next moves, or perhaps even through the interview with his wife—and we've moved you completely out of town, we lose our chance to get Hansen."

She jumped immediately to where she could see his mind going and said, "In which case, you think you're using me as bait." And it was killing him.

His eyes more intent, more serious than she'd ever seen them while trained on her, he said, "I know I am, Kara. But the shit of it is that if I don't, I could be putting you in more danger. Here, we have the means to protect you. If you're off with your sisters, there are three of you to protect, and people unfamiliar with the case protecting you. Added to that, we know so little about Hansen, we can't predict what he'll do next. He just seems to have appeared out of nowhere. He and Tina are renting the house. They haven't been there long. And his identity has no trail whatsoever. We wouldn't even have known he existed if not for Miller rolling on him."

Kara's heart thudded hard as new waves of fright hit. "Are you even sure he exists, then?" Surely, Ben wouldn't be pinning everything on the word of a serial killer.

"Miller told us where to find the murder weapon with Hansen's prints on it. We verified them through a confiscated glass he used at the bar where he hangs out. We had surveillance camera footage from where we found the body that gave us a partial of his face, and the bartender, as well as customers, confirmed that it was Hansen."

She was finally keeping up with him. "The prosecution has enough to hold Miller, but they don't think they have enough to convict him, or they wouldn't have hired you. If Hansen was a close associate of his, Hansen probably knows that they don't have enough at this point to convict him, either. Assuming he doesn't know Miller rolled on him. That is, if you're going with the theory that Hansen's in hiding just because of the murder he committed."

"That's the hope." He didn't sound hopeful.

And she continued in the way she'd done many times when discussing an investigation with him. "Unless Miller has someone on the outside still working for him. Has a way of getting prosecutorial information and passing that on to Hansen."

Chin tight, lips jutting out, he nodded.

"I'm safest right here, Ben, with an entire police force that knows the area, and the people, like the backs of their hands. I will abide by your dictates. And... I'm grateful for your plans on my behalf. For going through all the trouble to make it possible for me to stay where I need to be. For understanding."

"Even if we find out that Hansen didn't fall for our ruse regarding your death, no work at the clinic, Kara. You're closed for the next two days. You can have someone put a message on the answering machine that says someone will be in touch to reschedule appointments or something equally vague. Not saying you're dead, but not indicating that you aren't. Not until this guy is caught. With any luck, we'll have him in custody by Tuesday."

She hated the words. Wanted to argue with him. But said aloud instead, "If I show myself as alive, and open up shop, I'd be putting not only myself but my clients' and patients' lives in danger as well." And as something else hit home, added, "Just as I did Maggie."

Nausea hit her then. Fiercely. She made a dash for the trash can. Knelt there hugging it. And the feeling subsided.

But it put the elephant on the table right there on the three feet of tile floor separating her and Ben.

Holding the can to her, she stood.

Turned slowly.

In time to see the door closing quietly behind him.

## Chapter Nine

Ben didn't see Kara again until the plans for her lodgings had been made. True to his word, he had suites in all three places rented, with protection protocol in place, before he returned to her.

Others had talked to her. Officer Allen had met with Kara to get a list of what she wanted from the clinic and from home, and was already back with a box of things. She'd had dinner brought in.

All that was left was for Ben to find out where Kara wanted to spend the first night.

No one but he, Doug, and the protection details would know. Not even hotel staff was going to be privy to who was staying in the suite. Food would be ordered, taken by an officer at the door, and consumed, at all three places for all three meals.

He'd thought of everything he could.

And couldn't think about his marriage. Or where the next few days would take him.

Just as he couldn't stop thinking about the baby that Kara was growing inside her. Whether she wanted the child or not, he knew that she'd die to keep it safe.

Hell, she'd die to keep a dog safe. That was just Kara.

He'd been standing outside the door of the room she was

waiting in for a full minute before he knocked. And still didn't feel ready.

"It's time to go," he told her as he took in the space. The lack of anything she might have been doing while she sat there. She'd been given a burner phone to use. He'd confiscated hers. Had had it taken back to the clinic and destroyed in the wreckage. The new phone wasn't in sight.

"Did you eat?" she asked him. And for a second there, he was home again—home in his marriage to the wife he adored. Any night he was working late, the first thing she'd ask when he called from the office, or arrived at home, was "Did you eat?"

And when he hadn't, she'd immediately jump up and get something ready for him.

Not because he expected it. Or couldn't do it himself. But because, as she'd put it, "it makes me feel good to do it for you."

"I did," he told her. Partial truth. He'd had dinner delivered, too. Just hadn't had a stomach for much of it. "Right now, I need to know where you want to be taken for the night."

"Where *I* want to be taken? Don't you mean us?"

His heart lurched. But he tightened his control over it and shook his head.

"Where will you be?"

"Home," he told her. "I'm a grieving husband, Kara," he reminded her. "If I stay at the resort, I give them a much better chance to suspect that you're there."

She frowned. And he felt…another spurt of hope. She wanted him close.

"Aren't they going to already suspect that with the protection detail?" she asked him. "I mean, with your wife having been a target, it's safe to assume that you could be next. You're the one digging up the information they don't want found."

"The men and women protecting you don't look like protection detail," he told her. "They look like hotel workers. And guests."

"Oh." She truly looked crestfallen, and Ben was tempted to amend his strategy. Except that he knew he couldn't. He had a part to play, and his wife's and child's safety depended on how well he played it.

"I'm going to be spending most of the night here," he told her. "I'll go home, but not be able to stay. I've got a cot here. I'll get some sleep, and then I'll be monitoring radio communications. Hansen would expect that of me, knowing what I do for a living. Which he obviously does, since this all started with his wife's threat to me."

He put the small pile of clothes he'd brought in with him on the table. "You need to get into this," he said. "It's a police uniform, your size. It's dark out. You'll be walking to the car with Officer Allen, and others who will be appearing to have a jocular conversation. Your hair needs to be up under the hat. And the brim down low. After you're safely in the vehicle, the others will disperse to their own cars.

"Other officers, in unmarked cars, are already positioned along the route to all three resorts, are watching for any suspicious activity, or appearance of a car following another car, until they get the all clear. None of these peripheral officers will know your actual location."

Looking between Ben and the clothes he'd put on the table, she said, "That sounds like a lot of officers, Ben. North Haven's department isn't that big."

"I've hired off-duty officers from Atlanta," he told her. "They know they're on protection detail. They don't know who they're protecting." It helped to own a law firm that had grown successful beyond his imagination. Both in terms of contacts, and having the money to hire them.

"And...me dead...is that going to be spread around town?

People will be talking about the explosion. My clinic's right on Main Street…"

"We don't know if anyone saw the sheeted body go in the ambulance. There might be speculation, but as of right now, everyone who knows what's going on is under a strict gag order."

"Including Maggie?"

"She asked about you. Doug told her that he wasn't at liberty to talk about it."

"The rumor mill's going to be running hot."

He shrugged. "It's likely in high gear already."

Her eyes narrowed on him. "And that works in your favor—if Hansen, or whoever, hears gossip from locals about my possible death."

The words hit him wrong, at a time when he needed to be doing all he could to make things right with her. "In *our* favor, Kara," he said, with a quick glance at her belly.

She'd said she was going to have the baby. No matter what was going on between the two of them, they were going to be parents.

Turning her back right then, to pick up the clothes, couldn't have been a mistake. Ben's heart took a brief stab. He hardened up quickly enough.

"What about my sisters?" Kara's question came at him as, clothes held to her chest in one hand, she grabbed her purse with the other. "People are going to be offering condolences…are they expected to lie to everyone?"

"They'd gladly do so, to protect you. You know that."

She nodded, chin jutting out, as though she was biting back a response. One his gut was telling him he needed to hear.

But he'd given himself a mandate not to push her. Had just failed himself with the "our favor" comment, to no good response. He was not going to repeat the mistake.

"Stella has another out-of-state rally to attend. Melanie

and Josh are going to be staying in Atlanta, near Darin's new place. You know as well as I do, they're going to do whatever it takes to keep you safe."

Tears filled her eyes at that, and Ben almost stepped forward to take her in his arms.

Almost.

He held her gaze instead. For the ten or so seconds she gave him.

And when she looked away, he turned around and left.

Was she dead? Was she alive?

Kara felt as though she was kind of both. Half dead. Half alive. With her life on suspension, her ability to choose her activities so severely limited, she woke up Sunday morning in limbo.

Numb.

But not quite as much as she'd been, arriving at the suite the night before, showering, and going to bed.

She'd roused herself enough before sleep to text Ben, telling him good-night. But had done so more from the head than the heart.

It had been the right thing to do. He was a good man. A great man. He didn't deserve any of the crap she was dealing him.

She hadn't waited for his response before turning over to cry herself to sleep.

And didn't grab for her phone first thing upon waking, either.

Missing Ben more than anything, she cried herself through her shower. And stepped out, needing something to do with her day. With her mind.

So that she didn't lean on Ben when she couldn't be complete for him. She couldn't use him for her own selfish comfort. Couldn't hurt him anymore than she was already doing.

He needed her to talk to him. To explain what had gone awry. But how could she when she didn't understand it herself? She could hear just how the conversation would go.

She'd tell him she was scared. He'd coddle her and assure her it's natural for a woman to be a bit frightened at the prospect of having her first child, that it was a normal part of the process.

She'd tell him that her feelings weren't that. They were different. Deeper. He'd humor her, lovingly, all the while being certain he had the right answer, with his greater wisdom gained from more years of living and…

Kara's eyes glistened at the thought, but no tears fell. She stepped into the stretch jeans and short-sleeved ribbed white top she'd found in her suitcase. Comfort clothes. Took care of hair and makeup. Glad to have her own bathroom things with her. And gazing at herself in the luxurious bathroom mirror, she told herself aloud, "I'm totally in love with Ben, he's my man. I'm just not sure I know how to be his woman."

Then, when she had no response for herself, she turned out the light and left the room.

She could cry.

Or she could take action.

Be proactive, as her dad and Melanie used to tell her.

She was their darling. Smart enough to be whatever and whoever she wanted to be. A lawyer. A doctor.

A veterinarian. With her own successful practice—albeit currently ravaged—at twenty-nine. She had insurance for the clinic. And other than one officer with a cut needing stitches, no one had been hurt during the explosion. As soon as she was free, she'd have the place set up for temporary practice while the rest of the repair work was done. She could finally get her waiting room and reception area enlarged.

She just couldn't seem to figure out how to feel like a mother.

Or trust herself to actually be a good one.

For that matter, she wasn't even sure she wanted to be one. She'd thought she did. Had been certain she did.

She wasn't certain of anything anymore.

Except that she had a new life growing inside her.

Her mother was alive.

And Kara almost hadn't been.

She needed to tell Ben about Tory. He was talking with her sisters. They were bound to tell him. If they hadn't already. The three of them seemed to think it fine to discuss their little darling behind her back. To assure themselves that she was fine. Or do what had to be done to make her fine.

Like three guardian angels.

And what in the hell was the matter with her that she wasn't eternally grateful and happy about that? How could she not feel how incredibly blessed she was? A ton of people would be grateful for even one guardian angel.

She could see it. She knew it.

And her heart was bearing very little witness.

Kara checked in with her protection detail. Ordered orange juice, oatmeal, fruit, and toast for breakfast—because she had to eat healthy, not due to any desire for the food.

And while she waited for her meal to arrive, she set up the laptop Barbara Allen had collected from the clinic's office, and put the folder she'd also requested on the desk next to the computer.

She was going to not pout. Not worry. With nothing else pressing on her, she could spend the entire day continuing her own investigation. Finding out anything she could about Tory Mitchell.

Homing in on what seemed to be stifling Kara's ability to move forward with her life. She'd thought it was the fact that she didn't know enough about her mother. And then that her mother had committed suicide, that she'd chosen to die rather than be Kara's mother. Not that she'd blamed her. People struggled. She had medical training. She knew things.

Postpartum issues were real and no one was at fault for them.

She'd thought she just needed more information.

Only to find that what she'd been missing was the truth.

A horrible, astounding, unbelievable truth.

Her mother had chosen to testify on behalf of a dead man over staying around to raise her three daughters. What had made the sacrifice important enough to abandon her family?

She presented herself to the desk. The work. But didn't begin. Not until after she got food down her. What she did instead was open her text messages to see if Ben had responded the night before.

Then, with the hand holding her phone shaking slightly, read, Sleep well, babe. I love you. No matter how it all plays out.

Blinking back more tears, she texted back, I love you, too.

Because if, in the next hours, anything happened to either one of them, she needed him to know that.

Even if it turned out she couldn't be the wife he needed, or he wasn't the husband she should have chosen, she loved him.

It was one truth her heart and mind agreed upon. Without doubt.

She loved him.

It wasn't enough.

But for the moment, it seemed to be all she had to give.

BEN WAS ALREADY at a desk in the office he'd been loaned at the North Haven police headquarters when Kara's text came through. It took every bit of self-control he had not to call her immediately.

To hear how she'd slept. How she was feeling.

But figuring that she'd think he was asking because she was pregnant—which in part, he would be—he refrained from following husbandly instincts.

She knew how to reach him. And would do so when she was ready. Until then, his job was to find the fiend who'd tried, twice, to take Kara away from him.

Ben's only job at the moment was to ensure his wife's physical safety.

Which had to be done before she could get on with her life, no matter whether that life lead her back to the home they shared, or elsewhere.

Keeping Kara safe meant finding Hansen. Or whoever Miller might have sent on Hansen's behalf.

Ben had shifted his investigation back to where he'd left off before Kara's abduction on Friday afternoon. Doug and the North Haven investigative team were all over the kidnapping, the fire, and the bombing. They were fully focused and more than capable of getting every clue there was to be found and following up on them.

Even with it being Sunday, Doug was reporting to him every hour with updates.

Ben, in the meantime, was pouring over every word of Tina's interview the day before. Watching, and rewatching, taking notes. Listening with his eyes closed, so that he could catch indistinct, but possibly telling changes in word choice, voice decibel, tone. Jotting down more impressions.

He went from there back to bar patrons' recorded accounts of John Hansen, and caught something. A phrase.

That both Tina and one of the drinking buddies had repeated when speaking of John. Almost as though it was something the man had said? Said of himself? Just a phrase he commonly used?

Or Tina had lied about never going to the bar with John? About not having ever met the guys he drank with.

*Men gotta be boys.*

Not guys have to be guys. Or men have to be men.

Men gotta be boys.

And…heart rate picking up a tad, Ben opened a browser, dropped his fingers to the keyboard and began to type. *Men gotta be boys, I tell ya', men gotta be boys.*

It was a video game quote. How Ben knew that, he wasn't sure. Probably a throwback to his college days. Stored there in his brain that didn't quit clicking, looking for pieces to complete whatever puzzle was in front of him.

Tina had used the phrase when asked if she was bothered by the fact that her husband spent so much time at the bar. And didn't invite her along.

Her response was a shrug and an easy tone as she'd said, "Men gotta be boys."

And the patron on the bar stool…he'd been asked what John talked about. And his response had been a grin, a shake of the head, and he said, "Men gotta be boys, man. He talked about fishing, his first lay, the tits on any good-looking broad that walked in. And motorcycles."

Ben had been the one in the bar asking the questions on that one. He hadn't specifically remembered the phrase until he'd listened to the recording, but he remembered the grin. It had seemed to include Ben. Like he got that all men ever thought about was getting off, fishing, and motorcycles.

Ben preferred expensive cars, making love with his wife—and the occasional afternoon of fishing at a remote cabin he and Kara had rented a few times to get away from it all. Mostly before they were married.

And before she'd told her sisters that she was dating Stella's husband's best friend.

Gaze on the screen, he searched the phrase he'd typed, didn't find what he wanted, and retyped his question, adding "early 2000s" to the video game portion of it.

And got a page of hits. Clicked the first link that came up, and was staring at a screen shot from a game he'd played as a kid: *Mindset*.

As minutes passed, his focus turned to a stare, but he stayed with it. There was something there for him to see, something that gave him a clue into Hansen's mind. He just had to clear his preformed vision so he could see whatever the hell it was.

He went for coffee. Went back to the computer. Flipped to other screens in the video game. Ended up buying an updated version of the damned thing so he could play through a level or two.

He looked for subliminal messages, and at the more obvious overall scope of the game…a man's gotta be a boy…a kid saving the world. Every level was another challenge for the boy to save men in danger they'd fallen into because they'd forgotten how to think like a kid. It was all about simple truths. Mixed in with a huge dose of imagination and stretching reality to the furthest degree.

Ben completed the second level. Waited for the third to populate and stood. There it was. Right in front of him. The third level. A private fishing pond, where the boy secretly played. The place where he always started from and went back to.

He'd seen it on the first two levels, too. Just hadn't been paying attention…

Out of the office and down the hall in seconds, he interrupted Doug's current telephone call to say, "Private fishing ponds within an hour from here."

The drive time was a guess. That was how it started. If nothing panned out, he'd go out farther.

A man's gotta be a boy. And the only other thing besides sex and motorcycles that John Hansen talked about was fishing.

He had him. Almost. He had to believe that.

Ponds were checked against private properties, narrowing them down to ones most likely not to have year-round occupation, based on location, dual home ownership, occupation of the owner, among other things. Homing in on those with back taxes, alluding to possible abandonment, Ben narrowed down the search even further.

He might not have a great relationship with his wife at the moment, but he was going to do everything humanly possible to ensure that the threat against her life was eliminated. It was something he believed he *could* do.

And afterward, in the next day or two, when he brought her the good news, he could try to force the other issues hanging between them.

To give her an ultimatum. Insist that she talk to him. He, of all people, had the right to know what was going on with her. How could he fix something without knowing what was broken?

But there were other choices. Ones that included honor, respect, patience. Being willing to live through the hard times, regardless of what was fair.

Loving even when it wasn't easy.

And that's what good men did.

Or what men who adored their wives did.

Either way, Ben was on a mission to give Kara the space she needed.

And leave the ultimate fate of his marriage off the table.

What he didn't touch, couldn't break.

# Chapter Ten

Between long bouts at the computer—finding little things that were beginning to form, if not a picture, at least the beginning of one—Kara heard from her sisters multiple times on Sunday via group text message. Stella, chomping at the bit in Tennessee, threatened to come home in spite of what Ben had said. And Melanie demanded that everyone just stay calm and do as Ben had directed. For the time being.

Mostly the texts were funny little tidbits, memories, intended to make Kara smile. To help her get through the tough time. To let her know she wasn't alone.

She already knew that. The plethora of "hotel staff" that had popped in and out of her suite, the "guests" she'd noticed repeatedly walking down the hallway when she'd taken glances out the peephole, were one thing. But there were two female officers locked in with her, too. Taking turns sleeping in a smaller bedroom off the living area.

Kara ventured out to the lovely, elegant communal area to eat but was spending the majority of the day in her room. Her research wasn't anything she wanted anyone else seeing.

And she was texting with Ben, as often as he'd text her back. She'd sent the first "just letting you know things are good here" message late morning.

Had heard back after lunch.

At which time she'd asked how he was doing.

Got a cryptic Good. Making progress shortly afterward.

But when she'd sent the last question, midafternoon, asking if she'd be sleeping in the same place that night, she hadn't heard a thing.

Until almost dinnertime. When he indicated that, yes, she'd be staying right where she was. He was working, she got that. Knowing him as she did, she understood that he was fully focused on taking down the threat to Kara's life, and loved him for that. And so many other things.

Which only made her more upset with herself, and her inability to jump with enthusiasm and happiness into the life they'd planned as it came to fruition. The frustration, and resulting fear at her inability to understand herself, drove her further and further into her search for information about her mother.

She discovered that the little brother her mother had seen killed was an adopted, not biological sibling. But had been willed half of the family empire. The motive for the murder, she surmised.

Reading that, she felt a tug at her heart. A deep one. Could feel deep empathy for a young man being murdered simply because his adoptive parents had loved him.

He'd been a happy ending until that point.

A parentless little one being made whole through a new set of loving parents.

Something Kara had never known. She'd had a parent who loved her. One.

But no set of them.

And what a baby she was being. She'd had two older sisters who had most definitely filled a mother's shoes. With an honorary—now foster—aunt who was always in the background, making certain that everyone was happy and loved.

She'd been adored.

And should be completely capable of adoring a child of her own.

She put her hand to her stomach, then snatched it away just as quickly, as though she'd been burned. And stared at herself in the mirror over the desk where she was sitting. It wasn't that she didn't love the child growing inside her.

It was that she didn't want to risk not being there for the baby. Not being enough.

Because she knew how incomplete she'd felt her entire life, how she'd seemed to have been born with a sense of grief, and didn't want anyone she loved going through that.

At least in part, that was it.

There was more. Her lack of any sense of herself being a good mother. As hard as she tried, she just wasn't seeing it.

She heard from Glenda Arainus, one of the two officers staying with her, that someone had broken into her home sometime after dinner that night. An alarm had gone off. Whoever had been there had been in her and Ben's bathroom.

Her vanity mirror, behind which she'd stored all her toiletries, had been left hanging open. Mostly empty. With a message written with one of the lipsticks left behind on the mirror.

*You can run. You can even hide. But not forever. I'll find you.*

On her side of the bathroom.

If the intruder had opened Ben's vanity on the opposite wall—and noticed his toiletries missing as well—he'd given no indication of having done so.

Ben was the one he was trying to stop. But he obviously had her husband pegged well enough to know that the only possible way to get Ben to quit would be to continue to amp up the pressure on Kara's life.

She texted him as soon as she heard about the break-in.

But by bedtime Sunday night, she still hadn't heard back from him. She didn't blame him. He had to get in his zone, tune out emotion, and focus solely on every aspect of the man for whom he was searching. Almost become him. It was the way he worked.

And with her as the hunted one's target, she knew Ben had to be doing his job on figurative steroids.

She tried to sleep. Turned over half a dozen times. She'd close her eyes and think about a young Tory. About an adopted younger son who'd just been living the life he'd been granted. Trying to do good in the world, from all accounts she'd seen. Which weren't many.

About Ben, who was most definitely the best, most decent, honorable man she'd ever met.

And when she could stand her silence no longer, hating that her husband didn't even know half of what was keeping her up that night, feeling guilty for the emotions she didn't want and couldn't seem to escape, she picked up her burner phone and dialed.

She hadn't been going to call him. If he was getting some rest, she didn't want to wake him. But if he was awake, if there was anything she could help with...

As soon as Ben picked up the phone, she knew she'd made a mistake. His voice was groggy as he said, "Kara, are you okay?"

"I'm fine," she quickly assured him. And then, feeling awkward, inanely blurted, "Did I wake you?"

"It's after midnight, Kara, I've been at it eighteen hours, and have to be up at four. What do you think?" His tone wasn't harsh. More like weary and hurting. He was working himself to exhaustion for her. For their baby, yes, but for her, too. She knew that with her whole heart.

She was not going to cry.

She was going to hang up.

Didn't feel any better after she'd done so.

Or much worse, either. He was being honest with her, which was their way. And that in itself was a comfort. Which was more than she'd been with him. The reminder came as she thought about how she'd spent her day. And the fact that she'd let two days go by without telling him about the bombshell her sisters had dropped on her.

Of course, considering the chain of events since that fateful coffee house lunch, she wasn't totally to blame. But if her sisters had told him…

He called back before she'd had time to get her phone from her stomach back to close enough to her face to text her love and wishes for good sleep.

"I'm sorry. That was uncalled for," he said as soon as she picked up. "I'm on edge and absolutely do not want to take it out on you. I hate that you're there… I'm here. I hate that we aren't talking about the walls between us, too. I should have seen it all coming…"

The words set her on edge. Maybe that was better than burning up with pain. "How could you possibly have seen into Hansen's mind, Ben? Or that Miller guy's? And as far as I go, how could you possibly see inside me to know…"

Know what? That she didn't want their baby?

But that wasn't it, either.

She didn't want to be pregnant.

Wasn't ready to be a mother.

She wasn't ready to have the conversation.

His soft "How are you?" rescued her from the unfinished sentence she'd left hanging in their conversation.

He was letting her know she was off the hook. When she wasn't sure she should be.

But calling him on it…what was the point when she didn't have the answers they both needed from her?

"They told me about the break-in at home. Were you there?"

"No." He sounded more than just physically tired, and she ached to hold him. "I've been out in the field since just before dinner."

"Did you find what you were looking for?"

"Not yet, but we've narrowed our location down to three possibilities."

Excitement shot through her for a brief moment. "You think you know where Hansen is?"

"I think I might." She hated how carefully he was choosing his words. As though she was a victim for whom he was working. Not his wife.

And it hit her, that, in that moment, that's exactly what she was. His victim. Not his wife. Because it was the way he could focus and get the job done.

"You think he's who broke into our house tonight?"

"It's pretty much a given."

She'd been afraid of that. "That means he knows I'm still alive." Her toiletries wouldn't have been missing if she was dead. Not with others still left on the shelves. And the note on the mirror…

She shivered. Looked at the light under her bedroom door, signifying a wide-awake officer right on the other side, up for the night, guarding her while she slept.

"Which is why I need to be up before dawn to get him before he's on the move again."

She needed to let him go. But had to let him know what her sisters had told her. If they'd told him, and he thought she was holding out on him, he'd be hurt.

"I found out something the other day," she blurted out instead of the "Then get some rest" a good wife would have offered. "At lunch with my sisters. I…it's been playing with me, and I should have told you."

Tory being alive had nothing to do with the initial distance between them—her lack of joy at finding out she was pregnant.

But the two weren't unrelated, either.

At his silence, she said, "I'm guessing Mel or Stella already told you…"

"They said you wanted to talk to them about your mom." His tone held compassion. Not anger.

"Did they tell you the rest?"

"Nooo." He drew out the word like he wasn't sure he wanted to hear.

"They said my mom's alive, Ben. She didn't die in a car accident. She left us." It wasn't at all how she'd intended to explain the situation. And yet, in her heart, it was the stopping point. The part that mattered.

But to Ben—who lived in the world Tory had chosen to walk into for a blip in time, and give up the life she'd known for having done so—the rest would be of interest.

He might even be able to help her understand Tory's decision. Something she hadn't thought of. But should have.

And so she quietly, in as few words as possible, told him, "She'd seen something that was key evidence in a murder trial. And after she testified, had to enter witness protection."

"What now?" Ben's words didn't sound the least bit sleepy anymore. She pictured him sitting straight up in bed—or on the cot he was using at the precinct.

She sat up, too. And told him almost word for word what Melanie had told her two days before. Just the facts that she was sure of.

The rest…her research, she didn't even know if she'd found the right case. She'd found another that fit the parameters after dinner. Was going to spend the next day looking at that one.

For one reason only—to see if anything she read helped

snap her back to herself. To a woman she knew. Recognized. Understood.

Maybe reading up on possible scenarios that could have prompted a woman to abandon her baby would bring her some insight. Some kind of *aha* moment that would settle her world back into a place where she could be happy.

Or at least leave her capable of being a good wife and mother.

Ben had a couple of questions. For which she had no answers. "She witnessed whatever she witnessed during a weeklong trip to Florida the year before I was born," she told him. "No one knows anything else. Which is the point of witness protection, right?"

"Yeah." He paused and then said, "I'm sorry, babe. I'm sorry for pushing, but even more that you're dealing with this at all. I wish you'd let me know…"

She wished she had, too. Talking to him, getting personal…she needed that. And couldn't just let his statement hang there. "Things aren't so…great…between us," she reminded him. "My fault, not yours."

She wasn't ready for the conversation. For the questions she'd just opened herself up to.

And was surprised, and relieved, when he said, "It's okay, Kara. You need some time, and I need you to take it, okay?"

She could hardly believe what she was hearing. But took a truly easy breath. And then said, "Are you sure?"

"I am." He paused, and then suggested, "Now get some sleep."

"Okay."

"And Kara? I love you."

"I love you, too," she said, feeling warmer inside than she had since she'd peed on the damned stick Friday morning. Then she disconnected the call.

Snuggling down into her covers, she closed her eyes. Fully

knowing that Ben had just comforted her as a parent would a child.

As one of her sisters would have done.

But she was too emotionally exhausted to do anything but accept the moment of comfort and go to sleep.

## Chapter Eleven

The showdown, when it arrived, turned out to be as anticlimactic as anything Ben had ever experienced or heard of. It was still dark outside in the wee hours of Monday morning, dawn not even on the horizon yet, when several cruisers, followed by him and Doug, pulled onto a two-lane dirt track, through an acre or two of woods, to a broken-down cabin with what they knew to be a mile-wide pond beyond. With his focus intent on the building, Ben saw Hansen peek through the window as the entourage arrived. By the time the first squad car pulled to a stop, the unkempt man had come outside, squinting against the blare of so many headlights, with both hands in the air.

Spotlights were turned on the wanted murderer as Doug stopped his unmarked car and he and Ben got out. Hansen looked haggard. Unshaven. In dirty, disheveled jeans and a partially unbuttoned flannel shirt. His hair skewed as though he hadn't combed it in days.

He hadn't showered, either, Ben guessed as, surrounded by officers with guns steadily aimed on their suspect, he walked up with Doug, who would formally arrest the man. The guy stunk. Like body odor mixed with chocolate and stale cigarette smoke. And had tried to cover it all up with some cheap cologne.

Doug walked right up to him and said simply, "John Hansen, you're under arrest for the murder to Tom Dolan." Then he read him his rights. Asked if he understood them. And when Hansen said, "Yes," told him to turn around and he cuffed the man.

He didn't ask any of the questions Ben needed to hurl at the man. Nor did Ben do so. Jaw clenched, mouth firmly shut, he kept his fisted hands firmly at his sides as he walked back to the cruiser and officers waiting to drive Hansen back to North Haven.

Where, once he was in an interrogation room and in front of a video camera, the barrage of questions would begin. And while he itched to call Kara, or to text her, at least, Ben knew he had to hold off. He needed her on full alert until he knew for certain that she needn't be.

The break-in at their home the night before was bothering him. The note on the mirror didn't fit Hansen's profile. Nor did it coincide with a man who'd just given himself up so easily.

Unless it was all part of Miller's plan. Had the serial killer been in touch with the man, as Ben half suspected? Had he instructed Hansen what to do at Ben's house and somehow convinced Hansen to turn himself in when they found him? Telling the murderer that with no evidence against him, he'd be free in hours? And no longer needing to hide?

If Ben hadn't figured out to look for Hansen at a pond, how long would the attacks against Kara have lasted?

Miller was twisted enough to enjoy the whole gig. Could have continued for as long as he got away with it as a way to pass time in jail. Except that he wanted out of jail and seemed pretty confident that Hansen was his key.

Not smart of Hansen to believe that guy. Miller needed Hansen in jail to pin the rest of the killings on him, believing he would then walk free himself.

Was it possible that Hansen was going to give them something that could indeed set Miller free? Some fact that the prosecution didn't know he had?

Watching the back of the man's head as he and Doug followed the squad car back to North Haven, Ben didn't start any conversations. He was focused.

The job wasn't done yet. Not by a long shot.

"You did it, man," Doug said as they reached city limits. "How you always manage to pull facts out of nothing, I have no idea, but if you ever decide you want to leave your fancy office and come work with me, you've got a job here…"

Ben shook his head. Chuckled. But didn't take his gaze off the man in the back seat of the car in front of him for a second.

He'd found his target.

Should be satisfied.

And he wasn't.

Something just did not feel right.

KARA SLEPT SOME, but was up early. Just as dawn was breaking. She was safe. She knew that. Living in a bubble of protection.

And yet, felt hunted.

Fallout from the two attempts on her life. She understood that. Her brain and emotions just weren't in sync with each other. And fear was winning out over logic.

She showered and dressed in the same pair of stretch jeans but a different top. It wasn't like she'd done anything the day before to get anything dirty. And with no idea how long her life would be on hold, she wanted to be conservative with the clean clothes she had.

As soon as she'd left the bathroom, she sat back down at her computer. She had the new case to research. More opportunity for something to gel within her. Maybe all she needed was time. Days or weeks to acclimate to the shockingly fast culmination of her and Ben's plans to start their family.

Maybe more women went through what she was experiencing than she knew. She'd researched that part, too, but hadn't found anything that resonated with her.

She should probably just tell her sisters that she was pregnant. Melanie had had a child. She'd have an immediate plethora of information to pass on to Kara. Along with questions. Concerns.

Kara would be smothered, and at the moment, the one thing she knew was that she needed a break. Most particularly from her sisters, who'd been lying to her her entire life.

Maybe when she'd been little, and their father had been in charge, they'd had no choice. Maybe Melanie had even made a promise to Tory that Kara would never know that her mother had deserted her as a baby. Maybe her father and Susan and Lila had as well.

But she was no longer a child. They should have told her years ago.

If they had, she might have adjusted to her motherless state in a new way. And could have been ready to have a child of her own.

Would have. Could have. Should have. She had to stop.

Forced herself to focus intently on the links she'd been scrolling through. And…found an official-looking website—it had the Florida state emblem on it—with a listing of capital murder criminal court cases. Hands shaking, she scrolled through dates and found the two cases she'd been looking at through new articles, as well as several more that fit her parameters.

Clicking on the first one, the one she'd originally accessed, she was just beginning to read when a chat bot appeared at the bottom left of her screen.

*If you want to know more about this case, call this num-*

*ber.* An 800 area code was listed, followed by the rest of the number.

Staring at that little conversation screen, Kara could hardly believe her luck. There was actually a number she could call? With someone on the other end of the line who'd know details that she couldn't find anywhere? Things she had to know?

Not where her mother was, of course. Clearly she wasn't ever going to know that. But could she know what Jane Doe had seen? A jury knew.

She had a burner phone. Could make the call without putting herself under any risk at all.

A random college kid could be making the call for research in a legal class. Or a lawyer looking for case law. Didn't have to be Jane Doe's daughter.

And even if someone knew it was her…it wasn't like anyone could find Tory. Or hurt her. And they had no reason whatsoever to hurt the family Tory had left behind. Melanie, Stella and Kara knew nothing.

And hurting them wouldn't affect Tory's new life at all. She'd never know.

Kara glanced at the burner phone. But didn't pick it up. She wrote down the number instead. She'd sit with the possibility. Think about specific questions she'd ask. Give herself time to calm down and make certain that she really wanted to take any further steps at all.

Maybe she had enough.

She jumped when her phone buzzed a text. Glanced guiltily at the number. Like the chat bot knew who she was and was texting her since she hadn't called?

Had all the thoughts of her mother somehow reverted her back to childhood? Judging by her behavior, it sure seemed to have done.

The text was from Ben. She pushed to open it immediately.

He's in custody. Stay put. More soon.

Shaking, she read it a second time. Blinked back tears of relief. And typed back, I love you.

That was all. Just the one truth she had to give him.

Her kidnapper was in custody. She was eternally grateful.

And her time-out was basically done. Life would be back to normal that night. She and Ben, at home together. Sleeping in the same bed. Showering in the same shower. Brushing their teeth at the double-sink vanity with the lovely, framed mirror that stretched over the entire wall in front of them.

Only...she'd peed on a stick, and nothing was ever going to be normal again. Not the old normal. The one where she was confident, successful, happy as just a wife and veterinarian.

There would be purchases. A plethora of them. She liked shopping. And smiled as she thought of some of the cute baby things she'd be choosing from.

Yeah, the shopping wouldn't bother her. And the nursery...she loved to decorate. One wall could be a light lavender, the other pale yellow. With fun animal decals.

The midnight feedings weren't the problem, either. Or having to adjust her schedule to accommodate her other duties.

It all went deeper than that. Hurt harder.

A child needed more than lovely surroundings, kindness, and care. The baby deserved some kind of connection at the core.

Something Kara was missing.

She couldn't go back home and pretend. And did not want to tell Ben that she needed time away from him. She and Ben—separated after just one year of marriage?

The idea didn't fit inside her. At all.

And yet...

No.

She had to do everything she possibly could to fix herself. To get right.

Be proactive. Find her missing pieces. How she could be so certain they were wrapped up with her mother, she couldn't explain. But she was…certain.

Picking up the note she'd written just before her husband's text had come through, Kara dialed.

She had to know.

"I TOLD TINA to threaten anyone who came looking for me, but I swear to you, that's all I did. I been holed up in that cabin since Miller's arrest. I knew he was going to try to pin whatever he was doin' on me. I ain't done none of it."

Ben paced the small room on the other side of the glass. Watching. Taking in. Waiting for the piece that would be the magnet that zapped the picture together in his brain.

The interview had been going on for hours. Three detectives, including Doug, had had their go at the man.

Hansen continued to claim, somewhat convincingly, that he'd had nothing to do with the attacks on Kara. Forensics from Atlanta had been sent by the prosecutor's office to the cabin by the pond where they'd arrested Hansen. Atlanta was next in line for the man, to arrest him on the murder charges for which there'd been a warrant, allowing law enforcement to bring him in. But North Haven got him first, on suspicion of kidnapping—as a favor to Ben.

Preliminary reports gave evidence of waste and food remains that indicated Hansen could feasibly have been staying at the cabin for the two weeks he'd claimed. The lab was currently running a larvae test on some spoiled leftovers that would be able to mark a more definitive timeline.

They'd also found a motorcycle stashed in a shed in the

back. The gas tank was nearly full and there were indications that the engine had been started as recently as the day before.

Hansen claimed he hadn't left the place, other than to go to the grocery store to meet his wife the Saturday of his first week in captivity. Tire tracks indicated otherwise.

He also claimed he hadn't killed anyone. They had videotape to prove otherwise. Which meant that while the man was a convincing storyteller, he was also a liar.

Ben sent off a quick text to Doug, then waited the couple of minutes for his question to be posed to the suspect. And didn't move, hardly breathed, was fully honed as he watched the man as Doug asked, "How did you know that Kara Latimer is still alive?"

Just out of the blue. More to the point than anyone had been that morning.

The confusion on Hansen's face looked remarkably real. Ben had misjudged the man. He was good. Damned good.

Which led him to consider something else as well. What if John Hansen wasn't a drunk at all? He'd appeared out of nowhere with his wife in tow. Paid cash to rent a house outside of town. Claimed a barstool in a dark brooding place where heavy drinkers hung out, forming a kind of brotherhood that solidified his persona.

What if it was all just that? A cover?

They had him on murder. They had his prints on the weapon. And videotape at the scene. Didn't mean he knew that. Doug had purposely not brought Atlanta's case, or any association with Stuart Miller into the picture.

They'd let Hansen assume the warrant for his arrest had had to do with Kara. Had been playing it like she'd died in the explosion. Until Ben had just sent in the question.

Changing tactics…

"I don't know no Kara Latimer," the man said, eyes open

wide and steady as he looked straight at Doug. "If she's dead or not dead… I don't know nothing about that."

Doug leaned in and Ben waited, a curious pass of anticipation shooting through him. "So why were you in hiding?" the detective asked.

A closing-in question. They'd let Hansen proclaim his innocence for hours. Time to show him his mistakes.

"I'm not sayin' no more 'til I talk to a lawyer."

It wasn't the confession Ben was hoping for, but it was confirmation that the man wasn't the innocent he'd been proclaiming.

No way the man was going to get a court-appointed lawyer before court the next day. So, Ben pulled out his phone and made a call.

He'd pay an attorney from a rival firm if that was what it took to get Kara's attacker locked up and his wife home with him.

Even if home meant they were sleeping in separate rooms.

## Chapter Twelve

Kara was eerily calm as she listened to the ringing on the other end of the line. It was Monday. Surely someone within the judicial system would be answering the phone.

"This is the US Marshals Service, to whom am I speaking?"

The Marshals Service! Official answers! Feeling lighter than she had since getting out of the shower Friday morning, she said, "I'm Dr. Kara Latimer." Using her honorific felt kind of cheap, but she needed him to know she was trusted in her community. "I'm a veterinarian."

"I'm Marshal Scott Nivens, Dr. Latimer. Before we go any further, I need you to verify that this is an official call with the US Marshals Service. Do you have access to a computer?"

She was sitting right in front of one. "I do," she told him gladly. Eager to hear whatever he could tell her. Feeling real hope that he held the key to her missing pieces.

"I'm going to call you back on a recorded line here at the office. When I do, I need you to go on to your computer and verify that the incoming number is from the Marshals Service. Can you do that?"

"Of course. Yes."

"I see you're calling from a burner phone," the man said next. "I'll need you to give me the number."

She rattled it off quickly. With confidence. Needing him to know that she was completely, one hundred percent on the up and up.

In spite of using a burner phone. And added, "This phone is only temporary. Mine was destroyed in an…accident… yesterday."

*Accident?* She'd just lied to the US Marshals Service. Not a smart move. But she was under a gag order regarding the explosion, too.

How in the hell had life gotten so complicated?

"I'll call you right back."

Kara's heart thudded as the call disconnected and she waited for a call back. Afraid Marshal Scott Nivens wasn't going to call back. She jumped when her phone rang.

It wasn't Ben. Or a number she recognized. "Hello?"

"Dr. Latimer?" She recognized the voice immediately. "Yes, it's me."

"This is Marshal Nivens. Are you looking up the number from which I'm calling?"

Her fingers were a bit shaky as she typed. "I am."

"Good."

She had to delete a number, retype, hit Return, and saw several listings for the US Marshals Service. Every one of them including the number on her screen.

She was really there.

And the Marshals were most definitely serious about protection. Feeling safer than she had in days, she said, "I've verified the number."

"So now I must tell you that you have engaged in activity that appears suspicious to the US Marshals Service, Dr. Latimer. I'm going to need you to be upfront and honest with me here. If we get disconnected, you don't call me. I will call you back. Do you understand?"

Frozen in place, Kara said, "Yes."

"I have to tell you that I am recording this call. Do you understand that anything you say will be part of an official US Marshals transcript?"

Oh, God. "Yes," she answered immediately. What had she done?

Ben. "Do I need an attorney?" She needed Ben.

"That is your choice, Dr. Latimer. If your answers to our questions check out, we can end this call quickly and not bother you again. If you choose to involve an attorney, we will issue a warrant for your arrest, based on suspicious internet activity involving sealed government records, at which time a Marshal will come to arrest you. And you will have the chance to call your attorney. I already have a Marshal in the area."

Her mind focused on one line at a time. "How do you know where I am? I'm using a burner phone." Not at all what mattered. Just what she could grasp.

A warrant for her arrest? What had she done? Oh God, what had she done?

She'd been right. She wasn't mother material. Two days knowing she was pregnant, and she was under arrest? Because she'd been so desperately driven to find out something that was none of her business?

Her sisters had told her to leave it alone.

They'd known.

She hadn't listened.

"Your phone gives us approximate location based on the cell tower it's pinging off from," Nivens was saying in his same steady, clear voice. "Your computer gives us more as you're signed on to the internet through the resort where you're staying."

Right. Law enforcement would have the means to know that.

Had Hansen had the means, too? Had he been some kind

of techie? Was that how he'd known she wasn't dead? And had left that note on her bathroom mirror?

He'd known where she was—at least which resort. Just not which room…

"Do you want to continue with the recorded questioning, Dr. Latimer? Or wait for a Marshal to come and take you into custody for a more formal interrogation with your lawyer present?"

She hadn't done anything criminal. She'd searched the regular web, not the dark web. Hadn't done anything with the information she'd found except collect it. And would happily burn it all up if they needed her to do so. She hadn't even talked to anyone about what she'd seen. "I'll answer your questions." She gave the obvious answer.

The only one, as far as she was concerned. No way in hell she was going to let her stupidity complicate an already out-of-control two days.

Nor did she want the Marshals to know she was involved in a murder investigation, one that was tied to a serial killer.

She'd done nothing wrong. Was being used to pressure her husband into manipulating the case to the murderer's benefit. But Ben would never do that.

"Are you ready, Dr. Latimer?"

"Yes." Sitting up straight, she most definitely was.

"You are aware that we're recording this conversation?"

Her desk chair felt like a witness stand. "Yes."

"Once we start this conversation, do you give your word that you will mention the content within it to no one?"

Not even her husband? But…it was the only way to end the situation immediately. "Yes," she said. No way she was involving Ben in the horrible mess she'd created out of an immature desperation for something she couldn't even name.

And so, for the next half hour, Kara sat and slowly went

through, step by step, every search she'd done over the past week. Listing the places she'd been when she'd initiated each search. The information she'd printed. The numbers of copies. Verifying that she'd told no one. Breathing a little easier when Nivens told her that was good. And followed the comment up with the assurance that she was doing fine.

She almost thanked him for the reassurance. He'd been kind from the first moment he'd answered the phone. Was making it clear that he didn't think she'd done anything wrong, that they were just clearing up the situation because protocol required that they follow up on every single suspicious act.

"Most of these situations turn out just like this one is doing. They end up being nothing. We're almost done here," he told her. "Just a couple more questions."

She nodded, heard a beep, and looked at her screen to see that Ben was calling.

"My husband's beeping in," she told the Marshal. "I need to at least let him know that I'll call him right back."

"I'm sorry, Dr. Latimer, but this call is being recorded. Any interruption negates the security of our conversation, and I'll need to send a Marshal to pick you up."

She swallowed. Nodded. Had a bad taste in her mouth as she glanced again to see Ben's call. He'd know she was there. She had armed guards protecting her. If they stood at the door, they'd hear her voice—not the words, but they'd be able to make out that she was talking.

What in the hell she was going to tell Ben when he asked her why she didn't pick up his call? It couldn't be the truth. She'd be arrested if she spoke about her interaction with the Marshals Service.

Which meant, on top of everything else, she was going to have to lie to the man she loved.

Dare she hope that he assumed she didn't pick up because she was avoiding personal conversation with him?

The hope was minute. Ben wasn't going to be calling just to check in. To ask how she was.

He'd be calling with news on Hansen.

Which meant she had to give Nivens exactly what he wanted and get off the phone.

"Okay," she said. "Let's get this done."

And heard a soft knock on her bedroom door.

TEETH GRITTED TOGETHER, Ben stood at the one-way window in the small room he'd been pacing during the seconds he'd waited for Kara to pick up his call. If looks good kill, he was pretty sure the glare from his gaze would knock John Hensen dead.

Ben wasn't taking his eyes off the man. Every move the man made while they all awaited his new attorney's arrival was testimony to Ben. Evidence to add to the quickly growing pile.

But he needed his mind free to compile, collate, and place the pieces he was collecting. Phone to his ear, he waited while North Haven police officer, Glenda Arainus, knocked on Kara's door.

He heard the door open. Heard Kara say, "Yes, that's right," before Arainus said a word. Followed by the distinct click of the door closing.

"What just happened?" he barked into the phone, past the point where civility came naturally.

"She's on the phone, sir," Arainus said. "She opened the door, smiled at me, rolled her eyes at the phone, and closed the door."

"'Yes, that's right'?" he shot back at her.

"A response to whoever she was talking to."

He had to put a trace on Kara's phone. Immediately. It

would take a bit more work, with it being a burner phone, but with law enforcement resources, doable.

Heading for the door, Ben stopped himself.

What was he doing? Kara had answered her guard's knock immediately. She'd smiled and rolled her eyes.

Letting him know that she was fine.

She'd seen his call come in. Knew he'd check up on her when she didn't answer. Just as he knew she'd phone him back as soon as she was off her call. He translated the eye roll to mean she was on with one of her sisters. If either one of them were on the verge of coming to North Haven to get more involved in what was going on with her, she'd have definitely stayed on with them until she'd convinced them to stay put as they'd agreed to do.

But she damned well better call him back as soon as she was off with them. Giving her space was one thing—not speaking to one another an entirely different set of circumstances. One he was not going to be able—or at least was not willing—to sign on to. Most particularly with the strenuous conditions they were living under, apart from the stick. A man could only take so much.

John Hansen appeared to be dozing. Based on the loud, phlegmy sound coming over the speaker, Ben figured the man was asleep. Even if he wasn't an alcoholic, he'd clearly been drinking a lot in the short go. There'd been at least ten empty liquor bottles in the cabin, along with one nearly empty one on the table.

Ben wondered if the man would be any more forthcoming after he'd slept it all off. If he'd see sense enough to realize that he had a much better shot of experiencing freedom again in that lifetime if he cooperated with police. One murder, with possibly exigent circumstances involved, attempted kidnapping, and a car bomb didn't generally mean life without parole.

If he ended up pegged with serial murder, he'd be spending the rest of his life locked up.

Which would be just fine with Ben. But not if it meant Miller walked free. His job was to make certain that didn't happen. He had to find a way to get Hansen to spill his guts. Including whatever he had on Miller that would help the state put Miller away forever.

He glanced at his watch. Two minutes had passed since he'd hung up from Officer Arainus. Two minutes when Kara had to know he was waiting.

He didn't feel good about that. About any of it.

Arainus was a well-trained cop with an exemplary performance record. Had worked Special Forces in the military. He needed to accept that Kara was fine.

And possibly just avoiding him.

But he didn't have to like…

His phone buzzed in his hand, interrupting the thought. *Kara.*

Relief was palpable. As was an awareness of his need to get a better hold on himself. "Hey, baby, how are you?" he asked in lieu of hello.

"Good." That was it. Just that one sentence. "I'm working this morning," she said then. "Had an emergency call. Ordinarily, I'd just meet them at the clinic, but…"

He heard the frustration in her tone. And felt downright foolish, even with the sister concoction he'd come up with to explain her not having answered his call. He'd said he'd give her space. That didn't just mean openly. It meant he had to do so in his heart and mind, too.

"No problem," he said then. "I was just calling to let you know it's going to be a bit longer. Hansen lawyered up."

"Okay," she said. "They're calling back, Ben, I need to get this," she said, gave him a quick "I love you." And hung up.

His heart lurched. As though reaching out for her. A reaction to the longing he'd thought he'd heard in her voice.

More overreaction because his wife was asserting an independence from him that he hadn't seen coming.

Dropping his phone in the inside pocket of his jacket, Ben went back to window sitting.

Determined to keep his mind on John Hansen. On getting the man to admit that he'd attacked Ben's wife. Twice. Finding out for certain that Kara would at least be safe.

Not on the little drama going on between them.

In spite of the rock weighing down his gut.

SCOTT NIVENS HAD to have a signature, attesting that she was who she said she was, and that she'd agreed to the phone interview with him. She had to show her driver's license, sign a form, and the whole mess would go away.

Her investigations had not led her any closer to her mother, not in any way that lessened the disconnect inside her. But they'd shown her how far off course she'd gone. Bordering on irrational.

She needed it all behind her.

Without involving anyone else. She'd gotten herself into the trouble—she had to get herself out. No way she was going to risk Ben's reputation, or that of the North Haven Police Department. She couldn't give John Hansen's or Stuart Miller's attorneys any chance at having work thrown out of court pursuant to the cases Ben and Doug were spearheading.

She couldn't risk Hansen being set free, to come back and succeed at killing Kara. Not with Ben's child's life also at stake.

Now that would be the act of a terrible mother.

Due to the sealed manner of the case, Nivens was equally eager to have the matter settled without any further involvement, or vetting needed, from anyone else. Due to the fact that there'd been no other recent hits on the cases she'd visited, and her verification of having been alone in her office, or hotel suite, every time she'd used her computer—and the fact that her IP address had been the only one used—he was willing to close his investigation.

As soon as he'd verified her identity and had her signature.

She had to grow up. Right then. Right there. No big sisters to run to. No Dad to call.

And not even Ben to lean on. She loved him forever. Wanted him forever. Wished that he could be a part of what she was doing. But knew that no one could.

For the first time in her life, she was completely on her own. No cheering section. No advice as she set forth.

She'd gone off the deep end all on her own, and she had to swim her way back. There was no other way for her to be anything for others until she righted her wrong and got herself put together.

Grabbing clean clothes out of her suitcase, she set them on the bathroom counter, turned on the shower, closed the curtain all the way across, and shut the door.

She moved quickly to the bolted door leading to the hallway that she'd been told not to open for any reason—even a fire alarm, as she'd be led out the other way, or someone would open that door from the outside and let her out—she watched through the peephole. Offering up a little prayer that she was embarking on a very quick journey that was a first step in taking her life back, not ruining every good thing she already had.

She waited for the next "guests" to pass by. Counting every second. Nivens would be waiting for her in the stairwell just down the hall.

The "guests" would continue past another three doors

at least before heading back to their room for something...
and there they were. Walking slowly, talking, surreptitiously
checking the walls, the floor, the doorways around the suite
Kara and her team occupied.

They passed on. Not looking back.

And Kara quietly let herself out.

## Chapter Thirteen

Ben was still waiting alone, silently staring down a sleeping man, when his phone buzzed another call. Recognizing Barbara Allen's number, he pushed to answer and said, "What?"

"The silent alarm on her door went off, sir. We ran straight for her room. The shower was running, clean clothes were there. The door to the hallway was closed…"

"Where is she?"

"We don't know." The dreaded words came, crushing Ben's chest, and he ripped open the door to the hallway. Heading toward his car in the lot.

"I was checking the shower," Allen said, frantically. "Glenda noticed the dead bolt wasn't fastened on the door. She ran out, alerted everyone on the floor, but she was just… gone. All agents are on deck, split, covering every floor, the lobby, the parking lot, and beach…"

In the parking lot of the police station, Ben was aware of Doug running after him, but didn't slow down as he bit out his next words to Allen. "The stairwell."

"We're looking at the tapes now," a male voice said. "Mangus here, sir. Of course, that was the only way she could go. She was alone when she entered the stairwell door."

"And from there?"

"Nothing, sir. The cameras in the stairwell were spray-painted gray."

To match the colors of the walls, which was all that would have been visible had someone been glancing at the camera footage. Reaching in his pants pocket for the car's fob, Ben clicked to unlock the doors of his Mercedes-Benz while he was still yards away. Was heading toward the driver's side when Doug passed him.

"I'll drive," the detective said, and Ben didn't argue. By the time he was fully seated on the passenger side, Doug had the car started and was throwing it into gear.

At which point his car's Bluetooth picked up the call. "We're on our way, Allen," Doug told his officer. "I want someone at all exits on every floor. And surrounding the parking lot. More are on their way. I want every license plate number on that lot, every security camera within a three-mile radius. We're going to get this bastard."

Ben didn't doubt the truth of Doug's words. Taking in every detail around him as Doug drove, he didn't let himself think about Kara. He thought about the fact that she'd left of her own accord.

Had deliberately left a running shower and clothes on the bathroom counter.

Had waited until the officers in the hall posing as guests had passed her door. She'd heard all the protocol. He'd insisted on her knowing, in case she needed to use any of it to save herself.

He'd never in a million years figured that she'd use it to escape her safe refuge.

Couldn't even begin to think of why. Didn't matter.

What he had to figure out was how someone had lured her away.

"The phone call," he said. "Have someone check her phone. Now!" he almost yelled the word, and took Doug's phone as his friend handed it to him without so much as a raised brow. They weren't in Doug's car equipped with a radio. Ben had been determined to get himself to Kara, and Doug hadn't wasted time diverting him.

"She'd said she had an emergency, mentioned work. A client. Probably on her answering machine," he shot information into the phone as soon as he'd connected to Doug's second-in-command.

He should have traced her damned call. He should have damn well traced that call.

"We're going to get her back," Doug said to him as he broke all speed limits, in spite of no bubble or siren, to get them to the resort.

Ben nodded. Took the words for what they were worth. Comfort. Nothing more.

He kept his mind focused. Running over every piece of information he had. About Kara. Her voice that morning. Her recent texts. The stick.

And the way she'd suddenly distanced herself from him.

He'd been so caught up in the kidnapping, right after Hansen's threat, that he hadn't even considered another scenario to Kara's off behavior. And someone's very determined, and desperate attempts to take her from Ben.

What if Kara had had an affair? What if the baby wasn't his?

The thoughts came.

And they went. Just as quickly. His gut told him. His head told him. His heart told him. If it was possible, Kara was telling him through some kind of mental telepathy.

Call him off his rocker or up a wall, didn't matter.

There was no way his wife had been unfaithful to him. Not only had their own sex lives been amazingly healthy, it just wasn't in Kara to do such a thing.

Which put him back to Tina Hansen's threat.

With John Hansen in custody, that meant Stuart Miller. Somehow, the man was directing shots from within prison.

And was determined to get Ben to make certain that he walked free.

Gritting his teeth, Ben hoped to hell they got the bastard before it was too late. And that Ben didn't have a second alone with him when they did.

He'd kill the man with his bare hands.

Ben didn't give a damn about lawyering up. Or interrogation protocol. When they got this guy, he was going to spill every bean he had.

KARA KNEW THE second she pushed through the stairwell door and saw blotches of wet on the wall that she was in trouble.

He came from under the stairs, with a housekeeping laundry hamper. Threw her in it, dumped dirty towels and sheets on top of her, but not before he'd made sure she saw the gun under the towel hanging over his hand. "Make a sound, you die."

It wasn't Niven's voice.

Someone else. She'd walked right into her abductor's hands?

Hansen was in custody. Someone that Miller guy hired then? On their behalf.

*Think like Ben.* The thought occurred, she let it. Whatever it took to hold panic at bay.

She was all on her own. It was time to prove herself or die.

And if she died, she'd be responsible for the death of her and Ben's baby.

She couldn't let that happen. It would be the culmination of what she feared most. Letting her baby down. Having it suffer pain because of her.

A less-than-three-month-old fetus wouldn't have a developed-enough brain to process pain. There was that. It would still be loss of life.

Stop!

Focus. Clues. Putting pieces together.

Dirty laundry clenched in her fists, she held on as she was bumped down a flight of stairs. She heard a door open. Only one flight. Fifth floor. They were on carpet. Another door opened. She was wheeled some more. The door shut. And then…nothing.

Wait. She heard movement. Something scraping along the floor? Tile, not carpet? She wasn't in a hotel room?

She wasn't alone.

She was just…lying there. As seconds turned into thirty, then a minute. She'd been counting her pulse. Estimated her elevated heart rate. And figured time passage from there. One minute, ticking toward two. Might matter later.

Hands on top of her… Grabbing at the laundry under which she lay. A gun appeared, inches from her nose, and a soft male voice said, "Get up, get in the dryer. You make a sound, you die."

Dryer?

Slowly, holding on to the sides of the laundry bin, she stood. Saw a big, commercial-size front-loading dryer on a wooden pallet, what looked to be the cardboard box it had come in right behind it. And a forklift, machinery. She was in some kind of…

"Move!" The word was issued in a soft hiss.

She couldn't get in that dryer. She'd suffocate.

He…she couldn't see his face. He wore a surgical mask. But the voice, the build, the structure and size of his gloved hands…he was male.

"Get in or die." The warning was low, barely audible, and yet completely clear.

Shaking inside, Kara held an armful of towels and stood her ground. "I get in, I die," she said. "I'll suffocate."

Keeping the gun on her, the man did an odd thing. He pointed inside the dryer. "Newly drilled air holes," he said. "Get in or I shoot."

There was a silencer on the gun. Her captor cocked the trigger release.

And Kara climbed in.

BEN HAD TIME warped into a never-ending nightmare. Wearing forensic gloves, he followed the crime scene photographers. As soon as they snapped their photo, he was right behind them, going through Kara's things. Careful not to disturb evidence, but searching for anything that stood out. He knew her better than anyone. Lived with her.

And knew that the notes at her computer were not work related. He dialed what was clearly a phone number written on a piece of slightly crumbled paper. Only to hear that it had been disconnected.

Her computer showed no recent searches.

Frowning, he clicked a few more keys, looking for recent activity. She hadn't been on her secure work portal. Hadn't accessed any client records...

She hadn't had a work emergency.

She'd lied to him?

"Rush this to Atlanta," he barked out to the room.

A crime scene investigator he knew, but only peripherally, was right there. "On it, sir."

And so it went. For the next hour, Ben was in a tunnel of complete focus. He couldn't think about where Kara might be. About what could be happening to her.

He had to know what had led her to that place. It was the only way to find her.

And he *would* find her. There was no doubt in his mind about that.

Doug and his investigators were covering the resort, from stairwells to beach, interviewing every employee, every guest before allowing anyone to leave. The lockdown had been put into effect seven minutes after the alarm had sounded. She had to be somewhere on the premises. That was the theory.

As the second hour started to tick by, Ben wasn't so sure the going train of thought was the right one. And while he fully acknowledged that nothing was making sense to him, as time passed he felt more and more strongly that Kara wasn't right there.

She'd left her room of her own accord. Whether under duress or not, he couldn't be sure. But the clothes she'd left on the bathroom counter, to make it look like she was underneath the running shower spray, weren't right. She didn't wear the black-and-white tie-dyed top with white pants. She wore them with black. Barbara Allen, who'd packed for her, wouldn't have known that. But the black pants that went with that top—the ones faded almost to gray—were still in the suitcase.

And the bra and panties tucked inside the folded pants... she didn't do that, either. She laid them on top. Always. Because she put them on first, she'd laughingly told him once, when he'd teased her about her process. And she didn't want her clothes creased.

She'd also left her curling iron on. She was a stickler for that one. Had gotten in trouble for having done so when she was a kid. There'd been a fire in her neighborhood started by a curling iron.

Out in the hallway, walking every inch of the path she'd have taken from her door to the stairwell, Ben forced himself to stay in his wife's frame of reference. To think how she thought, to the best of his ability. She'd left of her own accord. But why?

What had been going on when he'd called her that morning? Something important enough to avoid picking up. And then, per their normal protocol, she'd called him back—she'd called him back…because if she hadn't, he'd have known something was wrong.

She hadn't wanted him to know…

She'd been on the phone.

*Yes, that's right.* The words he'd heard her say over the line when he'd called to make sure she was fine when she hadn't answered.

What was she confirming? To whom?

And her voice…it hadn't been a friendly conversation. She'd been assuring someone of something. He'd thought her sisters, but…

Heading down the stairs, Ben attempted to keep Kara front and center, staying in her skin, as he followed what had to have been her path. Presumably, since there'd only been seven or eight minutes in which for her to escape, she'd gone straight down. Again, just a theory.

But one that, so far, was leading nowhere. And so, he'd stop on every floor. He'd study every inch of them, if that's what it took. Professional criminals made mistakes. Someone like Kara—so trusting and existing in a world where covering her tracks wasn't even a blip on the radar—she'd done a damn fine job of it.

Or had she?

Those clothes. The curling iron. Was it possibly she'd been talking to him? Purposely leaving tracks?

Someone had gotten to her. Had to be through her phone or computer. They'd threatened her. And she was carrying a child inside her. They could have told her they'd get Ben and/or her sisters, too. Those would be the only reason Kara would suddenly just put herself in danger.

On the phone with the forensics lab in Atlanta, which included top-rated computer forensic capabilities, Ben insisted on being kept up to date every fifteen minutes. He walked the hallways of all five floors between Kara's floor and the ground. Teams were covering the outside of the property. He'd get there. He had to know where it had started. How she'd disappeared. That would give him a clue as to who had her and why.

She had no means of transportation from the hotel. One had to have been provided to her or for her. There was no sign of any struggle. No sign of dragging in the sand. Or wheels being rolled through it, either.

Stopping to speak with Doug on the ground floor, Ben secured a master key to all the hotel's mechanical rooms. The workspaces. They'd all been searched during the first fifteen minutes after the call went out. He was going back. Not looking for Kara, as others had done, or any obvious signs of intrusion, either. He needed his mind fully in the story. As though he was the one luring Kara out and snatching her away. Starting on the fifth floor—because it would have been only one flight down, and therefore, the most obvious stop if one only had seconds to work—he went through housekeeping quarters. Looked over racks of clean towels, cleaning supplies, a couple of unused carts. Talked to a woman who'd been on the floor all morning and had already been cleared to go back to work.

And when he asked if there was any other place on the floor where someone could slip unseen, maybe a vent, an access way to system repair, she shook her head and said, "No, sir. Just the actual laundry room, at the end of the hall. But it's been off-limits all morning. One of the dryers shorted out yesterday afternoon. Almost caused a fire.

New dryer was supposed to be delivered this morning, but it came in damaged…"

She was still talking when he tore out of the room, finding the last door—one that looked like any other guest room door. They had all been searched within the first half hour of disappearance, but he pulled out his master key. Ben threw the door open so hard it banged against the stopper mounted in the wall.

And with a precision eye, stood in the doorway, making note of the entire room. The haphazard collection of filled laundry bins, awaiting attention. There were five of them. All filled to the brim.

Except one. They'd all been searched. He'd seen a report.

But he homed in on that one bin that wasn't the same as the others. It was filled to the top, but not overflowing like the rest of them. Adrenaline pumping, he approached the bin and, pulling fresh gloves on, started hauling out the towels, one by one. Studying every one of them.

Freezing when he noticed a familiar smell. Lilies and jasmine. Kara had told him they were the scents in her perfume. She'd been in the bin?

Clawing his way down to the bottom, he looked for any other sign of his wife.

And found one. An earring. Half of the pair he'd given her for Christmas. A big heart, with a smaller heart encased in it. He'd meant it to represent her and the child they would be starting to try for sometime that next year. She'd thought it represented him and her. She'd been so happy with the gift, an avowal of his love, that he hadn't corrected her assessment.

With the small piece of jewelry in hand, he was out the door and taking the stairs back down, skipping every other one as he ran. Whether the earring had become dislodged, or Kara had purposely left it there to be found didn't matter. She'd been in that laundry bin.

He had his starting point.

# Chapter Fourteen

Kara didn't have the luxury of fear. She had intelligence. Training by proxy from living with a highly successful special investigator. And as long as she was alive and Ben was out there looking for her, she had hope.

She'd have more of it if she could keep herself thinking like Ben. She allowed herself to close her eyes now and then to send him subliminal messages. They were wordless. Bouts of intense emotion that she felt when she focused her mind and heart only on him.

Her dryer prison had been lifted into what she'd assumed was the box she'd had a brief glimpse of in the workroom. She'd been wheeled to what had to have been some kind of service elevator right there in that room. Then after a ride down another short distance, and up what had to have been a ramp. She heard what sounded like a big metal garage door close and then there'd been driving.

Clutching towels to her as she lay in an awkward, bent fetal position in the dryer drum, Kara made note of every move. Tried to keep a pulse-based timeline.

They hadn't gone far when the vehicle had stopped. She'd been set free of her appliance confinement in to some kind of dark metal container. A storage garage, she'd soon figured out.

From there, with her hands tied behind her, she'd been shoved into a windowless van, and had been inside ever since. They'd moved. They'd stopped for up to fifteen minutes at a time. With a dark curtain between her and the driver, she couldn't see much.

But when he spoke, she could hear him. "Yeah, I've got her. We're on our way" had been the first thing she'd made out.

And then, twelve minutes later, by her calculation, "Almost there."

Who the man was talking to, she had no idea. Knew she had to care. That she'd have a better chance of survival if she could figure it out.

She wasn't Ben.

Something that became blatantly obvious when the van stopped and she was hauled out. Squinting against the sudden brightness, sunlight coming from directly above, she noted that it was noon. Tried not to think about her pounding heart, the butterflies in her stomach as she took in her surroundings. Dirt ground. Small old white house. Fields and trees.

"Where are we?" She spoke to know that she was real. Alive. Capable of acting under her own power. Reminding herself that she had some.

"A place," the man said, his mask firmly in place. For her benefit, she surmised. Though, with changing times, mask wearing while driving wouldn't have garnered all that much attention—his face covering included eyebrows and forehead. With a bandana around his hair.

He had brown eyes. Which was more than she'd known about her accoster on the beach. Was it the same man?

She wanted to be able to discern, one way or the other. To have that information to report to Ben when they were back together. Searched her memory bank for any hint of recognition as the man, with a firm hand on her elbow, and a gun in his other hand, propelled her forward.

"What do you want from me?" she said then, finding that she felt stronger when she spoke. She might be confined but at least her words weren't trapped in her head.

"I can't speak to the end result," the man said. "But right now, you're going to do something for me."

She stopped, pulling her arm away. No way was she going to walk in that house and let that man take…

The baby.

"Just shoot me now," she said, her voice strong, as conviction flowed from her heart to wipe out all other sensation. "I will not walk in there with you."

"My friend is in there. He got shot. You're a doctor. And you're going to fix him."

Oh. She thought about keeping the fact that she was a veterinarian to herself. Decided it was the way to go. If she had access to a scalpel…

"Sorry if the ride was a bit rough back there," the man said then. "I swerved to avoid hitting a dog." A dog? Yeah, there'd been an uncomfortable swerve that had banged her up against the side of the van.

A guy who abducted women wouldn't go out of his way to save a dog's life. He had to be playing her. Probably knew she was a veterinarian and was trying to get her to cooperate with him by appearing to care about animals.

But his voice sounded…human. Not kind, maybe, but with a tiny hint of decency. Ben there, in her head, talking about how much you could discern from a person's voice. The various changes it made.

"And afterward?" she asked as they approached the broken cement outside the front door of the house.

"Then I deliver you to my boss."

Dare she hope that his boss was a US Marshal? Named Scott Nivens? And that some lower-level deputy person had just gone rogue to save a friend?

The Marshals Service, to protect the sanctity of the witness protection program, needed to make certain that Kara knew nothing more than she'd already disclosed.

She hadn't told them that she was under protection herself. Hadn't expected some big extraction effort.

But it was possible that Marshal Nivens, who was clearly good at his job or he wouldn't have it, had found out more about her. Enough to know that…she'd been in protective custody?

And her best chance at staying alive—at giving Ben time to follow the trail—was to keep her mind firmly focused in reality. It was more probable that someone connected to Stuart Miller and John Hansen was awaiting her arrival.

She had to accept that fact.

Along with another she saw the second she stepped into that old, musty-smelling house. Not only was there no patient there, there wasn't any furniture, either.

Just a dirty floor, littered with what looked like rat droppings.

Horror filled her. Her limbs felt weak. Tears threatened. He was going to…

No. Ben. The baby. Needed her strong.

If he…it would be after she was dead.

Letting go of Kara's arm, the man moved toward the door he'd left open. Giving her a chance to…

He pulled out his phone. "Delivered. I'm on my way," he said, and, walking out, closed and then bolted the door behind him.

That's when she noticed the back of the door, the part facing the inside of the house. There were no knobs. Her gaze flew to the room's two windows as her body followed just half a beat behind.

There was no glass there. Only bars that appeared to be wired to…she couldn't see where the wire went.

She'd been delivered.

To be blown up? At an old one-room house in the middle of nowhere? One that appeared to have once had a kitchen corner, based on the ancient wooden cupboard with a slatted wood counter on top, and what appeared to be part of a well pump.

Walking around, she calmed herself. Took in every detail she could. Cloning Ben. Or at least pretending to herself that she could. She was keeping him close, and it helped.

She had to find a way out. Broke a piece of rotted wood from the counter and threw it at the window. Heard the spark and watched it sizzle and fall to the ground.

At which point she stomped on it, burning the bottom of her tennis shoe in the process. She twisted and turned on the damned thing. Making certain that there was no chance of another spark, of sending herself up in flames along with the rest of what clearly was meant to be her incinerator.

She had to find a way out. There'd be more rotted wood. She pushed on walls. Went through one of the weather-damaged sheets of drywall, but ended up against a beam. And whatever else was between walls and the outside world. Wood for one. If she had a saw…even a table knife…

She had to find something.

Because it was becoming clear to her that it was up to her to do whatever it took to keep herself alive.

Which meant getting out.

Before someone flipped a switch and the little house went up in flames.

THE TRAIL WASN'T that difficult to follow. Which worried Ben. It was almost as if whoever had taken Kara had wanted him to go after her.

Knowing he'd be at the front of the line.

Hansen was in custody. Sitting with his lawyer while they awaited Doug's return from the newest crime scene.

Meaning Stuart Miller had been behind the attacks on Kara? Or had, upon Hansen's arrest, put another soldier in the field?

Whoever had Kara had planned well. He'd found a way to get in and out of the resort without issue. In spite of Kara's protection detail. And had known enough to figure out that all hands would be on-site first, hoping to find Kara there. It had been the most logical conclusion.

Who'd have thought to report a fried dryer and a damaged replacement in the midst of a life-and-death crisis?

The truck had already been in place, the driver vetted as having been on a legitimate repair call, before Kara's alarm went off. The man had had her out of there while searches were being organized. Before Ben had even arrived.

And had ditched the truck just a couple of miles away. In a wooded pull off just outside of town. He hadn't even tried to hide it.

He'd known they'd be on to him soon. He'd just needed time to get away. To do with Kara whatever it was he intended to do. Following whatever orders had gone awry with Friday's miscalculated kidnapping from the beach?

Doug's team was on the service repair company that owned the truck. And that regularly serviced resorts and hotels in Atlanta and surrounding regions. Some answers were taking a bit longer to come by. Which also had to have been part of the plan.

What the predator wouldn't have expected, however, was for Ben to be on him as quickly. When the ruckus died down, and all employees returned to their duties, the hotel would have discovered that their dryer problem was not resolved. That whoever had taken the new but damaged dryer out wasn't returning with another one.

Or Doug's team, upon viewing resort camera footage, or traffic cams from the area, would have found the appliance truck's exit too close to time of abduction, and made a follow-up visit.

But Kara, bless her, had lost an earring. And the fiend who'd stolen her had made a fatal error—he'd failed to fill up the bin after hauling his captive out of it.

Didn't mean Ben was going to find her alive. But it increased his chances. His gut was telling him she was still out there, waiting for him. And whether or not it was fantasy on his part, some kind of self-professed thing, he didn't really give a damn. The sense was propelling him forward like never before.

Leaving Doug and his team to handle the formal investigation, Ben changed quickly into jeans, shirt, and work boots before heading out on his own, just after noon on Monday. In the car by himself, following his choice of leads—but with a team of forensic specialists, and Doug, reporting in, too. Keeping him up to date.

He was to do the same with them. Teams were standing by, ready to storm any fortress necessary to bring Kara home.

Currently, he was following the very obvious leads being handed to him from traffic cameras, and minus those, surveillance cameras from various businesses—and one farmhouse close to the road that he stopped at to find welcoming and helpful homesteaders—to follow a van that had driven down the road on which the appliance truck had been found, just minutes after the truck had also been seen.

The blue cargo van had no windows in the back. And from one camera image, showing the windshield of the van, they'd been able to determine that a curtain had been hung just behind the two seats in front.

The plates had been run and the team had confirmed what Ben had assumed. They'd been stolen off another vehicle two days before.

That car had then been burned. The owner was recently deceased.

All clean work of an experienced criminal—a description that definitely fit Stuart Miller, if not John Hansen—except this last bit. The disposal of the appliance truck. Exposure of the getaway van. None of it was giving any clues to the identity of the perpetrator. But they were all leading Ben straight to Kara. Rather quickly.

Either they'd already killed her or otherwise had obtained what they needed from her. Or he was speeding his way into a trap that could prove lethal for both of them.

And the tiny fetus they'd created together. A living organism trying to grow into human life.

Ben saw the house even before receiving the coordinates being sent to his vehicle for the blue van that had passed another surveillance camera just half a mile away. It had stopped in between that sighting and the previous one.

Ben experienced a dangerous flash of weakening relief when he saw through his binoculars that the building was still intact. Not only that, he noticed what were clearly brand-new tire tracks in the dust on the one part of the dirt drive that was in clear view. His gut was telling him she was there. Or had been there just minutes ago.

His brain calculated what might be just ahead. The house was standing, but that didn't mean it would be for long. Twice Kara had been taken by being encased and wheeled past would-be witnesses. There'd been a fire. And a car explosion.

Reports on the bomb forensics had given indication that an individual who'd purchased like materials hadn't just bought enough for one bomb. But it was one report of said sales among many. Detectives were still following up on all of that.

And Ben had to move under the assumption that Kara could be rigged to explode.

He was missing that one critical piece. What was Miller hoping to gain from getting to Ben? The most logical theory was that Ben had, or was about to stumble on, something that would assure Miller's conviction. If so, he might need to take Ben alive, to find out what he knew. To find out what, if anything, he might already have done with the information.

To destroy said proof before it made its way to official channels.

Ben, after all, was only a hired PI. Working outside law enforcement channels.

With every muscle in his body tensed to run to his wife, to grab her in his arms and keep running for the rest of their lives, Ben pulled the Mercedes-Benz down into an embankment while he was still almost an eighth of a mile away. Before anyone watching the road from inside the small, clearly abandoned house would see him.

And then, keeping cover in trees, bushes, and undergrowth, he traveled the entire perimeter with enough control to study every aspect of the landscape, the space between him and the house. He was looking for any possible dangers, as well as best possible escape routes were something to go wrong.

The van had left, but he had no way of knowing whether it had left more than just Kara behind. Or how many more. If she was there at all.

He also had no way of knowing if or when the van, or another vehicle would be back.

And couldn't think about what could be happening to her inside those walls while he stood out there. If he blew in on a burst of emotion, he could get them both killed. As he got closer to the house, he found a tree to climb and pulled the binoculars hanging around his neck up to peer through them. Looking for footprints in the dirt.

Then, with another flash of weakness prompted by relief,

counted just two sets of them. One smaller than the other. Thinner. Male and female.

Two going in.

One heading out.

Didn't mean there was no one else there. That someone hadn't approached just as he was doing. Through grass and brush. Though he noticed none that was broken down, as the path he was leaving behind portrayed.

Fighting harder with himself to continue his perusal, to make certain he had a full picture of the outside landscape—including any trap that could be mounted to a tree, or a drone that would drop a firebomb—Ben continued forward. Keeping thoughts of Kara with him but not allowing himself to focus on them.

He'd seen the left, front, and right side of the house, and rounded ground that would allow him a study of the back of the building. And froze.

His worst nightmare smacked him in the face. Drawing breath up out of his lungs with difficulty, Ben stared through the magnifying lenses, taking stock of the wiring running between the two windows on the house—both in the back.

The lines running between the two openings were new enough that they were both brightly colored silver with no signs of weathering. No dirt or dust marring the bars where glass had been in those cutouts, either. Those wires told him that there could be similar ones in the walls on the sides of the house.

The door latch was probably rigged as well.

While he had no way of knowing how the kidnapper was keeping Kara hostage inside the house, he saw clearly what her likely fate was meant to be.

He'd seen no cameras in the trees around the property, or on the house. Didn't mean there weren't any. Could be they were set up inside. Though he'd been told no electronic signal had been detected coming from the area when he'd been given final coordinates, signals could be turned on and off at will.

So what was going to trigger whoever had set her up to die, to actually turn the switch meant to make it happen? His arrival?

How would anyone know he was there?

Or was Kara wired? And if she saw him, reacted, the bomb would go off?

He had to know more. He plotted a route in the trees, ones that were close enough for him to climb from one branch to another. Giving him enough of a view, with his lenses, to be able to see what he could inside the house.

If he was lucky… Ben didn't allow the thought to reach its conclusion as he climbed, scraping the top of his hand, ignoring the blood. He couldn't get to the V-shaped branch for which he was heading fast enough. And once there, he hardly secured his balance as he raised his binoculars once more.

And nearly dropped them, blinking back a blur in his vision, as he laid eyes on his darling Kara. She was at a wall. Had an oddly shaped something in both hands and was frantically trying to do something to the wall.

He slid down the tree, scraping his stomach on bark as his shirt slid up.

She was alive! But…

That one glance had told him two other things. Based on her current activity and the fact that he hadn't seen anyone else in the one room, there was a better chance than not that she was alone. For the moment.

And he had to stop her from doing whatever it was she was trying to do before she tripped a wire and blew herself up.

## Chapter Fifteen

The wiring wasn't intricate. Just appeared as a major danger to her because there didn't seem to be any kind of discernible plan in the running of it. The home had had electricity at one point, but the older wires were easily distinguishable from what was obviously new.

Mostly, Kara saw them all, tried to avoid them, and continued to turn the pointed end of her third piece of broken-off countertop through the rotted drywall, over or between the two-by-four framing studs, depending on the direction they were going and out toward the piece of rotted stuff that served as the outside of the house.

After she'd reached a dead end with her first attempt to break through, she'd studied more carefully, from the ceiling down. Had followed the worst of the water damage to a space closer to the front door, but still on the side wall. And with however many punches it took, she'd be through to the outside. Where she went from there, she didn't even care. Not right then.

First step was to get out alive.

Aiming carefully between wires for the patch of rotted outer whatever it was—some kind of special woodstuff that covered the outside of homes—Kara stayed focused and shoved. She could die with any push. She knew that.

It didn't take an electrician to figure out that she was in a home that was booby-trapped to explode.

She still had choice.

She could stand up and try. Or give up and die.

She was not going to go out as someone who didn't try to save the child inside her. Who just sat down and allowed the child's life to be snuffed out.

The next stab was harder than the last, breaking open the blister that had formed on her palm. She hardly acknowledged it. Stabbed again. And again.

Thinking like Ben. Keeping her mind on the task. Refusing to allow herself to get sidetracked by thought or purpose.

On the next stab, her makeshift tool broke and she ran back to the counter. Kicked upward with all her might and broke off another piece. Nodding when the break created another pointed edge. She was on the right track. The boards were showing her the way.

Back over at the hole she'd made, she didn't stop to look at progress. Couldn't let herself get discouraged in the event there wasn't enough. She had no idea what she was pushing through. How it would break. She could see the rotted outer edges and had to hope that the normally dreaded state, dry rot, went all the way through.

Another stab and she heard a pop. A sizzle. An old wire? Or a new one?

Either way, she could be out of time.

Backing up to the middle of the room, Kara grabbed one of her discarded boards. Shoved it down into the front of her jeans so it stood upright to her ribs. Then, positioning her newest tool perpendicular to it up high enough to break a rib, but not hurt the baby, point outward, she held the one to the other, kept her eye on her target, and ran her entire body into it.

The jolt just between her ribs knocked the air out of her. She fell.

And landed...on hard dirt. With a weed up her nose.

She'd made it out. Was free.

She was trying to breathe, to ready for her next steps, when she heard the sizzle directly behind her.

And the world around her turned orange.

BEN RAN WITHOUT a plan. Without thought. He saw Kara fly out of the side of the house and he ran. Feet passing so quickly past each other, back and forth, that they barely touched ground.

No training came to the fore. Nothing but getting to Kara. He didn't slow down until he was a foot away, and only then to bend down, scoop her up, and continue running.

He didn't feel her weight. Or her warmth. Just held on. One foot in front of the other at lightning speed. Stretching his stride as far as he could.

The blast hit him in the back with a force that knocked him to the ground, and, arms around Kara, he rolled. Over and over, like a kid down a hill in the summertime. Holding his heavier weight off from her as much as he could, he rolled until he reached brush too high to roll through, and then, only then, he allowed himself a quick glance back.

The house was in flames. A good twenty-five yards away. The mostly hard dirt ground surrounding the burning structure would help stem the fire's spread, but Ben had no idea how much time they had before someone showed up. Either firefighters to put out the flames, or someone responsible for setting them.

Checking to make certain that his prey was dead?

"We have to go," Kara said, extricating herself from his body and standing up. "They'll be back..."

Because she'd triggered the explosion, not them.

And he saw the chance right in front of him. "We have to go," he told her. "But not yet." Pulling his cell phone out of his pocket, he ran toward the flame, got close enough that he knew he could trust his old pitching arm to pull through for him, and let go.

The phone landed in flames just outside the perimeter of the house. By the front door.

Turning, he rushed back to Kara, grabbed her arm, and holding on to her, ran into the woods.

KARA DIDN'T WANT to run anymore. She wanted Ben to hold her. To tell her everything was going to be alright. But knew that even if he stopped, grabbed her up and said those words to her, they wouldn't be true. Not while whoever was working on behalf of Stuart Miller, and possibly John Hansen, was still out there.

And unknown to them. She wasn't superhuman. At some point, she was going to be seriously hurt. Or killed.

"What about your car?" she asked him. And then as another thought occurred to her, added, "Or did someone come with you? Is that where we're going? Is someone waiting for us?"

She'd seen the dirt drive in the yard where her small prison had been standing. There hadn't been a vehicle in sight. But neither had she expected to see one. Ben wouldn't have just driven up and shown himself.

He could have been shot for his effort.

"I drove," he said, not slowing down as he pressed on right in front of her, breaking down brush with his hands as he walked briskly through trees and small clearings. "The Mercedes is parked in a ditch."

Relief palpitated through her. "Is that where we're heading?"

His headshake wasn't as much of a surprise as it might have been. Ben was…different…somehow.

He'd spent two days investigating, listening to interviews from both Hansen and his wife. Researching. He was on the job. She'd never been on it with him before.

She'd never been the job.

And…he'd likely drawn his own conclusions regarding her reaction to her pregnancy, too. Their personal challenges couldn't be on the table they were being hunted and threatened, but they were lingering between them.

"The car's forty-five minutes behind us, Kar," he said, forging forward. "Obviously, the body in the ambulance didn't work, but I'm hoping a house burned to ash, with you known to be trapped inside, and me known by authorities to be close by and my cell phone burned just outside the front door, that we'll be assumed dead."

Dead. Twice in three days. She was beginning to feel like some kind of bad horror movie.

And if they were dead…her steps slowed…as more of her senses returned to a seminormal state. They had to stay completely out of sight. "So where are we going?"

His steps slowed, too, but he kept moving. Barely glancing back at her. "I'm still working on that," he told her. "I have a burner phone in my sock. Once we get far enough away so that I'm certain it won't ping off any tower near the house, I can phone Doug. Right now, Doug, his people, and local law enforcement are probably all over the scene. Doug's team led me there. Knew that's where I was headed. The heavy police presence will help to build your kidnapper's assumption I'm dead. Most particularly if, at the scene, it's determined that our bodies are part of the ashes. That there was no way of escape. The longer we stay dead, the safer we are."

*We.* She held on to that word. Not ignoring the rest of what he'd said. Just not letting it rob her of her strength and ability to press forward.

She walked harder. Faster. And tried to make sense of all the horrendous turns her life had taken since she'd peed on a stick.

Leading her and Ben to that moment, out in the wild, running for their lives.

"You left protective custody." His words came baldly, almost like gunshots, into the silence that had fallen between them.

He'd come for her. Risked his life to save her. But he was holding himself apart from her, too.

She didn't blame him. And knew, as soon as the answer she had to give him became clear, that she was only going to be making things worse between them.

"Yes."

"Why?"

"It's complicated, Ben. I'll talk to you about it, but now isn't the time. I can assure you that it's personal, nothing to do with our current challenges, and we... I...need to get through this first."

He said nothing, didn't even slow down his step. If anything, he increased his pace.

Her heart cried out for the man she loved so desperately, even as parts of her knew that she couldn't give him everything he wanted. She wasn't excited about being pregnant or raising a family. She was scared, unsure about herself.

"I'm sorry," she said then. "Please, just let's do this together and then we can talk."

She had to get back to safety, get with Marshal Nivens, and somehow wrangle permission for her husband to know that she'd been suspected of trying to find a person in the witness protection program, but had been vetted and cleared.

She'd given the Marshal her word that she hadn't been doing so, and stood by that with every fiber of her being. She hadn't been looking for Tory. Didn't need or want to see her.

She'd been seeking answers as to her own abandonment. Period.

And perhaps she'd found them. At least in part. That call with Marshal Nivens had sure given her an entirely different understanding of the utmost seriousness, and overly large scale, of whatever her mother had gotten mixed up in.

Ben didn't respond to her plea. But he let the topic go. And continued to watch out for her as they hiked.

She tired, some. Wanted a break, but didn't say so. They'd been on the move for more than an hour. So long that she could no longer see the smoke billowing up from the fire they'd left behind.

After those initial exchanges, they hadn't spoken much. When he asked, she described everything she could remember from the time she'd stepped out from the door of her suite into the hallway at the resort, until he'd seen her go careening out the side wall of a house.

And then other than to check up on each other, or discuss a possible turn, there was no conversation at all. Part of her was grateful. Mostly she needed a good cry.

As though tears would somehow fix what was broken inside her.

Ben had stopped. Kara, so lost in her thoughts, had almost run into him as she rounded a tree that led them into the next clearing. Maybe two feet of it.

"We need to eat and drink," he said. And then looked her in the eye for the first time since they'd been reunited. Looked as though he was seeing her, not just seeing that she was okay. "When was the last time you had anything?"

"This morning, breakfast," she said, and then shook her head. "I have no idea what time it is." She hadn't put on her watch that morning. Just her earrings. Reaching up, she felt for them. And remembered...

Looking up at Ben, she met those piercing blue eyes and

had no words. She'd broken up the pair. Their hearts. Hoping. And that, at least had come to fruition. Ben had found her.

She didn't think anything of it when Ben reached into his pocket. But when he lifted his hand to her, palm up, and she saw what was lying there, she was hit with an eerie calmness. New strength.

And a bout of tears, too, that sprang to her eyes as she took the small piece of jewelry and put it back in her ear. Searching for something to say to make things right between them. He'd found the clue she'd left. They were bound, a pair, communicating even when there didn't seem to be words to heal the pain hanging between them.

Needing to say something, anything, she had an *I love you* on the tip of her tongue.

But when she looked at Ben again, he'd turned away. "I think there's an old inn just over this crest and down the road about half a mile," he told her. "I noted it on my way to the house. I'm hoping to pay cash for a room for the night. There was a gas station convenience store on the corner. And a few other little shops across the street. A taco stand, for one. If nothing else, we can shower and get something to eat while I contact Doug and figure out our next moves."

He was all business.

Right after returning her earring to her.

Kara didn't know what to make of that, what to take from it, do with it, so she let it go.

Just nodded.

And when he started walking, she followed him.

THE ROOM HAD one bed. Threadbare carpet. Rusty drains in the sink and tub. Hard water stains in the toilet.

But it was clean.

And being run by a retired cop. Ben hadn't known that part ahead of time. And didn't disclose his identity as he checked in, either. He just recognized the look in the six-foot-six man's pointed gaze, and took note of his warning that he didn't put up with any crap at his establishment, humble as it was. The man was wearing a Glock, in plain sight in a holster at his waist.

And when Ben had shown his own gun, asking the man to please keep his presence there between the two of them, the man had nodded, disclosed his retired-cop status, and handed over a key. Ben didn't say who or what he was. Just nodded and took the key.

He'd put Ben on the back side of the property. In a room that he normally reserved for his hunting buddies. Ben had collected Kara from behind the dumpster where he'd left her armed with his knife and walked her back through the tunnel of bushes they'd come through to get to their room. He'd handed her both a juice and a water bottle, purchased from a machine in the small office, and opened his own as well.

"You can take your hair down for now," he told her as he returned to the small living quarters from the bathroom. And watched as she removed the makeshift scarf he'd made for her head from a sleeve torn from his shirt. He'd dirtied up both of their faces, and clothes, too. Not the caught in a fire, ash type dirt. More like days of living on the streets filth.

"I paid extra for some clothes and food," he told her. "They'll be left in the laundry bin on the walk outside. With no parking lot and no cameras back here, we should be relatively out of sight."

She nodded. Looked around without flinching.

"Not your usual accommodation," he said, the first words that came to his mind when so many others should have.

His tone intimated that Kara was some spoiled little rich girl who couldn't take a bit of hard, old minimalism now and then. He knew better. Dug at her anyway.

Because the room was the best he could provide under

the circumstances. And since she hadn't been thrilled with the baby he'd put inside her...

The thought wasn't fair. Nor was the fact that after the past hours they'd spent, all he wanted to do was hold his wife, and didn't feel as though she was his to hold.

Didn't even feel right taking her in his arms with her secrets between them.

"I'm alive and not trapped in a house bomb," she said. "Besides, it's kind of cozy." She walked past him into the bathroom and shut the door.

Not something she'd ever done in their own home. From day one of their marriage, doors had been left open between them.

But she was no longer who she'd been then.

And as much as he loved her, he wasn't sure he knew her like he'd thought he had.

Never in a million lifetimes would he have thought she'd leave protective custody of her own accord. Yet, she'd admitted it. And that her reasons had been personal.

He'd thought *he* was personal.

Yet he hadn't known that his pregnant wife was putting her life, and that of their unborn child, in danger. And still didn't know why. He wasn't sure he was going to ask a second time.

Because she was right about one thing. They had to conquer the beast on their tails before expending energy and focusing on personal matters.

He'd be risking their lives to do elsewise.

With Kara still in the bathroom, he phoned Doug's private line. His friend picked up on the first ring. Ben hung up and immediately called back. Twice more. On the third pickup Doug said, "Thank God you're alive."

"The house was wired, with her trapped inside," he said, not knowing how long they'd have to talk. Not trusting the new burner phone he'd taken from his glove compartment. Nor much of anything else at the moment.

Doug's pause felt heavy, and Ben was ready to demand more with a curt *what* when Doug said, "We're all so sorry, man. No words."

And Ben almost felt a bout of something halfway good. The plan had worked. Doug thought Kara was dead. Next choice, did he leave her there? The more who knew that she was alive and with him, the more danger she'd be in.

Her sisters...

They'd be ripped up.

More so if Kara really was killed.

As hard as it was, he needed everyone to believe that she'd died in the explosion, her body burned to ashes. It was his only way to protect her.

And himself?

"I'd like to stay dead, too, Doug," he spoke slowly, somberly, but with fight in his tone. "At least until I can figure out who's working for Miller and for Hansen."

"You need to come in, man," Doug said then. "You just lost your wife."

He considered telling Doug the truth for a second. But shook his head. Realized he couldn't be seen, and said, "You know me better than that. I need to do this."

"You don't sound right."

Maybe because his wife had just walked out of the bathroom. And he didn't like lying to one of the few men he'd trust with her life.

"I just lost my wife." He played the card. In spite of the bad taste it left in his mouth.

Kara, for her part, hardly blinked at his words. Instead, her face lost a few of its worry lines as she pulled out the plain wooden desk chair and sat. Leaving the two-seater couch unoccupied.

He wouldn't blame her for thinking that being presumed dead was a good thing at the moment. He'd felt the same relief. Just hated that others had to suffer due to the lie.

But only for a few hours. A day at the most. He made the silent promise as Doug filled him in on what they knew, which, at that point was very little. Most of the manpower had been assigned to the murder of Kara and Ben Latimer over the past couple of hours.

Doug relayed that the prosecutor on the Miller case had hired a team to replace Ben, starting with finding out who'd murdered Ben and Kara. They were planning to add the two new murder charges to both Miller and Hansen to see which one of them wanted to make a deal.

Promising to keep in touch with his friend, Ben disconnected. On edge. Not feeling good about the call, or being replaced, either.

Ben had never ever not completed an assignment. Gritted his teeth at the thought of the part he needed to play. But knew he'd made the right choices, too. He'd quit working for the rest of his life if that was what it took to keep Kara out of danger.

Whether she ended up living with him or not.

## Chapter Sixteen

Kara washed up. Ate one the packages of peanut butter crackers Ben had brought in with the water. Ham sandwiches and fruit from the convenience store across from the motel would be arriving within the hour.

In the meantime, the room was small, Ben's persona was not, and Kara couldn't stand the distance between them. They'd almost died. Her more than him. They should be holding each other.

They should have kissed.

The fact that they were acting as though they were strangers—Ben checking out every aspect of the room, her sitting on the hard wooden chair because it was the only place to roost that was just suited for one—was her fault.

It was up to her to fix it. How did she repair the two of them when she couldn't heal herself?

"I'm sorry," she said. Just that. No qualifier.

Checking out a corner of the room by the window, Ben lifted a finger to poke at the ceiling. As though he hadn't heard her.

Trying to figure out what to say, how to explain that which she didn't understand, Kara watched as he slowly turned around. Glanced at her, and then away.

"You don't want the baby," he said, as though telling her

she didn't like pickles. As though the news wasn't earth-shattering.

And that's when she knew that her response, as lame as it was, was a given. Ben was an analyzer. He'd done the job for her. "I'm dreading the idea of being a mother," she told him.

Waited for his next question. One for which she had no answer.

"Why didn't you tell me this from the beginning?" Not the query she'd expected.

Shaking her head, eyes wide, she said, "Because I didn't know, Ben!" He thought she'd been lying to him? Pretending she was all in with their plan?

Frowning at her, he crossed his arms, stood there looking straight at her. "How could you not know? We talked about it from the beginning."

She nodded. Shrugged. "That's the big mystery," she said, at a loss. "I was on board. I've always thought I'd have kids. And when you wanted to start trying at the year mark of our marriage so you'd be young enough to enjoy them as much as I would, I thought the plan made total sense. It's not like I'm a kid. I'll be thirty by the time the baby's born…"

She was rambling. Letting go of the thoughts that had been going around and around in her head since she'd first been late for her cycle. And even hearing them aloud, sharing them with the person she trusted more than any other—by far now that she knew her sisters had been lying to her—didn't render them any more clear. Or ease her dismay.

Ben's jaw tightened visibly, as though he was holding back words.

Holding back judgment?

He lifted a fist beneath his chin, resting his elbow on the other still-crossed arm. "It's probably normal for people to fear childbirth," he finally said. A rendition of what she'd expected to hear every time she'd thought about telling him how she was feeling. "Maybe if you'd told your sisters, asked them about it…"

Irritation rose within Kara, lifting her up out of her seat to stand eye to eye with Ben. "This right here is why I felt like I couldn't tell you this on Friday, Ben. You…my sisters… to an extent my father and Susan, too…everyone wants to guide and protect me. Even you. I love you all for loving me, but you treat me like a precious being, not an equal. I'm not a child, Ben! I'm an accomplished professional."

She stopped, staring at him, as it hit her that she was being far too hard on him. What she'd said was true…but the impetus behind her intensity wasn't just Ben.

"My sisters have been lying to me my entire life to protect me," she said aloud. And they'd lost some of her trust for having done so.

Had Ben been slowly losing her trust, too? Maybe even before she'd suspected she could be pregnant? The way she'd pegged his response to her current struggles…that hadn't just come to her out of the blue. It had been there. Sitting with her. Percolating subconsciously within her. Maybe even before their marriage.

Her entire life she'd had sisters a decade or more older than her protecting her. Overprotecting her. Ben's doing so had felt…normal.

Until it hadn't.

"I need you to treat me like an equal," she said then, looking him straight in the eye. Her voice firm.

"I already do," he said back, equally implacable. "Since the first time we went out."

Yeah, things had changed between them when she'd come home from college, and they'd started dating. A lot. Amazingly so.

But equals? She'd never thought specifically about it until right then. And suddenly so many things made sense. Not the uneasiness about being a mother, but so much more. Her need for independence in her career. The way she looked forward, every day, to her time at the clinic where she was the boss. And respected and admired for her ability to take charge of a situation and make it better.

She hadn't minded coming home to be coddled. At least not on the surface. Hadn't really even seen it happening. Because it had been that way her entire life.

The family who'd raised her had taught her to be proactive, to act rather than react, but they hadn't encouraged her independence. Rather, they'd all been uneasy anytime she'd asserted some.

Because of what had happened with Tory?

Maybe the mothering thing was a part of it, too. How could a baby have a baby? Maybe things had been building up in her for a long time and had finally surfaced because of the baby.

"I know what I'm feeling, Ben," she said. "And I know what types of things women experience during the first months of pregnancy. I've had medical training. And I've done a lot of reading, too," she said slowly. "But the bigger problem here is that you don't trust me to know my own mind. You think you and my sisters, with your greater life experience, all know better than I do."

Right there. She'd hit on something vitally important that she hadn't even allowed herself to acknowledge inside.

Maybe because finding out her entire life had been a lie had shown her how very dangerous that coddling could be.

Still didn't resolve her inability to feel good about being a mother. Yet Kara felt stronger. Had a far better understanding of herself. Felt like she was finally getting in touch with the person she'd seemed to have lost.

Ben took a step closer, his gaze softening. "You're overwrought, babe." His words were like a death knell. He wasn't hearing what she was trying to tell him.

Just as her sisters often failed to do. At which point, she had to separate from them and do what she thought best.

But Ben was her husband. Her partner. The love of her life. That didn't change just because he didn't understand.

Did it?

And was that moment, the two of them running for their lives from the same enemy, the right one to make such decisions? To have that particular showdown?

Shaking her head, Kara sat down. Knowing full well that the action showed her giving in to him. "I just need some time, Ben," she said then. And received his understanding nod.

Which made the fight come out in her all over again. The time might not be right, but Kara had just come to some life-changing realizations that—perhaps as a result of looking death in the face—weren't there beforehand.

The pregnancy, finding out about her mother, having her life threatened three times in three days—they'd all shown her a truth about herself that had already been there. Needing her to see it.

How could she become a mother when those who loved her most didn't trust her judgment?

Beyond that, she couldn't settle for a relationship without total honesty. Or live like her mother had, hurting everyone. She and Ben had to have trust or be done, and trust wasn't something you could just wish upon someone. Her heart was breaking, even as she knew that somehow things were going to have to change between her and her husband. She couldn't be with someone who didn't fully trust her to know her own mind, or trust her to be able to take care of herself. Mostly, she couldn't be with someone who doubted her because she had needs counterproductive to what he thought she should need.

And that thought scared her most of all.

BEN'S HEART MELTED as he watched expressions chase themselves across Kara's face. Poor sweetie had been through so much. He physically hurt, not being able to help her more. To take her burdens on himself so she didn't have to suffer. The woman was a dynamo, spending pretty much all her waking hours looking out for others. From all the animal owners whose hearts she soothed with her gentle and talented care of their family members, to her staff, her own sisters, and Ben, too. Kara spent her days trying to please everyone, to make sure they were all happy, cared for.

And she'd reached a point where she had to take the time, expend the energy, to take care of herself. The realization hit him and was followed by wave after wave of relief. All she needed was some time.

And that he was going to make damned sure he could give her.

To do that, he had to get them through their current hell, and back home. Which meant...

Ben sat down on the corner of the bed, rested his elbows on his knees, clasped his hands together, and said, "I need to know why you left the suite this morning, Kara."

She'd said her reasons were personal. He'd just vowed to give her the space she needed, and was already reneging on the point. Just to get her home.

Only to get her home.

He had to know how someone had breached protocols and been in the exact right place at the exact right time to grab her up.

Saw her nod.

Prepared to accept whatever she told him without personal feedback for the time being.

And felt his phone vibrate against his chest.

Only one person had the number. Grabbing the phone from his pocket, he verified the number and said, "What's up?"

And, seeing Kara's concerned gaze on him, turned away so however bad the news, he could break it to her gently. Giving her what space he could until she could take all she needed.

The call only took seconds, and he turned back to her. Saw her brows raised in question, and said, "They got the guy who kidnapped you on the beach," he said, his senses speeding ahead to find other pieces to go with the news. "Turned out to be a city worker, who had a criminal record he'd lied about. Said a guy came up to him and paid him a thousand dollars to tie you up, get you into the trash bin, wheel you to a point on the other side of the beach, and leave you there."

Kara's entire face lined in instant perplexity. "What?"

"The guy who hired him was older, fit Hansen's description."

"Was he paid in cash?" Kara asked, and Ben wanted to think her thoughts went immediately to the next key investigative point because she'd paid so much attention to his daily life. That she'd cared enough to take it all in. Just as he'd noted hers.

"He was," he said aloud, knowing he had to get his head out of personal territory and fully on the job. Just as she'd intimated earlier, when she'd let him know her struggles were personal and could wait. He didn't want to tell her the rest, but said, "He had a rock-solid alibi for the clinic bombing and this morning's kidnapping. But it stands to reason, based on the forms of attack being wheeled apparatus used by workers in the area, that the same person is behind the hiring of all of them."

"Bombs and fire were involved in two of the three as well," Kara pointed out, her tone almost sterile. Because she was shutting down?

Ben had to be aware that she was completely out of her element. Living in a world she only ever heard about through him.

At the same time, he needed her to know what they were up against. And had learned to appreciate, to seek out, her thought processes on his cases. So he said, "Exactly. We believe we're looking at one person in charge."

"Miller."

He nodded. And then said, "Doug took the city worker in for a lineup with Hansen, and while he said it could be him, he couldn't definitely identify him."

Standing, Kara said, "But we know it was."

He shrugged. "We assume so." They didn't know until they had a confession from Hansen. Or Miller, who had to be running the show somehow. "But at least you know that one of your attackers is in custody." Not Hansen, just as the man had said. But hired by him.

Kara hugged her arms to herself as though she was cold. Nodded. Moved as though to head toward the window, and Ben put himself between her and the wall that housed both the door and the window. Between her and any possible breach.

As he would for anyone he was protecting on the job.

But he wasn't just doing the job. He'd die for Kara. The fact was just a part of loving her.

"You think if I hadn't been making so much noise inside the barrel, that Hansen would have come and wheeled me someplace where he could have taken me hostage?"

Ben wished he could tell her exactly what Hansen's intentions had been. He couldn't lie to her. "I don't know, Kara." But he could give her a better scenario that was as much as possibility. "It could be that the first attempt was just to show me that he meant business."

"To scare you off the case." She stood there, rubbing her shoulders, and he ached to make the moment better for her.

"It's also possible that he or Miller think I know something, or that I do know it and just haven't yet connected the dots to know how it's pertinent to the case, which makes this far more than just getting an investigator off the case."

"It makes it personal to you. Something worth killing you for." She looked him in the eye then, and he read the very clear fear in her gaze. She didn't want to lose him.

And that was all he needed to keep him there, giving her time, for as long as it took.

## Chapter Seventeen

"They're not just using me to scare you," Kara blurted what she suspected her husband had already surmised. Maybe in recent minutes, more likely before that, and he just hadn't wanted to upset her with the theory. "They're taking me, but not killing me, because they know that you'll find me. Come after me. That's how they get you."

The wired house. It all made sense.

And if she hadn't pushed her way through the rotted wall, if Ben had tried to breach that house with her inside…they'd both be dead. They'd bought some time.

Had to use it wisely. Bickering over personal affronts wasn't that.

"We don't know that…" Ben glanced away briefly as he said the words, and Kara almost stamped her foot. Demanded that he be completely straight with her.

But didn't want to fight with him. Their issues didn't matter at the moment. Keeping him alive did.

Suddenly the idea of them both being thought dead meant more than ever. And she understood why he'd made the difficult decision to let the word get out around town—including to her sisters.

She hurt for them. A ton. But agreed wholeheartedly with Ben's choice.

And got back to the only critical topic. "The second attack—a couple…posing as Maggie's neighbors… Hansen wasn't in custody yet. So how do we figure out who he hired? And how? If they can positively ID him…"

Ben studied her for a long enough moment that Kara started to get uptight again, but calmed down when he said, "Doug said the first attacker had done time last year in the same jail where Miller is being held in Atlanta until a grand jury hearing to formally charge him."

"That's too much of a coincidence." Kara jumped in where she might otherwise have let Ben tell the story in his own way.

Was gratified when he nodded, and said, "Doug's in touch with law enforcement and they're running searches on anyone who's been incarcerated there during the past couple of years, and checking alibis for any who are a possible fit. For the bombing at your clinic and for this morning's kidnapping as well."

"This morning's should be easier, if he hired someone who would be normally pushing around a laundry cart, you know, inside help, like he did the city worker. There can't be that many people who served in that jail in the past couple of years who now work at a North Haven beach resort."

"Yes, but Hansen likely didn't hire him. He was already in custody."

"Maybe the couple did. The woman could have been staged somewhere close, saw me leave the clinic, knew I wasn't dead, they could have passed on the news and been hired for a second gig. No one was looking for a woman. Someone concerned, curious, who saw the smoke…"

"There are a lot of ifs, babe," Ben said then, as though he was going to shut down the conversation. A week ago, she might have taken the chance to let him do just that. To leave the heavy thinking to him since it was his job. One that he excelled at.

But she wasn't going to be shut out anymore. If she was going to have another human being dependent upon her, she had to force others to let her deal with the hard stuff. How else could she be sure she'd be able to protect a helpless child?

How else did she teach that child to be independent?

And if she was going to stand up, she had more she had to tell him. How could she expect Ben to be forthright with her, when she was holding back?

Beyond that, with her husband's life on the line, she'd rather be arrested than continue to hold back information that could help someone find a missing piece.

"Whoever was in that stairwell this morning..." She paused as a slice of fear shot through her. But swallowed and continued, "He couldn't have known that I'd come walking into his trap." The timing had been bothering her for hours. "He had to have been planning something, Ben, some way to get into that suite. If he was a hotel employee, working in housekeeping, he still would have had to know that there was about to be a sink leak, or something, a sprinkler system set off that would require my sheets to have been changed..." She was spitballing, but if they could find any evidence of something else having been tampered with...

Ben had taken a step closer and then stopped. His gaze was all business, intently so, as he studied her. "How are you so certain that he didn't know you'd be leaving the suite?"

"Because I'd just made the choice to do so. I'm also the one who chose the stairwell. About two or three minutes before I was actually there." She'd told Nivens where, when, and how she'd meet him. "This guy had to have been there, waiting for whatever plan to happen, so that he could quickly go in and get me out. No way he had time to get the laundry bin, and get himself positioned in that amount of time."

Frowning, Ben took Kara's hand, sat on the end of the bed and pulled her gently down beside him.

"You're the one who chose the stairwell?" he asked, a stranger to her suddenly. "You were meeting someone?"

She held his gaze steadily as she nodded, and said, "A US Marshal." There. She'd done it. If telling Ben the truth got her jail time, then it did. Just saying the words seemed to loosen some of the tension tying her up inside. "His name is Scott Nivens," she told him. And quickly explained about experiencing the first moments of dread regarding her pregnancy when she was two days past her cycle. Ignoring his frown as she revealed that she'd been struggling for a couple of weeks before he'd known.

She told him about going for the box of maternity clothes, finding the hotel note in the bottom of the box, which started her down a path to find out more about the mother no one talked to her about. With the investigative information she'd learned from Ben, she'd started searching for the car accident that had supposedly killed her mother. How, finding none, she'd been certain there'd been some cover up in the story because her mother had killed herself. Which had led her to call the emergency lunch meeting with her sisters on Friday.

She could see Ben's face getting tighter and tighter. His eyes narrower. Harder. But she didn't stop. Nor did he interrupt her.

"After… Friday morning… I panicked," she told him. "You were so excited and all I wanted to do was cry. You knew something was wrong. I can't even explain to myself what it was, let alone expect you to understand. And all I keep coming back to is that it has to have something to do with unresolved issues regarding my own mother. I thought, if I could just understand what had happened, understand her choices, how or why she'd been taken away from me..."

She paused, and Ben sat there beside her. Turned partially to face her. Watching her as though he could read every thought she had. Feel every breath she took. It was like he even noted when she blinked.

"Then when my sisters told me the truth... I just...it felt like my whole life was a lie, Ben. How could I be anything to you, or to a baby, when I couldn't even find myself?"

He pursed his lips. Said nothing. And she had to finish what she'd started.

"Then I was abducted, and things between you and I were so different. I knew it was up to me to fix myself and so I started investigating murder trials that were based in the area of the hotel note I'd found..."

She started to give more details, the county records she'd accessed, but Ben's eyes softened, and he asked, "You called the Marshals Service? You asked them to meet with you?"

"No!" She stood up. Stood before him as she said, "I was on this website, some official judicial thing, and a chat box popped up with a number to call if you wanted to know about that case."

Eyes narrowing again, Ben stood, too. "You called the number."

She nodded, and said, "Marshal Nivens answered. Turned out it's a site the US Marshals Service monitors for anyone they suspect could be a danger to any of their participants. Once I explained why I was there, what I was looking for—just my own inner peace, not my mother—he was less fierce. I had no idea I was making myself a suspect, that's for damned sure," she added. And stopped. Needing Ben to say something. Anything.

"I need the number, Kara." His tone was nothing she'd ever heard before.

"I don't have it. It's not the one we actually talked on," she told him. "He needed me to know that I was in serious trouble, that I was truly talking to the US Marshals Service. It was protocol. So he called me back on a different number. Had me look it up on my computer to confirm that it was indeed the office number of the US Marshals Service. And it was."

Ben's face relaxed some. Not a lot. "You're sure," he said. Not quite a question.

"Positive. I checked multiple times while I was speaking to him."

"And the reason you left the suite?"

"He told me that he needed my signature on the official report, needed to verify my identity with my driver's license, and then he'd close the investigation. He told me that I wasn't to speak of our conversation with anyone, or he'd need to investigate them as well..."

Ben was no longer listening.

He'd turned his back. Pulled out his phone.

And she assumed he was talking to Doug when he said, "Look up US Marshal Scott Nivens. Get back to me."

She assumed because he was no longer talking to her. He paced the room. Glanced through the edge of the curtain a few times. Checked his phone. Paced some more.

Until, less than two minutes later, his phone rang.

He listened. Then told Doug to check all employees at the resort against jail records immediately. Including family members in the search.

And then, with a deep breath she could actually see in the rise and fall of his chest, he turned to her.

"Marshal Scott Nivens is away from his desk right now. Doug left a message for him," he said, sitting back down. Seeming a bit more like himself.

And her heart nearly broke when he said, "I'm a state-renowned investigator, Kara. Why didn't you come to me? I could have found the case. And probably more details than you'd ever have found in a search of public records."

He could have. She'd known that. But the whole point had been her doing for herself.

Or rather, doing it separate and apart from those who were caging her in their protective arms.

She saw the second he figured that out. His eyes closed for longer than a blink.

She braced for his withdrawal. And when he took her in his arms instead, cradling her in his strong, manly embrace, she held on to him, too.

Whether they were meant to be together, whether they stayed together, she loved him.

That was a truth that was not going to change.

HE'D THOUGHT SHE'D walked into a trap. Still wasn't completely convinced she hadn't, though he'd relaxed a whole lot on the idea once he'd known that Nivens checked out.

That there was a US Marshal named Scott Nivens.

Not many criminals were bold enough to impersonate an existing law enforcement officer. The fact that the phone number had been verified was good, too.

But...pulling back from Kara as his relief abated somewhat...he said, "It's possible for anyone to clone any phone number, babe. Someone could call you with my number showing up on your screen." He needed her to know that, first and foremost.

Had never thought he'd see the day where phone number cloning would become an everyday worry in his life.

Eyes wide with horror, Kara stared at him. "You're saying I wasn't talking to a US Marshal?"

"No," he reassured her quickly, as was his way with her. "I'm fairly certain you were." Because Nivens was on the job. He'd feel a whole lot better when the guy returned Doug's call.

Beyond that, with a few lucid moments to put pieces together, get a mental look at the timeline, Ben could see that Kara's case search hadn't started until after she'd been kidnapped off the beach. And with the similarities between the threats on her life, his gut was telling him that the three incidents were definitely related.

Which brought him back to Miller. And Hansen.

But he put in another call to Doug anyway. "I need Kara's laptop from the suite," he ordered, knowing that in the grieving state Doug thought Ben was in, his friend wouldn't take offense. "If not that one, any one. And a vehicle. Get me a rental, borrow something, buy something, just get me something to drive. Park it on the side of the building at the PicWay Convenience Mart. Leave the keys you know where. I'll get it from there." He gave Doug the crossroads, and hung up.

Not sure why he was suddenly being so covert and curt with his friend. Not sure of a lot of things at the moment.

Except that he didn't have time to figure out what in the hell was crapping all over his life. And Kara's, too. He had no way to predict how soon there'd be another explosion.

One that could be life ending.

For both of them.

SHE'D TOLD HIM her secrets. Ben knew she wasn't on board with their happy life plan. At least not the happy part. And he was still there.

Fighting to get them free from threat.

He slipped outside shortly after talking to Doug and came in less than a minute later with a shopping bag with new clothes, men's and women's sizes, an outfit each. Ham sandwiches with chips and fruit. Ready-made chef salads that he put in the small refrigerator under the television set, and several more bottles of juice and water. In the bottom there were toothbrushes and toothpaste. And a package of her favorite cookies. Which he liked, too.

He'd thought of everything, not that that surprised her. Ben was an incredibly thoughtful, kind, and honorable human being. It wasn't his fault that she responded to those who babied her as though she was fine with their doing so.

Was she to blame for not consciously realizing how much it bothered her?

Or was it only getting at her so much because of the tension she was living under?

And it wasn't like she didn't want his loving attention. She did. The thought of living without it was suffocating her all over again.

At the same time, now that she'd come face-to-face with the fact that she needed to be treated like an equal, she knew she wasn't going to be able to settle for anything less than that.

Not and be happy and healthy.

Or be able to give a healthy life to one she was raising.

Ben asked her questions about her mother as they ate. Wanting to know everything she'd found, or thought she'd found. Asking about the specific cases she'd perused, as well as anything she'd found in storage.

She told him again about the note written on the hotel pad. Significant to her because it had the hotel's address on it.

"What did the note say?" he asked her.

And she shook her head. "Nothing, really. Just scribbling. It looked more like someone was trying to get a pen to write, and then when it did, they used it somewhere else. Which is what made me curious to begin with. Who saved a piece of paper used to scribble on to get ink from a pen?"

Sitting at the desk, where Ben had placed her food, she

took a bite of sandwich. Watched him pace a few steps back and forth in front of where his food was perched, the top of the small dresser next to the television stand and refrigerator. And when he said nothing to her rhetorical question, she said, "That's why I thought the hotel name or address must have been important to her."

It felt good, talking to him about it all. One on one. With no need to guard herself against his need to tell her what to think.

Or rather, telling her what he thought about whatever it was based on his life's experience. A normal thing for anyone to do. Was it her who'd given more weight to his opinion, over her own on topics that weren't in her field of expertise?

Either way, she'd been bracing herself against if for a while. Not all the time. But when it came to suppositions about things.

She'd been subconsciously protecting herself against something she hadn't even realized was happening. And if she hadn't known, how could he have?

He'd merely been telling her what he thought.

At least some of the time. There were others when he'd deliberately spared her from information. Like when Thane had told him that he and Stella were talking about divorce, and Kara had been the last to know...

Ben's phone rang before they'd finished their meal. Tensing, Kara waited. Was there more trouble? Someone right outside their door?

The caller was Doug Zellers. The only person who had Ben's number. That much she knew.

The detective had had the car and a laptop delivered. Not Kara's. That was with forensics as detectives searched for any reason she'd have left her protective custody that morning. It wasn't like Ben could tell them. He'd died in the fire that had killed her. And as far as Doug knew, she'd died before Ben had been able to get to her.

Ben's Mercedes-Benz had been towed, was also with forensics, and then would be safely stored.

It was all just so exhausting. The head trips. Figuring out what other people were thinking. Guessing their motives. Keeping secrets. Finding out those you trusted had been lying to you.

Knowing someone was determined to imprison you, with death imminent.

Someone who was locked up and still bearing enough power to call the shots?

Doug would be calling Ben with updated case information as it came in. Though Ben, thought to be dead, was off the case, Doug still intended to lean on him as much as he had been.

To use him in any way he could.

Kara didn't know the detective well, was uneasy about trusting anyone. Most particularly a man who'd had three chances to catch a kidnapper and was still no closer to doing so.

And said as much to Ben as he was getting ready to leave her in the room alone just after dark to get to the convenience store a quarter of a block away and retrieve the laptop.

"I need the information he's feeding me," Ben said as he put on the baggy jeans, dark shirt, and baseball cap he'd pulled out of the shopping bag. Along with a pair of cheap black tennis shoes.

He looked good, even in the ill-fitting clothes. Too good. "You stopped short of saying you trust him."

Ben studied her for a long moment. Too long. And then turned to the door. "Do not open this door for any reason," he told her. "Even if you think it's me. I'll kick the bottom of the door twice when I'm coming back in." He put his gun on the decrepit scarred coffee table in front of the little couch. "If anyone attempts to open that door, or break through the window, you use this. No exceptions." He glanced at her as he rose back to his full height. "I need your word, Kara."

"You trust me enough to believe me if I give it to you?"

She was being querulous. Maybe childishly so.

Unfairly so. They were in their current predicament, had both almost lost their lives, because of her having broken protocol that morning.

She'd never given her word that she wouldn't. And couldn't then, either. One had to have autonomy to assess a situation and act accordingly.

"I'll do my best," she replied. Watched him take the few steps to the door.

She understood his need for the computer, but she didn't want him to go.

And didn't say so.

But before the door shut behind him, she said, "I love you."

If he gave her a response, she didn't hear it.

## Chapter Eighteen

Walking behind the run-down motel to the woods that ran along the road, Ben slid quickly and quietly along until he was parallel with the convenience store. He spotted the older beige sedan Doug had described to him. A loan from a local car dealer for the night. Doug would pay cash for the vehicle in the morning. Have it titled in his dad's name.

Ben stayed in the shadows as he moved from the woods to the car. Grabbed the key stuck with black electrical tape to the inside rubber on the back left tire. Opening the door, he silently commended Doug for having the interior light disconnected. Grabbed the laptop from the inside zipper compartment on a well-used cooler, shoved it in the waistband of his jeans, under his shirt, and, reaching up to lock the door, slid out of the vehicle to a crouching position on the ground.

Grabbing his knife from inside his sock, Ben remained completely still. Listening. A breath, a step, the crunch of a single pebble and he'd be under the car with blade ready.

When he was certain he was alone, he carefully slid through shadows to make his way back to Kara. A woman he could no longer count on to follow his edicts.

But did that mean he didn't trust her?

She'd asked the question. He'd had no immediate answer.

He hadn't told her he loved her, either. He did. And should

have. Sudden tension pushing from within him, Ben hurried his step. He had to get back to her. To tell her that he loved her.

If something happened…if his last act with her was to hold back his love…

In his hurry to have the chance to blurt out feelings, Ben almost missed the pickup truck driving without headlights in the parking lot of the motel. He'd have barreled himself right across its path had his instincts not kicked in at the last second.

The phone in his shirt pocket buzzed a call, almost as though Doug was reaching out to remind him that he had to have his own back.

Fully in tune then, he stood as still as the tree trunk behind which he was standing. Watched as the truck drove around a second time, and then, flipping on its lights, headed out to the street. And under a light that showed him the blue hood.

Not Maggie's truck. That had blown up at Kara's office. But did Miller have a front man who had a penchant for the color blue?

If nothing else, that vehicle was a warning to him. He couldn't afford to be off his mark, not even for second.

And he had to keep his personal house in enough order to be able to do his job without distraction.

How he managed that, he wasn't sure, but he'd learned one thing.

He was never leaving Kara again without telling her he loved her.

*Kara!*

What if she'd been in that blue truck?

Driving without lights on, out in the street, turning them on…

Unless the truck had just pulled out of a parking space

before Ben had noticed it. And hadn't yet flipped on the lights...

He had no idea who'd checked in since he'd last been to the office. Nor who rented rooms by the week as a place to live.

He'd caught half the plate number, though.

Sliding along the wall of the back side of the motel, Ben got himself to their room. Noted that the window and doorknob were intact. And, with his back to the building, he reached his leg sideways to kick the door twice. Knife out, blade ready, he stood to the side, watching outward, noting stillness, and unlocked the door, rounding the entryway so that his back went from outer building to inside wall.

And stared into the barrel of his own gun.

"THANK GOD IT'S YOU!" Kara dropped arms suddenly weak with relief as she saw Ben slide into the room. "There's been a truck out there, it was blue and..."

Door closed and bolted behind him, Doug took his wife in his arms. Conceivably to comfort her. But he held on as much for himself as well. Whether he and Kara were able to make it as husband and wife or not, he loved her.

He'd always love her.

"I kicked twice," he said softly, reassuringly, against her hair.

"Yes, but whoever is stalking me has managed to find out exactly where I am, what I'm doing, at almost the exact moment that I decide to do it," she told him, pulling away. Staying close but no longer touching him.

He missed the warmth. The softness. But knew her choice had been the right one. He had to call Doug back. Pulled the laptop out of the back of his jeans and set it on the desk, first.

"I've checked myself for any kind of tracking device implantation," Kara said then. "I inject chips all the time. It only takes a second, hardly hurts, but the needle is large and leaves a definite mark, a sore spot, and a little bleeding. Depending on his device, it could have happened when he was tying my hands and putting me in the barrel. It hurt. I wasn't thinking about the pain. And when you're in shock, you don't always recognize pain..."

He stared at her. Hadn't even considered the possibility.

Suddenly, that blue truck was a much bigger deal.

"Strip, now," he said, ripping off his own shirt. Kicking off his shoes, shedding his pants and underwear, his socks. He hadn't been the initial point of contact, but anything was possible and after days without answers, he was ready to consider any angle.

In less than thirty seconds, Kara was standing before him naked. He went over every inch of her body. Under her arms, soles of her feet. Her butt. The insides of her legs. Any place she couldn't see clearly. And he rechecked the rest of her, too.

His body grew hard. The evidence was hanging right there in the open, but it didn't slow him down. At all.

She was the initial target to get to him.

"There's nothing," he told her, relief bringing a headiness that urged him to take her into his arms. To say with his body what he couldn't put into words he was certain he could stand by.

As he had the thought, Kara was perusing the back of him. Heels to thighs, butt, and back. The backs of his arms, elbows, shoulders, neck. And on around. His gaze looked for hers when she was in front of him. And saw...the gaze of a medical professional trained to look at the body as a business. Not something more personal.

She didn't say anything about his erection. If she was affected by the evidence of his desire for her, she didn't show it.

And the second she indicated that she'd not found evidence of a recent injection on him, he was climbing back into his clothes. And grabbing his phone.

Doug's message was short and not at all sweet. After asking his friend to see if he could get a hit on the partial plate he'd seen on the truck, Ben hung up. Seeing no reason to weigh Kara down with news that benefitted her in no way at all, and would most definitely alarm her.

He opened the computer instead, noting the hot spot allowing encrypted internet access first and foremost. Booted up. Was just starting to type when Kara said, "What did Doug have to say?"

The first word out of her mouth told him he'd made a mistake. A big one. Not the *what* but the tone in which it was delivered.

She was angry.

He understood. She was under a lot of pressure. Bubbling over with fear-based tension. And…right then, something else hit him.

Something she'd said earlier. Needing to be an equal.

Her life was in danger. She was on the case with him. She *was* the case. And though he didn't like it, he said, "A man's body was found in a ditch outside of town. He'd run his car into a tree. Further investigation showed that the car had been tampered with. Maggie identified the car as the one that had been left to her, when her new neighbor borrowed her truck—"

"If you think Maggie tampered with a car, you're way off base—" Kara interrupted and he held up a hand.

"She identified the car after having identified the dead body as the neighbor, Kara. She's helping with the case, not a suspect in it."

Her face straightened. Her mouth dropped, but not much. "You're telling me that the person responsible for blowing up part of my clinic is dead."

Looking her straight in the eye, he nodded.

"So he won't be able to identify Hansen."

Another hope dashed. Something she didn't need at the moment.

"What about his supposed wife?" she asked, as Ben tried to lose himself in computer research.

"She wasn't in the truck when we saw it following us. Nor when it pulled onto the lot. But, as we said, she could have been stationed close by. But we have no way of knowing whether or not she ever met or knew about Hansen. Maggie's description of her is all we have to go on and there's been no hits on facial recognition from the sketch."

Kara didn't need to be worrying about things over which she had no impact.

"Did Doug have anything else to say?"

"Hansen's being charged with murder and transported to Atlanta."

She'd plopped down to the end of the bed. He saw peripherally through the mirror above the desk. Didn't turn around. He had no idea how to help her. What she needed from him.

Kara seemed to be changing so fast he wasn't completely sure he knew her as well as he'd thought he had.

And yet, parts of her were exactly as he knew her to be. Like when she said, "It's breaking my heart, thinking about what Melanie and Stella are going through right now." He felt her pain acutely. Needed to hold her.

Before he turned around, she said, "Miller's getting what he wanted."

Glancing at her through the mirror, he asked, "How so?"

"He wanted Hansen charged with murder, right? And then plans to pin the other killings on him?"

"That's the theory." And left Ben with a critical job to do. He had to figure out what he knew, what Miller thought he knew, that could keep the serial killer in jail.

What connection was he missing? For an ace investigator, he was showing a remarkable lack of ability to get the job done.

"In the meantime," Kara continued, "if he's calling the shots, and that seems to be the only logical conclusion at this point, he's continuing to fulfill his serial killing lust even while locked up."

He turned then. Stared at her. Feeling as though her words put him on the cusp of something, but it remained just out of reach.

As did she.

KARA NEEDED TO stay busy. To keep her mind focused on getting the answers that were going to allow her to take back control of her life. She wasn't a detective, or an investigator, but she could put facts together and draw conclusions just like anyone else.

She was the only one who'd been witness to her kidnappings. There had to be something there that she could give Ben to lead him to something that could fill in his missing pieces.

While he worked on the computer, she forced herself to relive all three incidents of attack against her, making herself remember as many little nuances as she could. Just as she'd heard him talk about doing with victims. As Doug's team had done with her on Friday. And again on Saturday, too, before she'd been shipped off to the resort.

Getting frustrated with her inability to conjure up anything new, she scooted over on the bed to see what Ben was working on. Hoping maybe it would trigger something for her. She was shocked to see the name of the hotel she'd been researching in Florida named at the top of some kind of official-looking document, followed by lists of names.

"What is that?" she asked him.

He turned, looked at her, turned back. And then said, "A list of people staying at the Arlington Beach Hotel in Florida during the week that you said your mother was there."

Her heart thudded. With shock. Anger that he hadn't told her what he was doing. And with a large dose of gratitude, too.

Getting up to look over his shoulder, she went with the easiest emotion to handle, first. "Why didn't you tell me you were looking into this?"

He shrugged. "I had no idea I'd find anything. And looking into things is what I do all day long, Kara. For cases, and otherwise. You know that."

She did know. He was right. Ben was the most curious human being she'd ever known. It was one of the traits that had captivated her about him. And still did.

"I thought you were working on current stuff," she said then. Confused.

"As soon as Doug gets me forensic reports from today, I will be."

Being Ben, he'd needed to keep his mind in gear. And he'd chosen to use that gift of his to help her. Tearing up, she swallowed hard. Blinked a couple of times, and pulled the coffee table over next to him to sit on.

He told her he'd written to the hotel, given his credentials, said he was working on a cold case, and had asked for any records they'd had. They'd sent him old files of scanned copies of registered guests.

She suspected there'd been more to it than that but didn't press the issue. "So what did you find?"

"No Tory Mitchell," he said, sounding disappointed.

And she remembered what her sisters had told her on Friday at lunch. "She was with Lila. And they used fake names."

Ben started typing. Opened a new document. A spreadsheet. Copied. Pasted. Several times. And then did a search for rooms with two guests.

From there they perused the list together. Deleting all male names.

Then those that weren't there for the whole week.

"They paid cash," Kara said then, feeling the first stirrings of excitement, of anything that didn't come accompanied with dread, that day.

Ben deleted all reservations that paid by credit card and check.

And they had one room left.

Karin and Amanda Moore. He then pulled up the full registration and found a line that asked what relation the guests were to each other. It said sisters.

"That's them," she told him. Staring in disbelief. Two weeks of trying to find anything concrete at all, and Kara had come up with multiple murder cases and a call from the US Marshals Service looking to charge her with a crime.

An hour and Ben had found her mom.

Only for a blip in time. But the signature was there. Either the Karin or the Amanda. Her mother had handwritten one of those two names. She blinked back tears again.

Tried to find the more professional self she'd morphed into over the past twelve hours. And ended up telling Ben, "When I talked to my sisters, they told me a bit more about what happened that summer."

She glanced at him, once, but then stared at the computer as she said, "My dad had just told my mom about Susan. They'd been having an affair for over a year and my dad had just asked for a divorce." Staring at the signatures in front of her, wishing she knew which belonged to Tory, she added, "She had to have been feeling desperate and alone when she wrote that."

Which pretty much described how Kara had been feeling for a good part of the past several days.

And suddenly, looking at that signature, she began to understand how a woman could convince herself that it was best for her children if she just disappeared.

## Chapter Nineteen

A note in Kara's voice called out to Ben. So strongly that he didn't question himself as he turned to his wife and pulled her onto his lap. Not to coddle her. Or protect her.

Just to find a way to connect to her on a level deep enough to ease some of her pain. Not just at the loss of her mother.

But due to the battle she was waging inside herself as well. He didn't pretend to understand it all. Couldn't give her words of assurance as he didn't even have those for himself. She had doubts. He was having them, too.

But there was one thing he didn't doubt. He loved her.

And knew that, on some level, she loved him, too.

Maybe he'd outgrown her—in that he'd grown too old to meet her where her life was taking her. Maybe her life had been driving her to the point of needing to define herself without anyone else playing a part in the definition.

For once in his memory, he not only had no answers, he didn't even have a working theory.

But what he did have was a heart and body that yearned to pull Kara out of hell and make her smile again. One more time.

To remind her that life held pleasure. And moments of ultimate connection.

He wanted her to remember the great joy they'd been bringing each other for the past three years.

When she wrapped her arms around his neck and, her gaze on his lips, slowly moved her face toward his, Ben felt himself grow beneath her. Ready to move forward and complete their kiss, to lead them to the magic they'd learned how to make together, he stilled. Driven by something inside him he didn't understand. But didn't question.

He knew what he wanted. And what, a month ago, he'd have believed she wanted. No longer sure, he sat back and let her lead.

To an almost kiss.

Or…her lips had stopped short of his, but she was still staring at his mouth. And slowly moved forward again, touching her lips to his. Tentatively. As though it was all new to her.

She kissed him softly. Lips to lips. Once. Twice. Butterfly touches. And rather than calming down at the sign of nothing more coming, his body jumped higher beneath her hip.

Hard muscle squeezed against feminine thigh.

Exquisite torture.

And yet, Ben was willing to sit right there in that hard wooden chair, feeling that sweet pain all night long if Kara would stay there with him.

Passing her lips softly across his.

She was alive. In his arms. Making a memory he was never going to forget.

One that would ease any pain that was yet to come.


KARA HAD PLAYFULLY been the aggressor many times during the years she and Ben had been making love. A kind of game where the ending was a foregone conclusion, and both parties won.

That night, sitting in the chair with Ben, she had no idea

where she was headed. How far he'd let her go before stopping her.

Or even how far she wanted to go. She just knew that she had to find out.

By following her heart.

And so she kissed him softly because it felt right to her. Because she was crying out for something more than sex. Far deeper than words. Maybe even beyond understanding.

At first, he sat there, allowing her exploration, but not participating. Not with his lips, at any rate. The hardening beneath her thigh pleased her.

His lips starting to move softly beneath hers pleased her even more. To the point that she had to reach further, deeper, and she so she did. Following instincts, she opened her lips, used her tongue against his, not with hunger, but with tenderness.

And felt a flame flash through her when his mouth opened and hers did the same. Ben had always been the perfect lover. Attentive. Aware. Giving more than he took. But he'd never been only gentle. There'd always been hunger and energy in his touch. Even at its most tender.

When their tongues touched, and explored, the gentleness was still sweet. But not enough. Standing, she put a hand on Ben's shoulder, then straddled him with hands on both of his shoulders, sat down so that her crotch was directly on top of his hardness, and bent to kiss him again. Harder. Deeper. Needing something more profound than she'd ever sought before.

His hands gripped her waist, holding her to him, and he kissed her back. Meeting her challenge with some of his own. Like he felt hungry, but not content to just accept what he was given. He was seeking, too. And she liked it. A lot.

Moaning, she rocked herself against him. Kissing him more urgently, filling with a different kind of hunger. One that didn't care about past. Or even the future. It was a now moment. One that existed for that exact time and place.

Not a husband and wife. Or a couple. Just her and Ben. Two people who belonged together out of space and time. Without careers or life plans.

No hurting. No expectations. Just...them. In all their rawness.

She rocked hard against him, dragging her crotch across him, exciting herself as much as him, and he growled like an animal, grabbed her with one arm around her waist and standing, knocked the chair to the ground behind him. With two steps he had them to the bed. Holding her as he threw down the spread and laid her in the middle of the sheet.

She'd expected him to strip off her jeans, release his fly and grind into her. But instead, he laid down beside her, rubbing his hardness against her thigh as he unbuttoned her blouse. Opened the front closure on her bra, and bent his head to suckle her breast, his tongue teasing her nipple exactly as she'd taught him to do to bring her the most pleasure.

But he didn't stop there. He moved to her other breast, suckled and teased, and then nipped her tender skin. Gently, and yet, with enough of a bite to spring her to life in a whole new way. Hardening her nipple more than before. She cried out. She couldn't help it.

Didn't want to help it.

She wanted to nip him back, and with trembling, urgent hands, opened his buttons and spread his shirt wide. Pushing him over to lie down beneath her, she lathered his nipples, tickling her face with his chest hair. Inhaling the masculine scent of him.

And then moved down lower. Her palms splaying over the hard muscles of his stomach she kissed and licked until she was at the metal button on his jeans. Bypassing it she found the zipper, pulled it downward, and reached inside.

"Ah, God, Kara!" he cried out, but didn't stop her. And she didn't stop. She teased. She licked. She caressed, and when she was flooding inside her jeans, she rose up to unfasten them, rip them off, and returned to see him naked and ready for her.

She met his gaze then. She had to. Was compelled to know that they were there, her and Ben, together. Different time. Different place. Different way. But only the two of them.

And when he held on to her with his hands at her waist and his blue eyes steady on hers, she slowly lowered herself on top of him.

Taking him in, up to her hilt.

She sat there, holding him inside her, and knew that she'd become someone new. Someone different.

Someone who didn't want to let him go.

But didn't know how to hold on to him forever, either.

So she moved. Slowly. Retreating. Advancing. Over and over. Needing to stay. While nature forced her to go, too. Desire was rocking her, driving her to find what she had to have.

When she couldn't hold off any longer, she exploded around him. Feeling him pulse within her.

And didn't want to move. Ever. Didn't want to see what damage had been done by their animalistic coupling. Didn't want to lose him.

Or know how to fix them.

She just laid there. Breathing. Feeling his warmth. The steady rhythm as his breathing steadied. Didn't think. Just continued to feel.

Until she drifted off.

SEX HAD BEEN INEVITABLE. Ben woke with the thought a few hours later. Lying there, holding Kara while she slept, Ben tried not to beat himself up for taking from the woman when she was at the lowest point in her life. No longer trusting her sisters, thinking her entire life had been a lie, being hunted—because of Ben—and he'd let his own need mingle with hers, rather than staying focused on being there for her.

Consoling himself with the idea that she hadn't seemed to mind, that, if anything, she'd wanted him to hunger for her, to take from her, he figured that the second they'd stripped to search each other for tracking devices, their fate had been sealed.

They'd always been a team of fire in bed.

From a strictly logical standpoint, it was good to know that at least that part of them was still intact.

Yeah, he was okay to blame it on the tracking device possibility. It had actually been a valid, and frightening, theory. One that Kara, with her experience, had known to consider.

The only one that had even come close to explaining how Stuart Miller continued to be right behind them. No matter where they went, how they got there, or what protections were in place.

Even at the resort, what had been the plan if Kara hadn't been talking to Scott Nivens and trying to take care of some trouble she'd gotten into without involving Ben? Trouble that, if he were a suspect, could be used by Miller's defense attorneys to discredit his testimony on the case. Or taint any evidence he'd touched.

He got why she'd done what she had. He didn't like it, but he understood.

What he did not, could not comprehend, was how they continued to be prey. No matter what precautions they took. Someone had been in their home, in their bathroom, and the house was loaded with security devices.

The intruder had managed to avoid most of them. Had been distinguishable only by gray-covered movement where he had been seen. And had been in and out before the alarm service had called him to let him know someone was inside.

They were dealing with a professional. They had to be. Whoever was helping Miller was one of them. It was the only thing that made sense.

Doug had been going over the defense attorney with microscopic precision and had so far found nothing that linked anything back to him or Miller. Not even coinciding with phone calls or visits. A guard on the take could be passing information. Likely was, but they'd been unable to find any money trace or transfers to corroborate the theory.

Nor had Doug's team found any links between the city worker—who still claimed he'd been randomly approached down at the beach—and the bombing at Kara's clinic. Ben hadn't yet heard anything regarding that morning's kidnapping. Or anyone associated with the house he'd found Kara trapped in.

And shouldn't he have? Doug should know more than he was telling Ben.

Unless... Doug was the one who was on the take?

Kara had intimated that she didn't trust him. He'd taken her words as coming from a place of irrational fear based on the past few days' events. Her own sisters had shattered her trust in them, how did she then trust a near stranger?

Or anyone?

No. The case. He had to stick to the case.

And there it was. Again. Doug.

The detective—his friend—didn't know their exact location, but he knew where Ben had had him drop off the car.

The car. Was it still there? Would it be by morning? None of the attacks had come during the night. So that was when they had to move.

Right, then. "Kara." He woke her without tenderness, or care. "We have to go," he said. As she was slowly rising up off him, Ben laid her to the side and was up off the bed. Pulling on clothes. Grabbing supplies. Sliding the laptop down the back of his jeans. Checking his gun, shoving it into the waistband of his jeans.

He was aware of Kara moving quickly, quietly around him. He heard the toilet flush. Saw her take the plastic bag he'd loaded off the small dresser, add something else inside and then throw the handle over her arm.

"I'm ready," she said, no more than three minutes after he'd roused her.

He was at the front wall, taking one final look at the room in case there was some clue he'd missed inside it. Something he needed to take with him, even if only mentally, to be of use in the future.

Then, yanking his gun from his jeans, holding it steady in front of him, he pulled Kara behind him. "Stay close," he whispered.

And opened the door.

KARA STUCK RIGHT at Ben's back as they slid more than walked along the side of the building, then in shadows of a light post, a trash bin, to a wall of woods that ran perpendicular behind the motel.

She didn't ask why he'd woken her in the middle of the night to run again. She trusted him. And she went. Just as she was trusting that he'd do all he could to keep them alive. That was her focus. Trusting Ben with her life. Sharing the responsibility of keeping their baby alive inside her.

The rest would come if they ever made it back to any kind of a regular life. The issues were there.

But so were their strengths. The past few days had shown her that.

He'd found her mother for her. Given her personal handwriting. Keeping her mind on the good things, she felt his warmth as they moved through trees toward what appeared to be an all-night gas station. The convenience store he'd talked about.

She saw the beige car before he motioned his head toward it, letting her know that it was their target. And didn't let herself think about the lifetime that could pass in the yards between them and that mode of transportation. Instead, she followed his every move. Precisely. Step for step, arms in at her sides, keeping watch all around her.

The night was quiet. Eerily so. She listened for all sounds. Watched every shadow. And crouched low, like an animal, when he indicated that she do so as they crossed over to the car. He unlocked the driver's door, helped her in before him and then crawled in behind her.

"Keep down," he said. "If I'm seen, recognized, they can't know I'm not alone."

There'd always been more of a chance that Miller and his hired hands wouldn't believe Ben was dead. A cell phone wasn't nearly as compelling evidence as a body trapped in a house becoming one with the pile of ashes that was left.

If anything was left of her mode of exit, signs that a rotted wall had been broken through, the damage would be blamed on the explosion she'd set off.

Kara slid down to the floor of the front passenger seat. She didn't like being there. Hugged her bag of goods to her. And prayed that when Ben started the car they didn't explode.

They had to take chances, she understood that. Had come to that very clear understanding as she walked around trapped inside a house bomb. You tried or you died.

It was just that simple.

And that horrifying.

She clenched when she heard him turn the key. Braced herself as the engine turned over and purred. And hardly breathed as Ben drove them off the lot. A minute or two down the road, she started to breathe a little easier.

"What happened back there?" she asked then. "Did you hear something, or see a shadow at the window?" It was the only thing that made sense to her.

She was staring up at him, mostly seeing the underside of his chin, his nose, eyes that were pointed forward, not down at her. She should be on the seat, helping him keep watch.

"Just a hunch," he said.

He had to focus. She knew that. If she didn't know what they were up against, she wouldn't be prepared to face whatever came. "If something happens to you, how will I know what to do? How do I protect myself?"

The question was more than just for that moment. She had to believe they were going to get through the threats, and the danger. She was fighting for her current chances, and for her future, too.

She watched the muscles in his jaw tighten by light of the dash. And saw them start to move, too, as he said, "Attacks have all happened during the day. Nights are quiet. Made most sense that quiet time is when we should move. This threat is always just one step behind us. Or, perhaps, sitting right with us. All the time. How is Miller able to call such a close game? Get players in perfect position, and not leave any trace that law enforcement can follow? I found Hansen, but Miller wanted us to get him. The most logical conclusion, and perhaps the only one, is that there's someone on the inside helping this all happen. Miller comes from money. He can afford to make greedy people rich. Or, perhaps there's another motive. Maybe someone just wants me out of the picture. Wants to punish me." He was giving her free thought. As he'd done occasionally on other cases.

But never, ever when it came to her, or anything that affected her personally. The thought passed by. He'd figured it out. Had no proof, hence his "hunch" comment, but…she had to know.

"Who do you suspect?"

"It's not so much that I suspect one person, as it is who I'm no longer ruling out."

And she knew. "Doug Zellers."

Kara swallowed hard when Ben nodded his head.

# Chapter Twenty

Ben knew, ten miles down the long, remote country road that he was being followed. He also knew there was little he could do about the fact except just keep driving. The alternative would be to stop and, not knowing his opponent, or how many of them there were, that option didn't bode well. By his calculation, he had another five miles or so before a turn that would lead him to a major highway. With more options along the way.

Any branches off the current road led to homesteads, or dirt roads that would likely be dead ends. He couldn't take a chance that he'd get Kara trapped with no way out.

But he didn't like their odds as they stood, either. Someone behind him could shoot forward a whole lot easier than he could maintain his seventy-five-mile-an-hour speed limit and shoot backward. And he could count on his pursuer having as good or better familiarity with their current route. Meaning, he'd probably make his move before Ben had a chance to get to safer ground.

He. Ben wanted there to be only one. He didn't count on it.

He glanced at Kara and knew that she'd made a valid point. She had to know how to protect herself. "If anything happens, and this car is still drivable, you get behind the wheel and floor it," he told her. "Don't worry about breaking laws. Having the police after you would be a good thing. And you don't look back," he added. "Even if I'm back there." He didn't glance over at her with that one. Or anymore. He couldn't afford the distraction.

Emotion slowing his mental precision could be his downfall. Their downfall.

"I left the burner phone at the motel," he told her. He'd left Doug behind. Other than that the detective had arranged for their mode of transportation.

"First chance you get, you pull into any place that's open and ask them to dial 911."

The truck behind him was closing in on them. Had the advantage of height. And a more powerful engine. Ben's car could fit through smaller openings and make easier turns. He'd been eyeing possibilities for a cross-country run for it for the past couple of miles.

"What's going on?" Kara's tone was sharp. But not panicked. Giving him confidence where it should already have been.

"We're being followed," he told her. "A blue truck."

"The one from last night?"

"Looks like it. I asked Doug to run the partial I thought I saw, but didn't hear back yet." And since he'd ditched the phone, which was the only way to communicate with the man, he wouldn't hear.

Doug knew their car. Could have put a tracking device on it before he'd had it dropped off. Miller could have someone else in the system, using Doug without Doug's knowledge.

The blue truck had had eyes on them last night. Why wait until Ben moved to come after them?

Because he'd needed them alone. He'd been biding his time. Doug knew that Ben had been planning to spend the night in the room. To reconvene early morning to get updates on what investigators working through the night had found, and from there to consider next moves.

The detective had already asked Ben to come in. More than once.

He didn't know Kara was alive.

And what if whoever was closing in behind him wasn't working through Doug Zellers? The possibility was there. Had to stay with him.

He'd taken the car purposely. It was the quickest getaway. And a way to hide Kara while they ran. He'd planned to ditch it all along. Had just hoped to be able to do so without company.

The whole reason he'd woken Kara at three in morning.

He'd been wrong about that one.

Keeping his gaze on the rearview mirror as much as on the road in front of him, and the foliage on both sides of him, Ben saw the flash a split second before he heard the shot's blast, and felt the car jolt, and sink.

"The back tire's been shot out," he said aloud. Kara wasn't going to be able to drive away. Which left Ben only one option. Slowing, so he could better control the vehicle with one hand, he pulled out his gun. Moved to the other lane, praying that a vehicle didn't come up over the hill going the opposite direction and hit them head-on. There'd been no traffic since they'd been on the road. He had to take the chance. He was only likely to get one shot. He needed it to be clean. Not going through a passenger window on the truck.

As he'd expected, the truck, in a clear position of power, drew alongside him. "Brace yourself," he said calmly. Just the two words. Saw another flash. Heard glass shatter. Hit to roll down the passenger window just as he pulled his own trigger.

Then, still moving slowly, watched the truck careen off the road into the ditch.

Ben didn't stop the car. Keeping his eye on the road in front and behind him, he rolled up the passenger window and bumped along on the blown tires rim as fast as the car would take him. "Are you okay?" he asked after ten seconds or so of silence had passed.

"Fine. Are we safe for now?" She didn't ask outright if Ben had just shot a man. But the question was there.

"We are," he told her.

And lips tight, continued to drive.

BEN WAS TAKING CHANCES. Kara didn't like it but had no other suggestions. They couldn't just run out into the woods, hide in a cave, and stay there for the rest of their lives. After stopping at the first ditch in the road he determined secure enough to hide in, putting on the spare tire, and then affixing dirty clothes from her bag into the window grooves to close off the shattered back passenger window, Ben had driven them to an all-night big-box store on the edge of a small town between North Haven and Atlanta to purchase another burner phone and an electronic bug sweeper. Leaving Kara on the floor of the car, covered by the remainder of their dirty clothes.

She'd complied with that one, but only after he'd put on his baseball cap and promised her he'd keep his face away from all security cameras. And had suggested that he buy baby formula—an explanation for the four-in-the-morning store run. One that would bring smiles of sympathy and also detract from suspicion. Unless a law enforcement officer had just been in looking for information regarding an infant kidnapping.

The thought hit her while she sat out in the dark alone. Ben had parked right by the front door, saying there was less chance that anyone would try anything with security right there. He'd said he was going to use self-checkout, so he didn't have to actually look at or talk to anyone.

But as she lay there, waiting, all she could think about were ways things could go wrong. When her usual way had always been to segue to the positive. She'd been teased about the penchant in high school. College. And had had clients at the clinic mention the trait with appreciation, too.

The past few days had changed her. In far too many ways.

Clutching the opened knife Ben had left her, Kara planned for possible breaches. Passenger window was easy, stab whatever came through it. Bullets…shove her head up behind the glove compartment as far as she could, clutch the computer to her stomach. And freeze.

Someone getting in…stabbing, quickly.

If they climbed in the back and pointed a gun at her?

Fear engulfed the interior of the car, sucking her in, suffocating her. Until a question suddenly slid through. Who pointed guns at a pile of dirty laundry?

Everyone thought she was dead. They were after Ben.

His plan was keeping her safe.

No more than five minutes had passed before the double-knuckle knock sounded on the door, but even then, Kara froze, knife at the ready.

"It's me," Ben said, and had the car moving before she'd unburied herself enough to see him. He drove silently, then slowed. "I'm checking for tracking devices," he said, and was out and back in without incident.

"There are none." The report came without her asking.

"Which kind of makes it look like Doug isn't in on it, right?" she asked. They needed some kind of contact with law enforcement, with forensic results, case updates—or look at the possibility of spending the rest of their lives on the run, feigning death.

"And yet leaves us with no explanation as to how someone knew where I was."

She'd uncovered herself, shivered, and with her head leaning against the side door, asked, "What next?"

He pulled a container out the bag he'd dropped on the seat beside him. "Get this open. You've got the knife." And then, with a brief glance in her direction added, "Please."

She felt a little smile inside at that. Even focused on staying alive, dealing with the fact that he'd just shot someone, Ben thought to use the niceties with her. Coddling her, maybe. But it was still nice. Something that had always made her feel as though she was special to him.

The hard plastic package contained a burner phone. She freed it, followed the instructions to get it working, and handed it to him.

Then listened as he spoke to Doug Zellers. Telling the man right off that he'd been followed by the truck with the partial plate he'd given the detective the night before. That the truck had fired on him. Twice. After which he'd fired a shot, and the truck had careened off the road. He gave the coordinates. Then asked if Doug had any new information for him.

He listened. Thanked the man. Said, "Not sure yet." And hung up.

"You were curt with him," she said. "If Doug's on the take, don't you want him to think that you still trust him?"

"That wasn't just Doug," he told her. "I dialed in the lead detective in Atlanta and Doug's second-in-command in North Haven, too. If any one of them is bad, the other two are going to know it by the misuse of the information I just gave them."

"You set a trap."

"Possibly," he said. And then added, "The tone would have been the same, regardless of my suspicions. As far as they all believe, I just lost my wife. Curt is the best they'd expect."

Right. So many sides of nothing clear. Except something hit her right then. Ben kind of *had* lost his wife. Just as she'd lost herself, he'd lost the woman he'd thought Kara to be.

She didn't say so.

Ben suggested that Kara climb into the back seat and get some rest. He was taking them to an abandoned cabin on a pond that he'd visited the other day in his search for Hansen. He'd done a thorough search of the area and thought it would be the safest place for them to hang low for the time being.

Kara didn't want to leave her cramped haven. It felt safe. But knew she'd be better protected strapped in a seat, and did as Ben suggested, staying loose as she strapped herself in just to the bottom strap, and then lay down.

She had way too much on her mind. Didn't expect to sleep. And yet, as the miles passed, she watched Ben's shoulders, the side of his face, and slowly drifted off.


THE CABIN WASN'T MUCH. Ben had already known that. There was no electricity. The only bathroom was an outhouse. But a well with an iron-hand pumped faucet outside the back door provided water. No way they'd use it for drinking, but for washing it would be better than nothing.

Owned by a deceased schoolteacher who'd never married or had a family, the property had been deserted for a couple of years. Using his knife, he jimmied the door, promising himself that if they made it back to normal life, he'd pay to have the door replaced. And then, once inside, he barricaded the door with wood, and a hammer and nails found in a dresser drawer along with other tools and repair items. He'd found a key to a deadbolt lock hanging on a hook by the back door. It fit the lock on the door.

They'd use the back entrance for coming and going.

If, indeed, they came and went.

The one bedroom was sparsely furnished. A mattress with plastic covering, and bedding in zippered containers on top. And a stool used as a nightstand. There was no furnace, just a fireplace. He didn't trust the flue, but they didn't need heat.

If they were still there when nighttime fell, and it got too cold, they'd use the blankets for warmth.

He didn't let him look that far ahead. Instead, he gave Kara another rundown on using his gun, and set her up in the front room, with full view of the one skinny dirt path that had been cut through the trees—the only way a vehicle could make it to the cabin. And then went to lie on the mattress and get some sleep. Three hours he told her. Then she was to wake him up.

He spent the first half hour of the time thinking about the woman sitting watch for him. She'd barely spoken since they'd arrived at the cabin but had been completely attentive.

And calm.

Eerily so.

So much of the woman, who was emerging from the woman he'd married, was unfamiliar to him. And yet, he admired the hell out of her. And was starting to see parts of his Kara in her, too.

She woke him at noon, four hours after he'd fallen asleep. Had their premade salads ready at the table, with peanut butter crackers as garnish. And one little tub each of prepackaged peaches, their tops already peeled off.

"I wasn't sure the salads would still be good, but they smell and look fine," she told him. "They were still cool." She seemed…okay. As though she had the strength to continue another day. Or as many as it took.

She was also holding herself apart from him. Polite. Kind. But no meeting of the eyes. No accidental touches.

Ben welcomed the distance. He had a case to solve, their

lives to save, before he even thought about tackling his marriage problems.

And needed an update from Doug before he knew where to turn. He'd regurgitated all that he already knew so much he was just going in circles. And with the whirlwind, losing sight of who he could trust.

A state that kept bringing him back to the fact that he wasn't hearing from Doug. Surely, they knew something. The driver Ben had shot after being shot at—had they found a body? Dead or alive? Any identity? Slugs in the area? They knew Ben's gun, but what about the other one? Any similarities to other crimes associated with Miller? And what about the truck? All questions he'd have had answers to within the first hour of being told there'd been a shooting.

Why wasn't Doug getting back with him?

He'd set a trap for the three top people on the case and had to wait to see how it played out. And he needed his mind occupied. Sharp. So he'd be ready when the battle came to him.

After lunch, he pulled out the computer again. Signed on to his encrypted hot spot, and, using Doug's credentials— because his friend had instructed him to do so a couple of days before—started to search law enforcement databases for murders that had taken place in Florida at the time that Karin and Amanda Moore had been there. Starting within a ten-mile radius of the Arlington Beach hotel. Kara's struggles stemmed from something missing inside her where her mother was concerned. Being pregnant with his child had brought her to that place. If he could help her find resolution in that area, he wanted to do so. For himself, for their marriage, their child—of course. But just for her, too.

He wasn't using his talents to try to hang on to Kara, though he'd greatly welcome that result. He was trying to help her because he loved her. Period.

She didn't ask what he was working on. She lay on the

couch across from the table where he sat. He was hoping she'd be able to get some more rest, but anytime he looked over, her eyes were open.

At one point they were staring right at him. "I'm sorry," she told him. "I never, in a million years, thought we'd ever come to this place in our relationship."

He was with her on that one. Nodded. Then said, "It's not your fault, Kara. Your feelings, your needs are genuine." There had to be more. Some way he could help her find her way back to them, but how could he do that when he wasn't sure she belonged there?

"I love you," she said then.

"I know. I love you, too."

"Then why isn't this working?"

The words cut through him. "I didn't realize we'd reached the point where we knew for sure that it wouldn't," he told her. "Are you telling me it has?"

She pretty much just had. Grayness settled over him like an invisible blanket. He'd lost her, then? They weren't just going through a rough patch?

"I can't go back to being who I was," she said, sounding far more sure about her future than he was about his. As though she knew where she was headed, where she had to go, while he sat there waiting for her to come back to him.

"You don't want to be married to me." He said the words, glancing at his screen because it was the only thing that made sense to him. Words on a screen about some murder that had taken place thirty years before.

"I do." She sat up. "So much. But I'm not ready to celebrate being pregnant. I'm not sure I ever will be, which is not what you want. Not what I would have expected from myself. And if I don't figure this all out, I'm not going to want to have more than one child."

He wanted a minimum of two, would prefer four. Which

she knew. Had said once that a house full of laughing little voices would be the perfect culmination of their love. And a direct opposite of her own growing up, where the only childish laughter had been her own.

"I'd rather only have one child than lose you," he said, and wanted to take the words back as soon as he said them. He was supposed to be giving her space. The freedom to figure out what she needed, to choose. Not make her feel as though she had to stay to make him happy.

"I have to be an equal, Ben," she said then, looking him right in the eye. "After all this, I can't go back to being cosseted. You're ten years older than I am, but that doesn't make you ten years wiser. Yes, we're at different stages of life. I'm not yet thirty, you're turning forty. I get that. But sometimes youth has a perspective that fits today better than not. And even if it didn't, my view on things is just as valid."

He heard her. Took her words with a grain of salt, knowing that she couldn't know what she didn't yet know. Life had shaped him. Taught him lessons she hadn't lived long enough to learn yet. The aging process alone gave its own changing views. Something he hadn't known until he'd found himself facing forty. There was some wisdom that only came with having lived each phase of life.

He was a full decade of phases ahead of her.

Still, he needed her to know. "I do think of you as an equal," he said. "You're my partner in life, Kara. I value your opinions, need your input, and want you by my side as I go through life. I'm just no longer sure I'm enough for you."

"You're enough," she said, but wasn't smiling. "But I'm not the kid sister anymore, Ben."

He nodded. Tried to hide the frustration building inside him. Maybe he'd been selfish, grabbing up his young wife, thinking he could have it all. He hadn't thought of her as

Thane's kid sister-in-law since she'd come home from college all grown up. But for some reason she couldn't see that.

How did you help someone see what they couldn't see? The question came. Sat there on his shoulder. Weighing him down.

And when Kara closed her eyes, on him, on their unfinished conversation, he went back to looking for the answers he *could* find. Hoping they'd be what she needed to find her peace.

But fearing that, for Kara, when it came to the kind of husband she'd grown to need, nothing he did ever would be enough.

## Chapter Twenty-One

Kara felt her marriage breaking and had no idea how to fix it. Ben kept talking about age, but his age wasn't the problem. Hers was. He would always see himself as having more wisdom than her because he'd lived longer. Which meant he'd put more weight in his take on things than hers. Thinking he knew better.

And she just couldn't live like that anymore.

The thought, while new in the past few days, didn't seem all that new. Like it had been dangling there, just behind her mind's eye, waiting for the right chance for it to appear.

Truth was, Ben did have ten years more of experiences, of learning than she did. She'd always liked that about him. Finding security in the fact that someone wise had her back.

Because…it's all she'd ever known. From the moment of her mother's desertion, Kara had been set apart, the only young child being protected, with everyone so much older, knowing the truth, protecting her from it. The truth hit her hard as she lay there trying to find a few minutes' respite in sleep.

They'd made a truce. All of them. And had been living by it ever since.

And Ben…when he'd taken a personal interest in her, it had felt natural to her for Ben to coddle her, too.

So, was she really in love with him? Benjamin Gregory Latimer? Or just in love with the role he'd played in her life? Was that why she was struggling so much with carrying his baby?

Because while she loved him dearly, was she *in* love with him?

The thought ricocheted through her. Over and over. Hitting her hard. Forcing her to sit up. Open her eyes. Get out of her darkness.

She blinked, but there were no tears. Just…nothingness. A rejection of what had been. And a staunch refusal to consider what might have been, too.

She'd die for Ben Latimer. Had never once been the least bit tempted by another man since she'd been with Ben. Their first date, first kiss, first time making love…were all engrained on her heart.

She just had to make sure, for her sake and his, for the sake of their baby, that she hadn't been a kid reaching out to him to dispel some kind of lack of parent complex.

Her heart couldn't even consider the theory. But her heart wasn't giving her any other solutions, either. Not about Ben. About their baby. Even about herself.

Which left her head, logic, to guide her. She could no longer trust her sisters to give her the truth if they thought keeping it from her was in her best interest. Was it that same way with Ben? She had to be able to trust him or there was no marriage. She couldn't spend her life playing head games with herself, wondering what he wasn't telling her. Or whether or not he was withholding something from her because he didn't want to hurt her.

Like if their child got hurt and the doctor gave Ben some earth-shattering news and he didn't tell her because he didn't want to hurt her.

No. That was fear talking. Not logic. That last bit…

"I found it, Kara!" The lilt in Ben's voice lit a fire in her heart and she jumped up.

"What?" she asked, heading toward him. He'd found the link to Miller? Was putting an end to the terror?

"The case," he told her, looking up to meet her gaze. "Your mother's case, the one she testified for. The answers you were looking for. I can't do any more with Miller until I have more information…"

He let the words drop off as she rounded the table and stared at the screen.

But before she could do more than glance, a crack sounded just outside the door. Like a stick being stepped on. Heart pounding, she stared at him.

"Go!" he whispered harshly. "Get under the bed and do not come out. No matter what. Not until at least an hour has passed with no sound. More if you can bear it. And then, come out prepared to kill or be killed." He handed her his knife. Gave her two sharp knives from the one drawer in the kitchen, and a small little pistol. "I found this in the bedroom," he told her. "It's loaded and ready to shoot. When I return, if all is well, I'll tell you I'm hungry."

He was moving toward the back door before she'd even left the room.

"I love you," she said.

His "I love you, too" was whispered, but there.

And Kara prayed that it wasn't the last time she heard those words from him.

BEN SPENT A good half hour checking out the property surrounding them. He wasn't the only one who'd heard the stick snap. Could have been an animal. He saw no tracks. No footprints, either. But the area directly around the cabin was more rock than dirt. With cement steps leading down to the pond.

And an old boat dock that had dislodged from shore and was caught in undergrowth a few yards out. He checked the shore around the several-acre pond. Keeping his eye on the house at all times. Anyone who tried to get to Kara under that bed better get a bullet in the face for his trouble.

He had to trust her to be able to get the shot off. He couldn't be in two places at once. And he was the one who had to be outside. He was the only one anyone knew was alive.

Was someone setting them up?

Watching even as he made his careful search of the area?

Making mental notes of any way anyone could gain access to the cabin. He'd noticed a boat on the water. The pond had been built in front a rock cliff, which was one of the main reasons he'd chosen the place over the others he'd investigated on his search for Hansen.

The only way anyone could know they were there was if Doug was somehow tracking him. With his old burner and now his new?

Just didn't make sense that his friend would do that. Doug lived for the job. Came from enough money that he sure didn't need to turn dirty to get it. He wasn't married. Didn't gamble. He was on the fast track to be North Haven Chief of Police.

He'd also once been in love with Kara. Not that Ben had ever said a word to his wife about that. It had been long ago, before she'd left for college. Doug had just come back to North Haven to accept a promotion from officer in Atlanta to detective. She'd just graduated high school. They'd met at one of Stella and Thane's rallies. Doug had been working protection detail. Had chatted with her for a while. And made a point to talk to her anytime he saw her in town after that, too. But with almost fifteen years between them, he'd been chicken to actually ask her out.

By the time Kara had come home from college, Ben had already worked his first case with Doug, but they weren't on friendly enough terms to discuss women in their lives.

Doug had actually told Ben about his infatuation one night over beers. The night Ben had given the other man an invitation to his wedding. Doug had told him that Ben was the better man. And jokingly added that Ben had Doug to thank for Kara being available and open to him. Who knew what might have happened if Doug had been as brave as Ben and had gotten up the guts to ask out a woman so much younger than he was.

Doug had also teased Ben that he was glad it was Ben and not Doug who'd have to worry about keeping a younger woman interested in him as he aged. Most particularly a woman as smart and savvy as Kara.

He'd assured Ben the infatuation was long over. Had never given any indication, even during the past few days, that Kara was any more to him than the wife of a friend.

Ben would never have believed that Doug was the type to harbor some kind of obsession. To the point of losing all sense of right and wrong.

But he'd never have believed that Kara would be dissatisfied in their relationship, either. Or unhappy to be carrying his child.

There was no sign of fresh tire tracks on the path that led into the cabin through the trees. Ben checked the perimeter of the yard one more time before unlocking the back door and heading inside.

The one room was easy to peruse. The bedroom, just off to his right also clearly visible. And seemingly empty.

"Kara? It's me," he said. "I'm hungry."

He heard a shuffle. A bump. Another shuffle, and saw her feet coming out from under the bed. Her long hair disheveled, she came out of the room squinting against the brightness, and with a gun in one hand and butcher knife in the other, walked up to him, threw her arms around his neck and started to cry.

For a second, she was his Kara again. Not because of the tears, but because he had the ability to offer her comfort and strength.

And Ben held on tight.

KARA WASN'T HUNGRY. But she wasn't just feeding herself, so she ate more fruit. Peaches and pears, discarding most of the heavy syrup in which they'd come.

She had a peanut butter sandwich, made with the bread and spread Ben had picked up with the baby formula that morning. Drank more water.

And snacked on a cookie for dessert.

Not the best choices for a newly pregnant woman to be making, but it wasn't the worst diet she could have, either. And was better than starving.

Mostly she stayed close to Ben. All that time under the bed, listening for the sound of gunfire—something she was never going to forget after having a shot go off right above her head that morning—all she'd wanted was to see Ben again.

To have him return safely to the cabin.

Not for her, but for him. Because he was a bright light in the world.

Her heart had made one thing quite clear during all those awful minutes in the dark. She was in love with her husband.

She didn't know that that was enough to make a marriage work. But it was a truth that was a part of who she was.

The realization that she was lying there prepared to shoot another human being had opened some doors into a psyche that was still partially hiding from her. Like all the different experiences she was living through were slowly showing her parts of herself that she hadn't acknowledged, but that had been living inside her all along.

And to that end, when they finished eating, and Ben had answered all the questions she'd asked about his trek outside, she moved on to the other thing she'd been thinking about under that bed.

"Tell me about my mother's case," she said, sitting perpendicular to him at the table in her ill-fitting clothes, still searching for pieces of herself.

"It involved a powerful family that ran multiple businesses. Some legitimate, some not. The patriarch brought his firstborn son up to be just like him. One who held a respected place in society and had a dark side that was just as active and respected. The father remarried after his first wife died. Adopted his second wife's young son. The adopted son was raised outside the illegal portions of the business. Has no known ties to them at all, according to what I could access of the file…"

"I'm guessing the second wife had something to do with that," Kara piped in. Then checked herself. How would she know what a mother might do to protect her child?

"Father dies, younger son inherits half of the fortune. Stumbles upon a hit his older brother had put out on someone. I couldn't see what happened from there. Only that shortly after that, the younger brother was dead. And the older brother was in jail for his murder."

She shook her head. "I don't get it."

Ben looked over at her, frowning, and yet she saw warmth in his eyes. Pity, maybe. But warmth. "Younger brother had a new girlfriend. Had been with her when a key piece of evidence had been exposed. Older brother hadn't known about the girlfriend, had never heard of her or seen her, but whatever she saw, or heard, had been able to later definitively prove that older brother had committed the murder. If

I were at work, I could get more. All I had access to was a summary. But I can tell you that the older brother has been locked up tight ever since."

She could hardly breathe. Her mother had had a boyfriend during the week she'd been away? A new one, apparently? She'd taken the heart her father had just broken, and had flown down to Florida and met another man? A rich one with a conscience? Kara didn't know how she felt about that.

She didn't blame Tory. The woman's high school sweetheart husband of almost seventeen years had just told her he'd been having an affair for a year and wanted a divorce. Her heart ached for the person her mother had been. One who'd, even with a broken heart, had the good judgment to choose a decent man.

That felt good, at least. Until she realized that it might not have been Tory. It's not like her name would have been in any court record.

And being on the verge of losing the little bit she'd just found, she suddenly had to try not to do so. "How are you so sure it's my mother's case?"

"The witness had been at the Arlington Beach Hotel, the location of whatever she witnessed. It all happened during the exact dates Amanda and Karin were there. Something we know because Melanie knew exactly when your mom and Lila left and came back. The witness testified as a Jane Doe. And her file is nonexistent."

Kara's heart lifted a bit more. "She went into witness protection."

"It's also the only case during that year that had any ties to the Arlington."

He was building a good case. One she suddenly wanted to believe.

"The man she put away was a really bad guy, Kara. He'd been the main suspect in more than thirty murders over the years. Always managed to walk away. And those are likely only the tip of the iceberg. Jane Doe's testimony saved innumerable lives."

Kara shivered, hugging herself. She rubbed her hands up and down her arms. But not just for herself. She and her mother…they had something in common besides biology. They'd both been up against powerful bad guys, murderers, who saw torture as a way to climb higher on their ladders. Or to maintain their godhood. Tory had to have been terrified.

Just as Kara had been standing in that house with a board in hand, jamming a wall full of potentially hot wires.

She'd have done anything to save the baby growing inside her.

Just as Tory had done? Saving her children from that very bad older brother, were he to find out that she was Karin or Amanda Moore? And from there, find Tory Mitchell? And what about Lila? Her life would have been in danger as well.

If Tory had remained in Georgia, hadn't come forward, they all could have lived happily ever after. While a powerful, horrible man continued to ravage numbers of innocent lives.

Criminals, like Stuart Miller. That men like Ben—Ben himself—spent their lives, risked their lives, to put behind bars so others could live safely and without fear.

Would she have Ben quit his job and stay home so that she'd never again face any possibility of terror from men like Stuart Miller? But maybe their child would, say, be approached by someone selling illegal drugs. Or be lured on the internet.

No.

She wouldn't have Ben—or any of the other heroes who risked their lives every day to make the world better—quit doing what they did. Good people couldn't turn blind eyes to…

"My mother was a good person," Kara said then, tearing up, lips trembling. "Melanie asked Stella if we'd blame Dad for deserting us if he'd gone off to war, died saving our country…" Her words trailed off.

She looked into Ben's eyes. Saw the admiration shining from his gaze as he watched her. And saw something else, too. Like he was waiting…

"She was a good mother," she said slowly. "The best kind of mother, breaking her own heart, giving up her own life, to protect ours…and so many others."

He shrugged. Nodded. Half smiled.

Kara's mind flashed quick memories. The way she'd made noise in that trash barrel, the splintery wood she'd used to plow through a rotted house wall, the earring she'd thought to leave in the laundry cart, even the way she'd stayed steady under a bed, knife and gun in hand, ready to use both…all to fight evil.

And to give her child a chance to be born. "I'm going to be a mother," she said then, as though just realizing that fact. And in a sense, she was.

Because for the first time, she'd actually felt like one.

## Chapter Twenty-Two

Ben felt the hairs on the back of his neck prickle as his skin grew tight. He'd been listening to Kara, had been fully engaged, following every word she'd said. With details of her mother's case still in the forefront of his mind.

Pieces started to congregate, to form lines in his mind… only to fall off into nothingness.

"Oh my God, Ben!" Her words had him on his feet, gun drawn and ready as his gaze darted around her, them, trying to follow her gaze.

Which was wide-eyed and focused on him. Her mouth open wide.

"What?" he asked, tense and ready to take action.

"The kidnappings…the bomb…it all started after I began doing internet searches on my mom's case. After I found that note in storage…"

Relaxing a tad, he nodded. "Yeah," he told her. "I was just thinking along those same lines…"

She wasn't relaxing. Moving toward him, her gaze on him intense, she said, "Every single time my safety was breached, I'd been on the internet. At the office…the resort…and in last night's hotel, you were searching. It had to be anytime we accessed anything that took us too close to that case.

And..." Her words dropped off as alarm filled her eyes and her gaze darted haphazardly around them.

"That stick cracking we just heard..." She stopped, looking horrified. Then, with a hard swallow, said, "It's not Stuart Miller. It's the older brother, Ben. He knows. Witness protection found me. He did, too. Only sooner. He's not going to rest until he gets his revenge. He's got money. Is hiring people, just as you thought Stuart Miller was. Getting some kind of sick satisfaction over making someone pay. He's here, Ben. Whoever he hired is here. Waiting. Planning. Oh my God, the cabin's going to blow up! We have to go!"

He wanted to grab her, hug her to him until she felt safe again. And he would, if she let him. Once he knew she was out of danger.

Taking a deep breath, he said, "I was just on the same track. Until it took me to the one reason this doesn't fit."

"What's that?"

"Prison records. The guy's been in isolation at his insistence, and for his own protection, for over a month. No way he could have known anything about internet searches or hired anyone to do anything."

The rest, though...

What was he missing?

The bombs. Kidnapping in wheeled maintenance containers. Internet searches. A dirty cop? He hadn't heard back on Scott Nivens. Granted, it had only been a day and with the bombed house, a supposed dead witness, and a targeted investigator, law enforcement had a lot on their plate. But had Doug even tried to check out the Marshal?

Maybe the FBI should be brought in. He had contacts...

The drone. The thought had been that a drone had been used to drop the smaller firebomb in the grass outside Kara's office. To distract from the blue truck returning just long enough to park it, get out, and detonate it.

Was a drone flying overhead, watching the cabin, targeting it, right then?

He and Kara had both heard something. Based on all the other times Kara had been attacked, the fact that her attacker appeared to be patient—waiting in a stairwell for an opportunity to move in, leaving her in a house until the right moment to blow it up…a chance she'd taken from him by blowing it up herself.

The truck that had been in the hotel parking lot the night before, but waited until morning to attack. How had he known they'd left the hotel, unless he had constant eyes on him?

Or his computer. Kara's could have been hacked. But Ben's?

Had just come from Doug.

He and Kara had both heard something. Ben came back to the thought. Over and over. And he knew. Someone was out there. Waiting to attack. Waiting for what? The perfect moment?

Or was he out there working on their demise? Setting bombs? Dropping them from drones?

If he knew the end goal, he'd be better able to assess.

But he knew one thing. Someone was out there.

What he had to do was determine what he did with the information. Did he get Kara out of the house? Into a compromised car? Into the woods where the perpetrator was hiding? Watching?

Whoever he was up against had already blown up a house. Had almost succeeded in taking Kara's life. And the life of Ben's unborn child, too.

In the woods, they'd be hunted animals and could be caught. But he'd have more options than he would trying not to blow up in a bomb.

Did he take a chance on the car? It was the fastest way

out. Could be rigged to blow the second he turned the key in the ignition.

He needed a trench. One deep enough for Kara to lie in and him to lie on top of her. Or to create a distraction long enough to get Kara to the pond. Unless a bomb landed directly on top of them, they wouldn't explode in the water.

They could be shot. But he could shoot back. Kara would be a moving target, swimming underwater and only coming up for air.

He needed a trench that led to the pond.

Or he could create an explosion of his own. In the front yard. While Kara ran in a haphazard fashion, covered by trees, to the pond.

No one knew she was still alive.

He had his plan.

The explosion was simple. He had plenty of bullets filled with gunpowder.

"*Ben!*" Kara, who'd walked to the front side of the cabin—no windows and no doors that could be breached—dropped down to the floor.

Pulling his gun, he dropped, too, to a crouching position, moving toward her and asked, "What?"

"I just heard something," she told him. "Right outside the front door. Like a shoe shuffling in the dirt."

His time was up. Standing, he headed toward the front door, grabbing a box of ammunition as he went. He'd open the door an inch, toss the box right in front of it, and shoot.

"Get your gun, and as soon as I remove the barricade on the front door, you head out that one." He motioned toward the only other exit. "You run as fast as you can to the trees and through them to the pond. You don't look back, no matter what you hear. There's going to be an explosion—don't worry, it's only me."

"What about you?"

"I'll be right behind you, Kara, but you don't look or wait for me. You dive into the pond, and swim. Stay underwater as much as possible. When you get to the other side, you keep yourself out of sight and get as far from here as you can."

"But…how will I find you?"

He couldn't think that far ahead. Not until he succeeded and the bastard who'd been terrorizing them was dead. "You get to a phone. A house with family in the yard, a car with a woman and kids. A store or gas station. Call 911. Send someone here. I'll find you."

"But…"

He was at the front door. Had no way of knowing if it was going to explode in his face. "Go now!" he hissed.

And heard her quick "I love you" as the back door opened.

Ben's "I love you, too" was lost in a barrage of gunfire.

KARA STUMBLED WHEN she heard the blast of gunfire, but she tripped forward and kept running. Made it to the trees, and then through them.

To almost total silence.

Shots, and then nothing. Was Ben still alive?

Shaking, crying, she continued forward. Confused. Frightened. Feeling like she was at the beach again, with a bag over her head. She shook her head. Stumbled a second time. Now wasn't the time to think back. She had to move forward. Run faster.

She made it a few steps from the pond, and stopped. There was something moving in the water. Small. Round. Too symmetrical to be a living organism.

Kara had no idea what, precisely, she was looking at. A remote-controlled something, she figured. Didn't matter what it was. Just that it was.

The pond wasn't safe.

Staying back in the trees, she looked up. Saw a sky of green leaves. Wanted to be lost in them. And…the beach. The bench.

She couldn't get caught again.

Shoving the gun in the waistband of her jeans as she'd seen Ben do, just above her butt, she took less than ten seconds to choose her tree and started to shimmy. Straight up. Thinking of her baby, of her mother, emblazoned with a strength that didn't feel like wholly her own, she dug her tennis shoes into bark, hugged the trunk, and moved up the foot it took to reach a branch. From there, she held on to nature, let it bear her weight, help her as she climbed higher and higher.

The beach. The hood.

Chocolate. Stale cigarette smoke. Musty cologne. Smells she'd remembered that day…

She'd just caught of slight whiff of the odd combination again. When she'd torn out the back door.

He was there.

But maybe hadn't seen her.

He'd been at the back door. Or close to it. But before she'd run out. The putrid scent had been more of a hint than anywhere near as strong as it had been that first day.

And maybe she was just hallucinating. The result of one trauma too many.

She climbed anyway.

Couldn't think about Ben out there dying. About the fact that she wasn't on her way to get help. Shook away thoughts of him lying in a pool of blood. The water wasn't safe. She wouldn't be able to help him if she was dead.

She was going to climb as high as she could, then check on him. With every branch higher, she prayed that when she got to the top, she'd be able to see her husband.

And that he'd be able to hang on, to keep breathing, until she could assess that it was safe to get back down to earth and save his life.

THE FIRST PERSON Ben saw after the dust settled was... Doug Zellers. Looking through the barest crack in the door, he caught a glimpse of the detective, behind a tree not far from the car, gun pointed toward the house.

He'd feel things about that at some point. In that moment, all Ben knew was that he had to pick his battle. If it was just going to be between him and Doug, he had to make certain that the man's duplicity was clear. Otherwise, even dead, the detective would win.

Ben would go down as a cop killer.

In the next second, Ben's attention was caught by another movement. Peripherally seen. But there. He had no doubts about that. A second person was out there. In Doug's view, but not Ben's. The person paying Doug under the table?

Then why was the detective's gun seeming to point more to the left of Ben, rather than directly at him?

While Ben remained frozen in position, Doug darted from one tree to another, motioning behind him with a hand down at his thigh.

Who was out there with him? Had he seen Ben?

Were they in the process of surrounding the house?

Did they know he was inside?

He needed a sense of what kind of play they were making. Had his distraction maneuver worked?

As long as Kara had made it to the pond, was safe, he'd go down fighting. If he had to. He wasn't giving up. Not with his wife reeling in trauma and a baby on the way. But if he had to die to save the two of them, he would do so.

She had her sisters. Stella and Melanie would always watch out for her. And lather the baby with love and care, too.

He'd been watching Doug for several minutes. Giving Kara time. Determining his own plan.

They weren't going to shoot him. If that was the plan, they'd have moved in already. They needed his death to look accidental.

Or like a suicide.

And he still didn't know why. Because things had gotten out of hand? Doug had agreed to make a quick buck off from Ben's suffering, and things had escalated from there? By the time the detective had known who he was really dealing with, he'd been in too deep?

The theory made sense.

Ben just wasn't buying into it.

Was he failing himself in his crowning moment?

Looking death straight in the eye, Ben couldn't believe that Doug Zellers was there to kill him. Logic, theory, they were what helped Ben put criminals away for life.

He needed to allow them to serve him when his own mortality was at stake.

Doug darted again. To the left, a couple of yards closer to the house. Looking slightly behind him and to his right as he planted his feet. Following that glance, Ben spotted a man on Doug's team, sliding from one tree to another, also moving closer to the house. And then movement caught his peripheral vision again. Another body. Moving in.

Barbara Allen. The officer in charge of Kara's on-site protection detail at the resort.

It was like they were…

Working. Doing their jobs.

And he knew, Doug had his back. His front. And both sides, too.

They had eyes on a target. Were closing in.

And he was right in the middle of their takedown.

Which meant…

Spinning, gun raised, he had his finger on the trigger, poised to shoot, and was surprised to see himself standing alone in the house.

Whoever Doug had in his sights wasn't in the house.

Ben's new burner phone buzzed against his chest, and he pulled it out of his pocket. Only one person knew the number.

We're here. He's on the roof. Get out.

Doug didn't know Ben was at the door watching him. Not taking time to answer, Ben slid out the front door. Looking to the ground for the sun's shadow on the man, he saw which way he was facing, chose the closest tree to himself in the opposite direction, and rushed to it. Then to the next.

And saw the body on the roof. Heading toward the edge, as though to climb back down. He also saw the pack he'd left behind.

Another explosive.

A shot rang out, and then a second, third, and fourth in quick succession before the man made it to the edge of the roof. He fell, slid down the incline, and to the ground.

One of Doug's people. Ben didn't know which. He ran to the body, getting there first. Saw the blood spurting from the perp's chest and arm. And then his gaze moved upward, to see cognition shining from the kidnapper's still-open eyes.

A gaze filled with a curious mix of hate and fear. Almost a plea.

He'd seen the look before. When someone was facing death, a final reckoning, with too many sins.

"Why?" The question was pulled out of him.

"She...was...his...daughter," the man gurgled. Coughed up blood as Doug and others rushed forward. But the perp didn't seem to notice them. He continued to look only at Ben. "Would get...the money..."

Doug pulled Ben aside as an ambulance came rushing up the path to the yard where they all stood.

"I thought we'd get him before he got close to you," Doug said, looking Ben in the eye. The detective's gaze was filled with apology. With sorrow.

And Ben knew it would be a while before he'd be able to forgive himself for doubting his friend. The thought came and was pushed back.

"Kara!" he yelled at the top of his lungs. Then turned to Doug. "She's in the water. I told her to swim for it…" He took off toward the pond as he said the words, Doug at his heels.

"Man, listen…"

"She's alive! Call for help…" His words dropped off as he caught his first glimpse of the woman walking toward him. Her face, her clothes, were a mess. Dirt. Grime. What looked like spots of blood.

But it was the agony on her face that had him racing toward her, bending to her, needing to wrap her in his arms, but afraid to hurt her further. "Get the paramedics over here!" he screamed.

"I'm…no," Kara said. "I don't need them."

Doug, who'd been running right beside Ben, put up a hand, forestalling the medical team, as Ben asked, "What's wrong?"

"I shot him, Ben. I was up in the tree. I… I… I just… killed a man." She held up the gun he'd given her.

There'd been a shot, softer sounding, and then three more. And he didn't need a forensics team to assure her. "No, you didn't, my love. That pistol doesn't have a far enough range…"

Nor was she the sniper it would have taken to make such a shot. But she'd tried. She hadn't run as he'd told her. She'd climbed a tree, and waited, ready to protect him from danger.

Cacophony broke out around them. Another ambulance

arrived, and Ben sent Kara off to be checked over, just in case. While he turned to Doug.

"I'm sorry—"

"I'm sorry—"

They spoke in unison, and Ben motioned for Doug to go first. "I thought she was dead. And as much as you loved her, you were more a danger to yourself than anything if you tried to take on this fiend," the man said. "We found the truck. The body wasn't in it, but his fingerprints were. He was in the system for some things thirty years ago. Had disappeared off the grid. But when forensics got a look at Kara's laptop, and saw the searches…then I heard from the Marshals Service that Nivens was on leave recovering from a bullet wound…all hands were on deck. FBI. Atlanta police. They're all here…"

Doug motioned and Ben turned and saw all of the men and women coming out of the woodwork. "We had him two miles back. Thought we had him surrounded. The plan was to get him without you ever knowing he'd gotten close…"

But they hadn't known that Kara was alive. That the man still had his target. But the bastard had known. He'd seen Ben load Kara in the car in the wee hours of that morning.

Hard to believe that only fifteen, sixteen hours had passed since then.

Shaken up, feeling himself start to weaken with relief, Ben thought of Kara out in the yard, running toward the pond. The sound he'd heard outside the door had been the perp. Ready to take them. Until Ben had set off so many rounds just as Doug and his teams had breached the property, were making their way in.

His shots had alerted them all. Bringing law enforcement to the cabin in droves. Sending the would-be killer into action. He'd have known even if they saw him on the roof, they wouldn't shoot him. Not with the bomb detonator in his possession.

Not until Ben was outside, that was.

The officers who'd shot him wouldn't have known that Kara could still have been in the house. Once Ben was outside, they'd taken their shots. Or, perhaps Kara's shot had alerted them. Had them thinking the perp had a partner.

It would all come out in the reports. But either way, Ben's distraction plan had worked. Had it not, had the man been out back, not the sound Kara had heard in front, then Ben would have just handed the stalker his prey.

He glanced over at Kara, saw her looking at him, and Ben knew, in the space of a heartbeat, that, as an investigator, he'd probably saved Kara's life a second time.

But as a husband, he'd been failing her for years.

# Chapter Twenty-Three

Kara stepped out of the shower and shivered. Partially from the chill after the massaging warmth from the hot spray. But only somewhat.

Hours had passed since Doug and all the men and women working with him had rescued her and Ben from the abandoned house on the pond.

Toweling off, she amended that last thought. Since they'd helped them bring down the man who'd been torturing her, and then escorted her and Ben back to North Haven.

To the hospital first, at Ben's insistence, and then home. At her and Ben's agreement to his offer, Doug had contacted her sisters. He'd actually gone to Melanie's home. To deliver the news that her sister was alive, in person, rather than over the phone. He'd assured them both that Kara was fine, but that she needed time alone with Ben, and to rest, before she saw them.

They'd both called while Kara was still at the hospital. Insisting that they just had to see her. If only for a second. She held strong. And had agreed to having breakfast with them, Ben included, in the morning.

Where she and Ben went after that, Kara didn't know. She'd always be in love with him. The fear she'd felt when she'd thought he was going to be blown up by a bomb on the roof and had taken her shot at her tormentor was going to be with her forever. Because Ben was a part of her heart.

But that didn't change the other things she'd learned about herself over the past days. A counselor who'd come to talk to her at the hospital—giving Kara a card and suggesting that she call if she wanted to chat—had talked about trauma releasing pent-up emotions and issues within a person. About the aftereffects of facing death bringing what she'd called "aha moments."

Kara had known immediately that she'd had them. She might still feel a step back from her ability to be the nucleus of her own family, but she no longer had any doubts that she could be a good mother.

Just as she'd been a good partner and wife to Ben. Even when he hadn't treated her in the same vein. She'd just accepted his treatment of her as part of who he was. Because she'd grown up with everyone else she'd loved deeply treating her the same way.

And at the same time, when she and Ben had been alone in that house earlier in the day, when she'd seen that he was seeing her in a new light, when he'd realized that he might lose her, she hadn't fallen apart.

Because no one ever got close enough to her to have that power.

The realization had hit while she was talking to the counselor and had been resonating with Kara ever since. Her whole life, she'd lived a step back—caring for dogs that others owned and loved, but never owning one. Her sisters, her dad, all had their spouses, their own immediate families. Her immediate family had blown up before she was born. The one person who'd borne her, who'd been her only source of nourishment for the six months of her life, and from whom she was still breastfeeding when Tory's world had blown apart, had just…left. Others had stepped in. In duplicate and triplicate. There'd never been a main one. A mother. She'd grown up holding herself apart.

Dressing in a pair of light silk pajamas Ben had bought her for Christmas—one with long pants and a short-sleeved top—Kara combed tangles out of her newly conditioned long hair. Her husband was waiting for her in the next room. Sitting up on his side of the bed. Wearing a pair of silk pajama trousers she'd bought for him.

He'd slept nude every one of the nights they'd ever spent together prior to her peeing on the stick.

She'd caught a glimpse of him through the mirror on the bathroom door, which had been angled just right to see the bed when she'd stepped out of the shower.

He'd showered in one of the guest baths.

Letting her know that he knew they were no longer who they'd been.

She couldn't be who she'd been. Could no longer participate in a relationship where her partner thought he was doing the right thing by protecting her from painful information, rather than giving her the right to process it. Who thought it was better handling things on his own than trusting her, *needing* her to share in his struggles with him.

She needed a partner who believed she had enough mental and emotional maturity to be of help to him.

And she and Ben were having a baby. Their baby.

They had to find a way to co-parent, no matter what happened between them.

Most of all, she had to be honest with him. Too many lies—lies by words that were said, and lies by withholding words, too—had been flying around in the past few days for her to ever feel safe in a relationship that harbored them.

Doug had told her and Ben, in the car ride to the hospital, that the city worker who'd kidnapped her had actually been the man who'd died on the ground at the abandoned house early that evening. He'd paid the city worker to let him use his uniform. It was *his* scent she'd recognized outside when she'd left the house late that afternoon for her run to the pond. Doug had been so distraught for the death of his friend's wife that he'd unloaded on the city worker the night before, who'd then confessed to being more afraid of Matthew Humbolt Grossman coming after him then going to jail. Jail time would have a limit—no one had been hurt, and there'd been no hint of murder. Turning on that guy would have been a death sentence.

The scent had turned out to be a scent Ben had remembered, too. From the house where Hansen had been staying. The man, Grossman, had done his homework on Ben and had shown up at Hansen's hideout, but the man had eluded him. After Kara's supposed death, Doug had gone back at Hansen, too, with a threat to charge him with her murder as well, and the man had confessed to everything he'd done with Stuart Miller. Including the one murder Hansen had committed, in self-defense, because Miller had a gun on him. It might not be enough to hang Miller yet, but they were steps closer. The DA's office was in talks about possibly cutting a deal with Hansen, who would then be offered entry into the witness protection program after Miller was tried.

The Atlanta tech team had found the trackers Grossman, who was a techie himself, had put on all websites having to do with the case that had put his boss, his mentor, the man for whom he'd do anything, in jail for life. He'd vowed that he'd preserve the man's fortune, and never stop working to find evidence to get his boss out of jail. And had been following all those sites since they'd first gone online.

He'd also set up the fake, official-looking site Kara had stumbled upon. Listing that case, and many others, as another net to catch anyone who might be looking at any cases that resembled the one who'd put his boss in jail. He'd attacked Nivens. And impersonated him.

And then paid someone to get Kara out of the resort when she stepped into that stairwell. Doug's team had found the supposed appliance man dead not far from the wired house where he'd left Kara. He still had had cash on him that could be traced to Grossman.

Everyone figured that Grossman had been unraveling at that point.

Kara didn't know about that. And didn't want to think about any of it anymore. She would. She had to process it all if she was going to be able to let go and be happy. It was up to her to do the work that would free her to live a productive life.

With healthy relationships.

And the first step in doing so was only...a step away.

She'd finished combing her hair. Had brushed her teeth. And had lost track of the minutes she'd just been standing there, shoring herself up to face the most traumatic, heartbreaking experience of her life.

Leaving Ben.

BEN KNEW THE showdown was coming. Kara always prevaricated when it came to facing any kind of drama.

There were parts of the woman he adored that would never change. He was discovering more and more of them. Had been since the moment he'd first heard she'd been kidnapped from the beach.

Like the fact that she was as in love with him as he was with her.

So much so that she'd risk losing him, over growing to resent him. Or lying to him.

She was going to leave him. He knew that was her plan. No logic involved. Just the same gut feeling that had told him that Doug wasn't a traitor. That he had to get up at three in the morning and leave the motel. And so many other things.

Like the fact that he didn't just have to sit back and watch her go. He had a chance. She'd never have come home with him, gotten into the shower in the bedroom suite they shared, if she'd already said her final goodbyes to their marriage.

Knowing that he might not get another opportunity to reach as deeply into Kara as he had to go—knowing, too, that he could lose her—Ben took a deep breath and said, "We need to talk."

Nodding, Kara leaned back against the counter, crossing her arms over her breasts. He read the language. Didn't let it deter him. He had a chance.

"I was wrong, Kara. All along, I was doing just as you said, thinking that I somehow knew better in certain circumstances, because I had more life experience than you did. That I'd been around longer. Had seen more, dealt with more…"

He stopped himself. He had to come clean, he didn't have to shoot himself in both feet. She was a smart woman. She'd get the point.

Her very large and continuous nod had tipped him off to that one.

"I didn't get it until this afternoon," he told her.

She frowned, and, afraid he'd lost her—that she'd think his change of heart was only momentary due to the near-death experiences they'd just lived through—he pressed forward. "Doug was on to Grossman last night." In rapid succession he laid out the facts he'd heard from Doug on the lawn of the house that had nearly killed them both. "He almost cost us our lives, Kara, by trying to shield me from something he thought would get me killed if he told me. He was certain, with all the people he'd called in, that he had me covered. But he didn't know that you were alive. That

I had much more resting on getting the guy than revenge." He stopped to draw a full breath.

And saw a light come into Kara's eyes he'd never seen before. A hint of mature sexuality.

One that reminded him of the very different lovemaking they'd shared in that motel room. He wanted to go back there. Prayed that he would.

But he had more to tell her.

Before they had breakfast with her sisters in the morning and told them that Kara was pregnant. They, aside from the medical staff they'd seen that day, would be the first to know.

"I've got some other news." He swallowed. "I'm never going to be good at hurting you, Kara." The words weren't at all what he'd intended. Nor was the moisture hitting his eyes. Not tears. A blink and it was gone.

But she'd seen it. He saw the mirror in the blue eyes looking back up at him as she said, "Whatever it is, Ben, tell me."

"Your father, the man who raised you as your father, is not your biological dad." There'd be more testing to do, but he'd had Doug check out the blood types, and more.

Falling back against the counter, Kara paled. Held on. He needed to reach for her. To cradle her. But didn't. She'd let him know what she needed.

He hoped.

"H…how do you know?"

"There are quick DNA tests," he told her. Figuring the science wasn't one of those things that were pertinent to telling all. "They're going to be doing more, even exhuming the body if necessary, but there's really only one other option."

Mouth open, she paled more. Stared at him in horror.

Ben had known it would be that way. That the news would drill holes in her that would never heal. Holes that needn't ever have been there. There was no reason Kara, or her sisters, had ever needed to know…

Ben continued to sit there. To hold on to Kara the only way he felt he could. Gaze to gaze. And frowned, confused, when her eyes seemed to clear.

Right before his eyes, she was changing again. Which scared the shit out of him.

What the…

When Kara straightened, Ben stood up, going toward her, then giving her room to get by him. And stood, poleaxed, arms out to his sides, when she walked right into him, wrapping her arms around him.

He looked down at her, saw the tears in her eyes, felt a familiar sense of knowing what to do about them, but then saw the hint of a smile on her face.

Not denoting joy. But something…

"Kara?" He had to ask. "What's going on?"

Still holding him, in spite of arms that were frozen jutted out from his body, Kara said, "I'm not sure, but…it's like everything else that's happened over the past few days. It's like another part of me makes sense."

She wasn't making any sense to him. He was busy wondering if that was something he was supposed to share when she said, "You never know the piece that you're missing until you find it."

Pieces. Puzzles. Those he got. So he nodded. And put his hands on the small of her back. Not holding her to him. But…touching her. Which helped. Immensely.

"I have no idea how I feel about the man my mother fell in love with, slept with, after my father said their marriage was over, or even how I feel about the man I thought was my father, who obviously turned his back on his own plans, his own needs, when my mom ended up pregnant, then taking me on as his own to protect me—or maybe I do know about that. He did a really bad thing, being unfaithful to Mom, but then he stood up, and took responsibility for the result of his actions. A choice that he's been true to ever since. He's loved me my whole life."

Ben wouldn't have been so forgiving of the man. But he hoped that Kara's ability to be would bode well for him. He didn't speak either thought.

And breathed a sigh of relief when Kara kept talking in spite of his silence. "But don't you see, Ben?"

He didn't. Firmly shook his head.

"My whole life, I've never been all in with anyone." She was looking him straight in eye as she spoke, and he held on to her gaze for all he was worth, willing to die drowning in it rather than hear her tell him that she was leaving.

That those arms around him were a hug goodbye. The kind way in which Kara would deliver such news.

"Because I wasn't who I'd been told I was, and everyone knew it but me. But also, because I never had the love of either of my parents. And yet, was being told that the man who cared for me was actually my dad when he knew he wasn't." She stopped, frowning, but then said, "I know this doesn't sound like I'm making any sense, but it's my missing piece, Ben. It's not me that's lacking. Unable to give my all to a family. It's that I've never been in a real one."

The world stopped spinning around him. Everything stilled.

Ben drew his wife to him, full throttle. He finally understood. What Kara needed. What he needed from her. And why neither of them had been giving their all.

He'd taken his cues from her sisters. And in part from her. Because it's all she'd asked of him. Which meant he risked less in loving her.

But he didn't want less. He wanted it all. And knew he had to give it to get it in return.

"I need you, Kara. More than you'll ever know. I need you to call me on it when I go into protective mode." He stopped

then, had a thought. And, with new insight, didn't even tense
up as he said, "Unless I'm protecting you from immediate
physical danger." That one wasn't ever going to change.

She smiled, tears in her eyes, and gazing at her with his
whole heart right there for her to see, he said, "I promise not
to shield you from the bad. Not just because you've told me
not to, but because you've shown me that in doing so, I rob
us both of the chance of you helping to find the good that
comes from it. And when there's physical danger, I promise
to keep you fully involved in the process of protecting you.
Doug's well-intentioned choices over the past twenty-four
hours have brought that one home loud and clear. Not a lesson I'm ever going to forget."

He had more to say. Years' worth of confessions and apol-
ogies to make. Like when he'd known that Thane was planning to leave Stella but while there'd still been hope that
they'd reconcile, hadn't told Kara.

But before he could even start forming the list, she'd
pressed herself more firmly against him. Breast to chest.
Pelvis to his already-growing penis.

Yet when her lips moved up toward his, he pulled his head
back an inch. "I need to know that this is forever, Kara. That
you're in this marriage with your whole heart. That you trust
me to be the husband you need."

"You gained my trust the moment you said 'I was wrong.'
I don't need, or ever want perfection, Ben. I can't be perfection. I just needed you to hear me. Really hear me. And to
know that you were willing to work on changing my status
in this relationship. I can't be part of the nucleus of our family if I'm being shut out…"

His stomach dropped. His heart rocked. And Ben heard a
roaring in his ears. Followed by the sweetest sense of right-
ness he'd ever known.

Something he'd been unaware even existed.

Kara had found her missing pieces.

And with her help, he'd just found his.

"I adore you, babe," he told her. Then stopped. "I don't mean that in any way to sound as though I think you're a child or—"

With a finger to his lips, Kara smiled and said, "The first time you called me that was the first time you saw me naked. It's gone straight to my heart ever since. Now, can we put all this behind us and get back to being the coolest married couple in North Haven?"

"You have no idea how badly I needed to hear those words," he said, but realized that, yeah, she probably had known.

So he gave her some, too. "In all things that matter most, I was the immature one, Kara. I will never ever underestimate you in any way. Or take away your autonomy. I swear that to you."

She nodded. Blinked back tears and said, "I just wish I hadn't robbed you—us—of one of our happiest moments. Every time we think about finding out that we're expecting our first child, we'll have these past several days to remember. Starting with my first reaction to the news."

"Unless…we change the memory with a do-over," he said. Leaving her standing in the bathroom to head to the nightstand where he'd just emptied a back pocket of the jeans he'd had on that day.

She'd followed him. Was watching him, frowning.

Ben took the wrinkled, folded, little forensic bag and walked back into the bathroom. Carefully straightening and then pulling the bag open, he pulled out the stick and put it on the counter.

"Let's look at the results together, Kara, shall we? Understanding who and what we are together, knowing what matters most, and fully cognizant of something neither of us knew last time around. That neither of us were ready to start a family then. And we both are, now."

She didn't mention that there'd only been a few days between the *then* and the *now* of which he spoke.

Instead, she looked him in the eyes, sharing her love and excitement with him, and she took his hand and together, they stared down at the stick.

Saw the plus sign.

And, throwing their arms around each other, celebrated with a kiss that was deeper, more expressive, and sexier than any they'd ever shared before.

Ben went to bed with his wife that night, made love to her, with a completely new understanding. In a more meaningful relationship. As an enlightened and better man.

He'd been willing to settle for less.

It had taken his wife to show him the way.

And knowing that the child they'd created in their collective ignorance was going to change the world.

All he had to do was look at the lives the kid had already saved to know that.

Lying there half asleep, listening to Kara's even breathing, feeling it where her body lay against his, Ben's eyes suddenly opened wide.

He wanted to scratch out that last thought. Hard. Out of existence. What kind of father was he going to be, putting so much pressure on a kid who hadn't even been born yet.

How was he ever...

"I love you, Ben," Kara said, sliding up his chest to kiss his lips. With more than just good-night in them.

Shaking his head, he looked at her in the near darkness and asked, "How'd you know?"

With a grin, she said, "I don't yet. Not exactly. You jerked. Woke me up. Told me something bothered you. Now's the time when you tell me what."

He almost groaned. Then said, "That conversation would keep us both up all night. Just having fatherhood worries." He kissed her. Smiled with a full heart. And asked, "Can it keep until tomorrow?"

Her hand had found his penis. "Yes," she said, "But I don't think this can."

She was right, of course. She'd made certain of it. After all, only Kara knew how to get him from zero to hero in no seconds flat.

Vowing silently to spend the rest of his life making certain that she knew that, Ben rolled over to lie face-to-face with the woman he adored.

And knew that, while he'd screw up now and then, ultimately, he wouldn't fail her. Or the family they created.

All he had to do was give them his whole heart.

Love would do the rest.

\* \* \* \* \*

# COMING SOON!

We really hope you enjoyed reading this book.
If you're looking for more romance
be sure to head to the shops when
new books are available on

## Thursday 26th February

## MILLS & BOON

# LET'S TALK
## Romance

For exclusive extracts, competitions and special offers, find us online:

**f** MillsandBoon

**X** @MillsandBoon

**⊙** @MillsandBoonUK

**♪** @MillsandBoonUK

Get in touch on 01413 063 232